THE CAPTAIN'S

DAUGHTER *and*

Other Great Stories

BY

ALEXANDER PUSHKIN

D0188559

VINTAGE BOOKS

A DIVISION OF RANDOM HOUSE

New York

Contents

The Captain's Daughter

Watch over your honor while you are young . . .

A PROVERB

I

A SERGEANT OF THE GUARDS

He would have been a Captain in the Guards tomorrow.
"I do not care for that; a common soldier let him be."
A splendid thing to say! He'll have much sorrow . . .

. . . . .

Who is his father, then?

KNYAZHNIN

MY FATHER, Andrey Petrovich Grinyov, had in his youth served under Count Münnich and retired with the rank of first major in the year 17—. From that time onward he lived on his estate in the province of Simbirsk, where he married Avdotya Vassilyevna U., daughter of a poor landowner of the district. There had been nine of us. All my brothers and sisters died in infancy. Through the kindness of Prince B., our near relative, who was a major of the Guards, I was registered as sergeant in the Semyonovsky regiment. I was supposed to be on leave until I had completed my studies. Our bringing-up in those days was very different from what it is now. At the age of five I was entrusted to the groom Savelyich, who was assigned to look after me, as a reward for the sobriety of his behavior. Under his supervision I had learned, by the age of twelve, to read and write Russian, and could judge very soundly the points of a borzoi dog. At that time my father hired for me a Frenchman, Monsieur Beaupré, who was fetched from Moscow together with a year's supply of wine and olive oil. Savelyich very much disliked his coming.

"The child, thank heaven, has his face washed and his hair combed, and his food given him," he grumbled to himself. "Much good it is to spend money on the Frenchman, as though the master hadn't enough servants of his own on the estate!"

In his native land Beaupré had been a hairdresser; afterward he was a soldier in Prussia, and then came to Russia *pour être outchitel,*[1] without clearly understanding the meaning of that word. He was a good fellow, but extremely thoughtless and flighty. His chief weakness was his passion for the fair sex; his attentions were often rewarded by blows, which made him groan for hours. Besides, "he was not an enemy of the bottle," as he put it; that is, he liked to take a drop too much. But since wine was only served in our house at dinner, and then only one glass to each person, and the tutor was generally passed over, my Beaupré soon grew accustomed to the Russian homemade brandy and, indeed, came to prefer it to the wines of his own country as being far better for the digestion. We made friends at once, and although he was supposed by the agreement to teach me "French, German, and all subjects," he preferred to pick up some Russian from me and, after that, we each followed

[1] To be a teacher (TRANSLATOR'S NOTE).

our own pursuits. We got on together capitally. I wished for no other mentor. But fate soon parted us, and this was how it happened.

The laundress, Palashka, a stout pock-marked girl, and the dairymaid, one-eyed Akulka, had agreed to throw themselves together at my mother's feet, confessing their culpable weakness and tearfully complaining of the *mossoo* who had seduced their innocence. My mother did not like to trifle with such things and complained to my father. My father was not one to lose time. He sent at once for that rascal, the Frenchman. They told him *mossoo* was giving me my lesson. My father went to my room. At that time Beaupré was sleeping the sleep of innocence on the bed; I was usefully employed. I ought to mention that a map of the world had been ordered for me from Moscow. It hung on the wall; no use was made of it, and I had long felt tempted by its width and thickness. I decided to make a kite of it and, taking advantage of Beaupré's slumbers, set to work upon it. My father came in just at the moment when I was fixing a tail of tow to the Cape of Good Hope. Seeing my exercises in geography, my father pulled me by the ear, then ran up to Beaupré, roused him none too gently, and overwhelmed him with reproaches. Covered with confusion, Beaupré tried to get up but could not: the unfortunate Frenchman was dead drunk. He paid all scores at once: my father lifted him off the bed by the collar, kicked him out of the room, and sent him away that same day, to the indescribable joy of Savelyich. This was the end of my education.

I was allowed to run wild, and spent my time chasing pigeons and playing leap-frog with the boys on the estate. Meanwhile I had turned sixteen. Then there came a change in my life.

One autumn day my mother was making jam with honey

in the drawing room, and I licked my lips as I looked at the boiling scum. My father sat by the window reading the *Court Calendar,* which he received every year. This book always had a great effect on him: he never read it without agitation, and the perusal of it invariably stirred his bile. My mother, who knew all his ways by heart, always tried to stow the unfortunate book as far away as possible, and sometimes the *Court Calendar* did not catch his eye for months. When, however, he did chance to find it, he would not let it out of his hands for hours. And so my father was reading the *Court Calendar,* shrugging his shoulders from time to time and saying in an undertone: "Lieutenant-General! . . . He was a sergeant in my company . . . a Companion of two Russian Orders! . . . And it isn't long since he and I . . ."

At last my father threw the *Calendar* on the sofa, and sank into a thoughtfulness which boded nothing good.

He suddenly turned to my mother: "Avdotya Vassilyevna, how old is Petrusha?"

"He is going on seventeen," my mother answered. "Petrusha was born the very year when Auntie Nastasya Gerasimovna lost her eye and when . . ."

"Very well," my father interrupted her; "it is time he went into the Service. He has been running about the servant-girls' quarters and climbing dovecotes long enough."

My mother was so overwhelmed at the thought of parting from me that she dropped the spoon into the saucepan and tears flowed down her cheeks. My delight, however, could hardly be described. The idea of military service was connected in my mind with thoughts of freedom and of the pleasures of Petersburg life. I imagined myself as an officer of the Guards, which, to my mind, was the height of human bliss.

My father did not like to change his plans or to put them

off. The day for my departure was fixed. On the eve of it my father said that he intended sending with me a letter to my future chief, and asked for paper and a pen.

"Don't forget, Andrey Petrovich, to send my greetings to Prince B.," said my mother, "and to tell him that I hope he will be kind to Petrusha."

"What nonsense!" my father answered, with a frown. "Why should I write to Prince B.?"

"Why, you said you were going to write to Petrusha's chief."

"Well, what of it?"

"But Petrusha's chief is Prince B., to be sure. Petrusha is registered in the Semyonovsky regiment."

"Registered! What do I care about it? Petrusha is not going to Petersburg. What would he learn if he did his service there? To be a spendthrift and a rake? No, let him serve in the army and learn the routine of it and know the smell of powder and be a soldier and not a fop! Registered in the Guards! Where is his passport? Give it to me."

My mother found my passport, which she kept put away in a chest together with my christening robe, and, with a trembling hand, gave it to my father. My father read it attentively, put it before him on the table, and began his letter.

I was consumed by curiosity. Where was I being sent if not to Petersburg? I did not take my eyes off my father's pen, which moved rather slowly. At last he finished, sealed the letter in the same envelope with the passport, took off his spectacles, called me and said: "Here is a letter for you to Andrey Karlovich R., my old friend and comrade. You are going to Orenburg to serve under him."

And so all my brilliant hopes were dashed to the ground! Instead of the gay Petersburg life, boredom in a distant and wild part of the country awaited me. Going into the army, of which I had thought with such delight only a moment before, now seemed to me a dreadful misfortune. But it was no use protesting! Next morning a traveling chaise drove up to the house; my bag, a box with tea things, and bundles of pies and rolls, the last tokens of family affection, were packed into it. My parents blessed me. My father said to me: "Good-bye, Pyotr. Carry out faithfully your oath of allegiance; obey your superiors; don't seek their favor; don't put yourself forward, and do not shirk your duty; remember the saying: 'Watch over your clothes while they are new, and over your honor while you are young.' "

My mother admonished me with tears to take care of myself, and bade Savelyich look after "the child." They dressed me in a hareskin jacket and a fox-fur overcoat. I stepped into the chaise with Savelyich and set off on my journey, weeping bitterly.

In the evening I arrived at Simbirsk, where I was to spend the next day in order to buy the things I needed; Savelyich was entrusted with the purchase of them. I put up at an inn. Savelyich went out shopping early in the morning. Bored with looking out of the window into the dirty street, I wandered about the inn. Coming into the billiard room I saw a tall man of about thirty-five, with a long black mustache, in a dressing-gown, a billiard cue in his hand, and a pipe in his mouth. He was playing with the marker, who drank a glass of vodka on winning and crawled under the billiard table on all fours when he lost. I watched their game. The longer it continued, the oftener the marker had to go on all fours, till at last he remained under the table altogether. The gentleman pronounced some expressive sentences by way of a funeral oration and asked me to have a game. I refused, saying I could not play. This seemed to strike him as strange. He looked at me with something like pity; nevertheless, we entered into conversation. I learned that his name was Ivan Ivanovich Zurin, that he was captain of a Hussar regiment, that he had come to Simbirsk to receive recruits, and was staying at the inn. Zurin invited me to share his dinner, such as it was, like a fellow-soldier. I readily agreed. We sat down to dinner. Zurin drank a great deal and treated me, saying that I must get used to army ways; he told me military anecdotes, which made me rock with laughter, and we got up from the table on the best of terms. Then he offered to teach me to play billiards.

"It is quite essential to us soldiers," he said. "On a march, for instance, one comes to some wretched little place; what is one to do? One can't be always beating Jews, you know. So there is nothing for it but to go to the inn and play billiards; and to do that one must be able to play!"

He convinced me completely and I set to work very diligently. Zurin encouraged me loudly, marveled at the rapid progress I was making, and after several lessons suggested we should play for money, at a penny a point, not for the sake of gain, but simply so as not to play for nothing, which, he said, was a most objectionable habit. I agreed to this, too, and Zurin ordered some punch and persuaded me to try it, repeating that I must get used to army life; what would the army be without punch! I did as he told me. We went on playing. The oftener I sipped from my glass, the more reckless I grew. My balls flew beyond the boundary every minute; I grew excited, abused the marker, who did not know how to count, kept raising the stakes—in short, behaved like a silly boy who was having his first taste of freedom. I did not notice how the time passed. Zurin looked at the clock, put down his cue, and told me that I had lost a hundred rubles. I was somewhat taken aback. My money was with Savelyich; I began to apologize; Zurin interrupted me:

"Please do not trouble, it does not matter at all. I can wait; and meanwhile let us go and see Arinushka."

What can I say? I finished the day as recklessly as I had begun it. We had supper at Arinushka's. Zurin kept filling my glass and repeating that I ought to get used to army ways. I could hardly stand when we got up from the table; at midnight Zurin drove me back to the inn.

Savelyich met us on the steps. He cried out when he saw the unmistakable signs of my zeal for the Service.

"What has come over you, sir?" he said in a shaking voice, "wherever did you get yourself into such a state? Good Lord! Such a dreadful thing has never happened to you before!"

"Be quiet, you old dodderer!" I mumbled. "You must be drunk; go and lie down . . . and put me to bed."

Next day I woke up with a headache, vaguely recalling the events of the day before. My reflections were interrupted by Savelyich, who came in to me with a cup of tea.

"It's early you have taken to drinking, Pyotr Andreyich," he said to me, shaking his head, "much too early. And whom do you get it from? Neither your father nor your grandfather were drunkards; and your mother, it goes without saying, never tastes anything stronger than kvass. And who is at the bottom of it all? That damned Frenchman. He kept running to Antipyevna: 'Madame, she voo pree vodka.' Here's a fine 'shu voo pree' for you! There is no gainsaying it, he has taught you some good, the cur! And much need there was to hire an infidel for a tutor! As though Master had not enough servants of his own!"

I was ashamed. I turned away and said to him: "Leave me, Savelyich, I don't want any tea." But it was not easy to stop Savelyich once he began sermonizing.

"You see now what it is to take too much, Pyotr Andrey-ich. Your head is heavy, and you have no appetite. A man

who drinks is no good for anything. . . . Have some cu-
cumber brine with honey or, better still, half a glass of homemade brandy. Shall I bring you some?"

At that moment a servant-boy came in and gave me a note
from Zurin.

Dear Pyotr Andreyich,

*Please send me by my boy the hundred rubles you lost to
me at billiards yesterday. I am in urgent need of money.*

Always at your service,

Ivan Zurin

There was nothing for it. Assuming an air of indifference
I turned to Savelyich, "the keeper of my money, linen, and
affairs," and told him to give the boy a hundred rubles.

"What! Why should I give it to him?"

"I owe it to him," I answered, as coolly as possible.

"Owe it!" repeated Savelyich, growing more and more
amazed. "But when did you have time to contract a debt,
sir? There's something wrong about this. You may say what
you like, but I won't give the money."

I thought that if at that decisive moment I did not get the
better of the obstinate old man, it would be difficult for me
in the future to free myself from his tutelage, and so I said,
looking at him haughtily: "I am your master, and you are my
servant. The money is mine. I lost it at billiards because it
was my pleasure to do so; and I advise you not to argue, but
to do as you are told."

Savelyich was so startled by my words that he clasped
his hands and remained motionless.

"Well, why don't you go?" I cried angrily.

Savelyich began to weep.

"My dear Pyotr Andreyich," he said, in a shaking voice,
"do not make me die of grief. My darling, do as I tell you,

old man that I am; write to that brigand that it was all a joke, and that we have no such sum. A hundred rubles! Good Lord! Tell him that your parents have strictly forbidden you to play unless it be for nuts . . . !"

"That will do," I interrupted him sternly; "give me the money or I will turn you out."

Savelyich looked at me with profound grief and went to fetch the money. I was sorry for the poor old man, but I wanted to assert my independence and to prove that I was no longer a child.

The money was delivered to Zurin. Savelyich hastened to get me out of the accursed inn. He came to tell me that horses were ready. I left Simbirsk with an uneasy conscience and silent remorse, not saying good-bye to my teacher and not expecting ever to meet him again.

II

THE GUIDE

Thou distant land, land unknown to me!
Not of my will have I come to thee,
Nor was it my steed that brought me here.
I've been led to thee by my recklessness,
By my courage and youth and my love for drink.
                                        AN OLD SONG

MY REFLECTIONS on the journey were not particularly pleasant. The sum I had lost was considerable according to the standards of thàt time. I could not help confessing to myself that I had behaved stupidly at the Simbirsk inn, and I felt that I had been in the wrong with Savelyich. It all made me wretched. The old man sat gloomily on the coach-box, his head turned away from me; occasionally he cleared his throat but said nothing. I was determined to make peace with him, but did not know how to begin. At last I said to him: "There, there, Savelyich, let us make it up! I am sorry; I see myself I was to blame. I got into mischief yesterday and offended you for nothing. I promise you I will be more sensible now and do as you tell me. There, don't be cross; let us make peace."

"Ah, my dear Pyotr Andreyich," he answered, with a deep sigh, "I am cross with myself—it was all my fault. How could I have left you alone at the inn! There it is—I yielded to temptation: I thought I would call on the deacon's wife, an old friend of mine. It's just as the proverb says—you go and see your friends and in jail your visit ends. It is simply dreadful! How shall I show myself before my master and mistress? What will they say when they hear that the child gambles and drinks?"

To comfort poor Savelyich I gave him my word not to dispose of a single farthing without his consent in the future. He calmed down after a time, though now and again he still muttered to himself, shaking his head: "A hundred rubles! It's no joke!"

I was approaching the place of my destination. A desolate plane intersected by hills and ravines stretched around. All was covered with snow . . . the sun was setting. The chaise was going along a narrow road, or, rather, a track made by peasant sledges. Suddenly the driver began looking anxiously at the horizon, and at last, taking off his cap, he turned to me and said: "Hadn't we better turn back, sir?"

"What for?"

"The weather is uncertain: the wind is rising; see how it sweeps the snow."

"But what of it?"

"Do you see that?"

The driver pointed with the whip to the east.

"I see nothing but the white steppe and a clear sky."

"Why, that little cloud there."

I certainly did see at the edge of the sky a white cloud which I had taken at first for a small hill in the distance. The driver explained to me that the cloud betokened a snowstorm.

I had heard about snowstorms in those parts, and knew that whole transports were sometimes buried by them. Savelyich, like the driver, thought that we ought to turn back. But the wind did not seem to me strong; I hoped to arrive in time at the station, and told the man to drive faster.

The driver set the horses at a gallop but still kept glancing eastward. The horses went well. Meanwhile the wind grew stronger and stronger every hour. The little cloud grew bigger and rose heavily, gradually enveloping the sky. Fine snow began to fall, and then suddenly came down in big flakes. The wind howled, the snowstorm burst upon us. In a single moment the dark sky melted into the sea of snow. Everything was lost to sight.

"It's a bad lookout, sir," the driver shouted. "Snowstorm!" I peeped out of the chaise: darkness and whirlwind were around us. The wind howled with such ferocious expressiveness that is seemed alive; Savelyich and I were covered with snow; the horses walked on slowly and soon stopped altogether.

"Why don't you go on?" I asked the driver impatiently.

"What's the good?" he answered, jumping off the box. "I don't know where we are as it is; there is no road and it is dark."

I began scolding him, but Savelyich took his side.

"Why ever didn't you take his advice?" he said angrily. "You would have returned to the inn, had some tea and slept in comfort till morning, and have gone on when the storm stopped. And what's the hurry? We aren't going to a wedding."

Savelyich was right. There was nothing to be done. Snow was falling fast. A great drift of it was being heaped beside the chaise. The horses stood with their heads down and shuddered from time to time. The driver walked around them setting the harness to rights for the sake of something to do. Savelyich was grumbling; I was looking around in the hope of seeing some sign of a homestead or of the road, but I could distinguish nothing in the opaque whirlwind of snow. Suddenly I caught sight of something black.

"Hey, driver!" I cried. "Look, what is that black thing over there?"

The driver stared into the distance.

"Heaven only knows, sir," he said, climbing back onto the box; "it's not a wagon and not a tree, and it seems to be moving. It must be a wolf or a man."

I told him to go toward the unknown object, which immediately began moving toward us. In two minutes we came upon a man.

"Hey, there, good man," the driver shouted to him, "do you know where the road is?"

"The road is here," the wayfarer answered. "I am standing on hard ground, but what's the good?"

"I say, my good fellow, do you know these parts?" I asked him. "Could you guide us to a night's lodging?"

"I know the country well enough," the wayfarer answered. "I should think I have trodden every inch if it. But you see what the weather is: we should be sure to lose our way. Better stop here and wait; maybe the snowstorm will stop and when the sky is clear we can find our bearings by the stars."

His coolness gave me courage. I decided to trust to Providence and spend the night in the steppe, when the wayfarer suddenly jumped onto the box and said to the driver: "Thank God, there's a village close by; turn to the right and make straight for it."

"And why should I go to the right?" the driver asked with annoyance. "Where do you see the road? It's easy enough to drive other people's horses."

The driver seemed to me to be right.

"Indeed, how do you know that we are close to a village?" I asked the man.

"Because the wind has brought a smell of smoke from over there," he answered, "so a village must be near."

His quickness and keenness of smell astonished me. I told the driver to go on. The horses stepped with difficulty in the deep snow. The chaise moved slowly, now going into a snowdrift, now dipping into a ravine and swaying from side to side. It was like being on a ship in a stormy sea. Savelyich groaned as he kept jolting against me. I put down the front curtain, wrapped my fur coat around me and dozed, lulled to sleep by the singing of the storm and the slow, swaying motion of the chaise.

I had a dream which I could never since forget and in which I still see a kind of prophecy when I reflect upon the strange vicissitudes of my life. The reader will forgive me, probably knowing from experience how natural it is for man to indulge in superstition, however great his contempt for all vain imaginings may be.

I was in that state of mind and feeling when reality gives way to dreams and merges into them in the shadowy visions of oncoming sleep. It seemed to me the storm was still raging and we were still wandering in the snowy desert. . . . Suddenly I saw a gateway and drove into the courtyard of our estate. My first thought was fear lest my father should be angry with me for my involuntary return and regard it as an intentional disobedience. Anxious, I jumped down from the chaise and saw my mother, who came out to meet me on the steps, with an air of profound grief.

"Don't make any noise," she said. "Your father is ill; he is dying and wants to say good-bye to you."

Terror-stricken, I followed her to the bedroom. It was dimly lighted; people with sad-looking faces were standing by the bed. I approached the bed quietly; my mother lifted the bed-curtain and said: "Andrey Petrovich! Petrusha has come; he returned when he heard of your illness; bless him." I knelt down and looked at the sick man. But what did I see? Instead of my father a black-bearded peasant lay on the bed looking at me merrily. I turned to my mother in perplexity, and said to her: "What does it mean? This is not my father. And why should I ask this peasant's blessing?"— "Never mind, Petrusha," my mother answered, "he takes your father's place for the wedding; kiss his hand and let him bless you." . . . I would not do it. Then the peasant jumped off the bed, seized an ax from behind his back, and began waving it about. I wanted to run away and could not; the room was full of dead bodies; I stumbled against them and slipped in the pools of blood. . . . The terrible peasant called to me kindly, saying: "Don't be afraid, come and let me bless you." Terror and confusion possessed me. . . . At that moment I woke up. The horses were standing still; Savelyich held me by the hand, saying: "Come out, sir; we have arrived."

"Where?" I asked, rubbing my eyes.

"At the inn. With the Lord's help we stumbled right

against the fence. Make haste, come and warm yourself, sir."

I stepped out of the chaise. The snowstorm was still raging though with less violence. It was pitch-dark. The landlord met us at the gate, holding a lantern under the skirt of his coat, and let us into a room that was small but clean enough; it was lighted by a burning splinter. A rifle and a tall Cossack cap hung on the wall.

The landlord, a Yaïk Cossack, was a man of about sixty, active and well-preserved. Savelyich brought in the box with the tea things and asked for a fire so that he could make tea, which had never seemed to me so welcome. The landlord went to look after things.

"Where is our guide?" I asked Savelyich.

"Here, your honor," answered a voice above me.

I looked up and on the shelf by the stove saw a black beard and two glittering eyes.

"You must have got chilled, brother?"

"I should think I did with nothing but a thin jerkin on! I did have a sheepskin coat, but I confess I pawned it yesterday in a tavern; the frost did not seem to be bad."

At that moment the landlord came in with a boiling samovar; I offered our guide a cup of tea; he climbed down from the shelf. His appearance, I thought, was striking. He was about forty, of medium height, lean and broad-shouldered. Gray was beginning to show in his black beard; his big, lively eyes were never still. His face had a pleasant but crafty expression. His hair was cropped like a peasant's; he wore a ragged jerkin and Turkish trousers. I handed him a cup of tea; he tasted it and made a grimace.

"Be so kind, your honor . . . tell them to give me a glass of vodka; tea is not a Cossack drink."

I readily complied with his wish. The landlord took a glass and bottle out of the cupboard, came up to the man, and said, glancing into his face: "Aha! you are in our parts again! Where do you come from?"

My guide winked significantly and answered in riddles: "I flew about the kitchen-garden, picking hemp seed; granny threw a pebble but missed me. And how are you fellows getting on?"

"Nothing much to be said of them," the landlord said, also speaking in metaphors. "They tried to ring the bells for vespers, but the priest's wife said they must not: the priest is on a visit and the devils are in the churchyard."

"Be quiet, uncle," the tramp answered; "if it rains, there will be mushrooms, and if there are mushrooms there will be a basket for them; and now" (he winked again) "put the ax behind your back: the forester is about. Your honor, here's a health to you!"

With these words he took the glass, crossed himself, and drank it at one gulp; then he bowed to me and returned to the shelf by the stove.

I could not at the time understand anything of this thieves' jargon, but later on I guessed they were talking of the affairs of the Yaïk Cossacks, who had just been subdued after their rebellion in 1772. Savelyich listened with an air of thorough disapproval. He looked suspiciously both at the landlord and at our guide. The inn stood in the steppe by itself, far from any village, and looked uncommonly like a robbers' den. But there was nothing else for it. There could be no question of continuing the journey. Savelyich's anxiety amused me greatly. Meanwhile I made ready for the night and lay down on the bench. Savelyich decided to sleep on the stove; the landlord lay down on the floor. Soon the room was full of snoring and I dropped fast asleep.

Waking up rather late in the morning I saw that the storm had subsided. The sun was shining. The boundless steppe was wrapped in a covering of dazzling snow. The horses were harnessed. I paid the landlord, who charged us so little that even Savelyich did not dispute about it or try to beat him down as was his wont; he completely forgot his suspicions of the evening before. I called our guide, thanked him for the help he had given us, and told Savelyich to give him half a ruble for vodka. Savelyich frowned.

"Half a ruble!" he said. "What for? Because you were pleased to give him a lift and bring him to the inn? You may say what you like, sir, we have no half-rubles to spare. If we give tips to everyone we shall soon have to starve."

I could not argue with Savelyich. I had promised that the money was to be wholly in his charge. I was annoyed, however, at not being able to thank the man who had saved me from a very unpleasant situation, if not from actual danger.

"Very well," I said calmly. "If you don't want to give him half a ruble, give him something out of my clothes. He is dressed much too lightly. Give him my hareskin coat."

"Mercy on us, Pyotr Andreyich!" Savelyich cried. "What is the good of your hareskin coat to him? He will sell it for drink at the next pot-house, the dog."

"That's no concern of yours, old fellow, whether I sell it for drink or not," said the tramp. "His honor gives me a fur coat of his own; it is your master's pleasure to do so, and your business, as a servant, is to obey and not to argue."

"You have no fear of God, you brigand!" Savelyich answered in an angry voice. "You see the child has no sense as yet and you are only too glad to take advantage of his good nature. What do you want with a gentleman's coat? You can't squeeze your hulking great shoulders into it, however you try!"

"Please don't argue," I said to the old man; "bring the coat at once."

"Good Lord!" my Savelyich groaned. "Why, the coat is almost new! To give it away, and not to a decent man either, but to a shameless drunkard!"

Nevertheless the hareskin coat appeared. The peasant immediately tried it on. The coat that I had slightly outgrown was certainly a little tight for him. He succeeded, however, in getting into it, bursting the seams as he did so. Savelyich almost howled when he heard the threads breaking. The tramp was extremely pleased with my present. He saw me to the chaise and said, with a low bow: "Thank you, your honor! May God reward you for your goodness; I shall not forget your kindness so long as I live."

He went his way and I drove on, taking no notice of Savelyich, and soon forgot the snowstorm of the day before, my guide, and the hareskin coat.

Arriving in Orenburg I went straight to the General. I saw a tall man, already bent by age. His long hair was perfectly white. An old and faded uniform reminded one of the soldiers of Empress Anna's time; he spoke with a strong German accent. I gave him my father's letter. When I mentioned my name, he threw a quick glance at me.

"*Du lieber Gott!*" he said. "It does not seem long since Andrey Petrovich was your age, and now, see, what a big son he has! Oh, how time flies!"

He opened the letter and began reading it in an undertone, interposing his own remarks: " 'My dear Sir, Andrey Karlovich, I hope that Your Excellency' . . . Why so formal? Fie, he should be ashamed of himself! Discipline is, of course, a thing of the first importance, but is this the way to write to an old *Kamerad?* . . . 'Your Excellency has not forgotten' . . . H'm . . . 'and . . . when . . . the late Field Marshal Münnich . . . the march . . . and also . . . Carolinchen' . . . Ehe, *Bruder!* so he still remembers our old escapades! 'Now to business . . . I am sending my young rascal to you' . . . H'm . . . 'hold him in hedgehog gloves' . . . What are hedgehog gloves! It must be a Russian saying. . . . What does it mean?" he asked me.

"That means," I answered, looking as innocent as possible, "to treat one kindly, not to be too stern, to give one plenty of freedom."

"H'm, I see . . . 'and do not give him too much rope.' No, evidently 'hedgehog gloves' means something different. . . . 'Herewith his passport' . . . Where is it? Ah, here. . . . 'Write to the Semyonovsky regiment.' . . . Very good, very good; it shall be done. . . . 'Allow me, forgetting your rank, to embrace you like an old friend and comrade' . . . Ah, at last he thought of it . . . and so on and so on. . . ."

"Well, my dear," he said, having finished the letter and put my passport aside, "it shall be done as your father wishes; you will be transferred, with the rank of an officer, to the N. regiment, and, not to lose time, you shall go tomorrow to the Belogorsky fortress to serve under Captain Mironov, a good and honorable man. You will see real service there and learn discipline. There is nothing for you to do at Orenburg; dissipation is bad for a young man. And tonight I shall be pleased to have you dine with me."

"I am going from bad to worse!" I thought. "What is the good of my having been a sergeant in the Guards almost before I was born! Where has it brought me? To the N. regiment and a desolate fortress on the border of the Kirghiz Steppes!"

I had dinner with Andrey Karlovich and his old aide-de-camp. Strict German economy reigned at his table, and I think the fear of seeing occasionally an additional guest at his bachelor meal had something to do with my hasty removal to the garrison. The following day I took leave of the General and set off for my destination.

III

THE FORTRESS

In this fortress fine we live;
Bread and water is our fare.
And when ferocious foes
Come to our table bare,
To a real feast we treat them.
Load the cannon and then beat them.
                    SOLDIERS' SONG

Old-fashioned people, sir.
                    FONVIZIN

THE BELOGORSKY FORTRESS was twenty-five miles from Orenburg. The road ran along the steep bank of the Yaïk. The river was not yet frozen and its leaden waves looked dark and mournful between the monotonous banks covered with white snow. Beyond it the Kirghiz Steppes stretched into the distance. I was absorbed in reflections, for the most part of a melancholy nature. Life in the fortress did not attract me. I tried to picture Captain Mironov, my future chief, and thought of him as a stern, bad-tempered old man who cared for nothing but discipline and was ready to put me under arrest on a diet of bread and water for the least little trifle. Meanwhile it was growing dark. We were driving rather fast.

"Is it far to the fortress?" I asked the driver.

"No, not far," he answered; "it's over there, you can see it."

I looked from side to side, expecting to see menacing battlements, towers, and a rampart, but saw nothing except a village surrounded by a log fence. On one side of it stood three or four haystacks, half covered with snow, on another a tumbledown windmill with wings of bark that hung idle.

"But where is the fortress?" I asked in surprise.

"Why here," answered the driver, pointing to the village, and as he spoke we drove into it.

At the gate I saw an old cannon made of cast iron; the streets were narrow and crooked, the cottages low and, for the most part, with thatched roofs. I told the driver to take me to the Commandant's, and in another minute the chaise stopped before a wooden house built upon rising ground close to a church, also made of wood.

No one came out to meet me. I walked into the entry and opened the door into the anteroom. An old soldier was sitting on the table, sewing a blue patch on the sleeve of a green uniform. I asked him to announce me.

"Go in, my dear," he said, "our people are at home."

I stepped into a clean little room, furnished in the old-fashioned style. In the corner stood a cupboard full of crockery; an officer's diploma in a frame under glass hung on the wall; colored prints, representing "The Taking of Ochakoff and Küstrin," "The Choosing of a Bride," and "The Cat's Funeral," made bright patches on each side of it. An elderly lady, dressed in a Russian jacket[2] and with a kerchief on her head, was sitting by the window. She was winding yarn which a one-eyed man in an officer's uniform held for her on his outstretched hands.

"What is your pleasure, sir?" she asked me, going on with her work.

I answered that I had come to serve in the army, and

[2] A padded or fur-lined jacket, with or without sleeves (EDITOR'S NOTE).

thought it my duty to present myself to the Captain, and with these words I turned to the one-eyed old man whom I took to be the Commandant, but the lady of the house interrupted the speech I had prepared.

"Ivan Kuzmich is not at home," she answered; "he has gone to see Father Gerasim; but it makes no difference, sir; I am his wife. You are very welcome. Please sit down."

She called the maid and asked her to call the sergeant. The old man kept looking at me inquisitively with his single eye.

"May I be so bold as to ask in what regiment you have been serving?"

I satisfied his curiosity.

"And may I ask," he continued, "why you have been transferred from the Guards to the garrison?"

I answered that such was the decision of my superiors.

"I presume it was for behavior unseemly in an officer of the Guards?" the persistent old man went on.

"That's enough nonsense," the Captain's lady interrupted him. "You see the young man is tired after the journey; he has other things to think of. . . . Hold your hands straight.

"And don't you worry, my dear, that you have been banished to these wilds," she went on, addressing herself to me. "You are not the first nor the last. You will like it better when you are used to it. Shvabrin, Alexey Ivanych, was transferred to us five years ago for killing a man. Heaven only knows what possessed him, but, would you believe it, he went out of town with a certain lieutenant and they both took swords and started prodding each other—and Alexey Ivanych did for the lieutenant, and before two witnesses, too! There it is—one never knows what one may do."

At that moment the sergeant, a young and well-built Cossack, came into the room.

"Maximych!" the Captain's lady said to him. "Find a lodging for this gentleman and mind it is clean."

"Yes, Vasilisa Yegorovna," the Cossack answered. "Shall I get rooms for his honor at Ivan Polezhayev's?"

"Certainly not, Maximych," said the lady. "Polezhayev is crowded as it is; besides, he is a friend and always remembers that we are his superiors. Take the gentleman . . . what is your name, sir?"

"Pyotr Andreyich."

"Take Pyotr Andreyich to Semyon Kuzov's. He let his horse into my kitchen-garden, the rascal. Well, Maximych, is everything in order?"

"All is well, thank God," the Cossack answered; "only Corporal Prokhorov had a fight in the bathhouse with Ustinya Negulina about a bucket of hot water."

"Ivan Ignatyich," said the Captain's lady to the one-eyed old man, "will you look into it and find out whether Ustinya or Prokhorov is to blame? And punish them both! Well, Maximych, you can go now. Pyotr Andreyich, Maximych will take you to your lodging."

I took leave of her. The Cossack brought me to a cottage that stood on the high bank of the river at the very edge of the fortress. Half of the cottage was occupied by Semyon Kuzov's family, the other was allotted to me. It consisted of one fairly clean room partitioned into two. Savelyich began unpacking; I looked out of the narrow window. The melancholy steppe stretched before me. On one side I could see a few cottages; several hens strutted about the street. An old woman stood on the steps with a trough, calling to pigs that answered her with friendly grunting. And this was the place where I was doomed to spend my youth! I suddenly felt wretched; I left the window and went to bed without any supper in spite of Savelyich's entreaties. He kept repeating in distress: "Merciful heavens, he won't eat! What will my mistress say if the child is taken ill?"

Next morning I had just begun to dress when the door opened and a young officer, short, swarthy, with a plain but extremely lively face, walked in.

"Excuse me," he said to me in French, "for coming without ceremony to make your acquaintance. Yesterday I heard of your arrival: I could not resist the desire to see at last a human face. You will understand this when you have lived here for a time."

I guessed that this was the officer who had been dismissed from the Guards on account of a duel. We made friends at once. Shvabrin was very intelligent. His conversation was witty and entertaining. He described to me in a most amusing way the Commandant's family, their friends, and the place to which fate had brought him. I was screaming with laughter when the old soldier, whom I had seen mending a uniform at the Commandant's, came in and gave me Vasilisa Yegorovna's invitation to dine with them. Shvabrin said he would go with me.

As we approached the Commandant's house we saw in the square some twenty old garrison soldiers in three-cornered hats and with long queues. They were standing at attention. The Commandant, a tall, vigorous old man, wearing a night-cap and a cotton dressing gown, stood facing them. When he saw us, he came up, said a few kind words to me, and went on drilling his men. We stopped to look on, but he asked us to go to his house, promising to come soon after.

"There's nothing here worth looking at," he added. Vasilisa Yegorovna gave us a kind and homely welcome, treating me as though she had known me all my life. The old veteran and the maid Palasha were laying the table.

"My Ivan Kuzmich is late with his drilling today," she said.

"Palasha, call your master to dinner. And where is Masha?"

At that moment a girl of eighteen, with a rosy round face, came in; her fair hair was smoothly combed behind her ears which at that moment were burning. I did not particularly like her at the first glance. I was prejudiced against her: Shvabrin had described Masha, the Captain's daughter, as quite stupid. Marya Ivanovna sat down in a corner and began sewing. Meanwhile cabbage soup was served. Not seeing her husband, Vasilisa Yegorovna sent Palasha a second time to call him.

"Tell your master that our guests are waiting and the soup will get cold; there is always time for drilling, thank heaven; he can shout to his heart's content later on."

The Captain soon appeared, accompanied by the one-eyed old man.

"What has come over you, my dear?" his wife said to him. "Dinner was served ages ago, and you wouldn't come."

"But I was busy drilling soldiers, Vasilisa Yegorovna, let me tell you."

"Come, come," his wife retorted, "all this drilling is mere pretense—your soldiers don't learn anything and you are no good at it either. You had much better sit at home and say your prayers. Dear guests, come to the table."

We sat down to dinner. Vasilisa Yegorovna was never silent for a minute and bombarded me with questions: who were my parents, were they living, where did they live, how big was their estate? When she heard that my father had three hundred serfs she said: "Just fancy! to think of there being rich people in the world! And we, my dear, have only one maid, Palasha, but we are comfortable enough, thank heaven. The only trouble is Masha ought to be getting married, and all she has by way of dowry is a comb and a broom and a brass farthing, just enough to go to the baths with. If the right man turns up, all well and good, but, if not, she will die an old maid."

I glanced at Marya Ivanovna; she flushed crimson and tears dropped into her plate. I felt sorry for her and hastened to change the conversation.

"I have heard," I said, rather inappropriately, "that the Bashkirs propose to attack your fortress."

"From whom have you heard it, my good sir?" Ivan Kuzmich asked.

"I was told it at Orenburg," I answered.

"Don't you believe it!" said the Commandant. "We have not heard anything of it for years. The Bashkirs have been scared and the Kirghiz, too, have had their lesson. No fear, they won't attack us; and if they do I will give them such a fright that they will keep quiet for another ten years."

"And you are not afraid," I continued, turning to Vasilisa Yegorovna, "to remain in a fortress subject to such dangers?"

"It's a habit, my dear," she answered. "Twenty years ago when we were transferred here from the regiment, I cannot tell you how I dreaded those accursed infidels! As soon as I saw their lynx caps and heard their squealing, my heart stood still, would you believe it! And now I have grown so used to it that I don't stir when they tell us the villains are prowling round the fortress."

"Vasilisa Yegorovna is a most courageous lady," Shvabrin remarked pompously. "Ivan Kuzmich can bear witness to it."

"Yes; she is not of the timid sort, let me tell you!" Ivan Kuzmich assented.

"And Marya Ivanovna? Is she as brave as you are?" I asked.

"Is Masha brave?" her mother answered. "No, Masha is a coward. She can't bear even now to hear a rifle shot; it makes her all of a tremble. And when, two years ago, Ivan Kuzmich took it into his head to fire our cannon on my name-day, she nearly died of fright, poor dear. Since then we haven't fired the cursed cannon any more."

We got up from the table. The Captain and his wife went to lie down, and I went to Shvabrin's and spent the whole evening with him.

IV

THE DUEL

*Oh, very well, take up then your position
And you shall see me pierce your body through.*

KNYAZHNIN

SEVERAL WEEKS had passed and my life in the Belogorsky fortress had grown not merely endurable but positively pleasant. I was received in the Commandant's house as one of the family. The husband and wife were most worthy people. Ivan Kuzmich, who had risen from the ranks to be an officer, was a plain and uneducated man, but most kind and honorable. His wife ruled him, which suited his easygoing disposition. Vasilisa Yegorovna looked upon her husband's military duties as her own concern and managed the fortress as she did her own home. Marya Ivanovna soon lost her shyness with me and we became friends. I found her to be a girl of feeling and good sense. Imperceptibly I grew attached to the kind family, and even to Ivan Ignatyich, the one-eyed lieutenant of the garrison; Shvabrin had said of him that he was on improper terms with Vasilisa Yegorovna, though there was not a semblance of truth in it; but Shvabrin did not care about that.

I received my commission. My military duties were not strenuous. In our blessed fortress there were no parades, no drills, no sentry duty. Occasionally the Commandant, of his own accord, taught the soldiers, but had not yet succeeded in teaching all of them to know their left hand from their right. Shvabrin had several French books. I began reading and developed a taste for literature. In the mornings I read, practiced translating, and sometimes composed verses; I almost always dined at the Commandant's and spent there the rest of the day; in the evenings, Father Gerasim and his wife, Akulina Pamfilovna, the biggest gossip in the neighborhood, sometimes came there also. Of course I saw Alexey Ivanych Shvabrin every day, but his conversation grew more and more distasteful to me as time went on. I disliked his constant jokes about the Commandant's family and, in particular, his derisive remarks about Marya Ivanovna. There was no other society in the fortress; and, indeed, I wished for no other.

In spite of the prophecies, the Bashkirs did not rise. Peace reigned around our fortress. But the peace was suddenly disturbed by an internal war.

I have already said that I tried my hand a literature. Judged by the standards of that period my attempts were quite creditable, and several years later Alexander Petrovich Sumarokov[8] thoroughly approved of them. One day I succeeded in writing a song that pleased me. Everybody knows that sometimes under the pretext of seeking advice writers try to find an appreciative listener. And so, having copied out my song, I took it to Shvabrin, who was the only person in

---

[8] Sumarokov, 1718-77, an early Russian poet of the pseudo-classical school (TRANSLATOR'S NOTE).

the fortress capable of doing justice to the poet's work. After a few preliminary remarks I took my notebook out of my pocket and read the following verses to him:

> *"Thoughts of love I try to banish*
> *And her beauty to forget,*
> *And, ah me! avoiding Masha*
> *Hope I shall my freedom get.*
>
> *But the eyes that have seduced me*
> *Are before me night and day,*
> *To confusion they've reduced me,*
> *Driven rest and peace away.*
>
> *When you hear of my misfortunes*
> *Pity, Masha, pity me!*
> *You can see my cruel torments:*
> *I am captive held by thee."*

"What do you think of it?" I asked Shvabrin, expecting praise as my rightful due. But to my extreme annoyance Shvabrin, who was usually a kind critic, declared that my song was bad.

"Why so?" I asked, concealing my vexation.

"Because such lines are worthy of my teacher, Vassily Kirilych Tretyakovsky,[4] and greatly remind me of his love verses."

He then took my notebook from me and began mercilessly criticizing every line and every word of the poem, mocking me in a most derisive manner. I could not endure it, snatched the notebook from him, and said I would never show him my verses again. Shvabrin laughed at this threat too.

"We shall see," he said, "whether you will keep your word. Poets need a listener as much as Ivan Kuzmich needs his de-

----

[4] One of the early Russian writers of poetry, remarkable for his unwearying zeal and utter lack of talent (TRANSLATOR'S NOTE).

canter of vodka before dinner. And who is this Masha to whom you declare your tender passion and lovesickness? Is it Marya Ivanovna, by any chance?"

"It's none of your business whoever she may be," I answered, frowning. "I want neither your opinion nor your conjectures."

"Oho! A touchy poet and a modest lover!" Shvabrin went on, irritating me more and more. "But take a friend's advice: if you want to succeed, you must have recourse to something better than songs."

"What do you mean, sir? Please explain yourself."

"Willingly. I mean that if you want Masha Mironov to visit you at dusk, present her with a pair of earrings instead of tender verses."

My blood boiled.

"And why have you such an opinion of her?" I asked, hardly able to restrain my indignation.

"Because I know her manners and morals from experience," he answered, with a fiendish smile.

"It's a lie, you scoundrel," I cried furiously. "It's a shameless lie!"

Shvabrin changed color.

"You'll have to pay for this," he said, gripping my arm; "you will give me satisfaction."

"Certainly—whenever you like," I answered, with relief. I was ready to tear him to pieces at that moment.

I went at once to Ivan Ignatyich, whom I found with a needle in his hands threading mushrooms to dry for the winter, at Vasilisa Yegorovna's request.

"Ah, Pyotr Andreyich! Pleased to see you!" he said, when he saw me. "What good fortune brings you? What business, may I ask?"

I explained to him briefly that I had quarreled with Alexey

Ivanych and was asking him, Ivan Ignatyich, to be my second. Ivan Ignatyich listened to me attentively, staring at me with his solitary eye.

"You are pleased to say," he answered, "that you intend to kill Alexey Ivanych and wish me to witness it? Is that so, may I ask?"

"Quite so."

"Good heavens, Pyotr Andreyich! What are you thinking about? You have quarreled with Alexey Ivanych? What ever does it matter? Bad words are of no consequence. He abuses you—you swear back at him; he hits you in the face—you hit him on the ear, twice, three times—and then go your own way; and we shall see to it that you make it up later on. But killing a fellow-creature—is that a right thing to do, let me ask you? And, anyway, if you killed him it wouldn't matter so much; I am not very fond of Alexey Ivanych myself, for the matter of that. But what if he makes a hole in you? What will that be like? Who will be made a fool of then, may I ask?"

The sensible old man's arguments did not shake me. I stuck to my intention.

"As you like," said Ivan Ignatyich. "Do what you think best. But why should I be your witness? What for? Two men fighting each other! What is there worth seeing in it, may I ask? I've been in the Swedish War and the Turkish, and, believe me, I've seen enough."

I tried to explain to him the duties of a second, but Ivan Ignatyich simply could not understand me.

"You may say what you like," he said, "but if I am to take part in this affair, it is only to go to Ivan Kuzmich and tell him, as duty bids me, that a crime contrary to the interests of the State is being planned in the fortress—and to ask if the Commandant would be pleased to take proper measures."

I was alarmed and begged Ivan Ignatyich to say nothing to the Commandant. I had difficulty in persuading him, but at last he gave me his word and I left him.

I spent the evening, as usual, at the Commandant's. I tried to appear cheerful and indifferent so as to escape inquisitive questions, and not give grounds for suspicion, but I confess I could not boast of the indifference which people in my position generally profess to feel. That evening I was inclined to be tender and emotional. Marya Ivanovna attracted me more than ever. The thought that I might be seeing her for the last time, made her seem particularly touching to me. Shvabrin was there also. I took him aside and told him of my conversation with Ivan Ignatyich.

"What do we want with seconds?" he said to me, dryly. "We will do without them."

We arranged to fight behind the corn stacks near the fortress and to meet there the following morning between six and seven. We appeared to be talking so amicably that Ivan Ignatyich, delighted, let out the secret.

"That's right!" he said to me, looking pleased; "a bad peace is better than a good quarrel; a damaged name is better than a damaged skin."

"What's this, what's this, Ivan Ignatyich?" asked Vasilisa Yegorovna, who was telling fortunes by cards in the corner. "I wasn't listening."

Ivan Ignatyich, seeing my look of annoyance and recalling his promise, was confused and did not know what to say. Shvabrin hastened to his assistance.

"Ivan Ignatyich approves of our making peace," he said.

"But with whom had you quarreled, my dear?"

"I had rather a serious quarrel with Pyotr Andreyich."

"What about?"

"About the merest trifle, Vasilisa Yegorovna: a song."

"That's a queer thing to quarrel about! A song! But how did it happen?"

"Why, this is how it was. Not long ago Pyotr Andreyich composed a song and today he began singing it in my presence, and I struck up my favorite:

> 'Captain's daughter, I warn you,
> Don't you go for midnight walks.'

"There was discord. Pyotr Andreyich was angry at first, but then he thought better of it, and decided that everyone may sing what he likes. And that was the end of it."

Shvabrin's impudence very nearly incensed me, but no one except me understood his coarse hints, or, at any rate, no one took any notice of them. From songs the conversation turned to poets; the Commandant remarked that they were a bad lot and bitter drunkards, and advised me, as a friend, to give up writing verses, for such an occupation did not accord with military duties and brought one to no good.

Shvabrin's presence was unendurable to me. I soon said good-bye to the Captain and his family. When I came home I examined my sword, felt the point of it, and went to bed, telling Savelyich to wake me at six o'clock.

The following morning I stood behind the corn stacks at the appointed hour waiting for my opponent. He arrived soon after me.

"We may be disturbed," he said. "We had better be quick."

We took off our uniforms and, dressed in our waistcoats only, bared our swords. At that moment Ivan Ignatyich with five soldiers of the garrison suddenly appeared from behind the stacks. He requested us to go to the Commandant's. We obeyed, vexed as we were; the soldiers surrounded us and we followed Ivan Ignatyich, who led us in triumph, stepping along with an air of extraordinary importance.

We entered the Commandant's house. Ivan Ignatyich opened the doors and solemnly proclaimed: "I have brought them!"

We were met by Vasilisa Yegorovna.

"Goodness me! What ever next? What? How could you? Planning murder in our fortress! Ivan Kuzmich, put them under arrest at once! Pyotr Andreyich, Alexey Ivanych! Give me your swords, give them up, give them up! Palasha, take these swords to the pantry! I did not expect this of you, Pyotr Andreyich; aren't you ashamed of yourself? It is all very well for Alexey Ivanych—he has been dismissed from the Guards for killing a man, and he does not believe in God, but fancy you doing a thing like this! Do you want to be like him?"

Ivan Kuzmich fully agreed with his wife, and kept repeating: "Vasilisa Yegorovna is quite right; let me tell you duels are explicitly forbidden in the army regulations."

Meanwhile Palasha took our swords and carried them to the pantry. I could not help laughing; Shvabrin retained his dignity.

"With all respect for you," he said coolly, "I must observe that you give yourself unnecessary trouble in passing judgment upon us. Leave it to Ivan Kuzmich—it is his business."

"But, my dear sir, aren't husband and wife one flesh and one spirit?" the Commandant's lady retorted. "Ivan Kuzmich, what are you thinking of? Put them under arrest at once in different corners and give them nothing but bread and water till they come to their senses! And let Father Gerasim set them a penance that they may beg God to forgive them and confess their sin to the people."

Ivan Kuzmich did not know what to do. Marya Ivanovna was extremely pale. Little by little the storm subsided; Vasilisa Yegorovna calmed down and made us kiss each other.

Palasha brought us back our swords. We left the Commandant's house, apparently reconciled. Ivan Ignatyich accompanied us.

"Aren't you ashamed," I said to him angrily, "to have betrayed us to the Commandant when you promised me not to?"

"God is my witness, I never said anything to Ivan Kuzmich," he answered; "Vasilisa Yegorovna wormed it all out of me. And she made all the arrangements without saying a word to Ivan Kuzmich. . . . But thank Heaven that it has all ended in this way."

With these words he turned home and Shvabrin and I were left alone.

"We cannot let it end at that," I said to him.

"Of course not," Shvabrin answered; "you will answer me with your blood for your insolence, but I expect we shall be watched. We shall have to pretend to be friends for a few days. Good-bye."

And we parted as though nothing had happened. Returning to the Commandant's I sat down, as usual, by Marya Ivanovna. Ivan Kuzmich was not at home; Vasilisa Yegorovna was busy with household matters. We spoke in undertones. Marya Ivanovna tenderly reproached me for the anxiety I had caused everyone by my quarrel with Shvabrin.

"I was quite overcome," she said, "when I heard you were going to fight. How strange men are! Because of a single word which they would be sure to forget in a week's time they are ready to kill each other and to sacrifice their lives and their conscience and the welfare of those who . . . But I am sure you did not begin the quarrel. Alexy Ivanych is probably to blame."

"And why do you think so, Marya Ivanovna?"

"Oh, I don't know . . . he always jeers at people. I don't

like Alexey Ivanych. He repels me and yet, strange to say, I would not, on any account, have him dislike me also. That would worry me dreadfully."

"And what do you think, Marya Ivanovna? Does he like you?"

Marya Ivanovna stammered and blushed.

"I think . . . " she said, "I believe he does like me."

"And why do you believe it?"

"Because he made me an offer of marriage."

"He made you an offer of marriage? When?"

"Last year. Some two months before you came."

"And you refused?"

"As you see. Of course, Alexey Ivanych is clever and rich, and of good family; but when I think that in church I should have to kiss him before all the people . . . not for anything! Nothing would induce me!"

Marya Ivanovna's words opened my eyes and explained a great deal to me. I understood the persistent slanders with which he pursued her. The words that gave rise to our quarrel seemed to me all the more vile when, instead of coarse and unseemly mockery, I saw in them deliberate calumny. My desire to punish the impudent slanderer grew more intense, and I waited impatiently for an opportunity.

I did not have to wait long. The following day as I sat composing an elegy, biting my pen as I searched for a rhyme, Shvabrin knocked at my window. I left my pen, picked up my sword, and went out to him.

"Why wait?" Shvabrin said. "We are not watched. Let us go down to the river. No one will disturb us there."

We walked in silence. Descending by a steep path we stopped at a river bank and bared our swords. Shvabrin was more skilled than I, but I was stronger and more daring; Monsieur Beaupré, who had once been a soldier, had given me a few lessons in fencing and I made use of them. Shvabrin had not expected to find in me so formidable an opponent. For a time we could neither of us do the other any harm; at last, observing that Shvabrin was weakening, I began to press him and almost drove him into the river. Suddenly I heard someone loudly calling my name. I turned round and saw Savelyich running toward me down the steep path . . . at that moment I felt a stab in my breast under the right shoulder, and fell down senseless.

V

L O V E

Ah, you young maiden, you maiden fair!
You must not marry while still so young
You must ask your father and mother first,
Your father and mother and all your kin.
You must grow in wisdom and keen good sense,
Must save up for yourself a rich dowry.

A FOLK SONG

If you find one better than me—you'll forget me,
If one who is worse—you'll remember.

A FOLK SONG

WHEN I REGAINED consciousness I could not grasp for a few minutes where I was, and what had happened to me. I was lying on a bed in a strange room, feeling very weak. Savelyich was standing before me with a candle in his hand. Someone was carefully unwrapping the bandages round my chest and shoulder. Gradually my thoughts cleared. I remembered my duel, and understood that I had been wounded. At that moment the door creaked.

"How is he?" whispered a voice which sent a tremor through me.

"Still the same," Savelyich answered, with a sigh. "Still unconscious. It's the fifth day."

I tried to turn my head, but could not.

"Where am I? Who is here?" I said, with an effort.

Marya Ivanovna came up to my bed and bent over me.

"Well, how do you feel?" she asked.

"God be thanked," I answered in a weak voice. "Is it you, Marya Ivanovna? Tell me . . ."

I had not the strength to go on, and broke off. Savelyich cried out. His face lit up with joy.

"He has come to his senses! Thank God! Well, my dear Pyotr Andreyich, you have given me a fright! Five days, it's no joke!"

Marya Ivanovna interrupted him.

"Don't talk to him too much, Savelyich," she said; "he is still weak." She went out and quietly closed the door.

My thoughts were in a turmoil. And so I was in the Commandant's house: Marya Ivanovna had come in to me. I wanted to ask Savelyich several questions, but the old man shook his head and stopped his ears. I closed my eyes in vexation and soon dropped asleep.

When I woke up I called Savelyich, but instead of him I saw Marya Ivanovna before me; her angelic voice greeted me. I cannot express the blissful feeling that possessed me at that moment. I seized her hand and covered it with kisses, wetting it with tears of tenderness. Masha did not withdraw her hand . . . and suddenly her lips touched my cheek and I felt their fresh and ardent kiss. A flame ran through me.

"Dear, kind Marya Ivanovna," I said to her, "be my wife, consent to make me happy."

She regained her self-possession.

"Calm yourself, for Heaven's sake," she said, taking her hand from me, "you are not out of danger yet—the wound may open. Take care of yourself, if only for my sake."

With these words she went out, leaving me in an ecstasy of delight. Happiness revived me. She would be mine! She loved me! My whole being was filled with this thought.

From that time onward I grew better every hour. I was treated by the regimental barber, for there was no other doctor in the fortress, and fortunately he did not attempt to be clever. Youth and nature hastened my recovery. The whole of the Commandant's family looked after me. Marya Ivanovna never left my side. Of course, at the first opportunity, I returned to our interrupted explanation, and Marya Ivanovna heard me out with more patience. Without any affectation she confessed her love for me and said that her parents would certainly be glad of her happiness.

"But think well," she added, "won't your parents raise objections?"

I pondered. I had no doubts of my mother's kindness; but knowing my father's views and disposition, I felt that my love would not particularly touch him and that he would look upon it as a young man's whim. I candidly admitted this to Marya Ivanovna, but decided to write to my father as eloquently as possible, asking him to give us his blessing. I showed my letter to Marya Ivanovna, who found it so touching and convincing that she never doubted of its success and abandoned herself to the feelings of her tender heart with all the trustfulness of youth and love.

I made peace with Shvabrin in the first days of my convalescence. In reprimanding me for the duel, Ivan Kuzmich had said to me: "Ah, Pyotr Andreyich, I ought really to put you under arrest, but you have been punished enough already. Alexey Ivanych, though, is shut up in the storehouse and Vasilisa Yegorovna has his sword under lock and key. It is just as well he should think things over and repent."

I was much too happy to retain any hostile feeling in my heart. I interceded for Shvabrin, and the kind Commandant, with his wife's consent, decided to release him. Shvabrin called on me; he expressed a profound regret for what had passed between us; he admitted that he had been entirely to blame and asked me to forget the past. It was not in my nature to harbor malice and I sincerely forgave him both our quarrel and the wound he had inflicted on me. I ascribed his slander to the vexation of wounded vanity and rejected love, and generously excused my unhappy rival.

I was soon quite well again and able to move into my lodgings. I awaited with impatience the answer to my last letter, not daring to hope, and trying to stifle melancholy forebodings. I had not yet declared my intentions to Vasilisa Yegorovna and her husband; but my offer was not likely to surprise them. Neither Marya Ivanovna nor I attempted to conceal our feelings from them, and we were certain of their consent beforehand.

At last, one morning Savelyich came in to me holding a letter. I seized it with a tremor. The address was written in my father's hand. This prepared me for something important, for as a rule it was my mother who wrote to me and my father only added a few lines at the end of the letter. Several minutes passed before I unsealed the envelope, reading over again and again the solemnly worded address: "To my son Pyotr Andreyich Grinyov, at the Belogorsky fortress in the Province of Orenburg." I tried to guess from the handwriting in what mood my father wrote the letter; at last I brought myself to open it and saw from the very first lines that all was lost. The letter was as follows:

My Son Pyotr!

On the 15th of this month we received the letter in which you ask for our parental blessing and consent to your marriage with Marya Ivanovna, Mironov's daughter; I do not intend to give you either my blessing or my consent, and, indeed, I mean to get at you and give you a thorough lesson as to a naughty boy for your pranks, not regarding your officer's rank, for you have proved that you are not yet worthy to wear the sword which has been given to you to defend your fatherland, and not to fight duels with scapegraces like yourself. I will write at once to Andrey Karlovich asking him to transfer you from the Belogorsky fortress to some remote place where you can get over your foolishness. When your mother heard of your duel and of your being wounded, she was taken ill with grief and is now in bed. What will become of you? I pray to God that you may be reformed although I dare not hope for this great mercy.

Your father,

A. G.

The perusal of this letter stirred various feelings in me. The cruel expressions, which my father did not stint, wounded me deeply. The contemptuous way in which he referred to Marya Ivanovna appeared to me as unseemly as it was unjust. The thought of my being transferred from the Belogorsky fortress terrified me; but most of all I was grieved by the news of my mother's illness. I felt indignant with Savelyich, never doubting it was he who had informed my parents of the duel. As I paced up and down in my tiny room I stopped before him and said, looking at him angrily: "So it's not enough for you that I have been wounded be-

cause of you, and lain for a whole month at death's door—
you want to kill my mother as well."

Savelyich was thunderstruck.

"Good heavens, sir, what are you saying?" he said, almost
sobbing. "You have been wounded because of me! God
knows I was running to shield you with my own breast from
Alexey Ivanych's sword! It was old age, curse it, that hin-
dered me. But what have I done to your mother?"

"What have you done?" I repeated. "Who asked you to
inform against me? Are you here to spy on me?"

"I informed against you?" Savelyich answered with tears.
"O Lord, King of Heaven! Very well, read then what Master
writes to me: you will see how I informed against you."

He pulled a letter out of his pocket and I read the
following:

*You should be ashamed, you old dog, not to have written
to me about my son, Pyotr Andreyich, in spite of my strict
orders; strangers have to inform me of his misdoings. So
this is how you carry out your duties and your master's will?
I will send you to look after pigs, you old dog, for concealing the truth, and conniving with the young man. As soon
as you receive this I command you to write to me at once
about his health, which, I am told, is better, in what place
exactly he was wounded, and whether his wound has healed
properly.*

It was obvious that Savelyich was innocent and I had
insulted him for nothing by my reproaches and suspicion.
I begged his pardon; but the old man was inconsolable.

"This is what I have come to," he kept repeating; "this is
the favor my masters show me for my services! I am an old
dog and a swineherd, and I am the cause of your wound!
. . . No, my dear Pyotr Andreyich, not I, but the damned

Frenchman is at the bottom of it: he taught you to prod people with iron spits, and to stamp with your feet, as though prodding and stamping could save one from an evil man! Much need there was to hire the Frenchman and spend money for nothing!"

But who, then, had taken the trouble to inform my father of my conduct? The General? But he did not seem to show much interest in me, and Ivan Kuzmich did not think it necessary to report my duel to him. I was lost in conjectures. My suspicions fixed upon Shvabrin. He alone could benefit by informing against me and thus causing me, perhaps, to be removed from the fortress and parted from the Commandant's family. I went to tell it all to Marya Ivanovna. She met me on the steps.

"What is the matter with you?" she said when she saw me. "How pale you are!"

"All is lost," I answered, and gave her my father's letter.

She turned pale, too. After reading the letter she returned it to me with a hand that shook, and said in a trembling voice: "It seems it is not to be. . . . Your parents do not want me in your family. God's will be done! God knows better than we do what is good for us. There is nothing for it. Pyotr Andreyich, may you at least be happy. . . ."

"This shall not be," I cried, seizing her hand; "you love me; I am ready to face any risk. Let us go and throw ourselves at your parents' feet; they are simple-hearted people, not hard and proud . . . they will bless us; we will be married . . . and then in time I am sure we will soften my father's heart; my mother will intercede for us; he will forgive me."

"No, Pyotr Andreyich," Masha answered, "I will not marry you without your parents' blessing. Without their blessing there can be no happiness for you. Let us submit to

God's will. If you find a wife, if you come to love another woman—God be with you, Pyotr Andreyich; I shall pray for you both. . . ."

She burst into tears and left me; I was about to follow her indoors, but feeling that I could not control myself, returned home.

I was sitting plunged in deep thought when Savelyich broke in upon my reflections.

"Here, sir," he said, giving me a piece of paper covered with writing, "see if I am an informer against my master and if I try to make mischief between father and son."

I took the paper from his hands: it was Savelyich's answer to my father's letter. Here it is, word for word:

Dear Sir, Andrey Petrovich, our Gracious Father!

I have received your gracious letter, in which you are pleased to be angry with me, your servant, saying that I ought to be ashamed not to obey my master's orders; I am not an old dog but your faithful servant; I obey your orders and have always served you zealously and have lived to be an old man. I have not written anything to you about Pyotr Andreyich's wound, so as not to alarm you needlessly, for I hear that, as it is, the mistress, our mother Avdotya Vassilyevna, has been taken ill with fright, and I shall pray for her health. Pyotr Andreyich was wounded in the chest under the right shoulder, just under the bone, three inches deep, and he lay in the Commandant's house where we carried him from the river bank, and the local barber, Stepan Paramonov, treated him, and now, thank God, Pyotr Andreyich is well and there is nothing but good to be said of him. His commanders, I hear, are pleased with him and Vasilisa Yegorovna treats him as though he were her own son. And as to his having got into trouble, that is no dis-

grace to him: a horse has four legs, and yet it stumbles. And you are pleased to write that you will send me to herd pigs. That is for you to decide as my master. Whereupon I humbly salute you.

Your faithful serf,
Arhip Savelyev

I could not help smiling more than once as I read the good old man's epistle. I felt I could not answer my father, and Savelyich's letter seemed to me sufficient to relieve my mother's anxiety.

From that time my position changed. Marya Ivanovna hardly spoke to me and did her utmost to avoid me. The Commandant's house lost all its attraction for me. I gradually accustomed myself to sit at home alone. Vasilisa Yegorovna chided me for it at first, but seeing my obstinacy, left me in peace. I only saw Ivan Kuzmich when my duties required it; I seldom met Shvabrin, and did so reluctantly, especially as I noticed his secret dislike of me, which confirmed my suspicions. Life became unbearable to me. I sank into despondent brooding, nurtured by idleness and isolation. My love grew more ardent in solitude and oppressed me more and more. I lost the taste for reading and composition. My spirits drooped. I was afraid that I should go out of my mind or plunge into dissipation. Unexpected events that had an important influence upon my life as a whole suddenly gave my mind a powerful and beneficial shock.

VI

PUGACHOV'S REBELLION

Listen now, young men, listen,
To what we old men shall tell you.

A FOLK SONG

BEFORE I BEGIN describing the strange events which I witnessed, I must say a few words about the situation in the Province of Orenburg at the end of 1773.

This vast and wealthy province was inhabited by a number of half-savage peoples who had but recently acknowledged the authority of the Russian sovereigns. Unused to the laws and habits of civilized life, cruel and reckless, they constantly rebelled, and the Government had to watch over them unremittingly to keep them in submission. Fortresses had been built in suitable places and settled for the most part with Cossacks, who had owned the shores of Yaïk for generations. But the Cossacks who were to guard the peace and safety of the place had themselves for some time past been a source of trouble and danger to the Government. In 1772 a rising took place in their chief town. It was caused by the stern measures adopted by Major-General Traubenberg in order to bring the Cossacks into due submission. The result was the barbarous assassination of Traubenberg, a mutinous change in the administration of the Cossack army, and, finally, the quelling of the mutiny by means of cannon and cruel punishments.

This had happened some time before I came to the Belogorsky fortress. All was quiet or seemed so; the authorities too easily believed the feigned repentance of the perfidious rebels, who concealed their malice and waited for an opportunity to make fresh trouble.

To return to my story.

One evening (it was the beginning of October, 1773) I sat at home alone, listening to the howling of the autumn wind, and watching through the window the clouds that raced past the moon. Someone came to call me to the Commandant's. I went at once. I found there Shvabrin, Ivan Ignatyich, and the Cossack sergeant, Maximych. Neither Vasilisa Yegorovna nor Marya Ivanovna was in the room. The Commandant looked troubled as he greeted me. He closed the doors, made us all sit down except the sergeant, who was standing by the door, pulled a letter out of his pocket and said: "Important news, gentlemen! Listen to what the General writes." He put on his spectacles and read the following:

To THE COMMANDANT OF THE BELOGORSKY FORTRESS, CAPTAIN MIRONOV

Confidential.

I inform you herewith that a runaway Don Cossack, an Old Believer, Emelyan Pugachov, has perpetrated the unpardonable outrage of assuming the name of the deceased Emperor Peter III and, assembling a criminal band, has caused a rising in the Yaïk settlements, and has already taken and sacked several fortresses, committing murders and robberies everywhere. In view of the above, you have, sir, on receipt of this, immediately to take the necessary measures for repulsing the aforementioned villain and pretender, and, if possible, for completely destroying him, should he attack the fortress entrusted to your care.

"Take the necessary measures," said the Commandant, removing his spectacles and folding the paper. "That's easy enough to say, let me tell you. The villain is evidently strong; and we have only a hundred and thirty men, not counting the Cossacks on whom there is no relying—no offense meant, Maximych." (The sergeant smiled.) "However, there is nothing for it, gentlemen! Carry out your duties scrupulously, arrange for sentry duty and night patrols; in case of attack shut the gates and lead the soldiers afield. And you, Maximych, keep a strict watch over your Cossacks. The cannon must be seen to and cleaned properly. And, above all, keep the whole thing secret so that no one in the fortress should know as yet."

Having given us these orders, Ivan Kuzmich dismissed us. Shvabrin and I walked out together, talking of what we had just heard.

"What will be the end of it, do you think?" I asked him.

"Heaven only knows," he answered. "We shall see. So far, I don't think there is much in it. But if . . ."

He sank into thought, and began absent-mindedly whistling a French tune.

In spite of all our precautions the news of Pugachov spread throughout the fortress. Although Ivan Kuzmich greatly respected his wife, he would not for anything in the world have disclosed to her a military secret entrusted to him. Having received the General's letter, he rather skillfully got rid of Vasilisa Yegorovna by telling her that Father Gerasim had had some startling news from Orenburg, which he was guarding jealously. Vasilisa Yegorovna at once decided to go and call on the priest's wife and, on Ivan Kuzmich's advice, took Masha with her lest the girl should feel lonely at home.

Finding himself master of the house, Ivan Kuzmich at

once sent for us and locked Palasha in the pantry so that she should not listen at the door.

Vasilisa Yegorovna had not succeeded in gaining any information from the priest's wife and, coming home, she learned that, in her absence, Ivan Kuzmich had held a council, and that Palasha had been locked up. She guessed that her husband had deceived her and began questioning him. Ivan Kuzmich, however, had been prepared for attack. He was not in the least abashed and boldly answered his inquisitive consort: "Our women, my dear, have taken to heating the stoves with straw, let me tell you; and since this may cause a fire I have given strict orders that in the future they should not use straw but wood."

"Then why did you lock up Palasha?" the Commandant's wife asked. "What had the poor girl done to have to sit in the pantry till our return?"

Ivan Kuzmich was not prepared for this question; he was confused and muttered something very incoherent. Vasilisa Yegorovna saw her husband's perfidy, but knowing that she would not succeed in learning anything from him, ceased her questions, and began talking of pickled cucumbers, which the priest's wife prepared in some very special way. Vasilisa Yegorovna could not sleep all night, trying to guess what could be in her husband's mind that she was not supposed to know.

The next day returning from Mass she saw Ivan Ignatyich pulling out of the cannon bits of rag, stones, splinters, knucklebones, and all kinds of rubbish that boys had thrust into it.

"What can these military preparations mean?" the Commandant's wife wondered. "Are they expecting another Kirghiz raid? But surely Ivan Kuzmich would not conceal such trifles from me!" She hailed Ivan Ignatyich with the firm intention of finding out from him the secret that tormented her feminine curiosity.

Vasilisa Yegorovna made several remarks to him about housekeeping, just as a magistrate who is cross-examining a prisoner begins with irrelevant questions so as to take him off his guard. Then, after a few moments' silence, she sighed deeply and said, shaking her head: "Oh dear, oh dear! Just think, what news! Whatever will come of it?"

"Don't you worry, madam," Ivan Ignatyich answered; "God willing, all will be well. We have soldiers enough, plenty of gunpowder, and I have cleaned the cannon. We may yet keep Pugachov at bay. Whom God helps, nobody can harm."

"And what sort of man is this Pugachov?" she asked.

Ivan Ignatyich saw that he had made a slip and tried not to answer. But it was too late. Vasilisa Yegorovna forced him to confess everything, promising not to repeat it to anyone.

She kept her promise and did not say a word to anyone except to the priest's wife, and that was only because her cow was still grazing in the steppe and might be seized by the rebels.

Soon everyone began talking about Pugachov. The rumors differed. The Commandant sent Maximych to find out all he could in the neighboring villages and fortresses. The sergeant returned after two days' absence and said that in the steppe, some forty miles from the fortress, he had seen a lot of lights and had heard from the Bashkirs that a host of unknown size was approaching. He could not, however, say anything definite, for he had not ventured to go any farther.

The Cossacks in the fortress were obviously in a state of great agitation; in every street they stood about in groups, whispering together, dispersing as soon as they saw a dragoon or a garrison soldier. Spies were sent among them. Yulay, a Kalmuck converted to the Christian faith, brought important information to the Commandant. Yulay said that the sergeant's report was false; on his return, the sly Cossack told his comrades that he had seen the rebels, presented himself to their leader, who gave him his hand to kiss, and held a long conversation with him. The Commandant immediately arrested Maximych and put Yulay in his place. This step was received with obvious displeasure by the Cossacks. They murmured aloud and Ivan Ignatyich, who had to carry out the Commandant's order, heard with his own ears how they said: "You will catch it presently, you garrison rat!" The Commandant had intended to question his prisoner the same day, but Maximych had escaped, probably with the help of his comrades.

Another thing helped to increase the Commandant's anxiety. A Bashkir was caught carrying seditious papers. On this occasion the Commandant thought of calling his officers together once more and again wanted to send Vasilisa Yegorovna away on some pretext. But since Ivan Kuzmich was a most truthful and straightforward man, he could think of no other device than the one he had used before.

"I say, Vasilisa Yegorovna," he began, clearing his throat, "Father Gerasim, I hear, has received from town . . ."

"Don't you tell stories, Ivan Kuzmich," his wife interrupted him. "I expect you want to call a council to talk about Emelyan Pugachov without me; but you won't decieve me."

Ivan Kuzmich stared at her.

"Well, my dear," he said, "if you know all about it already, you may as well stay; we will talk before you."

"That's better, man," she answered. "You are no hand at deception; send for the officers."

We assembled again. Ivan Kuzmich read to us, in his wife's presence, Pugachov's manifesto written by some half-literate Cossack. The villain declared his intention to march against our fortress at once, invited the Cossacks and the soldiers to join his band, and exhorted the commanders not to resist him, threatening to put them to death if they did. The manifesto was written in crude but forceful language, and must have produced a strong impression upon the minds of simple people.

"The rascal!" cried Vasilisa Yegorovna. "To think of his daring to make us such offers! We are to go and meet him and lay the banners at his feet! Ah, the dog! Doesn't he know that we've been forty years in the army and have seen a thing or two? Surely no commanders have listened to the brigand?"

"I should not have thought so," Ivan Kuzmich answered, "but it appears the villain has already taken many fortresses."

"He must really be strong, then," Shvabrin remarked.

"We are just going to find out his real strength," said the Commandant. "Vasilisa Yegorovna, give me the key of the storehouse. Ivan Ignatyich, bring the Bashkir and tell Yulay to bring the whip."

"Wait, Ivan Kuzmich," said the Commandant's wife, getting up. "Let me take Masha out of the house; she will be terrified if she hears the screams. And, to tell the truth, I don't care for the business myself. Good luck to you."

In the old days torture formed so integral a part of judicial procedure that the beneficent law which abolished it long remained a dead letter. It used to be thought that the criminal's own confession was necessary for convicting him, which is both groundless and wholly opposed to judicial good sense; for if the accused person's denial of the charge is not considered a proof of his innocence, there is still less reason to regard his confession a proof of his guilt. Even now I sometimes hear old judges regretting the abolition of the barbarous custom. But in those days no one doubted the necessity of torture—neither the judges nor the accused. And so the Commandant's order did not surprise or alarm us. Ivan Ignatyich went to fetch the Bashkir, who was locked up in Vasilisa Yegorovna's storehouse, and a few minutes later the prisoner was led into the entry. The Commandant gave word for him to be brought into the room.

The Bashkir crossed the threshold with difficulty (he was wearing fetters) and, taking off his tall cap, stood by the door. I glanced at him and shuddered. I shall never forget that man. He seemed to be over seventy. He had neither nose nor ears. His head was shaven; instead of a beard, a few gray hairs stuck out; he was small, thin and bent, but his narrow eyes still had a gleam in them.

"Aha!" said the Commandant, recognizing by the terrible marks one of the rebels punished in 1741. "I see you are an old wolf and have been in our snares. Rebelling must be an old game to you, to judge by the look of your head. Come nearer; tell me, who sent you?"

The old Bashkir was silent and gazed at the Commandant with an utterly senseless expression.

"Why don't you speak?" Ivan Kuzmich continued. "Don't you understand Russian? Yulay, ask him in your language who sent him to our fortress?"

Yulay repeated Ivan Kuzmich's question in Tatar. But the Bashkir looked at him with the same expression and did not answer a word.

"Very well!" the Commandant said. "I will make you speak! Lads, take off his stupid striped gown and streak his back. Mind you do it thoroughly, Yulay!"

Two veterans began undressing the Bashkir. The unfortunate man's face expressed anxiety. He looked about him like some wild creature caught by children. But when the old man was made to put his hands round the veteran's neck and was lifted off the ground and Yulay brandished the whip, the Bashkir groaned in a weak, imploring voice, and, nodding his head, opened his mouth in which a short stump could be seen instead of a tongue.

When I recall that this happened in my lifetime and that now I have lived to see the gentle reign of the Emperor Alexander, I cannot but marvel at the rapid progress of enlightenment and the diffusion of humane principles. Young man! If my notes ever fall into your hands, remember that the best and most permanent changes are those due to the softening of manners and morals and not to any violent upheavals.

It was a shock to all of us.

"Well," said the Commandant, "we evidently cannot learn much from him. Yulay, take the Bashkir back to the storehouse. We have a few more things to talk over, gentlemen."

We began discussing our position when suddenly Vasilisa Yegorovna came into the room, breathless and looking extremely alarmed.

"What is the matter with you?" the Commandant asked in surprise.

"My dear, dreadful news!" Vasilisa Yegorovna answered. "The Nizhneozerny fortress was taken this morning. Father Gerasim's servant has just returned from there. He saw it being taken. The Commandant and all the officers were hanged. All the soldiers were taken prisoners. The villains may be here any minute."

The unexpected news was a great shock to me. I knew the Commandant of the Nizhneozerny fortress, a modest and quiet young man; some two months before he had put up at

Ivan Kuzmich's on his way from Orenburg with his young wife. The Nizhneozerny fortress was some fifteen miles from our fortress. Pugachov might attack us any moment now. I vividly imagined Marya Ivanovna's fate and my heart sank.

"Listen, Ivan Kuzmich," I said to the Commandant, "it is our duty to defend the fortress to our last breath; this goes without saying. But we must think of the women's safety. Send them to Orenburg if the road is still free, or to some reliable fortress farther away out of the villain's reach."

Ivan Kuzmich turned to his wife and said: "I say, my dear, hadn't I indeed better send you and Masha away while we settle the rebels?"

"Oh, nonsense!" she replied. "No fortress is safe from bullets. What's wrong with the Belogorsky? We have lived in it for twenty-two years, thank Heaven! We have seen the Bashkirs and the Kirghiz; God willing, Pugachov won't harm us either."

"Well, my dear," Ivan Kuzmich replied, "stay if you like, since you rely on our fortress. But what are we to do about Masha? It is all very well if we ward them off or last out till reinforcements come; but what if the villains take the fortress?"

"Well, then . . ."

Vasilisa Yegorovna stopped with an air of extreme agitation.

"No, Vasilisa Yegorovna," the Commandant continued, noting that his words had produced an effect perhaps for the first time in his life, "it is not fit for Masha to stay here. Let us send her to Orenburg, to her godmother's: there are plenty of soldiers there, and enough artillery and a stone wall. And I would advise you to go with her: you may be an old woman, but you'll see what they'll do to you, if they take the fortress."

"Very well," said the Commandant's wife, "so be it, let us send Masha away. But don't you dream of asking me—I won't go; I wouldn't think of parting from you in my old age and seeking a lonely grave far away. Live together, die together."

"There is something in that," said the Commandant. "Well, we must not waste time. You had better get Masha ready for the journey. We will send her at daybreak tomorrow and give her an escort, though we have no men to spare. But where is Masha?"

"At Akulina Pamfilovna's," the Commandant's wife answered. "She fainted when she heard about the Nizhneozerny being taken; I am afraid of her falling ill."

Vasilisa Yegorovna went to see about her daughter's departure. The conversation continued, but I took no part in it, and did not listen. Marya Ivanovna came in to supper, pale and with tear-stained eyes. We ate supper in silence and rose from the table sooner than usual; saying good-bye to the family, we went to our lodgings. But I purposely left my sword behind and went back for it; I had a feeling that I should find Marya Ivanovna alone. Indeed, she met me at the door and handed me my sword.

"Good-bye, Pyotr Andreyich," she said to me, with tears. "I am being sent to Orenburg. May you live and be happy; perhaps God will grant that we meet again, and if not . . . "

She broke into sobs; I embraced her.

"Good-bye, my angel," I said, "good-bye, my sweet, my darling! Whatever happens to me, believe that my last thought and my last prayer will be for you!"

Masha sobbed with her head on my shoulder. I kissed her ardently and hastened out of the room.

VII

THE ATTACK

Oh, my poor head, a soldier's head!
It served the Czar truly and faithfully
For thirty years and three years more.
It won for itself neither gold nor joy,
No word of praise and no high rank.
All it has won is a gallows high
With a cross-beam made of maple wood
And a noose of twisted silk.

A FOLK SONG

I DID NOT undress or sleep that night. I intended to go
at dawn to the fortress gate from which Marya Ivanovna
was to start on her journey, and there to say good-bye to
her for the last time. I was conscious of a great change in
myself; the agitation of my mind was much less oppressive
than the gloom in which I had but recently been plunged.
The grief of parting was mingled with vague but delicious
hope, with eager expectation of danger and a feeling of noble
ambition. The night passed imperceptibly. I was on the point
of going out when my door opened and the corporal came
to tell me that our Cossacks had left the fortress in the night,
taking Yulay with them by force, and that strange men were
riding about outside the fortress. The thought that Marya
Ivanovna might not have time to leave terrified me; I hastily
gave a few instructions to the corporal and rushed off to
the Commandant's.

It was already daybreak. As I ran down the street I heard
someone calling me. I stopped.

"Where are you going?" Ivan Ignatyich asked, overtaking me. "Ivan Kuzmich is on the rampart and has sent me for you. Pugachov has come."

"Has Marya Ivanovna left?" I asked, with a sinking heart.

"She has not had time," Ivan Ignatyich answered. "The road to Orenburg is cut off; the fortress is surrounded. It is a bad lookout, Pyotr Andreyich!"

We went to the rampart—a natural rise in the ground reinforced by palisading. All the inhabitants of the fortress were crowding there. The garrison stood under arms. The cannon had been moved there the day before. The Commandant was walking up and down in front of his small detachment. The presence of danger inspired the old soldier with extraordinary vigor. Some twenty men on horseback were riding to and fro in the steppe not far from the fortress. They seemed to be Cossacks, but there were Bashkirs among them, easily recognized by their lynx caps and quivers. The Commandant walked through the ranks, saying to the soldiers: "Well, children, let us stand up for our Empress and prove to all the world that we are brave and loyal men!" The soldiers loudly expressed their zeal. Shvabrin stood next to me, looking intently at the enemy. Noticing the commotion in the fortress, the horsemen in the steppe met together and began talking. The Commandant told Ivan Ignatyich to aim the cannon at the group and fired it himself. The cannonball flew with a buzzing sound over their heads without doing any damage. The horsemen dispersed and instantly galloped away, and the steppe was empty.

At that moment Vasilisa Yegorovna appeared on the rampart, followed by Masha, who would not leave her.

"Well, what's happening?" the Commandant's wife asked. "How is the battle going? Where is the enemy?"

"The enemy is not far," Ivan Kuzmich answered. "God willing, all shall be well. Well, Masha, aren't you afraid?"

"No, Father," Marya Ivanovna answered. "It is worse at home by myself."

She looked at me and made an effort to smile. I clasped the hilt of my sword, remembering that the day before I had received it from her hands, as though for the protection of my lady love. My heart was glowing, I fancied myself her knight. I longed to prove that I was worthy of her trust and waited impatiently for the decisive moment.

Just then fresh crowds of horsemen appeared from behind a hill that was less than half a mile from the fortress, and soon the steppe was covered with a multitude of men armed with spears and bows and arrows. A man in a red coat, with a bare sword in his hand, was riding among them mounted on a white horse: it was Pugachov. He stopped; the others surrounded him. Four men galloped at full speed, evidently at his command, right up to the fortress. We recognized them as our own treacherous Cossacks. One of them was holding a sheet of paper over his cap; another carried on the point of his spear Yulay's head, which he shook off and threw to us over the palisade. The poor Kalmuck's head fell at the Commandant's feet; the traitors shouted: "Don't shoot, come out to greet the Czar! The Czar is here!"

"I'll give it to you!" Ivan Kuzmich shouted. "Shoot, lads!"

Our soldiers fired a volley. The Cossack who held the letter reeled and fell off his horse; others galloped away. I glanced at Marya Ivanovna. Horrified by the sight of Yulay's bloodstained head and stunned by the volley, she seemed dazed. The Commandant called the corporal and told him to take the paper out of the dead Cossack's hands. The corporal went out into the field and returned leading the dead man's horse by the bridle. He handed the letter to the Commandant. Ivan Kuzmich read it to himself and then tore it to bits. Meanwhile the rebels were evidently making ready for action. In a few minutes bullets whizzed in our

ears, and a few arrows stuck into the ground and the palisade near us.

"Vasilisa Yegorovna," said the Commandant, "this is no
place for women, take Masha home; you see the girl is
more dead than alive."

Vasilisa Yegorovna, who had grown quiet when the bullets
began to fly, glanced at the steppe where a great deal of
movement was noticeable; then she turned to her husband
and said: "Ivan Kuzmich, life and death are in God's hands;
bless Masha. Masha, go to your father!"

Masha, pale and trembling, went up to Ivan Kuzmich,
knelt before him, and bowed down to the ground. The old
Commandant made the sign of the cross over her three times,
then he raised her and, kissing her, said in a changed voice:
"Well, Masha, may you be happy. Pray to God; He will not
forsake you. If you find a good man, may God give you
love and concord. Live as Vasilisa Yegorovna and I have
lived. Well, good-bye, Masha. Vasilisa Yegorovna, make
haste and take her away!"

Masha flung her arms round his neck and sobbed.

"Let us kiss each other, too," said the Commandant's
wife, bursting into tears. "Good-bye, my Ivan Kuzmich.
Forgive me if I have vexed you in any way."

"Good-bye, good-bye, my dear," said the Commandant,
embracing his old wife. "Well, that will do! Make haste and
go home; and, if you have time, dress Masha in a sarafan."

The Commandant's wife and daughter went away. I followed Marya Ivanovna with my eyes; she looked round and
nodded to me. Then Ivan Kuzmich turned to us and all his
attention centered on the enemy. The rebels assembled round
their leader and suddenly began dismounting.

"Now, stand firm," the Commandant said. "They are
going to attack."

At that moment terrible shouting and yelling was heard;

the rebels were running fast toward the fortress. Our cannon was loaded with grapeshot. The Commandant let them come quite near and then fired again. The shot fell right in the middle of the crowd; the rebels scattered and rushed back; their leader alone did not retreat. . . . He waved his saber and seemed to be persuading them. . . . The yelling and shouting that had stopped for a moment began again.

"Well, lads," the Commandant said, "now open the gates, beat the drum. Forward, lads; come out, follow me!"

The Commandant, Ivan Ignatyich, and I were instantly beyond the rampart; but the garrison lost their nerve and did not move.

"Why do you stand still, children?" Ivan Kuzmich shouted. "If we must die, we must—it's all in the day's work!"

At that moment the rebels ran up to us and rushed into the fortress. The drum stopped; the soldiers threw down their rifles; I was knocked down, but got up again and walked into the fortress together with the rebels. The Commandant, wounded in the head, was surrounded by the villains, who demanded the keys; I rushed to his assistance; several burly Cossacks seized me and bound me with their belts, saying: "You will catch it presently, you enemies of the Czar!"

They dragged us along the streets; the townspeople came out of their houses with offerings of bread and salt. Church bells were ringing. Suddenly they shouted in the crowd that the Czar was awaiting the prisoners in the square and receiving the oath of allegiance. The people rushed to the square; we were driven there also.

Pugachov was sitting in an armchair on the steps of the Commandant's house. He was wearing a red Cossack *caftan* trimmed with gold braid. A tall sable cap with golden tassels was pushed low over his glittering eyes. His face seemed

familiar to me. The Cossack elders surrounded him. Father
Gerasim, pale and trembling, was standing by the steps with
a cross in his hands and seemed to be silently imploring
mercy for future victims. Gallows were being hastily put up
in the square. As we approached, the Bashkirs dispersed the
crowd and brought us before Pugachov. The bells stopped
ringing: there was a profound stillness.

"Which is the Commandant?" the Pretender asked.

Our Cossack sergeant stepped out of the crowd and
pointed to Ivan Kuzmich. Pugachov looked at the old man
menacingly and said to him: "How did you dare resist me,
your Czar?"

Exhausted by his wound the Commandant mustered his
last strength and answered in a firm voice: "You are not my
Czar; you are a thief and an impostor, let me tell you!"

Pugachov frowned darkly and waved a white handkerchief. Several Cossacks seized the old Captain and dragged
him to the gallows. The old Bashkir, whom we had questioned the night before, was sitting astride on the cross-beam.
He was holding a rope and a minute later I saw poor Ivan
Kuzmich swing in the air. Then Ivan Ignatyich was brought
before Pugachov.

"Take the oath of allegiance to the Czar Peter III!"
Pugachov said to him.

"You are not our monarch," Ivan Ignatyich answered.
repeating his captain's words; "you are a thief and an impostor, my dear!"

Pugachov waved his handkerchief again, and the good
lieutenant swung by the side of his old chief.

It was my turn next. I boldly looked at Pugachov, making ready to repeat the answer of my noble comrades. At
that moment, to my extreme surprise, I saw Shvabrin among
the rebellious Cossacks; he was wearing a Cossack coat and

had his hair cropped like theirs. He went up to Pugachov and whispered something in his ear.

"Hang him!" said Pugachov, without looking at me.

My head was put through the noose. I began to pray silently, sincerely repenting before God of all my sins and begging Him to save all those dear to my heart. I was dragged under the gallows.

"Never you fear," the assassins repeated to me, perhaps really wishing to cheer me.

Suddenly I heard a shout: "Stop, you wretches! Wait!" The hangmen stopped. I saw Savelyich lying at Pugachov's feet.

"Dear father," the poor old man said, "what would a gentle-born child's death profit you? Let him go; they will give you a ransom for him; and as an example and a warning to others, hang me—an old man!"

Pugachov made a sign and they instantly untied me and let go of me. "Our father pardons you," they told me.

I cannot say that at that moment I rejoiced at being saved; nor would I say that I regretted it. My feelings were too confused. I was brought before the Pretender once more and made to kneel down. Pugachov stretched out his sinewy hand to me.

"Kiss his hand, kiss his hand," people around me said. But I would have preferred the most cruel death to such vile humiliation.

"Pyotr Andreyich, my dear," Savelyich whispered, standing behind me and pushing me forward, "don't be obstinate! What does it matter? Spit and kiss the vill— I mean, kiss his hand!"

I did not stir. Pugachov let his hand drop, saying with a laugh: "His honor must have gone crazy with joy. Raise him!"

They pulled me up and left me in peace. I began watching the terrible comedy.

The townspeople were swearing allegiance. They came up one after another, kissed the cross and then bowed to the Pretender. The garrison soldiers were there, too. The regimental tailor, armed with his blunt scissors, was cutting off their plaits. Shaking themselves they came to kiss Pugachov's hand; he granted them his pardon and enlisted them in his gang. All this went on for about three hours. At last Pugachov got up from the armchair and came down the steps accompanied by his elders. A white horse in a rich harness was brought to him. Two Cossacks took him by the arms and put him on the horse. He announced to Father Gerasim that he would have dinner at his house. At that moment a woman's cry was heard. Several brigands had dragged Vasilisa Yegorovna, naked and disheveled, onto the steps. One of them had already donned her coat. Others were carrying featherbeds, boxes, crockery, linen, and all sorts of household goods.

"My dears, let me go!" the poor old lady cried. "Have mercy, let me go to Ivan Kuzmich!"

Suddenly she saw the gallows and recognized her husband.

"Villains!" she cried in a frenzy. "What have you done to him! Ivan Kuzmich, light of my eyes, soldier brave and bold! You came to no harm from Prussian swords, or from Turkish guns; you laid down your life not in a fair combat, but perished from a runaway thief!"

"Silence the old witch!" said Pugachov.

A young Cossack hit her on the head with his saber and she fell dead on the steps. Pugachov rode away; the people rushed after him.

VIII

AN UNBIDDEN GUEST

An unbidden guest is worse than a Tatar.
A PROVERB

THE SQUARE EMPTIED. I was still standing there, unable
to collect my thoughts, confused by the terrible impressions
of the day.

Uncertainty as to Marya Ivanovna's fate tortured me most.
Where was she? What had happened to her? Had she had
time to hide? Was her refuge secure? Full of anxious
thoughts I entered the Commandant's house. All was empty;
chairs, tables, boxes had been smashed, crockery broken;
everything had been taken. I ran up the short stairway that
led to the top floor and for the first time in my life entered
Marya Ivanovna's room. I saw her bed pulled to pieces by
the brigands; the wardrobe had been broken and pillaged; the
sanctuary lamp was still burning before the empty ikon stand.
The little mirror that hung between the windows had been
left, too. . . . Where was the mistress of this humble vir-
ginal cell? A terrible thought flashed through my mind: I
imagined her in the brigands' hands . . . my heart sank.
. . . I wept bitterly and called aloud my beloved's name.
. . . At that moment I heard a slight noise and Palasha,
pale and trembling, appeared from behind the wardrobe.

"Ah, Pyotr Andreyich!" she cried, clasping her hands.
"What a day! What horrors!"

"And Marya Ivanovna?" I asked impatiently. "What has happened to her?"

"She is alive," Palasha answered; "she is hiding in Akulina Pamfilovna's house."

"At the priest's!" I cried, in horror. "Good God! Pugachov is there!"

I dashed out of the room, instantly found myself in the street and ran headlong to the priest's house, not seeing or feeling anything. Shouts, laughter, and songs came from there. . . . Pugachov was feasting with his comrades. Palasha followed me. I sent her to call out Akulina Pamfilovna without attracting attention. A minute later the priest's wife came into the entry to speak to me, with an empty bottle in her hands.

"For God's sake, where is Marya Ivanovna?" I asked, with inexpressible anxiety.

"She is lying on my bed there, behind the partition, poor darling," the priest's wife answered. "Well, Pyotr Andreyich, we very nearly had trouble, but thank God, all passed off well: the villain had just sat down to dinner when she, poor thing, came to herself and groaned. I simply gasped! He heard. 'Who is it groaning there, old woman?' he said. I made a deep bow to the thief: 'My niece is ill, sire, she has been in bed for a fortnight.' 'And is your niece young?' 'She is, sire.' 'Show me your niece, old woman.' My heart sank, but there was nothing for it. 'Certainly, sire; only the girl cannot get up and come into your presence.' 'Never mind, old woman, I will go and have a look at her myself.' And, you know, the wretch did go behind the partition. What do you think? He drew back the curtain, glanced at her with hawk's eyes—and nothing happened. . . . God saved us! But, would you believe it, both my husband and I had prepared to die a martyr's death. Fortunately the dear girl did not know who he was. Good Lord, what things we have lived to see! Poor Ivan Kuzmich! Who would have thought it! And Vasilisa Yegorovna! And Ivan Ignatyich! What did they hang him for? How is it you were spared? And what do you think of Shvabrin? You know, he cropped his hair like a Cossack and is sitting here with them feasting! He is a sharp one, there's no gainsaying! And when I spoke about my sick niece, his eyes, would you believe it, went through me like a knife; but he hasn't betrayed us, and that's something to be thankful for."

At that moment the drunken shouts of the guests were heard, and Father Gerasim's voice. The guests were clamoring for more drink and the priest was calling his wife. Akulina Pamfilovna was in a flutter.

"You go home now, Pyotr Andreyich," she said. "I haven't any time for you; the villains are drinking. It might be the end of you if they met you now. Good-bye, Pyotr Andreyich. What is to be, will be; I hope God will not forsake us!"

The priest's wife left me. I set off to my lodgings feeling somewhat calmer. As I passed through the market place I saw several Bashkirs, who crowded round the gallows, pulling the boots off the hanged men's feet; I had difficulty in suppressing my indignation, but I knew that it would have been useless to intervene. The brigands were running about the fortress, plundering the officers' quarters. The shouts of the drunken rebels resounded everywhere. I reached my lodgings. Savelyich met me at the threshold.

"Thank God!" he cried, when he saw me. "I was afraid the villains had seized you again. Well, Pyotr Andreyich, my dear! Would you believe it, the rascals have robbed us of everything: clothes, linen, crockery—they have left nothing. But there! Thank God they let you off with your life! Did you recognize their leader, sir?"

"No, I didn't; why, who is he?"

"What, sir? You have forgotten that drunkard who took the hareskin jacket from you at the inn? The coat was as good as new, and the brute tore it along the seams as he struggled into it!"

I was surprised. Indeed, Pugachov had a striking resemblance to my guide. I felt certain Pugachov and he were the same person and understood the reason for his sparing me. I could not help marveling at the strange concatenation of circumstances: a child's coat given to a tramp had saved me from the gallows, and a drunkard who had wandered from inn to inn was besieging fortresses and shaking the foundations of the State!

"Won't you have something to eat?" asked Savelyich, true to his habit. "There is nothing at home; I will look about and prepare something for you."

Left alone, I sank into thought. What was I to do? It was not fitting for an officer to remain in a fortress that belonged to the villain or to follow his gang. It was my duty to go where my services could be of use to my country in the present trying circumstances . . . But love prompted me to stay by Marya Ivanovna to protect and defend her. Although I had no doubt that things would soon change, I could not help shuddering at the thought of the danger she was in.

My reflections were interrupted by the arrival of a Cossack, who had run to tell me that "the great Czar was asking for me."

"Where is he?" I said, making ready to obey.

"In the Commandant's house," the Cossack answered. "After dinner our father went to the bathhouse and now he is resting. Well, your honor, one can see by everything that he is a person of importance: at dinner he was pleased to eat two roast suckling pigs, and he likes the bathhouse so hot that even Taras Kurochkin could not stand it—he passed on the birch to Fomka Bikbaev, and had to have cold water poured over him. There's no denying it, all his ways are so grand. . . . And they say, in the bathhouse, he showed them the royal marks on his breast: on one side the two-headed eagle, the size of a penny, and on the other his own likeness."

I did not think it necessary to dispute the Cossack's opinion and, together with him, went to the Commandant's house, trying to picture my meeting with Pugachov and wondering how it would end. The reader may well guess that I was not altogether calm.

It was growing dusk when I reached the Commandant's house. The gallows, with its victims, loomed menacingly in the dark. Poor Vasilisa Yegorovna's body was still lying at the bottom of the steps, where two Cossacks were mounting guard. The Cossack who had brought me went to announce me and returning at once, led me into the room where the night before I had taken such tender leave of Marya Ivanovna.

An extraordinary scene was before me. Pugachov and a dozen Cossack elders, wearing colored shirts and caps, were sitting round a table covered with a cloth and littered with bottles and glasses; their faces were flushed with drink and their eyes glittered. Neither Shvabrin nor our sergeant—the freshly recruited traitors—were among them.

"Ah, your honor!" said Pugachov, when he saw me, "come and be my guest; here is a place for you, you are very welcome."

The company made room for me. I sat down at the end of the table without speaking. My neighbor, a slim and good-looking young Cossack, poured out a glass of vodka for me, which I did not touch. I looked at my companions with curiosity. Pugachov sat in the place of honor leaning on the table, his black beard propped up with his broad fist. His features, regular and rather pleasant, had nothing ferocious about them. He often turned to a man of fifty, addressing him sometimes as Count, sometimes as Timofeich, and occasionally calling him uncle. They all treated one another as comrades and showed no particular deference to their leader. They talked of the morning's attack, of the success of the rising, and of the plans for the future. Everyone boasted, offered his opinion, and freely argued with Pugachov. At this strange council of war it was decided to go to Orenburg: a bold move which was very nearly crowned with disastrous success! The march was to begin the following day.

"Well, brothers," Pugachov said, "let us have my favorite song before we go to bed. Chumakov, strike up!"

My neighbor began in a high-pitched voice a mournful boatmen's song and all joined in:

> "Murmur not, mother-forest of rustling green leaves,
> Hinder not a brave lad thinking his thoughts,
> For tomorrow I go before the judgment seat,
> Before the dreaded judge, our sovereign Czar,
> And the Czar, our lord, will ask me:
> Tell me now, good lad, tell me, peasant's son,
> With whom didst thou go robbing and plundering,
> And how many were thy comrades bold?
> I shall tell thee the whole truth and naught but truth.
> Four in number were my comrades bold:
> My first trusty comrade was the dark night,
> And my second true comrade—my knife of steel,
> And my third one was my faithful steed,
> And the fourth one was my stout bow,
> And my messengers were my arrows sharp.

Then our Christian Czar will thus speak to me:
Well done, good lad, thou peasant's son!
Thou knowest how to rob and to answer for it,
And a fine reward is in store for thee—
A mansion high in the open plain,
Two pillars and a cross-beam I grant thee."

I cannot describe how affected I was by this peasant song about the gallows, sung by men doomed to the gallows. Their menacing faces, their tuneful voices, the mournful expression they gave to the words expressive enough in themselves—it all thrilled me with a feeling akin to awe.

The guests drank one more glass, got up from the table, and took leave of Pugachov. I was about to follow them when Pugachov said to me: "Sit still, I want to talk to you."

We were left alone. We were both silent for a few minutes; Pugachov was watching me intently, occasionally screwing up his left eye with an extraordinary expression of slyness and mockery. At last he laughed with such unaffected gaiety that, as I looked at him, I laughed, too, without knowing why.

"Well, your honor?" he said to me. "Confess you had a bit of a fright when my lads put your head in the noose? I expect the sky seemed no bigger than a sheepskin to you. . . . And you would have certainly swung if it had not been for your servant. I knew the old creature at once. Well, did you think, your honor, that the man who brought you to the inn was the great Czar himself?" (He assumed an air of mystery and importance.) "You are very much at fault," he continued, "but I have spared you for your kindness, for your having done me a service when I had to hide from my enemies. But this is nothing to what you shall see! It's not to

be compared to the favor I'll show you when I obtain my
kingdom! Do you promise to serve me zealously?"

The rascal's question and his impudence struck me as so
amusing that I could not help smiling.

"What are you smiling at?" he asked, with a frown. "Don't
you believe I am the Czar? Answer me plainly."

I was confused. I felt I could not acknowledge the tramp
as Czar: to do so seemed to me unpardonable cowardice.
To call him an impostor to his face meant certain death; and
what I was ready to do under the gallows, in sight of all the
people and in the first flush of indignation, now seemed to
me useless bravado. I hesitated. Pugachov gloomily awaited
my reply. At last (and to this day I recall that moment with
self-satisfaction) the feeling of duty triumphed over human
weakness. I said to Pugachov: "Listen, I will tell you the
whole truth. Think, how can I acknowledge you as Czar?
You are an intelligent man; you would see I was pretending."

"Who, then, do you think I am?"

"God only knows; but whoever you may be, you are playing a dangerous game."

Pugachov threw a swift glance at me.

"So you don't believe," he said, "that I am the Czar Peter
III? Very well. But there is such a thing as success for the
bold. Didn't Grishka Otrepyev[5] reign in the old days? Think
of me what you like, but follow me. What does it matter to
you? One master is as good as another. Serve me truly and
faithfully, and I'll make you Field Marshal and Prince. What
do you say?"

"No," I answered firmly. "I am a gentleman by birth; I
swore allegiance to the Empress: I cannot serve you. If you
really wish me well, let me go to Orenburg."

[5] Pseudo-Demetrius I, an alleged impostor who ruled Russia in 1605-
1606 (EDITOR'S NOTE).

Pugachov was thoughtful.

"And if I let you go," he said, "will you promise, at any rate, not to fight against me?"

"How can I promise that?" I answered. "You know yourself I am not free to do as I like; if they send me against you, I shall go, there is nothing for it. You yourself are a leader now; you require obedience from those who serve under you. What would you call it if I refused to fight when my service was required? My life is in your hands; if you let me go, I will thank you; if you hang me, God be your judge; but I have told you the truth."

My sincerity impressed Pugachov.

"So be it," he said, clapping me on the shoulder. "I don't do things by halves. Go wherever you like and do what you think best. Come tomorrow to say good-bye to me and now go to bed; I, too, am sleepy."

I left Pugachov and went out into the street. The night was still and frosty. The moon and the stars shone brightly, shedding their light on the square and the gallows. In the fortress all was dark and quiet. Only the tavern windows were lighted and the shouts of late revelers came from there. I looked at the priest's house. The gates and shutters were closed. All seemed quiet there.

I went home and found Savelyich grieving for my absence. The news of my freedom delighted him more than I can say.

"Thanks be to God!" he said, crossing himself. "We shall leave the fortress as soon as it is light and go straight away. I have prepared some supper for you, my dear; have something to eat and then sleep peacefully till morning."

I followed his advice, and having eaten my supper with great relish went to sleep on the bare floor, exhausted both in mind and body.

IX

THE PARTING

Sweet it was, O dear heart,
To meet and learn to love thee.
But sad it was from thee to part—
As though my soul fled from me.

                                        KHERASKOV

EARLY in the morning I was wakened by the drum. I went
to the square. Pugachov's crowds were already forming into
ranks by the gallows, where the victims of the day before
were still hanging. The Cossacks were on horseback, the
soldiers under arms. Banners were flying. Several cannon,
among which I recognized ours, were placed on their carriages. All the inhabitants were there, too, waiting for the
impostor. A Cossack stood at the steps of the Commandant's
house, holding a beautiful white Kirghiz horse by the bridle.
I searched with my eyes for Vasilisa Yegorovna's body. It
had been moved a little to one side and covered with a piece
of matting. At last Pugachov appeared in the doorway. The
people took off their caps. Pugachov stood on the steps and
greeted them all. One of the elders gave him a bag of coppers
and he began throwing them down in handfuls. The crowd
rushed to pick them up, shouting; some were hurt in the
scramble. Pugachov was surrounded by his chief confed-
erates. Shvabrin was among them. Our eyes met; he could
read contempt in mine, and he turned away with an expression of sincere malice and feigned mockery. Catching sight

of me in the crowd, Pugachov nodded and beckoned to me.

"Listen," he said to me. "Go at once to Orenburg and tell the Governor and all his generals from me that they are to expect me in a week. Advise them to meet me with childlike love and obedience, else they will not escape a cruel death. A pleasant journey to you, your honor!"

Then he turned to the people and said, pointing to Shvabrin: "Here, children, is your new commandant. Obey him in everything, and he will be answerable to me for you and the fortress."

I heard these words with horror; Shvabrin was put in command of the fortress; Marya Ivanovna would be in his power! My God! What would become of her? Pugachov came down the steps. His horse was brought to him. He quickly jumped into the saddle without waiting for the Cossacks to help him. At that moment I saw my Savelyich step out of the crowd and hand Pugachov a sheet of paper. I could not imagine what this would lead to.

"What is this?" Pugachov asked, with an air of importance.

"Read and you will see," Savelyich answered.

Pugachov took the paper and gazed at it significantly for a few moments.

"Why do you write so illegibly?" he said at last. "Our bright eyes can make nothing of it. Where is my chief secretary?"

A young man in a corporal's uniform at once ran up to Pugachov.

"Read it aloud," said the impostor, giving him the paper. I was extremely curious to know what Savelyich could have written to Pugachov. The chief secretary began reading aloud, syllable by syllable: "Two dressing gowns, one cotton and one striped silk, worth six rubles."

"What does this mean?" Pugachov asked, with a frown.

"Tell him to read on," Savelyich answered calmly.

The chief secretary continued: "A uniform coat of fine green cloth, worth seven rubles. White cloth trousers, worth five rubles. Twelve fine linen shirts with frilled cuffs, worth ten rubles. A tea set worth two and a half rubles. . . ."

"What nonsense is this?" Pugachov interrupted him. "What do I care about tea sets and frilled cuffs and trousers?"

Savelyich cleared his throat and began explaining: "Well, you see, sir, this is a list of my master's goods stolen by the villains. . . ."

"What villains?" Pugachov said menacingly.

"I am sorry; it was a slip of the tongue," Savelyich answered. "They are not villains, of course, your men, but they rummaged about and took these things. Don't be angry: a horse has four legs and yet it stumbles. Tell him to read to the end anyway."

"Read on," Pugachov said.

The secretary continued: "A cotton bedspread, a silk eiderdown, worth four rubles. A red cloth coat lined with fox fur, worth forty rubles. Also a hareskin jacket given to your honor at the inn, worth fifteen rubles. . . ."

"What next!" Pugachov shouted, with blazing eyes.

I confess I was alarmed for Savelyich. He was about to give more explanations, but Pugachov interrupted him.

"How dare you trouble me with such trifles!" he cried, seizing the paper from the secretary's hands and throwing it in Savelyich's face. "Stupid old man! They have been robbed—as though it mattered! Why, you old dodderer, you ought to pray for the rest of your life for me and my men, and thank your stars that you and your master are not swinging here together with those who rebelled against me. . . . Hareskin jacket, indeed! I'll give you a hareskin jacket! Why,

I'll have you flayed alive and make a jacket of your skin!"

"As you please," Savelyich answered. "But I am a bond·man, and have to answer for my master's property."

Pugachov was evidently in a generous mood. He turned away and rode off without saying another word. Shvabrin and the Cossack elders followed him. The gang left the fortress in an orderly fashion. The townspeople walked out some distance after Pugachov. Savelyich and I were left alone in the square. He was holding the paper in his hands, and examining it with an air of deep regret.

Seeing that I was on good terms with Pugachov, he had decided to take advantage of it; but his wise intention did not meet with success. I tried to scold him for his misplaced zeal, but could not help laughing.

"It's all very well to laugh, sir," Savelyich answered. "It won't be so amusing when we shall have to buy everything afresh!"

I hastened to the priest's house to see Marya Ivanovna. The priest's wife had bad news for me. In the night Marya Ivanovna had developed a fever. She lay unconscious and delirious. Akulina Pamfilovna took me into her room. I walked quietly to the bedside. The change in her face struck me. She did not know me. I stood beside her for some time without listening to Father Gerasim and his kind wife, who were, I think, trying to comfort me. Gloomy thoughts tormented me. The condition of the poor defenseless orphan left among the vindictive rebels, and my own helplessness, terrified me. The thought of Shvabrin tortured my imagination more than anything. Given power by the Pretender, put in charge of the fortress where the unhappy girl—the innocent object of his hatred—remained, he might do anything. What was I to do? How could I help her? How could I free her from the villain's hands? There was only one thing left me: I decided to go to Orenburg that very hour and do my utmost to hasten the relief of the Belogorsky fortress. I said good-bye to the priest and to Akulina Pamfilovna, begging them to take care of Marya Ivanovna, whom I already regarded as my wife. I took the poor girl's hand and kissed it, wetting it with my tears.

"Good-bye," said the priest's wife, taking leave of me, "good-bye, Pyotr Andreyich. I hope we shall meet in better times. Don't forget us and write to us often. Poor Marya Ivanovna has now no one to comfort and defend her but you."

Coming out into the square I stopped for a moment to look at the gallows, bowed down before it, and left the fortress by the Orenburg road, accompanied by Savelyich, who kept pace with me.

I walked on, occupied with my thoughts, when I suddenly heard the sound of a horse's hoofs behind me. I turned round and saw a Cossack galloping from the fortress; he was leading a Bashkir horse by the bridle and signaling to me from a distance. I stopped and soon recognized our sergeant. Overtaking me he dismounted and said, giving me the reins of the other horse: "Your honor, our father presents you with a horse and a fur coat of his own" (a sheepskin coat was tied to the saddle), "and he also presents you"—Maximych hesitated—"with fifty kopecks in money . . . but I lost it on the way; kindly forgive me."

Savelyich looked at him askance and grumbled: "Lost it on the way! And what is this rattling in the breast of your coat? You've got no conscience!"

"What is rattling in the breast of my coat?" replied the sergeant, not in the least abashed. "Why, mercy on us, my good man! That's my bridle and not the fifty kopecks!"

"Very well," I said, interrupting the argument. "Give my

thanks to him who sent you; and on your way back try to pick up the money you dropped and take it for vodka."

"Thank you very much, your honor," he answered, turning his horse; "I shall pray for you as long as I live."

With these words he galloped back, holding with one hand the breast of his coat, and in another minute was lost to sight. I put on the sheepskin and mounted the horse, making Savelyich sit behind me.

"You see now, sir," the old man said, "it was not for nothing I presented the petition to the rascal; the thief's conscience pricked him. It's true, the long-legged Bashkir nag and the sheepskin coat are not worth half of what they have stolen from us, the rascals, and what you had yourself given him, but it will come in useful; one may as well get a piece of wool off a fierce dog."

X

THE SIEGE OF THE TOWN

He pitched his camp upon the hills and meadows
And, eagle-like, he gazed upon the city;
He had a mound made beyond the camp
Concealing fire, which at night he brought to city walls.

KHERASKOV

AS WE APPROACHED Orenburg we saw a crowd of convicts with shaven heads and faces disfigured by the branding iron. They were working at the fortifications under the supervision of garrison soldiers. Some were carting away the rubbish with which the moat had been filled, others were

digging; on the ramparts masons were carrying bricks, mending the town wall. At the gates we were stopped by the sentries, who asked for our passports. As soon as the sergeant
heard that I came from the Belogorsky fortress, he took me
straight to the General's house.

I found the General in the garden. He was examining the
apple trees already bared by the breath of autumn and, with
the help of an old gardener, was carefully wrapping them up
in warm straw. His face wore a look of serenity, health, and
good nature. He was pleased to see me and began questioning me about the terrible happenings I had witnessed. I told
him everything. The old man listened to me attentively as
he pruned the trees.

"Poor Mironov!" he said, when I finished my sad story.
"I am sorry for him, he was a fine officer; and Madam
Mironov was an excellent woman and so good at pickling
mushrooms! And what has become of Masha, the Captain's
daughter?"

I answered that she remained at the fortress, in the charge
of the priest's wife.

"Aïe, aïe, aïe!" the General remarked, "that's bad, very
bad. There is certainly no relying on the brigands' discipline.
What will become of the poor girl?"

I answered that the Belogorsky fortress was not far and
that probably his Excellency would not delay in sending
troops to deliver its poor inhabitants. The General shook his
head doubtfully. "We shall see, we shall see," he said. "There
will be time enough to talk of this. Please come and have a
cup of tea with me; I am having a council of war today. You
can give us exact information about the rascal Pugachov and
his troops. And, meanwhile, go and have a rest!"

I went to the quarters allotted to me, where Savelyich
was already setting things to rights, and waited impatiently

for the appointed hour. The reader may well imagine that I did not fail to appear at the council which was of such importance to my future. At the appointed time I was at the General's.

I found there one of the town officials, the director of the customs house, if I remember rightly, a stout, rosy-cheeked old man in a brocade coat. He asked me about the fate of Ivan Kuzmich, with whom he was connected, and often interrupted me with fresh questions and moral observations which, proved, if not his skill in the art of war, at any rate his natural quickness and intelligence. Meanwhile other guests arrived. When all had sat down and cups of tea had been handed around, the General explained at great length and very clearly the nature of the business.

"Now, gentlemen, we must decide how we are to act against the rebels; must we take the offensive or the defensive? Each of these methods has its advantages and disadvantages. The offensive offers more hope of exterminating the enemy in the shortest time; the defensive is safer and more reliable. . . . And so let us take votes in the proper manner; that is, beginning with the youngest in rank. Ensign!" he continued, addressing himself to me, "please give us your opinion."

I got up and began by saying a few words about Pugachov and his gang; I said positively that the impostor had no means of resisting regular troops.

My opinion was received by the officials with obvious disfavor. They saw in it the defiance and rashness of youth. There was a murmur, and I clearly heard the word "greenhorn" uttered by someone in an undertone.

The General turned to me and said, with a smile: "Ensign, the first votes in councils of war are generally in favor of the offensive; this is as it should be. Now let us go on collecting votes. Mr. Collegiate Councilor! tell us your opinion."

The little old man in the brocade coat hastily finished his third cup of tea, considerably diluted with rum, and said in answer to the General: "I think, your Excellency, we need not take either the offensive or the defensive."

"How so, sir?" the General retorted in surprise. "No other tactics are possible; one must either take the offensive or be on the defensive. . . ."

"Your Excellency, take the way of bribery."

"Ha! ha! ha! Your suggestion is very reasonable. Bribery is permitted by military tactics and we will follow your advice. We can offer seventy rubles . . . or, perhaps, a hundred for the rascal's head . . . to be paid from the secret fund."

"And then," the chief customs officer interrupted, "may I be a Kirghiz sheep and not a collegiate councilor, if those thieves do not surrender their leader to us, bound hand and foot!"

"We will think of it again and talk it over," the General answered; "but we must, in any case, take military measures. Gentlemen, please vote in the usual manner!"

All the opinions were opposed to mine. All the officials spoke of troops being unreliable and luck changeable, of caution and such like things. All thought it wiser to remain behind strong stone walls defended by cannon rather than venture into the open field. At last, when the General had heard all the opinions, he shook the ashes out of his pipe and made the following speech: "My dear sirs! I must tell you that for my part I entirely agree with the Ensign's opinion, for it is based upon all the rules of sound military tactics, according to which it is almost always preferable to take up the offensive rather than to remain on the defensive."

At this point he stopped and began filling his pipe once more. My vanity was gratified. I proudly looked at the officials, who whispered to one another with an air of vexation and anxiety.

"But, my dear sirs," he continued, letting out, together with a deep sigh, a big whiff of tobacco smoke, "I dare not take upon myself so great a responsibility when the security of provinces entrusted to me by Her Imperial Majesty, our gracious sovereign, is at stake. And so I agree with the majority, which has decided that it is wiser and safer to await a siege within the city walls, repulsing the enemy's attacks by artillery and, if possible, by sallies."

The officials, in their turn, looked mockingly at me. The council dispersed. I could not help regretting the weakness of the venerable soldier who decided against his own conviction to follow the opinion of ignorant and inexperienced men.

Several days after this famous council we learned that Pugachov, true to his promise, was approaching Orenburg. From the top of the town hall I saw the rebels' army. It seemed to me their numbers had increased tenfold since the last attack which I witnessed. They now had artillery, brought by Pugachov from the small fortresses he had taken. Recalling the council's decision, I foresaw a prolonged confinement within the town walls and nearly wept with vexation.

I will not describe the siege of Orenburg, which belongs to history, and is not a subject for family memoirs. I will only say that, owing to the carelessness of the local authorities, the siege was disastrous for the inhabitants, who suffered famine and all sort of calamities. One may well imagine that life in Orenburg was simply unendurable. All were despondently waiting for their fate to be decided; all complained of the prices, which were, indeed, exorbitant. The inhabitants had grown used to cannonballs falling into their back yards; even Pugachov's assaults no longer excited general interest. I was dying of boredom. Time was passing. I received no letter from the Belogorsky fortress. All the roads were cut off. Separation from Marya Ivanovna was growing unbearable. Uncertainty about her fate tormented me. The skirmishes were my only distractions; thanks to Pugachov I had a good horse with which I shared my scanty fare, and I rode it every day to exchange shots with Pugachov's men. As a rule the advantage in these skirmishes was on the side of the villains, who were well fed, had plenty to drink, and rode good horses. The starving cavalry of the town could not get the better of them. Sometimes our hungry infantry also went afield, but the thick snow prevented it from acting successfully against the horsemen scattered all over the plain. Artillery thundered in vain from the top of the rampart, and in the field it stuck in the snow and could not move because the horses were too exhausted to pull it along. This is what our military operations were like! And this was what the Orenburg officials called being cautious and sensible.

One day when we succeeded in scattering and driving away a rather thick crowd, I overtook a Cossack who had lagged behind; I was on the point of striking him with my Turkish sword, when he suddenly took off his cap and cried: "Good morning, Pyotr Andreyich! How are you getting on?"

I looked at him and recognized our Cossack sergeant. I was overjoyed to see him.

"How do you do, Maximych," I said to him. "Have you been in the Belogorsky lately?"

"Yes, sir, I was there only yesterday; I have a letter for you, Pyotr Andreyich."

"Where is it?" I asked, flushing all over.

"Here," said Maximych, thrusting his hand in the breast of his coat. "I promised Palasha I would manage somehow to give it to you."

He gave me a folded paper and galloped away. I opened it and read, with a tremor, the following lines:

It has pleased God to deprive me suddenly of both father and mother; I have no friends or relatives in this world. I appeal to you, knowing that you have always wished me well and that you are ready to help everyone. I pray that this letter may reach you! Maximych has promised to take it to you. Palasha has heard from Maximych that he often sees you from a distance during the sallies and that you do not take any care of yourself or think of those who pray for you with tears. I was ill for a long time, and when I recovered, Alexey Ivanovich, who is now commandant instead of my father, forced Father Gerasim to give me up to him, threatening him with Pugachov! I live in our house as a prisoner. Alexey Ivanovich is forcing me to marry him. He says he saved my life because he did not betray Akulina Pamfilovna when she told the villains I was her niece. And I would rather die than marry a man like Alexey Ivanovich. He treats me very cruelly and threatens that if I don't change my mind and marry him he will take me to the villains' camp and there the same thing will happen to me as to Lizaveta Kharlova. I have asked Alexey Ivanovich to give me time to think. He agreed to wait three more days and if I don't marry him in three days' time he will have no pity on me. Dear Pyotr Andreyich! You alone are my protector; help me in my distress. Persuade the General and all the commanders to make haste and send a relief party to us, and come yourself if you can. I remain yours obediently,

A poor orphan,
Marya Mironov

I almost went out of my mind when I read this letter. I galloped back to the town, spurring my poor horse mercilessly. On the way I racked my brain for the means of saving the poor girl, but could think of nothing. When I reached the town I rode straight to the General's and rushed headlong into his house.

The General was walking up and down the room, smoking his pipe. He stopped when he saw me. He must have been struck by my appearance; he inquired with concern about the reason for my coming in such a hurry.

"Your Excellency," I said to him. "I appeal to you as to my own father; for God's sake don't refuse me, the happiness of my whole life is at stake."

"What is it, my dear?" the old man asked in surprise. "What can I do for you? Tell me."

"Your Excellency, allow me to have a detachment of soldiers and fifty Cossacks and let me go and clear the Belogorsky fortress."

The General looked at me attentively, probably thinking that I had gone out of my mind—he was not far wrong.

"How do you mean—to clear the Belogorsky fortress?" he brought out at last.

"I vouch for success," I said eagerly, "only let me go."

"No, young man," he said, shaking his head; "at so great a distance the enemy will find it easy to cut off your communication with the main strategic point and to secure a complete victory over you. Once the communication has been cut off . . ."

I was afraid he would enter upon a military discussion and made haste to interrupt him.

"Captain Mironov's daughter," I said to him, "has sent me a letter; she begs for help; Shvabrin is forcing her to marry him."

"Really? Oh, that Shvabrin is a great *Schelm,* and if he falls into my hands I will have him court-martialed within twenty-four hours and we will shoot him on the fortress wall! But meanwhile you must have patience. . . ."

"Have patience!" I cried, beside myself. "But meanwhile he will marry Marya Ivanovna!"

"Oh, that won't be so bad," the General retorted; "it will be better for her to be Shvabrin's wife for the time being; he will be able to look after her at present, and afterwards, when we shoot him, she will find plenty of suitors, God willing. Charming widows don't remain old maids; I mean a young widow will find a husband sooner than a girl would."

"I would rather die," I cried in a rage, "than give her up to Shvabrin!"

"Oh, I see!" said the old man, "now I understand. . . . You are evidently in love with Marya Ivanovna. Oh, that's another matter! Poor boy! But all the same, I cannot possibly give you a detachment of soldiers and fifty Cossacks. Such an expedition would be unreasonable; I cannot take the responsibility for it."

I bowed my head; I was in despair. Suddenly an idea flashed through my mind. The reader will learn from the following chapter what it was—as the old-fashioned novelists put it.

XI

THE REBELS' CAMP

The lion has just had a meal;
Ferocious as he is, he asked me kindly:
"What brings you to my lair?"

SUMAROKOV

I LEFT the General and hastened to my lodgings. Savelyich met me with his usual admonitions.

"Why ever do you go fighting those drunken brigands, sir? It isn't the thing for a gentleman. You may perish for nothing any day. If at least they were Turks or Swedes—but these wretches are not fit to be mentioned. . . ."

I interrupted him by asking how much money we had.

"We have enough," he said, with an air of satisfaction; "the rascals rummaged everywhere, but I have managed to hide it from them." With these words he took out of his pocket a long knitted purse full of silver.

"Well, Savelyich," said I to him, "give me half of it and take the rest for yourself. I am going to the Belogorsky fortress."

"My dear Pyotr Andreyich!" said the kind old man in a shaking voice, "What are you thinking of! How can you go at a time like this, when the brigands are all over the place? Have pity on your parents if you don't care about yourself. How can you go? What for? Wait a little; troops will come and catch the rascals; then go anywhere you like."

But my decision was firm.

"It is too late to argue," I answered; "I must go, I cannot help it. Don't grieve, Savelyich; God willing, we will meet again. Now don't be overscrupulous or stint yourself. Buy everything you need, even if you have to pay three times the price. I make you a present of that money. If I don't return in three days . . ."

"What, sir!" Savelyich interrupted me. "Do you imagine I would let you go alone? Don't you dream of asking that. Since you have decided to go, I will follow you; if I have to walk I won't leave you. To think of my sitting behind a stone wall without you! I haven't taken leave of my senses yet. Say what you like, sir, but I will go with you."

I knew it was useless to argue with Savelyich and so I allowed him to prepare for the journey. Half an hour later I mounted my good horse, and Savelyich a lame and skinny nag which one of the townspeople presented to him, not having the means to feed it. We rode to the town gates; the sentries let us pass; we left Orenburg.

It was growing dark. My way lay through the village of Berda, which was occupied by Pugachov's troops. The main road was covered with snowdrifts, but traces of horses' hoofs were all over the steppe, marked afresh each day. I was riding at a quick trot, Savelyich could hardly follow me at a distance, and kept shouting: "Not so fast, sir; for God's sake not so fast! My cursed nag cannot keep up with your long-legged devil. Where are you hurrying to? It's not to a feast we are going—more likely to our funeral! Pyotr Andreyich! . . . Pyotr Andreyich, my dear! . . . Good Lord, that child will come to grief!"

The lights of Berda soon came into sight. We rode up to the ravines that formed the natural defenses of the village. Savelyich kept pace with me, never ceasing from his pitiful entreaties. I was hoping to get round the village when suddenly I saw before me in the twilight some five peasants armed with clubs: it was the advance guard of Pugachov's camp. They called to us. Not knowing their password, I wanted to ride past them without saying anything; but they immediately surrounded me and one of them seized my horse by the bridle. I seized my sword and hit the peasant on the head; his cap saved him, but he staggered and let go the bridle. The others were confused and ran away; I took advantage of that moment, spurred my horse and galloped on. The darkness of the approaching night might have saved me from all danger, when turning round I suddenly saw that Savelyich was not with me. The poor old man could not ride away from the brigands on his lame horse. What was I to do? After waiting a few minutes and making certain that he had been detained, I turned my horse back and went to his rescue.

As I rode up to the ravine I heard a noise, shouts and my Savelyich's voice. I rode faster and soon found myself once more among the peasant watchmen who had stopped me a few minutes before. Savelyich was with them. They had pulled the old man off his nag and were preparing to bind him. My return pleased them. They rushed at me with a shout and instantly pulled me off my horse. One of them, evidently the chief, said that he would take us to the Czar at once.

"And it is for the Father Czar to decide," he added, "whether we are to hang you at once or wait till dawn."

I offered no resistance; Savelyich followed my example, and the watchmen led us along in triumph.

We crossed the ravine and entered the village. Lights were burning in all the windows. Noise and shouting came from everywhere. We met a number of people in the streets, but in the dark no one noticed us or recognized me for an officer from Orenburg. We were brought straight to a cottage that stood at the crossroads. There were several wine barrels and two cannon at the gate.

"Here is the palace," one of the peasants said. "I'll go and announce you."

He went in. I glanced at Savelyich; the old man was silently repeating a prayer and crossing himself. I waited a long time; at last the peasant returned and said to me: "Walk in, our father says he will see the officer."

I went into the cottage, or the palace, as the peasants called it. It was lighted by two tallow candles and the walls were papered with gold paper; but the benches, the table, the washing arrangements, the towel on a nail, the oven fork in the corner and the broad stove shelf covered with pots, were just as in any other cottage. Pugachov, wearing a red coat and a tall cap, was sitting under the ikons with an air of importance, his arms akimbo. Several of his chief associates were standing by him with an expression of feigned servility: news of the arrival of an officer from Orenburg had evidently aroused the rebels' curiosity and they had prepared an impressive reception for me. Pugachov recognized me at the first glance. His assumed air of importance suddenly disappeared.

"Ah, your honor!" he said genially. "How are you? What brings you here?"

I answered that I was traveling on my own business and that his men had detained me.

"And what is your business?" he asked me.

I did not know what to say. Thinking I did not want to speak before witnesses, Pugachov turned to his comrades and ordered them to leave the room. All obeyed except two who did not stir.

"Speak boldly in their presence," Pugachov said to me, "I hide nothing from them."

I threw a sidelong glance at the impostor's confidants. One

of them, a puny, bent old man with a gray beard, had nothing remarkable about him except a blue ribbon worn across the shoulder over a gray peasant coat. But I shall never forget his comrade. He was tall, stout, and broad-shouldered, and seemed to be about forty-five. A thick red beard, gray glittering eyes, a nose without nostrils, and reddish marks on the forehead and the cheeks gave an indescribable expression to his broad, pock-marked face. He wore a red shirt, a Kirghiz gown and Cossack trousers. As I learned later, the first was a runaway corporal, Beloborodov; the second, Afanasy Sokolov, nicknamed Khlopusha, a convict who had escaped three times from the Siberian mines. In spite of the feelings which absorbed me, the company in which I so unexpectedly found myself strongly appealed to my imagination. But Pugachov brought me back to myself by repeating: "Tell me on what business have you left Orenburg?"

A strange idea came into my head: it seemed to me that Providence, which had brought me for the second time to Pugachov, was giving me an opportunity to carry out my intention. I decided to take advantage of it and, without stopping to consider my decision, said in answer to Pugachov: "I was going to the Belogorsky fortress to rescue an orphan who is being ill-treated there."

Pugachov's eyes glittered.

"Which of my men dares to ill-treat an orphan?" he cried. "He may be as clever as you please, but he won't escape my sentence. Tell me, who is the guilty man?"

"Shvabrin," I answered. "He keeps under lock and key the girl whom you saw lying ill at the priest's house, and wants to marry her by force."

"I'll teach Shvabrin!" said Pugachov menacingly. "I'll show him what it is to take the law into his own hands and to ill-treat people. I will hang him!"

"Allow me to say a word," Khlopusha said, in a hoarse

voice. "You were in a hurry to put Shvabrin in command of the fortress and now you are in a hurry to hang him. You have already offended the Cossacks by putting a gentleman over them; do not now frighten the gentry by hanging him at the first accusation."

"One need not pity them nor show them favors!" said the old man with the blue ribbon. "There is no harm in hanging Shvabrin; but it wouldn't be amiss to question this officer thoroughly, too. Why has he come here? If he doesn't recognize you as Czar he need not seek justice from you; and if he does acknowledge you, why has he sat till today with your enemies in Orenburg? Won't you let me take him to the office and light a fire under his toes? It seems to me his honor has been sent to us by the Orenburg commanders."

The old villain's logic struck me as rather convincing. A shiver ran down my back when I thought in whose hands I was. Pugachov noticed my confusion.

"Eh, your honor?" he said to me, with a wink. "I fancy my field marshal is talking sense. What do you think?"

Pugachov's mockery gave me back my courage. I calmly answered that I was in his power and that he was free to do what he liked with me.

"Good," said Pugachov, "and now tell me how are things going with you in the town?"

"Thank Heaven, all is well," I answered.

"All is well?" Pugachov repeated. "And people are dying of starvation?" The Pretender was right; but in accordance with my duty I began assuring him that this was an empty rumor and that there were plenty of provisions in Orenburg.

"You see," the old man chimed in, "he is deceiving you to your face. All refugees say with one voice that there is famine and pestilence in Orenburg; people eat carcasses, and even that is a treat; and his honor assures you they have plenty of everything. If you want to hang Shvabrin, hang this fellow, too, on the same gallows so as to be fair to both!"

The cursed old man's words seemed to have shaken Pugachov. Fortunately Khlopusha began contradicting his comrade.

"Come, Naumych," he said to him, "you always want to
be hanging and murdering. And you are not much of a man
to look at—you can hardly keep body and soul together. You
have one foot in the grave and yet you are destroying others.
Isn't there enough blood on your conscience?"

"You are a fine saint!" Beloborodov retorted. "Why
should you have pity?"

"Of course, I, too, have things on my conscience," Khlopusha answered, "and this hand" (he clenched his bony fist
and, turning up his sleeve, showed a hairy arm) "has been
guilty of shedding Christian blood. But I destroyed enemies,
not guests; on a high road and in the dark forest and not at
home behind the stove; with a club and an ax and not with
womanish slander."

The old man turned away and muttered: "Torn nostrils . . ."

"What are you muttering, you old wretch?" Khlopusha
shouted. "I'll give you 'torn nostrils'! Wait a bit, your time
will come, too; God willing, you, too, will sniff the hangman's
pincers. . . . And, meanwhile, take care I don't pull out
your scurvy beard!"

"My Generals," Pugachov said pompously, "that's enough
quarreling! It does not matter if all the Orenburg pack
wriggle under the same gallows; but it does matter if our
dogs are at one another's throats. There, make peace!"

Khlopusha and Beloborodov did not say a word and
looked at each other gloomily. I saw that it was necessary to
change the subject of a conversation which might end very
badly for me and, turning to Pugachov, I said to him with
a cheerful air: "Oh, I have forgotten to thank you for the

horse and the sheepskin. Had it not been for you I could not have found the road and should have been frozen on the way."

My ruse succeeded. Pugachov's good humor was restored.

"One good turn deserves another," he said, with a wink. "And tell me now why are you concerned about the girl whom Shvabrin is ill-treating? Is she your sweetheart, by any chance?"

"She is my betrothed!" I answered, seeing the favorable change in the weather and not thinking it necessary to conceal the truth.

"Your betrothed!" Pugachov shouted. "Why didn't you say so before? Why, we'll have you married and make merry at your wedding!"

Then he turned to Beloborodov and said: "Listen, Field Marshal! His honor and I are old friends, so let us sit down to supper. Morning is wiser than evening; we shall see tomorrow what we are to do with him."

I should have been glad to refuse the honor, but there was nothing for it. Two young girls, daughters of the Cossack to whom the hut belonged, spread a white cloth on the table, brought bread, fish soup, and several bottles of vodka and beer. Once more I found myself at the same table with Pugachov and his terrible comrades.

The orgy of which I was an involuntary witness lasted far into the night. At last the company were overpowered with drink. Pugachov dozed; his friends got up and made me a sign to leave him. I went with them out of the room. At Khlopusha's orders the watchman took me into the cottage that served as office; I found Savelyich there and we were locked up together for the night. The old man was so amazed at all that was happening that he did not ask me a single question. He lay down in the dark and was a long time sighing and groaning; at last he snored, and I gave myself ıp to thoughts which did not give me a wink of sleep all night.

In the morning Pugachov sent for me. I went to him. A chaise, drawn by three Tatar horses, was standing at his gate. There was a crowd in the street. I met Pugachov in the entry; he was dressed for the journey in a fur coat and a Kirghiz cap. His comrades of the day before surrounded him with an air of servility which little accorded with all that I had seen the night before. Pugachov greeted me cheerfully and told me to step into the chaise with him. We took our seats.

"To the Belogorsky fortress!" Pugachov said to the broad-shouldered Tatar who drove the troika standing.

My heart beat violently. The horses set off, the bell clanged, the chaise flew along. . . .

"Stop! Stop!" a familiar voice called out, and I saw Savelyich running toward us. Pugachov told the driver to stop.

"My dear Pyotr Andreyich!" Savelyich cried. "Don't abandon me in my old age among these rascals!"

"Ah, you old creature!" Pugachov said to him. "So God has brought us together again. Well, climb onto the box!"

"Thank you, sire, thank you, our father!" said Savelyich, climbing up. "May God let you live to be a hundred for your kindness to an old man. I will pray for you as long as I live and will never mention the hareskin jacket again."

This hareskin jacket might anger Pugachov in earnest at last. Fortunately he had not heard or took no notice of the inopportune remark. The horses set off at a gallop; the people in the street stopped and bowed. Pugachov nodded right and left. A minute later we left the village and flew along the smooth road.

One may well imagine what I was feeling at that moment. In a few hours I was to see her whom I had already considered as lost to me. I was picturing the moment of our meeting. . . . I was also thinking of the man in whose hands I was and who was mysteriously connected with me through a strange combination of circumstances. I was recalling the thoughtless cruelty, the bloodthirsty habits of the would-be rescuer of my beloved. Pugachov did not know that she was Captain Mironov's daughter; Shvabrin in his bitterness might tell him; or Pugachov might discover the truth in other ways. . . . What would become of Marya Ivanovna then? A shiver ran down my back and my hair stood on end.

Suddenly Pugachov interrupted my reflections with a question: "What are you thinking of so deeply, your honor?"

"How can I help thinking," I answered. "I am an officer and a gentleman; only yesterday I was fighting against you and today I am driving beside you and the happiness of my whole life depends upon you."

"Well, are you afraid?" Pugachov asked.

I answered that since he had spared me once, I was hoping he would do so again and would, indeed, help me.

"And you are right, upon my soul, you are right!" Pugachov said. "You saw that my men were looking askance at you; and the old man again insisted this morning that you were a spy and ought to be tortured and hanged; but I did not agree," he added, lowering his voice so that Savelyich and the Tatar should not hear him, "remembering your glass of vodka and the hareskin jacket. You see, I am not so bloodthirsty as your people make me out."

I recalled the taking of the Belogorsky fortress but did not think it necessary to contradict him and did not answer.

"What do they say of me in Orenburg?" Pugachov asked, after a silence.

"They say it's not easy to get the better of you. There's no denying it, you've made your presence felt."

The Pretender's face assumed an expression of satisfied vanity.

"Yes," he said cheerfully, "I am quite a hand at fighting! Do they know at Orenburg about the battle at Yuzeyeva? Forty generals were killed, four armies taken captive. What do you think—would the Prussian king be a match for me?"

The brigand's boasting amused me.

"What do you think yourself?" I asked him. "Could you beat Frederick?"

"Why not? I beat your generals and they used to beat him. So far I have been lucky in war. Wait, you'll see even better things when I march on Moscow."

"Are you thinking of doing that?"

Pugachov pondered and said in a low voice: "God only knows. I am cramped; I cannot do as I like. My men are too independent. They are thieves. I have to keep a sharp lookout: at the first defeat they will ransom their necks with my head."

"That's just it!" I said. "Hadn't you better leave them yourself in good time and appeal to the Empress' mercy?"

Pugachov smiled bitterly.

"No," he said; "it is too late for me to repent. There will be no mercy for me. I will go on as I have begun. Who knows? I may succeed after all! Grishka Otrepyev did reign over Moscow, you know."

"And do you know what his end was? They threw him out of the window, killed him, burned his body and fired a cannon with his ashes."

"Listen," Pugachov said, with a kind of wild inspiration, "I will tell you a fairy tale which in my childhood an old Kalmuck woman told me. The eagle asked the raven one day: 'Tell me, raven-bird, why do you live in the world for three hundred years and I only for thirty-three?'—'Because, father-eagle, you drink living blood,' the raven said, 'and I feed on things that are dead.' The eagle thought: 'I will try and feed as he does.' Very well. The eagle and the raven flew along. They saw the carcass of a horse, came down and perched on it. The raven plucked and praised the food. The eagle took a peck or two, then waved his wing and said: 'No, brother raven, rather than feed on carrion flesh for three hundred years, I would have one drink of living blood—and leave the rest to God!' What do you think of the Kalmuck tale?"

"It is clever," I answered. "But to live by murder and brigandage is, to my mind, just pecking carrion."

Pugachov looked at me with surprise and made no answer. We both sank into silence, each absorbed in his own reflections. The Tatar struck up a doleful song; Savelyich dozed as he sat, rocking to and fro on the box. The chaise flew along the smooth winter road. . . . Suddenly I saw on the steep bank of the Yaïk a village with a palisade round it and a belfry rising above it—and in another quarter of an hour we drove into the Belogorsky fortress.

XII

AN ORPHAN

Our slender young apple tree
Has no spreading branch nor top to it,
Our tender young bride to be
Has no father nor mother to care for her,
She has no one to see her off,
No one to bestow a blessing on her.

A WEDDING SONG

THE CHAISE drove up to the Commandant's house. The people recognized the sound of Pugachov's bell and ran after us in a crowd. Shvabrin met the Pretender on the steps. He was dressed like a Cossack and had grown a beard. The traitor helped Pugachov to step out of the chaise, speaking in servile expressions of his delight and devotion. He was confused when he saw me, but soon recovered and gave me his hand, saying: "So you, too, are one of us? Time you were!"

I turned away and made no answer.

My heart ached when we came into the familiar room; the certificate of the late Commandant still hung on the wall as a sad epitaph of bygone days. Pugachov sat down on the sofa where Ivan Kuzmich used to doze, lulled to sleep by his wife's grumbling. Shvabrin brought him some vodka. Pugachov drank a glass and said, pointing to me: "Offer some to his honor, too."

Shvabrin came up to me with the tray, but I turned away again. He was obviously very uneasy. With his usual quickness he guessed, of course, that Pugachov was displeased with him; he was afraid, and looked at me with distrust. Pugachov asked about the state of the fortress, the news of the enemy's troops and such like things, and suddenly asked him: "Tell me, brother, who is the girl you are keeping prisoner in your house? Show her to me."

Shvabrin turned white as death.

"Sire," he said in a shaking voice, "sire, she is not a prisoner. She is ill . . . she is upstairs, in bed."

"Take me to her," the Pretender said, getting up.

It was impossible to refuse him. Shvabrin led Pugachov to Marya Ivanovna's room. I followed them.

Shvabrin stopped on the stairs.

"Sire," he said, "you may require of me whatever you wish, but do not allow a stranger to enter my wife's bedroom."

I shuddered.

"So you are married?" I said to Shvabrin, ready to tear him to pieces.

"Keep quiet!" Pugachov interrupted me. "It is my affair. And don't you try to be clever," he went on, addressing Shvabrin, "or invent excuses; wife or not, I take to her whomsoever I like. Follow me, your honor."

At Marya Ivanovna's door Shvabrin stopped again and said in a breaking voice: "Sire, I warn you, she has brain fever and has been raving for the last three days."

"Open the door!" said Pugachov.

Shvabrin began searching in his pockets and said he had not brought the key. Pugachov pushed the door with his foot, the lock fell off, the door opened, and we went in.

I looked—and was aghast. Marya Ivanovna, pale and thin, with disheveled hair and dressed like a peasant, was sitting on the floor; a jug of water, covered with a piece of bread, stood before her. When she saw me she started and cried out. What I felt then I cannot describe.

Pugachov looked at Shvabrin and said, with a bitter smile: "Fine hospital you have here!" Then he went up to Marya Ivanovna and said: "Tell me, my dear, what is your husband punishing you for? What wrong have you done to him?"

"My husband!" she repeated. "He is not my husband. I will never be his wife. I would rather die, and I shall die if I am not saved from him."

Pugachov looked menacingly at Shvabrin.

"And you dared to deceive me!" he said. "Do you know what you deserve, you wretch?"

Shvabrin dropped on his knees. . . . At that moment a feeling of contempt outweighed my hatred and anger. I looked with disgust upon a gentleman groveling at the feet of an escaped convict. Pugachov was softened.

"I will spare you this time," he said to Shvabrin, "but next time you are at fault, this wrong will be remembered against you."

Then he turned to Marya Ivanovna and said kindly: "Come away, my pretty maid. I set you free. I am the Czar!"

Marya Ivanovna glanced at him and understood that her parents' murderer was before her. She buried her face in her hands and fell down senseless. I rushed to her, but at that moment my old friend Palasha very boldly made her way into the room and began attending to her mistress. Pugachov walked out and the three of us went downstairs.

"Well, your honor," Pugachov said, laughing, "we've delivered the fair maiden! What do you think, hadn't we better send for the priest and tell him to marry you to his niece? I'll give her away if you like, and Shvabrin will be best man; we'll make merry and drink, and give the guests no time to think!"

The very thing that I feared happened. Shvabrin was beside himself when he heard Pugachov's suggestion.

"Sire!" he cried in a frenzy. "I am to blame; I have lied to you, but Grinyov, too, is deceiving you. This girl is not the priest's niece; she is the daughter of Captain Mironov who was hanged when the fortress was taken."

Pugachov fixed on me his fiery eye.

"What's this?" he asked, in perplexity.

"Shvabrin is right," I answered firmly.

"You hadn't told me," remarked Pugachov, and his face clouded.

"But consider," I answered him. "How could I have said in your men's presence that Mironov's daughter was living? They would have torn her to pieces. Nothing would have saved her!"

"That's true enough," Pugachov said, laughing. "My

drunkards would not have spared the poor girl. The priest's wife did well to deceive them."

"Listen," I said, seeing that he was in a kind mood. "I do not know what to call you and I don't want to know. . . . But God knows I would gladly pay you with my life for what you have done for me. Only don't ask of me what is against my honor and Christian conscience. You are my benefactor. Finish as you have begun; let me go with the poor orphan whither God may lead us. And whatever happens to you and wherever you may be, we shall pray to Him every day of our lives to save your sinful soul."

It seemed that Pugachov's stern heart was touched.

"So be it!" he said. "I don't believe in stopping halfway, be it in vengeance or in mercy. Take your sweetheart; go with her where you will and God grant you love and concord!"

Then he turned to Shvabrin and told him to give me a pass through all the villages and fortresses subject to his rule.

Shvabrin, utterly overwhelmed, stood like one dumfounded. Pugachov went to look at the fortress. Shvabrin accompanied him and I remained behind under the pretext of making ready for the journey.

I ran upstairs. The door was locked. I knocked.

"Who is there?" Palasha asked.

I gave my name. Marya Ivanovna's sweet voice came from behind the door: "Wait a little, Pyotr Andreyich; I am changing my dress. Go to Akulina Pamfilovna's. I shall be there directly."

I obeyed and went to Father Gerasim's house. Both he and his wife ran out to meet me. Savelyich had already given them the news.

"How do you do, Pyotr Andreyich?" the priest's wife said. "God has brought us together again! How are you?

We have talked of you every day. Marya Ivanovna has been through a dreadful time without you, poor darling! . . . But tell me, my dear, how did you hit it off with Pugachov? How is it he hasn't made an end of you? It's something to the villain's credit!"

"That will do, my dear," Father Gerasim interrupted her. "Don't blurt out all you know. There is no salvation in speaking overmuch. Please come in, Pyotr Andreyich! You are very welcome. We haven't seen you for months!"

The priest's wife offered me what food there was and talked incessantly as she did so. She told me how Shvabrin had forced them to give up Marya Ivanovna; how Marya Ivanovna wept and did not want to part from them; how Marya Ivanovna always kept in touch with her through Palasha (a spirited girl who made the sergeant himself dance to her tune); how she had advised Marya Ivanovna to write a letter to me, and so on. I, in my turn, briefly told her my story. The priest and his wife crossed themselves when they heard that Pugachov knew of their deception.

"The power of the Holy Cross be with us!" said Akulina Pamfilovna. "May the Lord let the storm go by! Fancy Alexey Ivanych betraying us! He is a fine one!"

At that moment the door opened and Marya Ivanovna came in, a smile on her pale face. She had laid aside peasant clothes and was dressed as before, simply and prettily.

I clasped her hand and for some moments could not utter a word. Our hearts were too full for speech. Our hosts felt that we had no thoughts to spare for them and left us. We were alone. All was forgotten. We talked and talked. Marya Ivanovna told me all that had happened to her after the fortress was taken; she described to me the horror of her position, and all that she had had to endure at the hands of her vile pursuer. We recalled the bygone happy days. . . . We were both weeping. . . . At last I put my plans before her. It was impossible for her to stay in a fortress subject to Pugachov and ruled by Shvabrin. It was no use thinking of Orenburg where the inhabitants were suffering all the horrors of the siege. She had no one belonging to her in the world. I suggested she go to my parents' estate. She hesitated at first; she knew my father's animosity toward her and was afraid. I reassured her. I knew that my father would be happy and consider it his duty to welcome the daughter of a veteran who had died for his country.

"Darling Marya Ivanovna," I said to her, at last. "I look upon you as my wife. Miraculous circumstances have united us forever; nothing in the world can part us."

Marya Ivanovna listened to me without coyness or feigned reluctance. She felt that her fate was united to mine. But she repeated that she would only marry me with my parents' consent. I did not contradict her about it. We kissed each other sincerely and ardently—and all was settled between us.

An hour later, Maximych brought me a pass signed with Pugachov's hieroglyphics and said that he wanted to see me. I found him ready for the journey. I cannot express what I felt on parting from this terrible man, a monster of evil to all but me. Why not confess the truth? At that moment I was drawn to him by warm sympathy. I longed to tear him away from the criminals whose leader he was and to save his head before it was too late. Shvabrin and the people who crowded around us prevented me from saying all that was in my heart.

We parted friends. Seeing Akulina Pamfilovna in the crowd, Pugachov shook his finger at her and winked significantly; then he stepped into the chaise, told the driver to go to Berda, and as the horses moved he put out his head from the chaise once more and shouted to me: "Good-bye, your honor! We may yet meet again."

We did meet again—but under what circumstances!

Pugachov drove away. I gazed for some time at the white steppe where his troika was galloping. The crowd dispersed. Shvabrin disappeared. I returned to the priest's house. Everything was ready for our departure. I did not want to delay any longer. All our belongings were packed in the old Commandant's carriage. The drivers harnessed the horses in a trice. Marya Ivanovna went to say good-bye to the graves of her parents, who were buried behind the church. I wanted to accompany her, but she asked me to let her go alone. She returned in a few minutes, silently weeping quiet tears. The carriage was brought before the house. Father Gerasim and his wife came out onto the steps. The three of us—Marya Ivanovna, Palasha, and I—sat inside the carriage and Savelyich climbed on the box.

"Good-bye, Marya Ivanovna, my darling! Good-bye, Pyotr Andreyich, our bright falcon!" kind Akulina Pamfilovna said to us. "A happy journey to you, and God grant you happiness!"

We set off. I saw Shvabrin standing at the window of the Commandant's house. His face was expressive of gloomy malice. I did not want to triumph over a defeated enemy and turned my eyes in another direction. At last we drove out of the fortress gates, and left the Belogorsky fortress for ever.

XIII

THE ARREST

"Do not be angry, sir; my duty bids me
To send you off to gaol this very day."
By all means, I am ready; but I trust
You will first allow me to have my say.

                                    KNYAZHNIN

UNITED so unexpectedly to the sweet girl about whom I had been terribly anxious only that morning, I could not believe my senses and fancied that all that had happened to me was an empty dream. Marya Ivanovna gazed thoughtfully now at me and now at the road: she did not seem to have come to herself as yet. We were silent. Our hearts were much too tired. We did not notice how in a couple of hours we found ourselves at the neighboring fortress, which also was in Pugachov's hands. We changed horses there. The quickness with which they were harnessed and the hurried servility of the bearded Cossack, promoted by Pugachov to the post of Commandant, proved that, owing to our driver's talkativeness, I was being taken for the Czar's favorite.

We continued our journey. Dusk was falling. We drew near a small town occupied, according to the bearded Commandant, by a strong detachment of Pugachov's supporters on their way to join him. We were stopped by the sentries. To the question, "Who goes there?" the driver answered, in a loud voice, "The Czar's friend with his lady." Suddenly a crowd of Hussars surrounded us, swearing fearfully.

"Come out, you devil's friend!" a sergeant, with a big

mustache said to me. "You will get it hot presently, and that girl of yours, too."

I stepped out of the chaise and demanded to be taken to the commanding officer. Seeing my uniform, the soldiers stopped swearing. The sergeant led me to the major. Savelyich went with me, muttering to himself: "There's a fine Czar's friend for you! Out of the frying pan into the fire. . . . Good Lord, what will the end of it be?" The chaise followed us at a walking pace. After five minutes' walk we came to a brilliantly lighted house. The sergeant left me with the sentries and went to announce me. He returned at once, saying the major had not time to see me, but that he ordered that I should be taken to jail and my lady brought to him.

"What's the meaning of this?" I cried, in a rage. "Has he gone off his head?"

"I cannot tell, your honor," the sergeant answered. "Only his honor said that your honor was to be taken to jail and her honor brought to his honor."

I rushed up the steps. The sentries made no attempt to detain me and I ran straight into the room where six officers of the Hussars were playing cards. The major was dealing. Imagine my surprise when I recognized him for Ivan Ivanovich Zurin who had won from me at billiards at the Simbirsk inn!

"Is it possible?" I cried. "Ivan Ivanych! Is that you?"

"Why, Pyotr Andreyich! What wind brings you? Where do you come from? Glad to see you, brother. Won't you join the game?"

"Thanks. Better tell them to give me a lodging."

"What lodging? Stay with me."

"I cannot; I am not alone."

"Well, bring your comrade along."

"It's not a comrade. I am with a lady."

"A lady! Where did you pick her up? Oho, brother!" At these words, Zurin whistled so expressively that everyone laughed. I was utterly confused.

"Well," Zurin went on, "so be it! You shall have a lodging, but it's a pity. . . . We could have had a gay time, as in the old days. . . . Hey, boy! Why don't they bring along Pugachov's sweetheart? Doesn't she want to come? Tell her she need not fear, the gentleman is very kind and will do her no harm—and give her a good kick to hurry her up."

"What are you talking about?" I said to Zurin. "Pugachov's sweetheart? It is the late Captain Mironov's daughter. I have rescued her and am now seeing her off to my father's estate where I shall leave her."

"What! So it was you they have just announced? Upon my word! What does it all mean?"

"I will tell you afterward. And now for Heaven's sake reassure the poor girl whom your Hussars have frightened."

Zurin made arrangements at once. He came out into the street to apologize to Marya Ivanovna for the misunderstanding and told the segeant to give her the best lodging in the town. I was to spend the night with him.

We had supper and when we were left alone I told him my adventures. Zurin listened with great attention. When I had finished, he shook his head and said: "That's all very good, brother; one thing only is not good: why the devil do you want to be married? I am an honest officer; I would not deceive you; believe me, marriage is a delusion. You don't want to be bothered with a wife and be nursing babies! Give it up! Do as I tell you: get rid of the Captain's daughter. The road to Simbirsk is safe now; I have cleared it. Send her tomorrow to your parents by herself and you stay in my detachment. There is no need for you to return to Orenburg. If you fall into the rebels' hands once more you may not escape this time. And so the love-foolishness will pass of itself and all will be well."

I did not altogether agree with him, but I felt that I was in duty bound to remain with the army. I decided to follow Zurin's advice and send Marya Ivanovna to the country while I remained in his detachment.

Savelyich came to undress me; I told him that he must be ready next day to continue the journey with Marya Ivanovna. He did not want to at first.

"What are you thinking of, sir? How can I leave you? Who will look after you? What will your parents say?"

Knowing Savelyich's obstinacy I decided to win him by affection and sincerity.

"Arhip Savelyich, my dear!" I said to him. "Don't refuse. You will be doing me a great kindness. I shall not need a servant, but I shall have no peace if Marya Ivanovna goes on her journey without you. In serving her you will be serving me, because I am determined to marry her as soon as circumstances allow."

Savelyich clasped his hands with an air of indescribable amazement.

"To marry!" he replied. "The child thinks of marrying! But what will your father say; what will your mother think?"

"They will agree; I am sure they will agree when they know Marya Ivanovna," I answered. "I rely on you, too. My father and mother trust you; you will intercede for us, won't you?"

Savelyich was touched.

"Ah, Pyotr Andreyich, dear," he answered, "though it is much too early for you to think of marrying, Marya Ivanovna is such a good young lady that it would be a sin to miss the opportunity. Have it your own way! I shall go with her, angel that she is, and will tell your parents faithfully that such a bride does not need a dowry."

I thanked Savelyich and went to bed in the same room with Zurin. My mind was in a turmoil and I talked and talked. At first Zurin answered me readily, but gradually his words became few and disconnected; at last in answer to a question he gave a snore with a whistle in it. I stopped talking and soon followed his example.

Next morning I went to Marya Ivanovna and told her of my plans. She recognized their reasonableness and agreed with me at once. Zurin's detachment was to leave the town that same day. There was no time to be lost. I said good-bye to Marya Ivanovna there and then, entrusting her to Savelyich and giving her a letter to my parents. Marya Ivanovna wept.

"Good-bye, Pyotr Andreyich," she said, in a low voice. "God only knows whether we shall meet again; but I will not forget you as long as I live; till death you alone shall remain in my heart."

I could not answer her. Other people were there. I did not want to abandon myself in their presence to the feelings that agitated me. At last she drove away. I returned to Zurin, sad and silent. He wanted to cheer me; I sought distraction; we spent the day in riotous gaiety and set out on the march in the evening.

It was the end of February. The winter, which had made military operations difficult, was coming to an end, and our generals were preparing for concerted action. Pugachov was still besieging Orenburg. Meanwhile the army detachments around him were joining forces and approaching the brigands' nest from all sides. Rebellious villages were restored to order at the sight of the soldiers, brigand bands dispersed on our approach, and everything indicated a speedy and successful end of the war.

Soon Prince Golitzyn defeated Pugachov at the Tatishcheva fortress, scattered his hordes, delivered Orenburg and dealt, it seemed, the last and decisive blow to the rebellion. Zurin was at that time sent against a gang of rebellious Bashkirs, who had dispersed before we caught sight of them. Spring found us in a Tatar village. Rivers were in flood and roads impassable. We could do nothing, but comforted ourselves with the thought that the petty and tedious war with brigands and savages would soon be over.

Pugachov was not caught, however. He appeared at the Siberian foundries, collected there fresh bands of followers and began his evil work once more. Again rumors of his success spread abroad. We heard of the fall of the Siberian fortresses. Soon afterward, the army leaders, who slumbered carefree in the hope that the contemptible rebel was powerless, were alarmed by the news of his taking Kazan and advancing toward Moscow. Zurin received an order to cross the Volga.

I will not describe our campaign and the end of the war. I shall say briefly that there was extreme misery. There was no lawful authority anywhere. The landowners were hiding in the forests. Bands of brigands were ransacking the country. The chiefs of separate detachments arbitrarily meted out punishments and granted pardons; the vast region where the conflagration had raged was in a terrible state. . . . God save us from seeing a Russian revolt, senseless and merciless!

Pugachov was in retreat, pursued by Ivan Ivanovich Michelson. Soon after we learned that he was utterly defeated. At last Zurin heard that he had been captured and at the same time received an order to halt. The war was over! I could go to my parents at last! The thought of embracing them and of seeing Marya Ivanovna, of whom I had had no news, delighted me. I danced with joy like a child. Zurin laughed and said, shrugging his shoulders: "No, you'll come to a bad end! You will be married and done for!"

And yet a strange feeling poisoned my joy: I could not help being troubled at the thought of the villain smeared with the blood of so many innocent victims and now awaiting his punishment. "Why didn't he fall on a bayonet? Or get hit with a cannonball?" I thought with vexation. "He could not have done anything better." What will you have? I could not think of Pugachov without remembering how he had spared me at one of the awful moments of my life and saved my betrothed from the vile Shvabrin's hands.

Zurin gave me leave of absence. In a few days I was to be once more with my family and see my Marya Ivanovna. Suddenly an unexpected storm burst upon me.

On the day of my departure, at the very minute when I was to go, Zurin came into my room with a paper in his hand, looking very much troubled. My heart sank. I was frightened without knowing why. He sent out my orderly and said he had something to tell me.

"What is it?" I asked anxiously.

"Something rather unpleasant," he answered, giving me the paper. "Read what I have just received."

I began reading it: it was a secret order to all commanding officers to arrest me wherever they might find me and to send me at once under escort to Kazan, to the Commission of Inquiry into the Pugachov rising.

The paper almost dropped out of my hands.

"There is nothing for it," Zurin said; "my duty is to obey the order. Probably the news of your friendly journeys with Pugachov has reached the authorities. I hope it will not have any consequences and that you will clear yourself before the Committee. Go, and don't be downhearted."

My conscience was clear; I was not afraid of the trial, but the thought of putting off, perhaps for several months the sweet moment of reunion, terrified me. The carriage was ready. Zurin bade me a friendly good-bye. I stepped into the carriage. Two Hussars, with bare swords, sat down beside me and we drove along the high road.

XIV

THE TRIAL

Popular rumor is like a sea-wave.
A PROVERB

I WAS CERTAIN it was all due to my leaving Orenburg without permission. I could easily justify myself: sallying out against the enemy had never been prohibited and was, indeed, encouraged in every way. I might be accused of too great rashness, but not of disobedience. My friendly relations with Pugachov, however, could be proved by a number of witnesses and must have seemed highly suspicious, to say the least of it. Throughout the journey I kept thinking of the questions I might be asked and pondering my answers; I decided to tell the plain truth at the trial, believing that this was the simplest and, at the same time, the most certain way of justifying myself.

I arrived at Kazan; it had been devastated and burned down. Instead of houses there were heaps of cinders in the streets and remnants of charred walls without roofs or windows. Such was the trail left by Pugachov! I was brought to the fortress that had remained intact in the midst of the burned city. The Hussars passed me on to the officer in charge. He called for the blacksmith. Shackles were put on

my feet and soldered together. Then I was taken to the prison
and left alone in the dark and narrow cell with bare walls and
a window with iron bars.

Such a beginning boded nothing good. I did not, however,
lose either hope or courage. I had recourse to the comfort of
all the sorrowful and, having tasted for the first time the
sweetness of prayer poured out from a pure but bleeding
heart, dropped calmly asleep without caring what would happen to me.

The next morning the warder woke me up, saying I was
wanted by the Commission. Two soldiers took me across the
yard to the Commandant's house; they stopped in the entry
and let me go into the inner room by myself.

I walked into a rather large room. Two men were sitting
at a table covered with papers: an elderly general who looked
cold and forbidding and a young captain of the Guards, a
good-looking man of about twenty-eight, with a pleasant and
easy manner. A secretary, with a pen behind his ear, sat at a
separate table, bending over the paper in readiness to write
down my answers. The examination began. I was asked my
name and rank. The General asked whether I was the son of
Andrey Petrovich Grinyov. When I said I was, he remarked
severely: "It is a pity that so estimable a man has such an
unworthy son!"

I calmly answered that whatever the accusation against me
might be, I hoped to clear myself by candidly telling the
truth. The General did not like my confidence.

"You are sharp, brother," he said to me, frowning; "but
we have seen cleverer ones than you!" Then the young man
asked me: "On what occasion and at what time did you enter
Pugachov's service, and on what commissions did he employ
you?"

I answered, with indignation, that as an officer and a gentleman I could not possibly have entered Pugachov's service or have carried out any commissions of his.

"How was it, then," my questioner continued, "that an officer and a gentleman was alone spared by the Pretender while all his comrades were villainously murdered? How was it that this same officer and gentleman feasted with the rebels, as their friend, and accepted presents from the villain—a sheepskin coat, a horse, and fifty kopecks in money? How had such a strange friendship arisen and what could it be based upon except treason or, at any rate, upon base and vile cowardice?"

I was deeply offended by the officer's words and warmly began my defense. I told them how I had first met Pugachov in the steppe in the snowstorm, and how he recognized and spared me at the taking of the Belogorsky fortress. I admitted that I had not scrupled to accept from the Pretender the horse and the sheepskin coat, but said that I had defended the Belogorsky fortress against him to the last extremity. At last I referred them to my General, who could testify to my zealous service during the perilous Orenburg siege.

The stern old man took an unsealed letter from the table and began reading it aloud:

"With regard to Your Excellency's inquiry concerning Ensign Grinyov, said to be involved in the present insurrection and to have had relations with the villain, contrary to the military law and to our oath of allegiance, I have the honor to report as follows: The said Ensign Grinyov served at Orenburg from the beginning of October, 1773, to February 24, 1774, upon which date he left the city and returned no more to serve under my command. I have heard from refugees that he had been in Pugachov's camp and went with him to the Belogorsky fortress, where he had served before; as to his conduct, I can . . ."

At this point he interrupted his reading and said to me sternly: "What can you say for yourself now?"

I wanted to go on as I had begun and to explain my connection with Marya Ivanovna as candidly as all the rest, but I suddenly felt an overwhelming repulsion. It occurred to me that if I mentioned her, she would be summoned by the Commission; and I was so overcome at the awful thought of connecting her name with the vile slanders of the villains, and of her being confronted with them, that I became confused and hesitated.

My judges, who seemed to have been listening to me with favor, were once more prejudiced against me by my confusion. The officer of the Guards asked that I should be faced with the chief informer. The General gave word that *yesterday's villain* should be brought in. I turned to the door with interest, waiting for the appearance of my accuser. A few minutes later there was a rattle of chains, the door opened, and Shvabrin walked in. I was surprised at the change in him. He was terribly pale and thin. His hair that had a short time ago been black as pitch was now white; his long beard was unkempt. He repeated his accusations in a weak but confident voice. According to him I had been sent by Pugachov to Orenburg as a spy; under the pretext of sallies, I had come out every day to give him written news of all that was happening in the town; at last I had openly joined the Pretender, had driven with him from fortress to fortress, doing my utmost to ruin my fellow-traitors so as to occupy their posts, and had taken presents from the Pretender. I heard him out in silence and was pleased with one thing only: Marya Ivanovna's name had not been uttered by the base villain, either because his vanity suffered at the thought of one who had scorned him, or because there lingered in his heart a spark of the same feeling which made me keep silent about her. In any case, the name of the Belogorsky Commandant's daughter was not mentioned before the Commission. I was more determined than ever not to bring it up, and when the judges asked me how I could disprove Shvabrin's accusations, I answered that I adhered to my original explanation and had nothing more to say in my defense. The General gave word for us to be led away. We went out together. I calmly looked at Shvabrin, but did not say a word to him. He gave a malignant smile and, lifting his chains, quickened his pace and left me behind. I was taken back to prison and not called for examination any more.

I have not witnessed the subsequent events of which I must inform the reader; but I had them told me so often that the least details are engraved on my memory and I feel as though I had been invisibly present.

Marya Ivanovna had been received by my parents with that sincere cordiality which distinguished people in former days. They held it to be a blessing that they had been afforded the opportunity of sheltering and comforting the poor orphan. They soon became truly attached to her, for it was impossible to know her and not to love her. My love for her no longer seemed to my father a mere whim, and my mother had but one wish—that her Petrusha should marry that dear creature, the Captain's daughter.

The news of my arrest was a shock to my family. Marya Ivanovna had told my parents of my strange acquaintance with Pugachov so simply that, so far from being troubled about it, they often laughed at it with whole-hearted amusement. My father refused to believe that I could have been implicated in vile rebellion the aim of which was to overthrow the throne and exterminate the gentry. He closely questioned Savelyich. The old man did not conceal the fact that I had been to see Pugachov and that the villain had been kind to me; but he swore that he had not heard of any treason. My parents were reassured and waited impatiently for favorable news. Marya Ivanovna was very much alarmed but said nothing, for she was extremely modest and prudent.

Several weeks passed. . . . Suddenly my father received a letter from our relative in Petersburg, Prince B. The Prince wrote about me. After beginning in the usual way he went on to say that, unfortunately, the suspicions about my complicity in the rebels' designs proved to be only too true and that I should have been put to death as an example to others had not the Empress, in consideration of my father's merits and advanced age, decided to spare the criminal son and commuted the shameful death penalty to a mere exile for life to a remote part of Siberia.

This unexpected blow very nearly killed my father. He lost his habitual self-control, and his grief, usually silent, found expression in bitter complaints.

"What!" he repeated, beside himself. "My son is an accomplice of Pugachov's! Merciful heavens, what have I lived to see! The Empress reprieves him! Does that make it any better for me? It's not the death penalty that is terrible. My great-grandfather died on the scaffold for what was to him a matter of conscience; my father suffered, together with Volynsky and Khrushchov.[6] But for a gentleman to betray his oath of allegiance and join brigands, murderers and runaway serfs! Shame and disgrace to our name!"

Terrified by his despair, my mother did not dare to weep in his presence and tried to cheer him by talking of the uncertainty of rumor and the small faith to be attached to people's opinions. My father was inconsolable.

Marya Ivanovna suffered most. She was certain that I could have cleared myself if I had chosen to do so, and, guessing the truth, considered herself the cause of my mis-

[6] Leaders of the Russian party against Bühren, the German favorite of the Empress Anna (TRANSLATOR'S NOTE).

fortune. She concealed her tears and sorrow from everyone, but was continually thinking of the means to save me.

One evening my father was sitting on the sofa turning over the leaves of the *Court Calendar,* but his thoughts were far away and the reading did not have its usual effect upon him. He was whistling an old march. My mother was knitting a woolen coat in silence, and now and again a tear dropped on her work. Suddenly Marya Ivanovna, who sat by her doing needlework, said that it was necessary for her to go to Petersburg, and asked for the means of traveling there. My mother was very much grieved.

"What do you want in Petersburg?" she said. "Can it be that you, too, want to leave us, Marya Ivanovna?"

Marya Ivanovna answered that her whole future depended upon this journey and that she was going to seek the help and protection of influential people, as the daughter of a man who had suffered for his loyalty.

My father bent his head: every word that reminded him of his son's alleged crime pained him and seemed to him a bitter reproach.

"Go, my dear," he said to her, with a sigh. "We don't want to stand in the way of your happiness. God grant you may have a good man for a husband and not a disgraced traitor."

He got up and walked out of the room.

Left alone with my mother, Marya Ivanovna partly explained her plan to her. My mother embraced her with tears and prayed for the success of her undertaking. Marya Ivanovna was made ready for the journey, and a few days later she set off with the faithful Palasha and the faithful Savelyich, who in his enforced parting from me comforted himself with the thought that, at least, he was serving my betrothed.

Marya Ivanovna safely arrived at Sofia and, hearing that the Court was at Czarkoe Selo, decided to stop there. At the posting-station, a tiny recess behind the partition was assigned to her. The stationmaster's wife immediately got into conversation with her, said that she was the niece of the man who tended the stoves at the Palace, and initiated her into the mysteries of Court life. She told her at what time the Empress woke up in the morning, took coffee, went for walks; what courtiers were with her at the time; what she had said at dinner the day before; whom she had received in the evening. In short, Anna Vlasyevna's conversation was as good as several pages of historical memoirs and would have been precious for posterity. Marya Ivanovna listened to her attentively. They went into the gardens. Anna Vlasyevna told the history of every avenue and every bridge, and they returned to the station after a long walk, much pleased with each other.

Marya Ivanovna woke up early the next morning, dressed, and slipped out into the gardens. It was a beautiful morning; the sun was lighting the tops of the lime trees that had already turned yellow under the fresh breath of autumn. The broad lake, without a ripple on it, glittered in the sunlight. The stately swans, just awake, came sailing out from under the bushes that covered the banks. Marya Ivanovna walked along a beautiful meadow where a monument had just been put up in honor of Count Rumyantzev's recent victories. Suddenly a little white dog of English breed ran toward her, barking. Marya Ivanovna was frightened and stood still. At that moment she heard a woman's pleasant voice: "Don't be afraid, he won't bite."

And Marya Ivanovna saw a lady sitting on a bench opposite the monument. Marya Ivanovna sat down at the other end of the bench. The lady was looking at her attentively; Marya Ivanovna, in her turn, cast several sidelong glances at her and succeeded in examining her from head to foot. She was wearing a white morning dress, a nightcap, and a Russian jacket. She seemed to be about forty. Her plump and rosy face wore an expression of calm and dignity, her blue eyes and slight smile had an indescribable charm. The lady was the first to break the silence.

"I expect you are a stranger here?" she asked.

"Yes, madam; I came from the country only yesterday."

"Have you come with your relatives?"

"No, madam; I have come alone."

"Alone! But you are so young. . . ."

"I have neither father nor mother."

"You are here on business, of course?"

"Yes, madam. I have come to present a petition to the Empress."

"You are an orphan; I suppose you are complaining of some wrong or injustice?"

"No, madam. I have come to ask for mercy, not justice."

"Allow me to ask, What is your name?"

"I am Captain Mironov's daughter."

"Captain Mironov's! The man who was Commandant in one of the Orenburg fortresses?"

"Yes, madam."

The lady was evidently touched.

"Excuse me," she said, still more kindly, "for interfering in your affairs, but I go to Court sometimes; tell me what your petition is and perhaps I may be able to help you."

Marya Ivanovna got up and respectfully thanked her.

Everything in the unknown lady instinctively attracted her and inspired her with confidence. Marya Ivanovna took a folded paper out of her pocket and gave it to the lady, who began reading it to herself.

At first she read with an attentive and kindly air, but suddenly her expression changed, and Marya Ivanovna, who was watching her every movement, was frightened at the stern look on her face, so calm and pleasant a moment before.

"You are interceding for Grinyov?" the lady said coldly.

"The Empress cannot forgive him. He joined the Pretender not from ignorance and credulity, but as a dangerous and immoral scoundrel."

"Oh, it isn't true!" Marya Ivanovna cried.

"How, it isn't true?" the lady repeated, flushing crimson.

"It isn't true; I swear to God it isn't! I know all about it; I will tell you everything. It was solely for my sake that he went through it all. And if he hasn't cleared himself before the judges, it was only because he did not want to implicate me."

And she told, with great warmth, all that is already known to the reader.

The lady listened to her attentively.

"Where have you put up?" she asked, and hearing that it was at Anna Vlasyevna's, said, with a smile: "Ah, I know. Good-bye, do not tell anyone of our meeting. I hope you will not have long to wait for an answer to your letter."

With these words, she rose and went into a covered alley and Marya Ivanovna, full of joyous hope, returned to Anna Vlasyevna's.

Her landlady chided her for her early walk which, she said, was not good for a young girl's health, as it was autumn. She brought the samovar and just began, over a cup of tea, her endless stories about the Court, when suddenly a Court carriage stopped at the door and a footman from the Palace came into the room, saying that the Empress invited Miss Mironov to her presence.

Anna Vlasyevna was surprised and flurried.

"Dear me!" she cried. "The Empress sends for you to come to the Palace! How has she heard of you? And how are you going to appear before the Empress, my dear? I expect you know nothing about Court manners. . . . Hadn't I better go with you? I could warn you about some things, at any rate. And how can you go in your traveling dress? Hadn't we better send to the midwife for her yellow gown?"

The footman announced that it was the Empress' pleasure that Marya Ivanovna should come alone and as she was. There was nothing else for it; Marya Ivanovna stepped into the carriage and drove to the Palace accompanied by Anna Vlasyevna's admonitions and blessings.

Marya Ivanovna felt that our fate was going to be decided; her heart was throbbing. A few minutes later the carriage stopped at the Palace. Marya Ivanovna walked up the stairs, trembling. The doors were flung wide open before her. She walked through a number of deserted, luxuriously furnished rooms; the footman was pointing out the way. At last, coming to a closed door, he said he would go in and announce her, and left her alone.

The thought of seeing the Empress face to face so terrified her that she could hardly keep on her feet. In another minute the door opened and she walked into the Empress' dressing room.

The Empress was seated in front of her dressing table. Several courtiers were standing round her, but they respectfully made way for Marya Ivanovna. The Empress turned to her kindly and Marya Ivanovna recognized her as the lady to whom she had been talking so freely not many minutes before. The Empress called her to her side and said, with a smile: "I am glad that I have been able to keep my promise to you and to grant your request. Your case is settled. I am convinced that your betrothed is innocent. Here is a letter which please take yourself to your future father-in-law."

Marya Ivanovna took the letter with a trembling hand and fell, weeping, at the feet of the Empress, who lifted her up, kissed her and engaged her in conversation.

"I know you are not rich," she said, "but I am in debt to Captain Mironov's daughter. Do not worry about the future. I will provide for you."

After saying many kind things to the poor orphan, the Empress dismissed her. Marya Ivanovna was driven back in the same Court carriage. Anna Vlasyevna, who had been eagerly awaiting her return, bombarded her with questions, to which Marya Ivanovna answered rather vaguely. Anna Vlasyevna was disappointed at her remembering so little, but ascribed it to provincial shyness and generously excused her. Marya Ivanovna went back to the country that same day, without troubling to have a look at Petersburg. . . .

The memoirs of Pyotr Andreyich Grinyov end at this point. It is known from the family tradition that he was released from confinement at the end of 1774, at the express order of the Empress; that he was present at the execution of Pugachov, who recognized him in the crowd and nodded to him a minute before his lifeless, bleeding head was held up before the people. Soon after, Pyotr Andreyich married Marya Ivanovna. Their descendants are flourishing in the Province of Simbirsk. Thirty miles from N. there is an estate belonging to ten owners. In one of the lodges a letter written by Catherine II may be seen in a frame under glass. It is addressed to Pyotr Andreyich's father; it affirms the innocence of his son and praises the heart and intelligence of Captain Mironov's daughter.

Pyotr Andreyich Grinyov's memoirs have been given to us by one of his grandchildren who had heard that we were engaged upon a work dealing with the period described by his grandfather. With the relatives' consent, we have decided to publish it separately, prefixing a suitable epigraph to each chapter and taking the liberty to change some of the proper names.

THE EDITOR

October 19, 1836

The Captain's Daughter

OMITTED CHAPTER[7]

WE WERE approaching the banks of the Volga. Our regiment entered the village of N. and halted to spend the night there. The village headman told me that all the villages on the other side had rebelled, and that Pugachov's bands were prowling about everywhere. I was very much alarmed at this news. We were to cross the river the following morning.

Impatience possessed me and I could not rest. My father's estate was on the other side of the river, some twenty miles away. I asked if anyone would row me across. All the peasants were fishermen; there were plenty of boats. I came to Zurin and told him of my intention.

"Take care," he said, "it is dangerous for you to go alone. Wait for the morning. We will be the first to cross and will pay a visit to your parents with fifty Hussars in case of emergency."

I insisted on going. The boat was ready. I stepped into it with two boatmen. They pushed off and plied their oars.

The sky was clear. The moon was shining brightly. The air was still. The Volga flowed calmly and evenly. Swaying

---

[7] This early variant of the latter part of Chapter XIII is offered here because of its intrinsic interest (EDITOR'S NOTE).

rhythmically, the boat glided over the dark waves. Half an hour passed. I sank into dreaming. I thought of the calm of nature and horrors of civil war; of love, and so on. We reached the middle of the river. . . . Suddenly the boatmen began whispering together.

"What is it?" I asked, coming to myself.

"Heaven only knows; we can't tell," the boatmen answered, looking into the distance.

I looked in the same direction and saw in the dark something floating down the river. The mysterious object was approaching us. I told the oarsmen to stop and wait.

The moon hid behind a cloud. The floating phantom seemed darker still. It was quite close to me and yet I could not distinguish it.

"Whatever can it be?" the boatmen said. "It isn't a sail nor a mast."

Suddenly the moon came out from behind the cloud and lighted a terrible sight. A gallows fixed to a raft was floating toward us. Three corpses were swinging on the cross-bar. A morbid curiosity possessed me. I wanted to look into the hanged men's faces. I told the oarsmen to hold the raft with a boat-hook, and my boat knocked against the floating gallows. I jumped out and found myself between the terrible posts. The full moon lighted the disfigured faces of the unfortunate creatures. . . . One of them was an old Chuvash, another a Russian peasant boy of about twenty, strong and healthy. I was shocked when I looked at the third and could not refrain from crying out: it was our servant Vanka—poor Vanka, who, in his foolishness, went over to Pugachov. A black board was nailed over the gallows and had written on it in white letters: "Thieves and rebels." The oarsmen waited for me, unconcerned, holding the raft with the hook. I stepped into the boat. The raft floated down the river. The gallows showed black in the dim night long after we passed it. At last it disappeared and my boat landed at the high and steep bank.

I paid the oarsmen handsomely. One of them took me to the headman of the village by the landing stage. We went into the hut together. When the headman heard that I was asking for horses he spoke to me rather rudely, but my guide whispered something to him and his sternness immediately gave way to hurried obsequiousness. The troika was ready in a minute. I stepped into the carriage and told the driver to take me to our estate.

We galloped along the high road past the sleeping villages. The only thing I feared was being stopped on the way. My night meeting on the Volga proved the presence of rebels in the district, but it also proved the strong counteraction on the part of the authorities. To meet all emergencies I had in my pocket the pass given me by Pugachov and Colonel Zurin's order. But I did not meet anyone, and, toward morning, I saw the river and the pine copse behind which lay our village. The driver whipped up the horses and in another quarter of an hour I drove into it. Our house stood at the other end. The horses were going at full speed. Suddenly in the middle of the village street the driver began pulling up.

"What is it?" I asked impatiently.

"A barrier, sir," the driver answered, with difficulty bringing the fuming horses to a standstill.

Indeed, I saw a barrier fixed across the road and a watchman with a club. The man came up to me and, taking off his hat, asked for my passport.

"What does this mean?" I asked him. "Why is this barrier here? Whom are you guarding?"

"Why, sir, we are in rebellion," he answered, scratching himself.

"And where are your masters?" I asked, with a sinking heart.

"Where are our masters?" the peasant repeated. "Master and mistress are in the granary."

"In the granary?"

"Why, Andryushka, the headman,[8] put them in stocks, you see, and wants to take them to our Father Czar."

"Good Heaven! Lift the bar, you blockhead! What are you gaping at?"

The watchman did not move. I jumped out of the carriage, gave him a box on the ear, I am sorry to say, and lifted the bar myself.

The peasant looked at me in stupid perplexity. I took my seat in the carriage once more and told the driver to drive to the house as fast as he could. Two peasants, armed with clubs, were standing by the locked doors of the granary. The carriage drew up just in front of them. I jumped out and rushed at them.

"Open the doors!" I said to them.

I must have looked formidable, for they threw down their clubs and ran away. I tried to knock the lock off the door or to pick it, but the doors were of oak and the huge lock was unbreakable. At that moment a young peasant came out of the servants' quarters and haughtily asked me how I dared to make a disturbance.

"Where is Andryushka, the headman?" I shouted to him. "Call him to me."

"I am Andrey Afanasyevich and not Andryushka," he answered proudly, with his arms akimbo. "What do you want?"

By way of an answer, I seized him by the collar, and dragging him to the granary doors told him to open them. He did not comply at once; but the "fatherly" chastisement had due effect upon him. He pulled out the key and unlocked the granary. I rushed over the threshold and saw in a dark corner

[8] "Headman," when applied to Andryushka, stands for *zemski*, an official, appointed by Pugachov (EDITOR'S NOTE).

dimly lighted by a narrow skylight my father and mother. Their hands were tied and their feet were in stocks. I flew to embrace them and could not utter a word. They both looked at me with amazement: three years of military life had so altered me that they could not recognize me.

Suddenly I heard the sweet voice I knew: "Pyotr Andreyich! It's you?"

I turned round and saw Marya Ivanovna in another corner, also bound hand and foot. I was dumfounded. My father looked at me in silence, not daring to believe his senses. His face lit up with joy.

"Welcome, Petrusha," he said, pressing me to his heart. "Thank God, we have lived to see you!"

My mother cried out and burst into tears.

"Petrusha, my darling!" she said. "How has the Lord brought you here? Are you well?"

I hastened to cut with my sword the ropes that bound them and to take them out of their prison; but when I came to the door I found that it had been locked again.

"Andryushka, open!" I shouted.

"No fear!" the man answered from behind the door. "You may as well sit here, too! We'll teach you how to be rowdy and drag the Czar's officials by the collar!"

I began looking round the granary to see if there was some way of getting out.

"Don't trouble," my father said to me. "It's not my way to have granaries into which thieves could find a way."

My mother, who had rejoiced a moment before at my coming, was overcome with despair at the thought that I, too, would have to perish with the rest of the family. But I was calmer now that I was with them and Marya Ivanovna. I had a sword and two pistols; I could withstand a siege. Zurin was due to arrive in the evening and would set us free. I told all this to my parents and succeeded in calming my mother and Marya Ivanovna. They gave themselves up completely to the joy of our meeting, and several hours passed for us imperceptibly in expressions of affection and continual conversation.

"Well, Pyotr," my father said, "you have been foolish enough, and I was quite angry with you at the time. But it's no use remembering old scores. I hope that you have sown your wild oats and are reformed. I know that you have served as an honest officer should. I thank you; you have comforted me in my old age. If I owe my deliverance to you, life will be doubly pleasant to me."

I kissed his hand with tears and gazed at Marya Ivanovna, who was so overjoyed at my presence that she seemed quite calm and happy.

About midday we heard extraordinary uproar and shouting. "What does this mean?" my father said. "Can it already be your colonel?"

"Impossible," I answered. "He won't come before evening."

The noise increased. The alarm bell was rung. We heard men on horseback galloping across the yard. At that moment Savelyich's gray head was thrust through the narrow opening cut in the wall and the poor old man said in a pitiful voice: "Andrey Petrovich! Pyotr Andreyich, my dear! Marya Ivanovna! We are lost! The villains have come into the village. And do you know who has brought them, Pyotr Andreyich? Shvabrin, Alexey Ivanych, damnation take him!"

When Marya Ivanovna heard the hated name she clasped her hands and remained motionless.

"Listen!" I said to Savelyich. "Send someone on horseback to the ferry to meet the Hussar regiment and to tell the Colonel of our danger."

"But whom can I send, sir? All the boys have joined the rebels, and the horses have all been seized. Oh, dear! There they are in the yard! They are coming to the granary."

As he said this, we heard several voices behind the door. I made a sign to my mother and Marya Ivanovna to move away into a corner, bared my sword, and leaned against the wall just by the door. My father took the pistols, cocked them both, and stood beside me. The lock rattled, the door opened and Andryushka's head showed. I hit it with my sword and he fell, blocking the doorway. At the same moment my father fired the pistol. The crowd that had besieged us ran away, cursing. I dragged the wounded man across the threshold and closed the door.

The courtyard was full of armed men. I recognized Shvabrin among them.

"Don't be afraid," I said to the women, "there is hope. And don't you shoot any more, Father. Let us save up the last shot."

My mother was praying silently. Marya Ivanovna stood beside her, waiting with angelic calm for her fate to be decided. Threats, abuse, and curses were heard behind the door. I was standing in the same place ready to hit the first man who dared to show himself. Suddenly the villains subsided. I heard Shvabrin's voice calling me by name.

"I am here. What do you want?"

"Surrender, Grinyov; resistance is impossible. Have pity on your old people. Obstinacy will not save you. I shall get at you!"

"Try, traitor!"

"I am not going to put myself forward for nothing or waste my men; I will set the granary on fire and then we'll see what you will do, Belogorsky Don Quixote. Now it is time to have dinner. Meanwhile you can sit and think it over at leisure. Good-bye! Marya Ivanovna, I do not apologize to you: you are probably not feeling bored with your knight beside you in the dark."

Shvabrin went away, leaving sentries at the door. We were

silent, each of us thinking his own thoughts, not daring to express them to the others. I was picturing to myself all that Shvabrin was capable of doing in his malice. I hardly cared about myself. Must I confess it? Even my parents' fate terrified me less than Marya Ivanovna's. I knew that my mother was adored by the peasants and the house serfs. My father, too, was loved in spite of his sternness, for he was just and knew the true needs of the men he owned. Their rebellion was a delusion, a passing intoxication, and not the expression of their resentment. It was possible that my parents would be spared. But Marya Ivanovna? What did the dissolute and unscrupulous man hold in store for her? I did not dare to dwell upon this awful thought and would have killed her (God forgive me!) sooner than see her fall once more into the hands of the cruel enemy.

Another hour passed. Drunken men could be heard singing in the village. Our sentries envied them, and in their annoyance abused us, threatening us with tortures and death. We were waiting for Shvabrin to carry out his threat. At last there was great commotion in the courtyard and we heard Shvabrin's voice once more.

"Well, have you thought better of it? Do you surrender to me of your own will?"

No one answered.

After waiting a while, Shvabrin ordered his men to bring some straw. In a few minutes flames appeared, lighting the dim granary. Smoke began to rise from under the door.

Then Marya Ivanovna came up to me and, taking me by the hand, said in a low voice: "Come, Pyotr Andreyich, don't let both yourself and your parents perish because of me. Shvabrin will listen to me. Let me out!"

"Never!" I cried angrily. "Do you know what awaits you?"

"I will not survive dishonor," she answered calmly, "but

perhaps I shall save my deliverer and the family that has so generously sheltered a poor orphan. Good-bye, Andrey Petrovich! Good-bye, Avdotya Vassilyevna! You have been more than benefactors to me. Bless me! Farewell to you, too, Pyotr Andreyich. Believe me that . . . that . . ."

She burst into tears and buried her face in her hands. . . . I was beside myself. My mother was weeping.

"Stop this nonsense, Marya Ivanovna," said my father. "Whoever would dream of letting you go alone to the brigands? Sit here and keep quiet. If we must die, we may as well die together. Listen! What is he saying now?"

"Do you surrender?" Shvabrin shouted. "You see you will be roasted in another five minutes."

"We won't surrender, you villain!" my father answered firmly.

His vigorous, deeply lined face was wonderfully animated. His eyes sparkled under the gray eyebrows. Turning to me, he said: "Now's the time!"

He opened the door. The flames rushed in and rose up to the beams whose chinks were stuffed with dry moss. My father fired the pistol, stepped over the burning threshold and shouted: "Follow me!" I took my mother and Marya Ivanovna by the hands and quickly led them out. Shvabrin, shot through by my father's feeble hand, was lying by the threshold. The crowd of brigands who had rushed away at our sudden sally took courage and began closing in upon us. I succeeded in dealing a few more blows; but a well-aimed brick hit me right on the chest. I fell down and lost consciousness for a few moments; I was surrounded and disarmed. Coming to myself I saw Shvabrin sitting on the bloodstained grass, with all our family standing before him.

I was supported under the arms. A crowd of peasants, Cossacks, and Bashkirs hemmed us in. Shvabrin was terribly pale. He was pressing one hand to his wounded side. His face expressed malice and pain. He slowly raised his head, glanced at me and said, in a weak, hardly audible voice: "Hang him . . . and all of them . . . except her."

The crowd surrounded us at once and dragged us to the gates. But suddenly they left us and scampered away: Zurin and a whole squadron of Hussars, with bared swords, rode into the courtyard.

The rebels were flying as fast as they could. The Hussars pursued them, striking right and left with their swords and taking prisoners. Zurin jumped off his horse, bowed to my father and mother, and warmly clasped me by the hand.

"I have come just in time," he said to me. "Ah, and here is your betrothed!"

Marya Ivanovna flushed crimson. My father went up to him and thanked him calmly, though he was obviously touched. My mother embraced him, calling him an angel-deliverer.

"Welcome to our home!" my father said to him, and led him toward the house.

Zurin stopped as he passed Shvabrin.

"Who is this?" he asked, looking at the wounded man.

"It is the leader of the gang," my father answered, with a certain pride that betokened an old soldier. "God has helped my feeble hand to punish the young villain and to avenge the blood of my son."

"It is Shvabrin," I said to Zurin.

"Shvabrin! I am very glad. Hussars, take him! Tell the leech to dress his wound and to take the utmost care of him. Shvabrin must certainly be sent to the Kazan Secret Commission. He is one of the chief criminals and his evidence may be of great importance. . . ."

Shvabrin wearily opened his eyes. His face expressed nothing but physical pain. The Hussars carried him away on an outspread cloak.

We went into the house. I looked about me with a tremor, remembering the years of my childhood. Nothing had changed in the house, everything was in its usual place: Shvabrin had not allowed it to be pillaged, preserving in his very degradation an unconscious aversion to base cupidity.

The servants came into the hall. They had taken no part in the rebellion and were genuinely glad of our deliverance. Savelyich was triumphant. It must be mentioned that during the alarm produced by the brigands' arrival he ran to the stables where Shvabrin's horse had been put, saddled it, led it out quietly and, unnoticed in the confusion, galloped toward the ferry. He met the regiment having a rest this side of the Volga. When Zurin heard from him of our danger, he ordered his men to mount, cried: "Off! Off! Gallop!" and, thank God, arrived in time.

Zurin insisted that Andryushka's head should be exposed for a few hours at the top of a pole by the tavern.

The Hussars returned from their pursuit bringing several prisoners with them. They were locked in the same granary where we had endured our memorable siege. We all went to our rooms. The old people needed a rest. As I had not slept the whole night, I flung myself on the bed and dropped fast asleep. Zurin went to make his arrangements.

In the evening we all met round the samovar in the drawing room, talking gaily of the past danger. Marya Ivanovna poured out the tea. I sat down beside her and devoted myself entirely to her. My parents seemed to look with favor upon the tenderness of our relations. That evening lives in my memory to this day. I was happy, completely happy—and are there many such moments in poor human life?

The following day my father was told that the peasants

had come to ask his pardon. My father went out on to the steps to talk to them. When the peasants saw him they knelt down.

"Well, you silly fools," he said to them, "whatever did you rebel for?"

"We are sorry, Master," they answered as one man.

"Sorry, are you? They get into mischief and then they are sorry! I forgive you for the sake of our family joy—God has allowed me to see my son, Pyotr Andreyich, again. So be it, a sin confessed is a sin forgiven."

"We did wrong; of course we did."

"God has sent fine weather. It is time for haymaking; and what have you been doing for the last three days, you fools? Headman! Send everyone to make hay; and mind that by St. John's Day all the hay is in stacks, you red-haired rascal! Begone!"

The peasants bowed and went to work as though nothing had happened. Shvabrin's wound proved not to be mortal. He was sent under escort to Kazan. I saw from the window how they laid him in a cart. Our eyes met. He bent his head and I made haste to move away from the window; I was afraid of looking as though I were triumphing over a humiliated and unhappy enemy.

Zurin had to go on farther. I decided to join him, in spite of my desire to spend a few more days with my family. On the eve of the march I came to my parents and, in accordance with the custom of the time, bowed down to the ground before them, asking their blessing on my marriage with Marya Ivanovna. The old people lifted me up, and with joyous tears gave their consent. 1 brought Marya Ivanovna, pale and trembling, to them. They blessed us. . . . I will not attempt to describe what I was feeling. Those who have been in my position will understand; as to those who have not, I can only pity them and advise them, while there is still time, to fall in love and receive their parents' blessing.

The following day our regiment was ready. Zurin took leave of our family. We were all certain that the military operations would soon be over. I was hoping to be married in another month's time. Marya Ivanovna kissed me in front of all as she said good-bye. I mounted my horse; Savelyich followed me again and the regiment marched off. For a long time I kept looking back at the country house that I was leaving once more. A gloomy foreboding tormented me. Something seemed to whisper to me that my misfortunes were not yet over. My heart felt that another storm was ahead.

I will not describe our campaign and the end of the Pugachov war. We passed through villages pillaged by Pugachov, and could not help taking from the poor inhabitants what the brigands had left them.

They did not know whom to obey. There was no lawful authority anywhere. The landowners were hiding in the forests. Bands of brigands were ransacking the country. The chiefs of separate detachments sent in pursuit of Pugachov, who was by then retreating toward Astrakhan, arbitrarily punished both the guilty and the innocent. The entire region where the conflagration had raged was in a terrible state. God save us from seeing a Russian revolt, senseless and merciless. Those who plot impossible upheavals among us, are either young and do not know our people or are hard-hearted men who do not care a straw either about their own lives or those of other people.

THE TALES OF THE LATE
Ivan Petrovich Belkin

MME. PROSTAKOVA: *My dear sir, from his childhood on, he has been fond of stories.*
SKOTININ: *Mitrofan takes after me.*

THE MINOR

EDITOR'S FOREWORD

HAVING undertaken to arrange the publication of the Tales of I. P. Belkin, which are herewith offered to the public, we wished to add to these a biography, however brief, of the late author, and thereby to satisfy, at least partly, the just curiosity of lovers of our native letters. To that end we addressed ourselves to Marya Alexeyevna Trafilina, the heiress of Ivan Petrovich Belkin and his nearest of kin; but unfortunately it was impossible for her to furnish any intelligence concerning him, inasmuch as she had never known the deceased. She advised us to confer on the matter with an esteemed person, who had been a friend of Ivan Petrovich. We followed this advice, and our letter elicited the following answer. We present it here without any changes or explanatory notes, as a precious testimony to a noble manner of thinking and a touching friendship, and at the same time as a sufficient biographical account.

————, Esq.

My dear sir!

On the twenty-third of this month I had the honor of receiving your most esteemed letter of the fifteenth, in which you express your desire to secure detailed information regarding the dates of birth and death, the career in the service, the domestic circumstances, as well as the occupations and the character of the late Ivan Petrovich Belkin, my late good friend and neighbor. I take great pleasure in complying with your request, and I am here setting forth, my dear sir, all that I can recall of our talks and my own observations.

Ivan Petrovich Belkin was born of honorable and noble parents in the year 1798 in the village of Goryukhino. His late father, second-major Piotr Ivanovich Belkin, was married to Pelageya Gavrilovna, *née* Trafilina. He was a man of moderate means, modest habits, very shrewd in business matters. Their son received his elementary education from a village beadle. To this esteemed man he owed, it would seem, his interest in reading and in Russian letters. In 1815 he entered the service in a Jaeger regiment of the infantry (I do not remember the number), in which he remained until the year 1823. The deaths of his parents, which occurred almost simultaneously, caused him to retire and settle at Goryukhino, his family estate.

Having undertaken the management of the estate, Ivan Petrovich, because of his inexperience and soft-heartedness, soon began to neglect his property, and relaxed the strict regime established by his late parent. Having dismissed the punctual and efficient steward with whom his peasants (as is their habit) were dissatisfied, he placed the management of the village in the hands of his old housekeeper, who had acquired his confidence through her ability to tell stories. This stupid old woman could not tell a twenty-five-ruble from a fifty-ruble note. She was godmother to the children of all the peasants, and so the latter were not in fear of her. The steward they had elected indulged them to such an extent, at the same time defrauding the master, that Ivan Petrovich was forced to abolish the corvée and introduce a very moderate quit-rent. Even then, the peasants, taking advantage of his weakness, obtained a special privilege the first year, and during the next two years paid more than two-thirds of the quit-rent in nuts, huckleberries, and the like; and even so they were in arrears.

Having been a friend of Ivan Petrovich's late parent, I deemed it my duty to offer my advice to the son, too, and repeatedly I volunteered to restore the order he had allowed to fall into decay. To that end, having come to see him one day, I demanded the account books, summoned the rascally steward, and, in the presence of Ivan Petrovich, started examining them. At first the young master followed me with all possible attention and diligence, but after we had ascertained from the accounts that in the last two years the number of peasants had increased, while the quantity of fowls and cattle had considerably diminished, Ivan Petrovich was satisfied with this bit of information, and no longer listened to me, and at the very moment when my investigation and strict questioning had reduced the thievish steward to extreme embarrassment, and indeed forced him to complete silence, to my extreme mortification I heard Ivan Petrovich snoring loudly in his chair. Thenceforward I ceased to intervene in his business affairs and entrusted them (as he did himself) to the care of the Almighty.

This, however, did not injure our friendly relations to any

degree; for, commiserating as I did his weakness and the ruinous negligence common to all our young noblemen, I sincerely loved Ivan Petrovich. It was indeed impossible not to like a young man so gentle and honorable. On his part, Ivan Petrovich showed respect to my years and was cordially attached to me. Until his very end he saw me nearly every day, prizing my simple conversation, although we did not resemble each other in habits, or manner of thinking, or character.

Ivan Petrovich lived in the most moderate fashion, and avoided excesses of any sort. I never chanced to see him tipsy (which in our parts may be accounted an unheard-of miracle); he had a strong leaning toward the female sex, but he was truly as bashful as a girl.[1]

Besides the tales which you are pleased to mention in your letter, Ivan Petrovich left many manuscripts, some of which are in my hands, the rest having been put by his housekeeper to various domestic uses. Thus, last winter all the windows in her own wing were pasted over with the first part of the novel which he did not complete. The above-mentioned tales were, it seems, his first effort. As Ivan Petrovich said, they are for the most part true stories, which he had heard from various persons.[2] But the names in them were almost all his own invention, while the names of the villages and hamlets were taken from our neighborhood, for which reason my village too is mentioned somewhere. This happened not because of

[1] Follows an anecdote, which we do not give, deeming it superfluous; we assure the reader, however, that it contains nothing prejudicial to the memory of Ivan Petrovich Belkin.

[2] Indeed, in Mr. Belkin's manuscript, there is an inscription, in the author's hand, over each tale: "Heard by me from such-and-such a person" (follow rank or title and initials of name and surname). We quote for the curious student: "The Postmaster" was told to him by Titular Counsellor A.G.N.; "The Shot" by Lieutenant I. L. P.; "The Undertaker" by B. V., shop-assistant; "The Snow Storm" and "Mistress into Maid" by Miss K. I. T.

any malicious design, but solely through lack of imagination.

In the autumn of 1828, Ivan Petrovich came down with a catarrhal fever, which took a bad turn, so that he died, in spite of the tireless efforts of our district doctor, a man very skillful, particularly in the treatment of inveterate diseases, such as bunions and the like. He died in my arms in the thirtieth year of his life, and was buried near his deceased parents in the churchyard of the village of Goryukhino.

Ivan Petrovich was of middle height, had gray eyes, blonde hair, a straight nose; his complexion was fair and his face lean.

Here, my dear sir, is all I can recall regarding the manner of life, the occupations, the character and the appearance of my late neighbor and friend. In case you should think fit to make some use of my letter, I respectfully beg you not to mention my name; for much as I esteem and admire authors, I deem it superfluous, and indeed at my age unseemly, to enter their ranks.

With every expression of sincere esteem, believe me, etc.

November 16, 1830

The village of Nenaradovo

Considering it our duty to respect the wish of our author's esteemed friend, we signalize our deepest gratitude to him for the intelligence furnished by him, and trust that the public will appreciate his candor and good nature.

A. P.

The Shot

We fought a duel.
BARATYNSKY

I swore to shoot him, as the code of dueling allows (it was my turn to fire)

EVENING AT CAMP

I

WE WERE stationed in the town of N——. The life of an officer in the army is well known. In the morning, drill and the riding school; dinner with the Colonel or at a Jewish restaurant; in the evening, punch and cards. In N—— there was not one open house, or a single marriageable girl. We used to meet in each other's rooms, where all we saw were men in uniform.

One civilian only was admitted into our society. He was about thirty-five years of age, and therefore we looked upon him as an old fellow. His experience gave him great advantage over us, and his habitual sullenness, stern disposition, and caustic tongue produced a deep impression upon our young minds. Some mystery surrounded his existence; he had the appearance of a Russian, although his name was a foreign one. He had formerly served in the Hussars, and with distinction. Nobody knew the cause that had induced him to retire from the service and settle in a wretched town, where he lived poorly and, at the same time, extravagantly. He always went on foot, and constantly wore a shabby black overcoat, but the officers of our regiment were ever welcome at his table. His dinners, it is true, never consisted of more than two or three dishes, prepared by a retired soldier, but the champagne flowed like water. Nobody knew what his circumstances were, or what his income was, and nobody dared to question him about them. He had a collection of books, chiefly works on military matters and novels. He willingly lent them to us to read, and never asked for their return; on the other hand, he never returned to the owner the books that were lent to him. His principal amusement was shooting with a pistol. The walls of his room were riddled with bullets, and were as full of holes as a honeycomb. A rich collection of pistols was the only luxury in the humble cottage where he lived. The skill which he had acquired with his favorite weapon was simply incredible; and if he had offered to shoot a pear off somebody's forage cap, not a man in our regiment would have hesitated to expose his head to the bullet.

Our conversation often turned upon duels. Silvio—so I will call him—never joined in it. When asked if he had ever fought, he drily replied that he had; but he entered into no particulars, and it was evident that such questions were not to his liking. We imagined that he had upon his conscience the memory of some unhappy victim of his terrible skill. It never entered into the head of any of us to suspect him of anything like cowardice. There are persons whose mere look is sufficient to repel such suspicions. But an unexpected incident occurred which astounded us all.

One day, about ten of our officers dined with Silvio. They drank as usual, that is to say, a great deal. After dinner we asked our host to hold the bank for a game at faro. For a long time he refused, as he hardly ever played, but at last he ordered cards to be brought, placed half a hundred gold coins upon the table, and sat down to deal. We took our places around him, and the game began. It was Silvio's custom to preserve complete silence when playing. He never argued, and never entered into explanations. If the punter made a mistake in calculating, he immediately paid him the difference or noted down the surplus. We were acquainted with this habit of his, and we always allowed him to have his own way; but among us on this occasion was an officer who had only recently been transferred to our regiment. During the course of the game, this officer absently scored one point too many. Silvio took the chalk and noted down the correct account, according to his usual custom. The officers, thinking that he had made a mistake, began to enter into explanations. Silvio continued dealing in silence. The officer, losing patience, took the brush and rubbed out what he considered an error. Silvio took the chalk and corrected the score again. The officer, heated with wine, play, and the laughter of his comrades, considered himself grossly insulted, and in his rage he seized a brass candlestick from the table, and hurled it at Silvio, who barely succeeded in avoiding the missile. We were filled with consternation. Silvio rose, white with rage, and with gleaming eyes, said: "My dear sir, have the goodness to withdraw, and thank God that this has happened in my house."

None of us entertained the slightest doubt as to what the result would be, and we already looked upon our new comrade as a dead man. The officer withdrew, saying that he was ready to answer for his offense in whatever way the banker liked. The play went on for a few minutes longer, but feeling that our host was too overwrought to care for the game, we withdrew one after the other, and repaired to our respective quarters, after having exchanged a few words upon the probability of there soon being a vacancy in the regiment.

The next day, at the riding school, we were already asking each other if the poor lieutenant was still alive, when he himself appeared among us. We put the same question to him, and he replied that he had not yet heard from Silvio. This astonished us. We went to Silvio's house and found him in the courtyard shooting bullet after bullet into an ace pasted upon the gate. He received us as usual, but did not utter a word about the event of the previous evening. Three days passed, and the lieutenant was still alive. We asked each other in astonishment: "Can it be possible that Silvio is not going to fight?"

Silvio did not fight. He was satisfied with a very lame explanation, and made peace with his assailant.

This lowered him very much in the opinion of all our young fellows. Want of courage is the last thing to be pardoned by young men, who usually look upon bravery as the chief of all human virtues, and the excuse for every possible fault. But, by degrees, everything was forgotten, and Silvio regained his former influence.

I alone could not approach him on the old footing. Being endowed by nature with a romantic imagination, I had become attached more than all the others to the man whose life was an enigma, and who seemed to me the hero of some mysterious tale. He was fond of me; at least, with me alone did he drop his customary sarcastic tone, and converse on different subjects in a simple and unusually agreeable manner. But after this unlucky evening, the thought that his honor had been tarnished, and that the stain had been allowed to remain upon it through his own fault, was ever present in my mind, and prevented me from treating him as before. I was ashamed to look at him. Silvio was too intelligent and experienced not to observe this and guess the cause of it. This seemed to vex him; at least, I observed once or twice a desire on his part to enter into an explanation with me, but I avoided such opportunities, and Silvio gave up the attempt. From that time forward I saw him only in the presence of my comrades, and our former confidential conversations came to an end.

Those who live amidst the excitements of the capital have no idea of the many experiences familiar to the inhabitants of villages and small towns, as, for instance, waiting for the arrival of the post. On Tuesdays and Fridays our regimental bureau used to be filled with officers: some expecting money, some letters, and others newspapers. The packets were usually opened on the spot, items of news were communicated from one to another, and the bureau used to present a very animated picture. Silvio used to have his letters addressed to our regiment, and he was generally there to receive them.

One day he received a letter, the seal of which he broke with a look of the greatest impatience. As he read the contents, his eyes sparkled. The officers, each occupied with his own mail, did not observe anything.

"Gentlemen," said Silvio, "circumstances demand my immediate departure; I leave tonight. I hope that you will not refuse to dine with me for the last time. I shall expect you, too," he added, turning toward me. "I shall expect you without fail."

With these words he hastily departed, and we, after agreeing to meet at Silvio's, dispersed to our various quarters.

I arrived at Silvio's house at the appointed time, and found nearly the whole regiment there. All his belongings were already packed; nothing remained but the bare, bullet-riddled walls. We sat down to table. Our host was in an excellent humor, and his gaiety was quickly communicated to the rest. Corks popped every moment, glasses foamed incessantly, and, with the utmost warmth, we wished our departing friend a pleasant journey and every happiness. When we rose from the table it was already late in the evening. After having wished everybody good-bye, Silvio took me by the hand and detained me just at the moment when I was preparing to depart.

"I want to speak to you," he said in a low voice.

I stopped behind.

The guests had departed, and we two were left alone. Sitting down opposite each other, we silently lit our pipes. Silvio seemed greatly troubled; not a trace remained of his former feverish gaiety. The intense pallor of his face, his sparkling eyes, and the thick smoke issuing from his mouth, gave him a truly diabolical appearance. Several minutes elapsed, and then Silvio broke the silence.

"Perhaps we shall never see each other again," said he; "before we part, I should like to explain something to you. You may have observed that I care very little for the opinion of other people, but I like you, and I feel that it would be painful to me to leave you with a wrong impression on your mind."

He paused, and began to refill his pipe. I sat gazing silently at the floor.

"You thought it strange," he continued, "that I did not demand satisfaction from that drunken idiot R——. You will admit, however, that since I had the choice of weapons, his life was in my hands, while my own was in no great danger. I could ascribe my forbearance to generosity alone, but I will not tell a lie. If I could have chastised R—— without the least risk to my own life, I should never have pardoned him."

I looked at Silvio with astonishment. Such a confession completely astounded me. Silvio continued: "Exactly so: I have no right to expose myself to death. Six years ago I received a slap in the face, and my enemy still lives."

My curiosity was greatly excited.

"Did you not fight with him?" I asked. "Circumstances probably separated you."

"I did fight with him," replied Silvio: "and here is a souvenir of our duel."

Silvio rose and took from a cardboard box a red cap with a gold tassel and galloon (what the French call a *bonnet de police*); he put it on—a bullet had passed through it about an inch above the forehead.

"You know," continued Silvio. "that I served in one of the Hussar regiments. My character is well known to you: I am accustomed to taking the lead. From my youth this has been my passion. In our time dissoluteness was the fashion, and I was the wildest man in the army. We used to boast of our drunkenness: I outdrank the famous B——,[1] of whom D. D——[2] has sung. In our regiment duels were constantly taking place, and in all of them I was either second or principal. My comrades adored me, while the regimental commanders, who were constantly being changed, looked upon me as a necessary evil.

"I was calmly, or rather boisterously enjoying my reputation, when a young man belonging to a wealthy and distinguished family—I will not mention his name—joined our regiment. Never in my life have I met with such a fortunate fellow! Imagine to yourself youth, wit, beauty, unbounded

[1] Burtzov, an officer of the Hussars, notorious for his drinking powers and escapades (TRANSLATOR'S NOTE).

[2] Denis Davydov, author, 1781-1839 (TRANSLATOR'S NOTE).

gaiety, the most reckless bravery, a famous name, untold wealth—imagine all these, and you can form some idea of the effect that he would be sure to produce among us. My supremacy was shaken. Dazzled by my reputation, he began to seek my friendship, but I received him coldly, and without the least regret he held aloof from me. I began to hate him. His success in the regiment and in the society of ladies brought me to the verge of despair. I began to seek a quarrel with him; to my epigrams he replied with epigrams which always seemed to me more spontaneous and more cutting than mine, and which were decidedly more amusing, for he joked while I fumed. At last, at a ball given by a Polish landed proprietor, seeing him the object of the attention of all the ladies, and especially the mistress of the house, with whom I was having a liaison, I whispered some grossly insulting remark in his ear. He flamed up and gave me a slap in the face. We grasped our swords; the ladies fainted; we were separated; and that same night we set out to fight.

"The dawn was just breaking. I was standing at the appointed place with my three seconds. With indescribable impatience I awaited my opponent. The spring sun rose, and it was already growing hot. I saw him coming in the distance. He was on foot, in uniform, wearing his sword, and was accompanied by one second. We advanced to meet him. He approached, holding his cap filled with black cherries. The seconds measured twelve paces for us. I had to fire first, but my agitation was so great, that I could not depend upon the steadiness of my hand; and in order to give myself time to become calm, I ceded to him the first shot. My adversary would not agree to this. It was decided that we should cast lots. The first number fell to him, the constant favorite of fortune. He took aim, and his bullet went through my cap. It was now my turn. His life at last was in my hands; I looked at him eagerly, endeavoring to detect if only the faintest shadow of uneasiness. But he stood in front of my pistol, picking out the ripest cherries from his cap and spitting out the stones, which flew almost as far as my feet. His indifference enraged me beyond measure. 'What is the use,' thought I, 'of depriving him of life, when he attaches no value whatever to it?' A malicious thought flashed through my mind. I lowered my pistol.

" 'You don't seem to be ready for death just at present,' I said to him: 'you wish to have your breakfast; I do not wish to hinder you.'

" 'You are not hindering me in the least,' he replied. 'Have the goodness to fire, or just as you please—you owe me a shot; I shall always be at your service.'

"I turned to the seconds, informing them that I had no intention of firing that day, and with that the duel came to an end.

"I resigned my commission and retired to this little place. Since then, not a day has passed that I have not thought of revenge. And now my hour has arrived."

Silvio took from his pocket the letter that he had received that morning, and gave it to me to read. Someone (it seemed to be his business agent) wrote to him from Moscow, that a *certain person* was going to be married to a young and beautiful girl.

"You can guess," said Silvio, "who the certain person is. I am going to Moscow. We shall see if he will look death in the face with as much indifference now, when he is on the eve of being married, as he did once when he was eating cherries!"

With these words, Silvio rose, threw his cap upon the floor, and began pacing up and down the room like a tiger in his cage. I had listened to him in silence; strange conflicting feelings agitated me.

The servant entered and announced that the horses were

ready. Silvio grasped my hand tightly, and we embraced each other. He seated himself in the carriage, in which there were two suitcases, one containing his pistols, the other his effects. We said good-bye once more, and the horses galloped off.

I I

SEVERAL years passed, and family circumstances compelled me to settled in a poor little village of the N—— district. Occupied with farming, I continued to sigh in secret for my former active and carefree life. The most difficult thing of all was having to accustom myself to passing the spring and winter evenings in perfect solitude. Until the hour for dinner I managed to pass away the time somehow or other, talking with the bailiff, riding about to inspect the work, or going around to look at the new buildings; but as soon as it began to get dark, I positively did not know what to do with myself. The few books that I had found in the cupboards and store-rooms, I already knew by heart. All the stories that my housekeeper Kirilovna could remember, I had heard over and over again. The songs of the peasant women made me feel depressed. I tried drinking spirits, but it made my head ache; and moreover, I confess I was afraid of becoming a drunkard from mere chagrin, that is to say, the saddest kind of drunkard, of which I had seen many examples in our district. I had no near neighbors, except two or three topers, whose conversation consisted for the most part of hiccups and sighs. Solitude was preferable to their society.

Four versts from my house there was a rich estate belonging to the Countess B——; but nobody lived there except the steward. The Countess had only visited her estate once, during the first year of her married life, and then she had remained there only a month. But in the second spring of my secluded life, a report was circulated that the Countess, with her husband, was coming to spend the summer on her estate. Indeed, they arrived at the beginning of June.

The arrival of a rich neighbor is an important event in the lives of country people. The landed proprietors and the people of their household talk about it for two months beforehand, and for three years afterwards. As for me, I must confess that the news of the arrival of a young and beautiful neighbor affected me strongly. I burned with impatience to see her, and the first Sunday after her arrival, I set out after dinner for the village of A——, to pay my respects to the Countess and her husband, as their nearest neighbor and most humble servant.

A lackey conducted me into the Count's study, and then went to announce me. The spacious room was furnished with every possible luxury. The walls were lined with bookcases, each surmounted by a bronze bust; over the marble mantelpiece was a large mirror; on the floor was a green cloth covered with carpets. Unaccustomed to luxury in my own poor corner, and not having seen the wealth of other people for a long time, I awaited the appearance of the Count with some little trepidation, as a suppliant from the provinces awaits the entrance of the minister. The door opened, and a handsome-looking man, of about thirty-two, entered the room. The Count approached me with a frank and friendly air: I tried to be self-possessed and began to introduce myself, but he anticipated me. We sat down. His conversation, which was easy and agreeable, soon dissipated my awkward bashfulness; and I was already beginning to recover my usual composure, when the Countess suddenly entered, and I became more confused than ever. She was indeed beautiful.

The Count presented me. I wished to appear at ease, but the more I tried to assume an air of unconstraint, the more awkward I felt. In order to give me time to recover myself and to become accustomed to my new acquaintances, they began to talk to each other, treating me as a good neighbor, and without ceremony. Meanwhile, I walked about the room, examining the books and pictures. I am no judge of pictures, but one of them attracted my attention. It represented some view in Switzerland, but it was not the painting that struck me, but the circumstance that the canvas was shot through by two bullets, one planted just above the other.

"A good shot, that!" said I, turning to the Count.

"Yes," replied he, "a very remarkable shot. . . . Do you shoot well?" he continued.

"Tolerably," I replied, rejoicing that the conversation had turned at last upon a subject that was familiar to me. "At thirty paces I can manage to hit a card without fail—I mean, of course, with a pistol that I am used to."

"Really?" said the Countess, with a look of the greatest interest. "And you, my dear, could you hit a card at thirty paces?"

"Some day," replied the Count, "we will try. In my time I did not shoot badly, but it is now four years since I touched a pistol."

"Oh!" I observed. "In that case, I don't mind laying a wager that Your Excellency will not hit the card at twenty paces: the pistol demands daily practice. I know that from experience. In our regiment I was reckoned one of the best shots. It once happened that I did not touch a pistol for a whole month, as I had sent mine to be mended; and would you believe it, Your Excellency, the first time I began to shoot again, I missed a bottle four times in succession at twenty paces! Our captain, a witty and amusing fellow, happened to be standing by, and he said to me: 'It is evident, my friend, that you will not lift your hand against the bottle.' No, Your Excellency, you must not neglect to practice, or your hand will soon lose its cunning. The best shot that I ever met used to shoot at least three times every day before dinner. It was as much his custom to do this, as it was to drink his daily glass of brandy."

The Count and Countess seemed pleased that I had begun to talk.

"And what sort of a shot was he?" asked the Count.

"Well, it was this way with him, Your Excellency: if he saw a fly settle on the wall—you smile, Countess, but, before Heaven, it is the truth—if he saw a fly, he would call out: 'Kuzka, my pistol!' Kuzka would bring him a loaded pistol—bang! and the fly would be crushed against the wall."

"Wonderful!" said the Count. "And what was his name?"

"Silvio, Your Excellency."

"Silvio!" exclaimed the Count, starting up. "Did you know Silvio?"

"How could I help knowing him, Your Excellency: we were intimate friends; he was received in our regiment like a brother officer, but it is now five years since I had any news of him. Then Your Excellency also knew him?"

"Oh, yes, I knew him very well. Did he ever tell you of one very strange incident in his life?"

"Does Your Excellency refer to the slap in the face that he received from some scamp at a ball?"

"Did he tell you the name of this scamp?"

"No, Your Excellency, he never mentioned his name. . . . Ah! Your Excellency," I continued, guessing the truth: "pardon me . . . I did not know . . . could it have been you?"

"Yes, I myself," replied the Count, wtih a look of extraordinary distress; "and that picture with a bullet through it is a memento of our last meeting."

"Ah, my dear," said the Countess, "for Heaven's sake, do not speak about that; it would be too terrible for me to listen to."

"No," replied the Count; "I will relate everything. He knows how I insulted his friend, and it is only right that he should know how Silvio revenged himself."

The Count pushed a chair toward me, and with the liveliest interest I listened to the following story:

"Five years ago I got married. The first month—the honeymoon—I spent here, in this village. To this house I am indebted for the happiest moments of my life, as well as for one of its most painful recollections.

"One evening we went out together for a ride on horseback. My wife's horse became restive; she grew frightened, gave the reins to me, and returned home on foot. I rode on before. In the courtyard I saw a traveling carriage, and I was told that in my study sat waiting for me a man who would not give his name, but who merely said that he had business with me. I entered the room and saw in the darkness a man, covered with dust and wearing a beard of several days' growth. He was standing there, near the fireplace. I approached him, trying to remember his features.

" 'You do not recognize me, Count?' said he, in a quivering voice.

" 'Silvio!' I cried, and I confess that I felt as if my hair had suddenly stood on end.

" 'Exactly,' continued he. 'There is a shot due me, and I have come to discharge my pistol. Are you ready?'

"His pistol protruded from a side pocket. I measured twelve paces and took my stand there in that corner, begging him to fire quickly, before my wife arrived. He hesitated, and asked for a light. Candles were brought in. I closed the doors, gave orders that nobody was to enter, and again begged him to fire. He drew out his pistol and took aim. . . . I counted the seconds . . . I thought of her . . . A terrible minute passed! Silvio lowered his hand.

" 'I regret,' said he, 'that the pistol is not loaded with cherry stones . . . the bullet is heavy. It seems to me that this is not a duel, but a murder. I am not accustomed to taking aim at unarmed men. Let us begin all over again; we will cast lots as to who shall fire first.' "My head went round . . . I think I raised some objection. . . . At last we loaded another pistol, and rolled up two pieces of paper. He placed these latter in his cap—the same through which I had once sent a bullet—and again I drew the first number.

" 'You are devilishly lucky, Count,' said he, with a smile that I shall never forget.

"I don't know what was the matter with me, or how it was that he managed to make me do it . . . but I fired and hit that picture."

The Count pointed with his finger to the perforated picture; his face burned like fire; the Countess was whiter than her own handkerchief; and I could not restrain an exclamation.

"I fired," continued the Count, "and, thank Heaven, missed my aim. Then Silvio—at that moment he was really terrible —Silvio raised his hand to take aim at me. Suddenly the door opens, Masha rushes into the room, and with a shriek throws herself upon my neck. Her presence restored to me all my courage.

" 'My dear,' said I to her, 'don't you see that we are joking? How frightened you are! Go and drink a glass of water and then come back to us; I will introduce you to an old friend and comrade.'

"Masha still doubted.

" 'Tell me, is my husband speaking the truth?' said she, turning to the terrible Silvio. 'Is it true that you are only joking?'

" 'He is always joking, Countess,' replied Silvio: 'once he gave me a slap in the face in jest; on another occasion he sent a bullet through my cap in jest; and just now, when he fired at me and missed me, it was all in jest. And now I feel inclined to have a joke.'

"With these words he raised his pistol to take aim at me—right before her! Masha threw herself at his feet.

" 'Rise, Masha; are you not ashamed!' I cried in a rage. 'And you, sir, will you stop making fun of a poor woman? Will you fire or not?'

" 'I will not,' replied Silvio. 'I am satisfied. I have seen your confusion, your alarm. I forced you to fire at me. That is sufficient. You will remember me. I leave you to your conscience.'

"Then he turned to go, but pausing in the doorway, and looking at the picture that my shot had passed through, he fired at it almost without taking aim, and disappeared. My wife had fainted away; the servants did not venture to stop him, the mere look of him filled them with terror. He went out upon the steps, called his coachman, and drove off before I could recover myself."

The Count fell silent. In this way I learned the end of the story, whose beginning had once made such a deep impression upon me. The hero of it I never saw again. It is said that Silvio commanded a detachment of Hetaerists during the revolt under Alexander Ypsilanti, and that he was killed in the battle of Skulyani.

The Snowstorm

Horses dash across the slopes,
Trampling snow deep-drifted . . .
By the wayside stands a church,
Lonely cross uplifted.

. . . .

Suddenly a snowstorm flings
Tufted flakes about us,
O'er the sledge with whistling wing
Flies a crow to flout us.
Weird his cry, foreboding grief!
Gathering their forces,
Manes upraised, toward the dark
Peer the speeding horses . . .

ZHUKOVSKY

TOWARD the end of the year 1811, a memorable period for us, the good Gavrila Gavrilovich R—— was living on his estate of Nenaradovo. He was celebrated throughout the district for his hospitality and kindheartedness. The neighbors were constantly visiting him: some to eat and drink; some to play "Boston" at five kopecks with his wife, Praskovya Petrovna; and some to look at their daughter, Marya Gavrilovna, a pale, slender girl of seventeen. She was considered wealthy, and many desired her for themselves or for their sons.

Marya Gavrilovna had been brought up on French novels, and consequently was in love. The object of her choice was a poor sub-lieutenant, who was then on leave of absence in his village. It need scarcely be mentioned that the young man returned her passion with equal ardor, and that the parents of his beloved one, observing their mutual inclination, forbade their daughter to think of him, and gave him a worse reception than if he were a retired assessor.

Our lovers corresponded with each other and daily saw each other alone in the little pine wood or near the old chapel. There they exchanged vows of eternal love, lamented their cruel fate, and formed various plans. Corresponding and conversing in this way, they arrived quite naturally at the following conclusion:

If we cannot exist without each other, and the will of hardhearted parents stands in the way of our happiness, why cannot we do without their consent?

Needless to mention that this happy idea originated in the mind of the young man, and that it was very congenial to the romantic imagination of Marya Gavrilovna.

The winter came and put a stop to their meetings, but their correspondence became all the more active. Vladimir Nikolayevich in every letter implored her to give herself up to him, to get married secretly, to hide for some time, and then throw themselves at the feet of their parents, who would, without any doubt, be touched at last by the heroic constancy and unhappiness of the lovers, and would assuredly say to them: "Children, come to our arms!"

Marya Gavrilovna hesitated for a long time, and many plans for elopement were rejected. At last she consented: on the appointed day she was not to take supper, but was to retire to her room under the pretext of a headache. Her maid was in the plot; they were both to go into the garden by the back stairs, and behind the garden, they would find ready a sledge, into which they were to get, and then drive straight to the church of Zhadrino, a village about five versts from Nenaradovo, where Vladimir would be waiting for them.

On the eve of the decisive day, Marya Gavrilovna did not sleep the whole night; she packed and tied up her linen and other articles of apparel, wrote a long letter to a sentimental young lady, a friend of hers, and another to her parents. She took leave of them in the most touching terms, urged the invincible strength of passion as an excuse for the step she was taking, and wound up with the assurance that she would consider it the happiest moment of her life, when she would be allowed to throw herself at the feet of her dear parents.

After having sealed both letters with a Tula seal, upon which were engraved two flaming hearts with a suitable inscription, she threw herself upon her bed just before daybreak, and dozed off: but even then she was constantly being awakened by terrible dreams. First it seemed to her that at the very moment when she seated herself in the sledge, in order to go and get married, her father stopped her, dragged her over the snow with agonizing rapidity, and threw her into a dark, bottomless abyss, down which she fell headlong with an indescribable sinking of the heart. Then she saw Vladimir lying on the grass, pale and bloodstained. With his dying breath he implored her in a piercing voice to make haste and marry him. . . . Other abominable and absurd visions floated before her one after another. At last she arose, paler than usual, and with an unfeigned headache. Her father and mother observed her uneasiness; their tender solicitude and incessant inquiries: "What is the matter with you, Masha? Are you ill, Masha?" cut her to the heart. She tried to reassure them and to appear cheerful, but in vain.

Evening came. The thought, that this was the last day she

would pass in the bosom of her family, weighed upon her heart. She was more dead than alive. In secret she took leave of everybody, of all the objects that surrounded her.

Supper was served; her heart began to beat violently. In a trembling voice she declared that she did not want any supper, and then took leave of her father and mother. They kissed her and blessed her as usual, and she could hardly restrain herself from weeping.

On reaching her own room, she threw herself into a chair and burst into tears. Her maid urged her to be calm and to take courage. Everything was ready. In half an hour Masha would leave forever her parents' house, her room, and her peaceful girlish life. . . .

Outside a snowstorm was raging; the wind howled, the shutters shook and rattled, and everything seemed to her to portend misfortune.

Soon all was quiet in the house: everyone was asleep. Masha wrapped herself in a shawl, put on a warm cloak, took her box in her hand, and went down the back staircase. Her maid followed her with two bundles. They descended into the garden. The snowstorm had not subsided; the wind blew in their faces, as if trying to stop the young criminal. With difficulty they reached the end of the garden. On the road a sledge awaited them. The chilled horses would not keep still; Vladimir's coachman was walking up and down in front of them, trying to restrain their impatience. He helped the young lady and her maid into the sledge, stowed away the box and the bundles, seized the reins, and the horses dashed off.

Having entrusted the young lady to the care of fate and to the skill of Teryoshka the coachman, we will return to our young lover.

All day long Vladimir had been driving about. In the

morning he paid a visit to the priest of Zhadrino, and having come to an agreement with him after a great deal of difficulty, he then set out to seek for witnesses among the neighboring landowners. The first to whom he presented himself, a retired officer about forty years old, whose name was Dravin, consented with pleasure. The adventure, he declared, reminded him of his young days and his pranks in the Hussars. He persuaded Vladimir to stay to dinner with him, and assured him that he would have no difficulty in finding the other two witnesses. And, indeed, immediately after dinner, appeared the surveyor Schmidt, wearing mustaches and spurs, and the son of the captain of police, a lad of sixteen, who had recently entered the Uhlans. They not only accepted Vladimir's proposal, but even vowed that they were ready to sacrifice their lives for him. Vladimir embraced them with rapture, and returned home to get everything ready.

It had been dark for some time. He dispatched his faithful Teryoshka to Nenaradovo with his troika and with detailed instructions, ordered for himself the one-horse sleigh and set out alone, without any coachman, for Zhadrino, where Marya Gavrilovna was due to arrive in about a couple of hours. He knew the road well, and it was only a twenty-minute ride.

But Vladimir scarcely found himself on the open road, when the wind rose and such a snowstorm came on that he could see nothing. In one minute the road was completely hidden; the landscape disappeared in a thick yellow fog, through which fell white flakes of snow; earth and sky merged into one. Vladimir found himself off the road, and tried vainly to get back to it. His horse went on at random, and at every moment climbed either a snowdrift or sank into a hole, so that the sledge kept turning over. Vladimir's one effort was not to lose the right direction. But it seemed to him that more than half an hour had already passed, and he had not yet reached the Zhadrino wood. Another ten minutes elapsed—still no wood was to be seen. Vladimir drove across a field intersected by deep ravines. The snowstorm did not abate, the sky did not become any clearer. The horse began to grow tired, and the sweat rolled from Vladimir in great drops, in spite of the fact that he was constantly being half buried in the snow.

At last Vladimir perceived that he was going in the wrong direction. He stopped, began to think, to recollect and compare, and he felt convinced that he ought to have turned to the right. He turned to the right now. His horse could scarcely move forward. He had now been on the road for more than an hour. Zhadrino could not be far off. But on and on he went, and still no end to the field—nothing but snowdrifts and ravines. The sledge was constantly turning over, and as constantly being set right again. The time was passing; Vladimir began to grow seriously uneasy.

At last something dark appeared in the distance. Vladimir directed his course toward it. On drawing near, he perceived that it was a wood.

"Thank Heaven!" he thought, "I am not far off now."

He drove along by the edge of the wood, hoping by and by to come upon the well-known road or to pass round the wood; Zhadrino was situated just behind it. He soon found the road, and plunged among the dark trees, now denuded of leaves by the winter. The wind could not rage here; the road was smooth; the horse recovered courage, and Vladimir felt reassured.

But he drove on and on, and Zhadrino was not to be seen; there was no end to the wood. Vladimir discovered with horror that he had entered an unknown forest. Despair took possession of him. He whipped the horse; the poor animal broke into a trot, but soon slackened its pace, and in about a quarter of an hour it was scarcely able to drag one leg after the other, in spite of all the exertions of the unfortunate Vladimir.

Gradually the trees began to get sparser, and Vladimir emerged from the forest; but Zhadrino was not to be seen. It must now have been about midnight. Tears gushed from his eyes; he drove on at random. Meanwhile the storm had subsided, the clouds dispersed, and before him lay a level plain covered with a white undulating carpet. The night was tolerably clear. He saw, not far off, a little village, consisting of four or five houses. Vladimir drove toward it. At the first cottage he jumped out of the sledge, ran to the window and began to knock. After a few minutes, the wooden shutter was raised, and an old man thrust out his gray beard.

"What do you want?"

"Is Zhadrino far from here?"

"Zhadrino? Far from here?"

"Yes, yes! Is it far?"

"Not far; about ten versts."

At this reply, Vladimir clutched his hair and stood motionless, like a man condemned to death.

"Where do you come from?" continued the old man.

Vladimir had not the heart to answer the question.

"Listen, old man," said he, "can you find any horses to take me to Zhadrino?"

"How should we have such things as horses?" replied the peasant.

"Can I at least get a guide? I will pay him whatever he asks."

"Wait," said the old man, closing the shutter, "I will send my son out to you; he will direct you."

Vladimir waited. But a minute had scarcely elapsed when he began knocking again. The shutter was raised, and the beard again appeared.

"What do you want?"

"What about your son?"

"He'll be out presently; he is putting on his boots. Are you cold? Come in and warm yourself."

"Thank you; send your son out quickly."

The door creaked: a lad came out with a cudgel and led the way, now pointing out the road, now searching for it among the snowdrifts.

"What time is it?" Vladimir asked him.

"It will soon be daylight," replied the young peasant. Vladimir did not say another word.

The cocks were crowing, and it was already light when they reached Zhadrino. The church was locked. Vladimir paid the guide and drove into the priest's courtyard. His troika was not there. What news awaited him! . . .

But let us return to the worthy proprietors of Nenaradovo, and see what is happening there.

Nothing.

The old people awoke and went into the parlor, Gavrila Gavrilovich in a nightcap and flannel doublet, Praskovya Petrovna in a wadded dressing gown. The samovar was brought in, and Gavrila Gavrilovich sent a servant to ask Marya Gavrilovna how she was and how she had passed the night. The servant returned, saying that the young lady had not slept very well, but that she felt better now, and that she would come down presently into the parlor. And, indeed, the door opened and Marya Gavrilovna entered the room and wished her father and mother good morning.

"How is your head, Masha?" asked Gavrila Gavrilovich.

"Better, Papa," replied Masha.

"You must have gotten your headache yesterday from charcoal fumes," said Praskaovya Petrovna.

"Very likely, Mamma," replied Masha.

The day passed happily enough, but in the night Masha was taken ill. They sent to town for a doctor. He arrived in the evening and found the sick girl delirious. A violent fever ensued, and for two weeks the poor patient hovered on the brink of the grave.

Nobody in the house knew anything about her intended elopement. The letters, written the evening before, had been burned; and her maid, dreading the wrath of her master, had not whispered a word about it to anybody. The priest, the retired officer, the mustached surveyor, and the little Uhlan were discreet, and not without reason. Teryoshka, the coachman, never uttered one word too much about it, even when he was drunk. Thus the secret was kept by more than half a dozen conspirators.

But Marya Gavrilovna herself divulged her secret during her delirious ravings. Her words were so disconnected, however, that her mother, who never left her bedside, could only understand from them that her daughter was deeply in love with Vladimir Nikolayevich, and that probably love was the cause of her illness. She consulted her husband and some of her neighbors, and at last it was unanimously decided that such was evidently Marya Gavrilovna's fate, that a woman cannot escape her destined husband even on horseback, that poverty is not a crime, that one does not marry wealth, but a man, etc., etc. Moral maxims are wonderfully useful in those cases where we can invent little in our own justification.

In the meantime the young lady began to recover. Vladimir had not been seen for a long time in the house of Gavrila Gavrilovich. He was afraid of the usual reception. It was resolved to send and announce to him an unexpected piece of good news: the consent of Marya's parents to his marriage with their daughter. But what was the astonishment of the proprietor of Nenaradovo, when, in reply to their invitation, they received from him a half-insane letter. He informed them that he would never set foot in their house again, and begged them to forget an unhappy creature whose only hope was death. A few days afterwards they heard that Vladimir had joined the army again. This was in the year 1812.

For a long time they did not dare to announce this to Masha, who was now convalescent. She never mentioned the name of Vladimir. Some months afterwards, finding his name in the list of those who had distinguished themselves and been severely wounded at Borodino, she fainted away, and it was feared that she would have another attack of fever. But, Heaven be thanked! the fainting fit had no serious consequences.

Another misfortune fell upon her: Gavrila Gavrilovich died, leaving her the heiress to all his property. But the inheritance did not console her; she shared sincerely the grief of poor Praskovya Petrovna, vowing that she would never leave her. They both quitted Nenaradovo, the scene of so many sad recollections, and went to live on another estate.

Suitors crowded round the charming heiress, but she gave not the slightest hope to any of them. Her mother sometimes exhorted her to make a choice; but Marya Gavrilovna shook her head and became pensive. Vladimir no longer existed: he had died in Moscow on the eve of the entry of the French. His memory seemed to be held sacred by Masha; at least, she treasured up everything that could remind her of him: books that he had once read, his drawings, his music, and verses that he had copied out for her. The neighbors, hearing of all this, were astonished at her constancy, and awaited with curiosity the hero who should at last triumph over the melancholy fidelity of this virgin Artemis.

Meanwhile the war had ended gloriously. Our regiments returned from abroad, and the people went out to meet them. The bands played the songs of the conquered: "Vive Henri-Quatre," Tyrolese waltzes and airs from "Joconde." Officers, who had set out for the war almost mere lads, returned, grown men in the martial air, their breasts hung with crosses. The soldiers chatted gaily among themselves, constantly using French and German words in their speech. Unforgettable time! Time of glory and enthusiasm! How the Russian heart throbbed at the word "Fatherland!" How sweet were the tears of reunion! With what unanimity did we mingle feelings of national pride with love for the Czar! And for him—what a moment!

The women, the Russian women, were then incomparable. Their usual coldness disappeared. Their enthusiasm was truly intoxicating, when welcoming the conquerors they cried "Hurrah!"

"And tossed their caps into the air!"

What officer of that time does not confess that to the Russian women he was indebted for his best and most precious reward?

At this brilliant period Marya Gavrilovna was living with her mother in the province of ——, and did not see how both capitals celebrated the return of the troops. But in the districts and villages the general enthusiasm was, if possible, even greater. The appearance of an officer in those sections was for him a veritable triumph, and the lover in a frock coat fared ill in his vicinity.

We have already said that, in spite of her coldness, Marya Gavrilovna was, as before, surrounded by suitors. But all had to withdraw when the wounded Colonel Burmin of the Hussars, with the Order of St. George in his buttonhole, and with an "interesting pallor," as the young ladies of the neighborhood observed, appeared at the manor. He was about twenty-six years of age. He had obtained leave of absence to visit his estate, which was near that of Marya Gavrilovna. Marya bestowed special attention upon him. In his presence her habitual pensiveness disappeared. It cannot be said that she flirted with him, but a poet, observing her behavior, would have said:

"*Se amor non è, che dunque?*"

Burmin was indeed a very charming young man. He had the sort of mind which pleases women: decorous and keen, without any pretensions, and inclined to carefree mockery. His behavior toward Marya Gavrilovna was simple and frank, but whatever she said or did, both his soul and his eyes followed her. He seemed to be of a quiet and modest disposition, though it was reported that he had once been a terrible rake; but this did not injure him in the opinion of Marya Gavrilovna, who—like all young ladies—excused with pleasure follies that gave indication of boldness and ardor of temperament.

But more than anything else—more than his tenderness, more than his agreeable conversation, more than his interesting pallor, more than his arm in a sling—the silence of the young Hussar excited her curiosity and imagination. She could not but confess that he pleased her very much; probably he, too, with his intelligence and experience, had already observed that she singled him out; how was it then that she had not yet seen him at her feet or heard his declaration? What restrained him? Was it timidity, or pride, or the coquetry of a crafty ladies' man? It was a puzzle to her. After long reflection, she came to the conclusion that timidity alone was the cause of it, and she resolved to encourage him by greater attention and, if circumstances should render it necessary, even by an exhibition of tenderness. She was preparing a startling dénouement, and waited with impatience for the moment of the romantic explanation. A secret, of whatever nature it may be, always presses heavily upon the female heart. Her strategy had the desired success; at least, Burmin fell into such a reverie, and his black eyes rested with such fire upon her, that the decisive moment seemed close at hand. The neighbors spoke about the marriage as if it were a settled matter, and good Praskovya Petrovna rejoiced that her daughter had at last found a worthy suitor.

On one occasion the old lady was sitting alone in the parlor, playing patience, when Burmin entered the room and immediately inquired for Marya Gavrilovna.

"She is in the garden," replied the old lady. "Go out to her, and I will wait here for you."

Burmin went, and the old lady made the sign of the cross and thought: "Perhaps the business will be settled today!"

Burmin found Marya Gavrilovna near the pond, under a willow tree, with a book in her hands, and in a white dress: a veritable heroine of a novel. After the first few questions, Marya Gavrilovna purposely allowed the conversation to drop, thereby increasing their mutual embarrassment, from which there was no possible way of escape except only by a sudden and decisive declaration.

And that is what happened: Burmin, feeling the difficulty of his position, declared that he had long sought an opportunity to open his heart to her, and requested a moment's attention. Marya Gavrilovna closed her book and cast down her eyes, as a sign of consent.

"I love you," said Burmin. "I love you passionately."

Marya Gavrilovna blushed and lowered her head still further. "I have acted imprudently in indulging the sweet habit of seeing and hearing you daily. . . ." Marya Gavrilovna recalled to mind the first letter of St. Preux. "But it is now too late to resist my fate; the remembrance of you, your dear incomparable image, will henceforth be the torment and the consolation of my life, but there still remains a painful duty for me to perform—to reveal to you a terrible secret which will place between us an insurmountable barrier. . . ."

"That barrier has always existed," interrupted Marya Gavrilovna hastily. "I could never be your wife."

"I know," he replied calmly. "I know that you once loved, but death and three years of mourning . . . Dear, kind Marya Gavrilovna, do not try to deprive me of my last consolation: the thought that you would have consented to make me happy, if . . ."

"Don't speak, for Heaven's sake, don't speak. You torture me."

"Yes, I know, I feel that you would have been mine, but —I am the most miserable creature under the sun—I am already married!"

Marya Gavrilovna looked at him in astonishment.

"I am already married," continued Burmin. "I have been married four years, and I do not know who my wife is, or where she is, or whether I shall ever see her again!"

"What are you saying?" exclaimed Marya Gavrilovna. "How very strange! Continue: I will relate to you afterwards. . . . But continue, I beg of you."

"At the beginning of the year 1812," said Burmin, "I was hastening to Vilna, where my regiment was stationed. Arriving late one evening at one of the post-stations, I ordered the horses to be got ready as quickly as possible, when suddenly a terrible snowstorm came on, and the postmaster and drivers advised me to wait till it had passed over. I followed their advice, but an unaccountable uneasiness took possession of me: it seemed as if someone were pushing me forward. Meanwhile the snowstorm did not subside; I could endure it no longer, and again ordering out the horses, I started off at the height of the storm. The driver conceived the idea of following the course of the river, which would shorten our journey by three versts. The banks were covered with snow: the driver drove past the place where we should have come out upon the road, and so we found ourselves in an unknown part of the country. . . . The storm did not abate; I saw a light in the distance, and I ordered the driver to proceed toward it. We reached a village; in the wooden church there was a light. The church was open. Outside the fence stood several sledges, and people were passing in and out through the porch.

" 'This way! this way!' cried several voices.

"I ordered the driver to proceed.

" 'In the name of Heaven, where have you been loitering?' somebody said to me. 'The bride has fainted away; the priest does not know what to do, and we were just getting ready to go back. Get out as quickly as you can.'

"I got out of the sledge without saying a word, and went into the church, which was feebly lit up by two or three tapers. A young girl was sitting on a bench in a dark corner of the church; another girl was rubbing her temples.

" 'Thank God!' said the latter, 'you have come at last. You have almost killed the young lady.'

"The old priest advanced toward me, and said: 'Do you wish me to begin?'

" 'Begin, begin, Father,' I replied absently.

"The young girl was raised up. She seemed to me not at all bad-looking. . . . Impelled by an incomprehensible, unpardonable levity, I placed myself by her side in front of the pulpit; the priest hurried on; three men and a maid supported the bride and only occupied themselves with her. We were married.

" 'Kiss each other!' said the witnesses to us.

"My wife turned her pale face toward me. I was about to kiss her, when she exclaimed: 'Oh, it is not he! It is not he!' and fell in a swoon.

"The witnesses gazed at me in alarm. I turned around and left the church without the least hindrance, flung myself into the *kibitka* and cried: 'Drive off!' "

"My God!" exclaimed Marya Gavrilovna. "And do you not know what became of your poor wife?"

"I do not know," replied Burmin; "neither do I know the name of the village where I was married, nor the post-station where I set out from. At that time I attached so little importance to my wicked prank, that on leaving the church, I fell asleep, and did not awake till the next morning after reaching the third station. The servant, who was then with me, died during the campaign, so that I have no hope of ever discovering the woman upon whom I played such a cruel joke, and who is now so cruelly avenged."

"My God, my God!" cried Marya Gavrilovna, seizing him by the hand. "Then it was you! And you do not recognize me?"

Burmin blenched—and threw himself at her feet.

The Undertaker

Are coffins not beheld each day,
The gray hairs of an aging world?
DERZHAVIN

THE LAST of the effects of the undertaker, Adrian Prokhorov, were piled upon the hearse, and a couple of
sorry-looking jades dragged themselves along for the fourth
time from Basmannaya to Nikitskaya, whither the undertaker was removing with all his household. After locking up
the shop, he posted upon the door a placard announcing
that the house was for sale or rent, and then made his way
on foot to his new abode. On approaching the little yellow
house, which had so long captivated his imagination, and
which at last he had bought for a considerable sum, the old
undertaker was astonished to find that his heart did not
rejoice. When he crossed the unfamiliar threshold and found
his new home in the greatest confusion, he sighed for his old
hovel, where for eighteen years the strictest order had pre-
vailed. He began to scold his two daughters and the servants
for their slowness, and then set to work to help them himself.
Order was soon established; the ikon case, the cupboard with
the crockery, the table, the sofa, and the bed occupied the
corners reserved for them in the back room; in the kitchen
and parlor were placed the master's wares—coffins of all

colors and of all sizes, together with cupboards containing mourning hats, cloaks and torches.

Over the gate was placed a sign representing a plump Cupid with an inverted torch in his hand and bearing this inscription: "Plain and colored coffins sold and upholstered here; coffins also let out on hire, and old ones repaired."

The girls retired to their bedroom; Adrian made a tour of inspection of his quarters, and then sat down by the window and ordered the samovar to be prepared.

The enlightened reader knows that Shakespeare and Walter Scott have both represented their grave-diggers as merry and facetious individuals, in order that the contrast might more forcibly strike our imagination. Out of respect for the truth, we cannot follow their example, and we are compelled to confess that the disposition of our undertaker was in perfect harmony with his gloomy métier. Adrian Prokhorov was usually sullen and pensive. He rarely opened his mouth, except to scold his daughters when he found them standing idle and gazing out of the window at the passers-by, or to ask for his wares an exorbitant price from those who had the misfortune—or sometimes the pleasure—of needing them. And so Adrian, sitting near the window and drinking his seventh cup of tea, was immersed as usual in melancholy reflections. He thought of the pouring rain which, just a week before, had commenced to beat down during the funeral of the retired brigadier. Many of the cloaks had shrunk in consequence of the downpour, and many of the hats had been put quite out of shape. He foresaw unavoidable expenses, for his old stock of funeral apparel was in a pitiable condition. He hoped to compensate himself for his losses by the burial of old Trukhina, the merchant's wife, who for more than a year had been upon the point of death. But Trukhina lay dying in Razgulyay, and Prokhorov was afraid that her heirs, in spite of their promise, would not take the trouble to send so far for him, but would make arrangements with the nearest undertaker.

These reflections were suddenly interrupted by three masonic knocks at the door.

"Who is there?" asked the undertaker.

The door opened, and a man, who at first glance could be recognized as a German artisan, entered the room, and with a jovial air advanced toward the undertaker.

"Pardon me, good neighbor," said he in that Russian dialect which to this day we cannot hear without a smile, "pardon me for disturbing you. . . . I wished to make your acquaintance as soon as possible. I am a shoemaker, my name is Gottlieb Schultz, and I live across the street, in that little house just facing your windows. Tomorrow I am going to celebrate my silver wedding, and I have come to invite you and your daughters to dine with us."

The invitation was cordially accepted. The undertaker asked the shoemaker to seat himself and take a cup of tea, and thanks to the open-hearted disposition of Gottlieb Schultz, they were soon engaged in friendly conversation.

"How is business with you?" asked Adrian.

"So so," replied Schultz; "I can't complain. But my wares are not like yours: the living can do without shoes, but the dead cannot do without coffins."

"Very true," observed Adrian; "but if a living person hasn't anything to buy shoes with, he goes barefoot, and holds his peace, if you please; but a dead beggar gets his coffin for nothing."

In this manner the conversation was carried on between them for some time; at last the shoemaker rose and took leave of the undertaker, renewing his invitation.

The next day, exactly at twelve o'clock, the undertaker

and his daughters issued from the wicket door of their newly purchased residence, and went to their neighbor's. I will not stop to describe the Russian *caftan* of Adrian Prokhorov, or the European toilettes of Akulina and Darya, deviating in this respect from the custom of modern novelists. But I do not think it superfluous to observe that the two girls had on the yellow hats and red shoes, which they were accustomed to don on solemn occasions only.

The shoemaker's little dwelling was filled with guests, consisting chiefly of German artisans with their wives and apprentices. Of the Russian officials there was present but one, Yurko the Finn, a constable, who, in spite of his humble calling, was the special object of the host's attention. Like Pogorelsky's postman,[1] for twenty-five years he had faithfully discharged his duties. The conflagration of 1812, which destroyed the ancient capital, destroyed also his little yellow booth. But immediately after the expulsion of the enemy, a new one appeared in its place, painted gray and with little white Doric columns, and Yurko again began to pace to and fro before it, *with his ax and armor of coarse cloth.* He was known to the greater part of the Germans who lived near the Nikitskaya Gate, and some of them had even spent Sunday night beneath his roof.

Adrian immediately made himself acquainted with him, as with a man whom, sooner or later, he might have need of, and when the guests took their places at the table, they sat down beside each other. Herr Schultz and his wife, and their daughter Lotchen, a young girl of seventeen, did the honors of the table and helped the cook to serve. The beer flowed in streams; Yurko ate like four, and Adrian in no way yielded to him; his daughters, however, stood upon their

[1] A character in a story by Pogorelsky, a contemporary of Pushkin (EDITOR'S NOTE).

dignity. The conversation, which was carried on in German, gradually grew more and more noisy. Suddenly the host requested a moment's attention, and uncorking a sealed bottle, he said loudly in Russian: "To the health of my good Louise!"

The imitation champagne foamed. The host tenderly kissed the fresh face of his partner, and the guests drank noisily to the health of the good Louise.

"To the health of my amiable guests!" exclaimed the host, uncorking a second bottle; and the guests thanked him by draining their glasses once more.

Then followed a succession of toasts. The health of each individual guest was drunk; they drank to Moscow and to a round dozen of little German towns; they drank to the health of all guilds in general and of each in particular; they drank to the health of the masters and apprentices. Adrian drank with assiduity, and became so jovial that he proposed a facetious toast himself. Suddenly one of the guests, a fat baker, raised his glass and exclaimed: "To the health of those for whom we work, our customers!"

This proposal, like all the others, was joyously and unanimously received. The guests began to salute each other; the tailor bowed to the shoemaker, the shoemaker to the tailor, the baker to both, the whole company to the baker, and so on. In the midst of these mutual congratulations, Yurko exclaimed, turning to his neighbor: "Come, little father! Drink to the health of your corpses!"

Everybody laughed, but the undertaker considered himself insulted, and frowned. Nobody noticed it, the guests continued to drink, and the bells had already rung for vespers when they rose from the table.

The guests dispersed at a late hour, the greater part of them in a very merry mood. The fat baker and the bookbinder, whose face seemed as if bound in red morocco, linked their arms in those of Yurko and conducted him back to his booth, thus observing the proverb: "One good turn deserves another."

The undertaker returned home drunk and angry.

"Why is it," he argued aloud, "why is it that my trade is not as honest as any other? Is an undertaker brother to the hangman? Why did those heathens laugh? Is an undertaker a buffoon? I wanted to invite them to my new house and give them a feast, but now I'll do nothing of the kind. Instead of inviting them, I will invite those for whom I work: the orthodox dead."

"What is the matter, Master?" said the servant, who was engaged at that moment in taking off his boots. "Why do you talk such nonsense? Make the sign of the cross! Invite the dead to your new house! What nonsense!"

"Yes, by God! I will invite them," continued Adrian. "And that, too, for tomorrow! . . . Do me the favor, my benefactors, to come and feast with me tomorrow evening; I will regale you with what God has sent me."

With these words the undertaker turned into bed and soon began to snore.

It was still dark when Adrian was roused out of his sleep. Trukhina, the merchant's wife, had died during the course of that very night, and a special messenger was sent off on horseback by her clerk to carry the news to Adrian. The undertaker gave him ten kopecks to buy brandy with, dressed himself as hastily as possible, took a *droshky* and set out for Razgulyay. At the gate of the house in which the deceased lay, the police had already taken their stand, and the tradespeople were busily moving back and forth, like ravens that smell a dead body. The deceased lay upon a table, yellow as wax, but not yet disfigured by decomposition. Around her stood her relatives, neighbors, and domestic servants. All the windows were open; tapers were burning; and the priests were reading the prayers for the dead. Adrian went up to the nephew of Trukhina, a young shopman in a fashionable jacket, and informed him that the coffin, wax candles, pall, and the other funeral accessories would be immediately delivered in good order. The heir thanked him in an absent-minded manner, saying that he would not bargain about the price, but would rely upon his acting in everything according to his conscience. The undertaker, in accordance with his custom, swore that he would not charge him too much, exchanged significant glances with the clerk, and then departed to commence operations.

The whole day was spent in passing to and fro between Razgulyay and the Nikitskaya Gate. Toward evening everything was finished, and he returned home on foot, after having dismissed his driver. It was a moonlight night. The undertaker reached the Nikitskaya Gate in safety. Near the Church of the Ascension he was hailed by our acquaintance Yurko, who, recognizing the undertaker, wished him good night. It was late. The undertaker was just approaching his house, when suddenly he fancied he saw someone approach his gate, open the wicket, and disappear within.

"What does that mean?" thought Adrian. "Who can be wanting me again? Can it be a thief come to rob me? Or have my foolish girls got lovers coming after them? It means no good, I fear!"

And the undertaker thought of calling his friend Yurko to his assistance. But at that moment, another person approached the wicket and was about to enter, but seeing the master of the house hastening toward him, he stopped and took off his three-cornered hat. His face seemed familiar to

Adrian, but in his hurry he was not able to examine it closely.

"You are favoring me with a visit," said Adrian, out of breath. "Walk in, I beg of you."

"Don't stand on ceremony, sir," replied the other, in a hollow voice; "you go first, and show your guests the way."

Adrian had no time to spend upon ceremony. The wicket was open; he ascended the steps followed by the other. Adrian thought he could hear people walking about in his rooms.

"What the devil does all this mean!" he thought to himself, and he hastened to enter. But the sight that met his eyes caused his legs to give way beneath him.

The room was full of corpses. The moon, shining through the windows, lit up their yellow and blue faces, sunken mouths, dim, half-closed eyes, and protruding noses. Adrian, with horror, recognized in them people that he himself had buried, and in the guest who had entered with him, the brigadier who had been buried during the pouring rain. They all, ladies and gentlemen, surrounded the undertaker, with bowings and salutations, except one poor man lately buried gratis, who, conscious and ashamed of his rags, did not venture to approach, but meekly kept to a corner. All the others were decently dressed: the female corpses in caps and ribbons, the officials in uniforms, but with their beards unshaven, the tradesmen in their holiday *caftans*.

"You see, Prokhorov," said the brigadier in the name of all the honorable company, "we have all risen in response to your invitation. Only those have stopped at home who were unable to come, who have crumbled to pieces and have nothing left but fleshless bones. But even of these there was one who hadn't the patience to remain behind—so much did he want to come and see you. . . ."

At this moment a little skeleton pushed his way through

the crowd and approached Adrian. His skull smiled affably at the undertaker. Shreds of green and red cloth and rotten linen hung on him here and there as on a pole, and the bones of his feet rattled inside his big jackboots, like pestles in mortars.

"You do not recognize me, Prokhorov," said the skeleton. "Don't you remember the retired sergeant of the Guard, Pyotr Petrovich Kurilkin, the same to whom, in the year 1799, you sold your first coffin, and a deal one at that, instead of oak as agreed?"

With these words the corpse stretched out his bony arms toward him; but Adrian, collecting all his strength, shrieked and pushed him away. Pyotr Petrovich staggered, fell and crumbled to pieces. Among the corpses arose a murmur of indignation; all stood up for the honor of their companion, and they overwhelmed Adrian with such threats and curses, that the poor host, deafened by their shrieks and almost crushed to death, lost his presence of mind, fell upon the bones of the retired sergeant of the Guard, and swooned away.

For some time the sun had been shining upon the bed on which the undertaker lay. At last he opened his eyes and saw before him the servant attending to the samovar. With horror, Adrian recalled all the incidents of the previous day. Trukhina, the brigadier, and the sergeant Kurilkin rose vaguely before his imagination. He waited in silence for the servant to open the conversation and inform him of the events of the night.

"How you have slept, Adrian Prokhorovich! said Aksinya, handing him his dressing gown. "Your neighbor, the tailor, has been here, and the constable also called to inform you that today is his name-day; but you were so sound asleep, that we did not wish to wake you."

"Did anyone come for me from the late Trukhina?"

"The late? Is she dead, then?"

"What a fool you are! Didn't you yourself help me yesterday to prepare the things for her funeral?"

"Have you taken leave of your senses, Master, or have you not yet recovered from the effects of yesterday's drinking bout? What funeral was there yesterday? You spent the whole day feasting at the German's, and then came home drunk and threw yourself upon the bed, and have slept till this hour, when the bells have already rung for Mass."

"Really!" said the undertaker, greatly relieved.

"Yes, indeed," replied the servant.

"Well, since that is the case, make tea as quickly as possible and call my daughters."

The Postmaster

This tyrant, a collegiate recorder,
Still keeps the posting station in good order.
PRINCE VYAZEMSKY

WHO HAS NOT cursed postmasters, who has not quarreled with them? Who, in a moment of anger, has not demanded from them the fatal book in order to record in it unavailing complaints of their extortions, rudeness and carelessness? Who does not look upon them as monsters of the human race, equal to the attorneys of old, or, at least, the Murom highwaymen? Let us, however, be just; let us place ourselves in their position, and perhaps we shall begin to judge them with more indulgence. What is a postmaster? A veritable martyr of the fourteenth class,[1] protected by his rank from blows only, and that not always (I appeal to the conscience of my readers). What is the function of this tyrant, as Prince Vyazemsky jokingly calls him? Is he not an actual galley slave? He has no rest either day or night. All the vexation accumulated during the course of a wearisome journey the traveler vents upon the postmaster. Should the weather prove intolerable, the road abominable, the driver obstinate, the horses stubborn—the postmaster is

[1] The officials of Russia were divided into fourteen classes, the fourteenth being the lowest (TRANSLATOR'S NOTE).

to blame. Entering into his poor abode, the traveler looks upon him as an enemy, and the postmaster is fortunate if he succeeds in soon getting rid of his unbidden guest; but if there should happen to be no horses! . . . Heavens! What volleys of abuse, what threats are showered upon his head! When it rains, when it is muddy, he is compelled to run about the village; during times of storm and bitter frost, he is glad to seek shelter in the entry, if only to enjoy a minute's repose from the shouting and jostling of incensed travelers.

A general arrives: the trembling postmaster gives him the last two troikas, including that intended for the courier. The general drives off without uttering a word of thanks. Five minutes afterwards—a bell! . . . And a courier throws down upon the table before him his order for fresh post horses! . . . Let us bear all this well in mind, and, instead of anger, our hearts will be filled with sincere compassion. A few words more. During a period of twenty years I have traversed Russia in every direction; I know nearly all the post roads, and I am acquainted with several generations of drivers. There are very few postmasters that I do not know personally, and few with whom I have not had something to do. I hope shortly to publish the curious observations that I have noted down during my travels. For the present I will only say that the class of postmasters is presented to the public in a very false light. These much-calumniated officials are generally very peaceful persons, obliging by nature, disposed to be sociable, modest in their pretensions to honors and not too greedy. From their conversation (which traveling gentlemen very unreasonably scorn) much may be learned that is both curious and instructive. For my own part, I confess that I prefer their talk to that of some official of the sixth class traveling on government business.

It may easily be supposed that I have friends among the honorable body of postmasters. Indeed, the memory of one of them is precious to me. Circumstances once brought us together, and it is of him that I now intend to tell my amiable readers.

In the month of May of the year 1816, I happened to be traveling through the X. Government, along a route that has since been abandoned. I then held an inferior rank, and I traveled by post stages, paying the fare for two horses. As a consequence, the postmasters treated me with very little ceremony, and I often had to take by force what, in my opinion, belonged to me by right. Being young and hot-tempered, I was indignant at the baseness and cowardice of the postmaster, when the latter harnessed to the coach of some gentleman of rank, the horses prepared for me. It was a long time, too, before I could get accustomed to being served out of my turn by a discriminating flunky at the governor's dinner. Today the one and the other seem to me to be in the natural order of things. Indeed, what would become of us if, instead of the generally observed rule: "Let rank honor rank," another were to be brought into use, as for example: "Let mind honor mind?" What disputes would arise! And whom would the butler serve first? But to return to my story.

The day was hot. About three versts from the N. station a drizzling rain came on, and in a few minutes it began to pour down in torrents and I was drenched to the skin. On arriving at the station, my first care was to change my clothes as quickly as possible, my second to ask for some tea.

"Hi! Dunya!"[2] cried the postmaster. "Prepare the samovar and go and get some cream."

At these words, a young girl of about fourteen years of age appeared from behind the partition; and ran out into the entry. Her beauty struck me.

"Is that your daughter?" I inquired of the postmaster.

[2] Diminutive of Avdotya (TRANSLATOR'S NOTE).

"That is my daughter," he replied, with a look of gratified pride; "and she is so sharp and sensible, just like her late mother."

Then he began to register my traveling passport, and I occupied myself with examining the pictures that adorned his humble but tidy abode. They illustrated the story of the Prodigal Son. In the first, a venerable old man, in a night-cap and dressing gown, was taking leave of the restless lad, who was hastily accepting his blessing and a bag of money. In the next picture, the dissolute conduct of the young man was depicted in vivid colors: he was represented sitting at table surrounded by false friends and shameless women. Further on, the ruined youth, in rags and a three-cornered hat, was tending swine and sharing with them their food: his face expressed deep grief and repentance. The last picture represented his return to his father: the good old man, in the same nightcap and dressing gown, runs forward to meet him; the prodigal son is on his knees; in the distance the cook is killing the fatted calf, and the elder brother is asking the servants the cause of all the rejoicing. Under each picture I read some suitable German verses. All this I have preserved in my memory to the present day, as well as the little pots of balsamine, the bed with gay curtains, and the other objects with which I was then surrounded. I can see, as though he were before me, the host himself, a man of about fifty years of age, healthy and vigorous, in his long green coat with three medals on faded ribbons.

I had scarcely settled my account with my old driver, when Dunya returned with the samovar. The little coquette saw at the second glance the impression she had produced upon me; she lowered her large blue eyes; I began to talk to her; she answered me without the least timidity, like a girl who has seen the world. I offered her father a glass of punch, to Dunya herself I gave a cup of tea, and then the three of us began to converse together, as if we were old acquaintances.

The horses had long been ready, but I felt reluctant to take leave of the postmaster and his daughter. At last I bade them good-bye, the father wished me a pleasant journey, the daughter accompanied me to the coach. In the entry I stopped and asked her permission to kiss her; Dunya consented. . . . I can reckon up a great many kisses

Since first I chose this occupation,

but not one which has left behind such a long, such a pleasant recollection.

Several years passed, and circumstances led me to the same route, and to the same neighborhood.

"But," thought I, "perhaps the old postmaster has been changed, and Dunya may already be married."

The thought that one or the other of them might be dead also flashed through my mind, and I approached the N. station with a sad foreboding. The horses drew up before the little post-house. On entering the room, I immediately recognized the pictures illustrating the story of the Prodigal Son. The table and the bed stood in the same places as before, but the flowers were no longer on the window sills, and everything around indicated decay and neglect.

The postmaster was asleep under his sheepskin coat; my arrival awoke him, and he stood up. . . . It was certainly Samoon Vyrin, but how aged! While he was preparing to register my traveling passport, I gazed at his gray hair, the deep wrinkles upon his face, that had not been shaved for a long time, his bent back, and I was astonished to see how three or four years had been able to transform a vigorous individual into a feeble old man.

"Do you recognize me?" I asked him. "We are old acquaintances."

"Maybe," replied he sullenly; "this is a high road, and many travelers have stopped here."

"Is your Dunya well?" I continued.

The old man frowned. "God knows," he replied.

"Probably she is married?" said I.

The old man pretended not to have heard my question, and went on reading my passport in a low tone. I ceased questioning him and ordered some tea. Curiosity began to torment me, and I hoped that the punch would loosen the tongue of my old acquaintance.

I was not mistaken; the old man did not refuse the proffered glass. I observed that the rum dispelled his sullenness. At the second glass he began to talk; he remembered me, or appeared to do so, and I heard from him a story, which at the time, deeply interested and affected me.

"So you knew my Dunya?" he began. "But who did not know her? Ah, Dunya, Dunya! What a girl she was! Everybody who passed this way praised her; nobody had a word to say against her. The ladies used to give her presents—now a handkerchief, now a pair of earrings. The gentlemen used to stop on purpose, as if to dine or to take supper, but in reality only to take a longer look at her. However angry a gentleman might be, in her presence he grew calm and spoke graciously to me. Would you believe it, sir: couriers and government messengers used to talk to her for half an hour at a stretch. It was she held the home together; she put everything in order, got everything ready, and looked after everything. And I, like an old fool, could not look at her enough, could not idolize her enough. Did I not love my Dunya? Did I not indulge my child? Was not her life a happy one? But no, there is no escaping misfortune; there is no evading what has been decreed."

Then he began to tell me the story of his trouble in detail. Three years earlier, one winter evening, when the postmaster was ruling a new register, and his daughter behind the partition was sewing a dress, a troika drove up, and a traveler in a Circassian cap and military cloak, and enveloped in a shawl, entered the room and demanded horses. The horses were all out. On being told this, the traveler raised his voice and whip; but Dunya, accustomed to such scenes, ran out from behind the partition and graciously inquired of the traveler whether he would not like something to eat and drink.

The appearance of Dunya produced the usual effect. The traveler's anger subsided; he consented to wait for horses, and ordered supper. Having taken off his wet shaggy cap, and divested himself of his shawl and cloak, the traveler was seen to be a tall, young Hussar with a small black mustache. He settled down, and began to converse gaily with the postmaster and his daughter. Supper was served. Meanwhile the horses returned, and the postmaster ordered them, without being fed, to be harnessed immediately to the traveler's *kibitka*. But on returning to the room, he found the young man lying almost unconscious on the bench; he had been taken ill, his head ached, it was impossible for him to continue on his journey. What was to be done? The postmaster gave up his own bed to him, and it was decided that if the sick man did not get better, they would send next day to S—— for the doctor.

The next day the Hussar was worse. His servant rode to town for a doctor. Dunya bound round his head a handkerchief soaked in vinegar, and sat with her needlework beside his bed. In the presence of the postmaster, the sick man groaned and scarcely uttered a word; but he drank two cups of coffee, and, groaning, ordered dinner. Dunya did not quit his side. He constantly asked for something to drink, and Dunya gave him a jug of lemonade prepared by herself. The sick man moistened his lips, and each time, on returning the jug, he feebly pressed Dunya's hand in token of gratitude.

About dinner time the doctor arrived. He felt the sick man's pulse, spoke to him in German, and declared in Russian that he only needed rest, and that in about a couple of days he would be able to set out on his journey. The Hussar gave him twenty-five rubles for his visit, and invited him to dinner; the doctor consented. They both ate with great appetite, drank a bottle of wine, and separated very well satisfied with each other.

Another day passed, and the Hussar felt quite himself again. He was extraordinarily gay, joked unceasingly, now with Dunya, now with the postmaster, whistled tunes, chatted with the travelers, copied their passports into the register, and the worthy postmaster took such a fancy to him that when the third day arrived, it was with regret that he parted with his amiable guest.

The day was Sunday; Dunya was preparing to go to Mass. The Hussar's *kibitka* stood ready. He took leave of the postmaster, after having generously recompensed him for his board and lodging, bade farewell to Dunya, and offered to drive her as far as the church, which was situated at the edge of the village. Dunya hesitated.

"What are you afraid of?" asked her father. "His Excellency is not a wolf: he won't eat you. Drive with him as far as the church."

Dunya seated herself in the *kibitka* by the side of the Hussar, the servant sprang upon the box, the driver whistled, and the horses started off at a gallop.

The poor postmaster could not understand how he could have allowed his Dunya to drive off with the Hussar, how he could have been so blind, and what had become of his senses at that moment. A half-hour had not elapsed, before his heart began to ache, and uneasiness took possession of him to such a degree that he could contain himself no longer, and started off for Mass himself. On reaching the church, he saw that the people were already beginning to disperse, but Dunya was neither in the churchyard nor in the porch. He hastened into the church: the priest was leaving the chancel, the sexton was blowing out the candles, two old women were still praying in a corner, but Dunya was not in the church. The poor father was scarcely able to summon up sufficient resolution to ask the sexton if she had been to Mass. The sexton replied that she had not. The postmaster returned home neither alive nor dead. One hope alone remained to him: Dunya, in the thoughtlessness of youth, might have taken it into her head to go on as far as the next station, where her godmother lived. In agonizing agitation he awaited the return of the troika in which he had let her set out. There was no sign of it. At last, in the evening, the driver arrived alone and intoxicated, with the terrible news: "Dunya went on with the Hussar from the next station."

The old man could not bear his misfortune: he immediately took to that very same bed where, the evening before, the young deceiver had lain. Taking all the circumstances into account, the postmaster now came to the conclusion that the illness had been a mere pretense. The poor man fell ill with a violent fever; he was removed to S——, and in his place another person was appointed for the time being. The same doctor, who had attended the Hussar, attended him also. He assured the postmaster that the young man had been perfectly well, and that at the time of his visit he had suspected him of some evil intention, but that he had kept silent through fear of his whip. Whether the German spoke the truth or only wished to boast of his perspicacity, his communication afforded no consolation to the poor invalid. Scarcely had the latter recovered from his illness, when he obtained from the postmaster of S—— two months' leave of

absence, and without saying a word to anybody of his intention, he set out on foot in search of his daughter.

From the traveling passport he knew that Captain Minsky
was journeying from Smolensk to St. Petersburg. The driver
with whom he had gone off said that Dunya had wept the
whole of the way, although she seemed to go of her own
free will.

"Perhaps," thought the postmaster, "I shall bring my lost
lamb home again."

With this thought he reached St. Petersburg, stopped in the
neighborhood of the Izmailovsky barracks, at the house of
a retired corporal, an old comrade of his, and began his
search. He soon discovered that Captain Minsky was in St.
Petersburg, and was living at Demoute's Inn. The postmaster
resolved to call upon him.

Early in the morning he went to Minsky's antechamber,
and requested that His Excellency might be informed that an
old soldier wished to see him. The orderly, who was just
then polishing a boot on a boot-tree, informed him that his
master was still asleep, and that he never received anybody
before eleven o'clock. The postmaster retired and returned
at the appointed time. Minsky himself came out to him in
his dressing gown and red skullcap.

"Well, brother, what do you want?" he asked.

The old man's heart was wrung, tears started to his eyes,
and he was only able to say in a trembling voice: "Your
Excellency! . . . Do me the great favor! . . ."

Minsky glanced quickly at him, flushed, took him by the
hand, led him into his study and locked the door.

"Your Excellency!" continued the old man. "What has
fallen from the load is lost; give me back at least my poor
Dunya. You have had your pleasure with her; do not ruin
her for nothing."

"What is done cannot be undone," said the young man, in the utmost confusion. "I am guilty before you, and am ready to ask your pardon, but do not think that I could forsake Dunya: she will be happy, I give you my word of honor. Why do you want her? She loves me; she has become unaccustomed to her former way of living. Neither you nor she will forget what has happened."

Then, pushing something into the old man's cuff, he opened the door, and the postmaster, without remembering how, found himself in the street again.

For a long time he stood motionless; at last he observed in the cuff of his sleeve a roll of papers; he drew them out and unrolled several fifty-ruble notes. Tears again filled his eyes, tears of indignation! He crushed the notes into a ball, flung them upon the ground, stamped upon them with the heel of his boot, and then walked away. . . . After having gone a few steps, he stopped, reflected, and returned . . . but the notes were no longer there. A well-dressed young man, noticing him, ran toward a *droshky,* jumped in hurriedly, and cried to the driver: "Go on!"

The postmaster did not pursue him. He resolved to return home to his station, but before doing so he wished to see his poor Dunya once more. For that purpose, he returned to Minsky's lodgings a couple of days later, but when he came the orderly told him roughly that his master received nobody, pushed him out of the antechamber and slammed the door in his face. The postmaster stood waiting for a long time, then he walked away.

That same day, in the evening, he was walking along Liteinaia Street, having been to a service at the Church of Our Lady of All the Sorrowing. Suddenly a smart *droshky* flew past him, and the postmaster recognized Minsky. The *droshky* stopped in front of a three-story house, close to the entrance, and the Hussar ran up the steps. A happy thought flashed through the mind of the postmaster. He returned, and, approaching the coachman.

"Whose horse is this, my friend?" asked he. "Doesn't it belong to Minsky?"

"Exactly so," replied the coachman. "What do you want?"

"Well, your master ordered me to carry a letter to his Dunya, and I have forgotten where his Dunya lives."

"She lives here, on the second floor. But you are late with your letter, my friend; he is with her himself just now."

"That doesn't matter," replied the postmaster, with an indescribable emotion. "Thanks for your information. I shall do as I was told." And with these words he ascended the staircase.

The door was locked; he rang. There was a painful delay of several seconds. The key rattled, and the door was opened.

"Does Avdotya Samsonovna live here?" he asked.

"Yes," replied a young maidservant. "What do you want with her?"

The postmaster, without replying, walked into the room.

"You mustn't go in, you mustn't go in!" the servant cried out after him. "Avdotya Samsonovna has visitors."

But the postmaster, without heeding her, walked straight on. The first two rooms were dark; in the third there was a light. He approached the open door and paused. In the room, which was beautifully furnished, Minsky sat, in deep thought. Dunya, attired in the most elegant fashion, was sitting upon the arm of his chair, like a lady rider upon her English saddle. She was gazing tenderly at Minsky, and winding his black curls round her dazzling fingers. Poor postmaster! Never had his daughter seemed to him so beautiful; he admired her against his will.

"Who is there?" she asked, without raising her head.

He remained silent. Receiving no reply, Dunya raised her head . . . and with a cry she fell upon the carpet. The alarmed Minsky hastened to pick her up, but suddenly catching sight of the old postmaster in the doorway, he left Dunya and approached him, trembling with rage.

"What do you want?" he said to him, clenching his teeth. "Why do you steal after me everywhere, like a thief? Or do you want to murder me? Be off!" And with a powerful hand he seized the old man by the collar and pushed him out onto the stairs.

The old man returned to his lodgings. His friend advised him to lodge a complaint, but the postmaster reflected, waved his hand, and resolved to abstain from taking any further steps in the matter. Two days afterward he left St. Petersburg and returned to his station to resume his duties.

"This is the third year," he concluded, "that I have been living without Dunya, and I have not heard a word about her. Whether she is alive or not—God only knows. So many things happen. She is not the first, nor yet the last, that a traveling scoundrel has seduced, kept for a little while, and then abandoned. There are many such young fools in St. Petersburg, today in satin and velvet, and tomorrow sweeping the streets along with the riff-raff of the dram shops. Sometimes, when I think that Dunya also may come to such an end, then, in spite of myself, I sin and wish her in her grave. . . ."

Such was the story of my friend, the old postmaster, a story more than once interrupted by tears, which he picturesquely wiped away with the skirt of his coat, like the zealous Terentyich in Dmitriyev's beautiful ballad. These tears were partly induced by the punch, of which he had drunk five glasses during the course of his narrative, but for all that, they moved me deeply. After taking leave of him, it was

a long time before I could forget the old postmaster, and
for a long time I thought of poor Dunya. . . .

Passing through the little town of X. a short time ago, I
remembered my friend. I heard that the station, over which
he ruled, had been done away with. To my question: "Is the
old postmaster still alive?" nobody could give me a satisfac-
tory reply. I resolved to pay a visit to the familiar place, and
having hired horses, I set out for the village of N——.

It was in the autumn. Gray clouds covered the sky; a cold
wind blew across the reaped fields, carrying along with it the
red and yellow leaves from the trees that it encountered. I
arrived in the village at sunset, and stopped at the little post-
house. In the entry (where Dunya had once kissed me) a
stout woman came out to meet me, and in answer to my
questions replied that the old postmaster had been dead for
about a year, that his house was occupied by a brewer, and
that she was the brewer's wife. I began to regret my useless
journey, and the seven rubles that I had spent in vain.

"Of what did he die?" I asked the brewer's wife.

"Of drink, sir," she replied.

"And where is he buried?"

"On the outskirts of the village, near his late wife."

"Could somebody take me to his grave?"

"To be sure! Hi, Vanka, you have played with that cat
long enough. Take this gentleman to the cemetery, and show
him the postmaster's grave."

At these words a ragged lad, with red hair, and blind in
one eye, ran up to me and immediately began to lead the way
toward the burial ground.

"Did you know the dead man?" I asked him on the road.

"Yes, indeed! He taught me how to cut whistles. When
he came out of the dram shop (God rest his soul!) we used

to run after him and call out: 'Grandfather! grandfather! some nuts!' and he used to throw nuts to us. He always used to play with us."

"And do the travelers remember him?"

"There are very few travelers now; the assessor passes this way sometimes, but he doesn't trouble himself about dead people. Last summer a lady passed through here, and she asked after the old postmaster, and went to his grave."

"What sort of a lady?" I asked with curiosity.

"A very beautiful lady," replied the lad. "She was in a carriage with six horses, and had along with her three little children, a nurse, and a little black lapdog; and when they told her that the old postmaster was dead, she began to cry, and said to the children: 'Sit still, I will go to the cemetery.' I offered to show her the way. But the lady said: 'I know the way.' And she gave me a five-kopeck piece. . . . such a kind lady!"

We reached the cemetery, a bare place, with no fence around it, dotted with wooden crosses, which were not shaded by a single tree. Never in my life had I seen such a dismal cemetery.

"This is the old postmaster's grave," said the lad to me, leaping upon a heap of sand, in which was planted a black cross with a bronze ikon.

"And did the lady come here?" I asked.

"Yes," replied Vanka; "I watched her from a distance. She cast herself down here, and remained lying down for a long time. Then she went back to the village, sent for the priest, gave him some money and drove off, after giving me a five-kopeck piece . . . such a kind lady!"

And I, too, gave the lad a five-kopeck piece, and I no longer regretted the journey or the seven rubles that I had spent on it.

Mistress into Maid

You're pretty, Dushenka, no matter what you wear.
BOGDANOVICH

IN ONE of our remote provinces was situated the estate of Ivan Petrovich Berestov. In his youth he had served in the Guards, but having quitted the service at the beginning of the year 1797, he repaired to his village, and since that time he had not stirred from it. He had been married to a penniless gentlewoman, who had died in childbed at a time when he was absent from home on a visit to one of the outlying fields of his estate. He soon found consolation in attending to his affairs. He built a house on a plan of his own, established a textile mill, tripled his revenues, and began to consider himself the most intelligent man in the whole country roundabout, and in this he was not contradicted by his neighbors, who came to visit him with their families and their dogs. On weekdays he wore a velveteen jacket, but on Sundays and holidays he appeared in a surtout of cloth that had been manufactured on his own premises. He himself kept an account of all his expenses, and he never read anything except the "Senate Bulletins."

In general he was liked, although he was considered proud. There was only one person who was not on good terms with him, and that was Grigory Ivanovich Muromsky, his nearest neighbor. This latter was a genuine Russian gentleman. After having squandered the greater part of his fortune in Moscow, and having become a widower about the same time, he retired to his last remaining estate, where he continued to indulge in habits of extravagance, but of a new kind. He laid out an English garden, on which he expended nearly the whole of his remaining revenue. His grooms were dressed like English jockeys, his daughter had an English governess, and his fields were cultivated after the English method.

But Russian corn fares ill when foreign ways are followed,

and in spite of a considerable reduction in his expenses, the revenues of Grigory Ivanovich did not increase. He found means, even in the country, of contracting new debts. Nevertheless he was not considered a fool, for he was the first landowner in his province who conceived the idea of mortgaging his estate in the Tutorial Council—a proceeding which at that time was considered exceedingly complicated and venturesome. Of all those who censured him, Berestov showed himself the most severe. Hatred of all innovation was a distinguishing trait in his character. He could not bring himself to speak calmly of his neighbor's Anglomania, and he constantly found occasion to criticize him. If he showed his possessions to a guest, in reply to the praises bestowed upon him for his economical arrangements, he would say with a sly smile: "Yes, sir, it is not the same with me as with my neighbor Grigory Ivanovich. What need have we to ruin ourselves in the English style, when we have enough to do to keep the wolf from the door in the Russian style?"

These and similar sarcastic remarks, thanks to the zeal of obliging neighbors, did not fail to reach the ears of Grigory Ivanovich greatly embellished. The Anglomaniac bore criticism as impatiently as our journalists. He became furious, and called his traducer a boor and a country bumpkin.

Such were the relations between the two proprietors, when Berestov's son came home. He had been educated at the University of ——, and intended to enter the military service, but to this his father would not give his consent. For the civil service the young man had not the slightest inclination, and as neither felt inclined to yield to the other, the young Alexey lived in the meantime like a gentleman, and at any rate allowed his mustache to grow.[1]

Alexey was indeed a fine young fellow, and it would really have been a pity were his slender frame never to be set off to advantage by a military uniform, and were he to be compelled to spend his youth in bending over the papers of the chancery office, instead of cutting a figure on horseback. The neighbors, observing how at the hunt he always dashed ahead across the fields, agreed that he would never make a proper clerk. The young ladies cast glances at him, and sometimes could not leave off looking at him, but Alexey troubled himself very little about them, and they attributed this insensibility to some secret love affair. Indeed, there passed from hand to hand a copy of the address on one of his letters: "To Akulina Petrovna Kurochkina in Moscow, opposite the Alexeyevsky Monastery, in the house of the coppersmith Savelyev, with the request that she hand this letter to A. N. R."

Those of my readers who have never lived in the country, cannot imagine how charming these provincial young ladies are! Brought up in the pure air, under the shadow of their own apple trees, they derive their knowledge of the world and of life from books. Solitude, freedom, and reading develop very early within them sentiments and passions unknown to our town-bred beauties. For the young ladies of the country the sound of harness bells is an event; a journey to the nearest town marks an epoch in their lives, and the visit of a guest leaves behind a long and sometimes an everlasting memory. Of course everybody is at liberty to laugh at some of their peculiarities, but the jokes of a superficial observer cannot nullify their essential merits, the chief of which is that quality of character, that *individualité*, without which, in Jean Paul's opinion, there can be no human greatness. In the capitals, women receive perhaps a better education, but intercourse with the world soon smooths down the character and makes their souls as uniform as their headdresses. This is said neither by way of judgment nor of censure, but *"nota nostra manet,"* as one of the old commentators writes.

It can easily be imagined what impression Alexey produced in the circle of our young ladies. He was the first who appeared before them gloomy and disenchanted, the first who spoke to them of lost happiness and of his blighted youth; in addition to which he wore a black ring engraved with a death's head. All this was something quite new in that province. The young ladies went mad over him.

But not one of them felt so much interest in him as the daughter of our Anglomaniac, Liza, or Betsy, as Grigory Ivanovich usually called her. As their parents did not visit each other, she had not yet seen Alexey, even when he had become the sole topic of conversation among all the young ladies of the neighborhood. She was seventeen years old. Dark eyes illuminated her swarthy and exceedingly pleasant countenance. She was an only and consequently a spoiled child. Her liveliness and continual pranks delighted her father and filled with despair the heart of Miss Jackson, her governess, an affected old maid of forty, who powdered her face and darkened her eyebrows, read through *Pamela* twice a year, for which she received two thousand rubles, and was dying of boredom in this barbarous Russia.

Liza was waited upon by Nastya, who, although somewhat

older, was quite as giddy as her mistress. Liza was very fond of her, confided to her all her secrets, and planned pranks together with her; in a word, Nastya was a far more important person in the village of Priluchino, than the trusted confidante in a French tragedy.

"Will you allow me to go out today on a visit?" said Nastya one morning, as she was dressing her mistress.

"Certainly; but where are you going to?"

"To Tugilovo, to the Berestovs'. The wife of their cook is going to celebrate her name-day today, and she came over yesterday to invite us to dinner."

"Well!" said Liza. "The masters are at odds with each other, but the servants entertain each other."

"What have the masters to do with us?" replied Nastya. "Besides, I belong to you, and not to your papa. You have not had any quarrel with young Berestov; let the old ones quarrel and fight, if it gives them any pleasure."

"Try and see Alexey Berestov, Nastya, and then tell me what he looks like and what sort of a person he is."

Nastya promised to do so, and all day long Liza waited with impatience for her return. In the evening Nastya made her appearance.

"Well, Lizaveta Grigoryevna," said she, on entering the room, "I have seen young Berestov, and I had ample opportunity for taking a good look at him, for we have been together all day."

"How did that happen? Tell me about it, tell me everything just as it happened."

"Very well. We set out, I, Anisya Yegorovna, Nenila, Dunka . . ."

"Yes, yes, I know. And then?"

"With your leave, I will tell you everything in detail. We arrived just in time for dinner. The room was full of people.

The folk from Kolbino were there, from Zakharyevo, the bailiff's wife and her daughters, the people from Khlupino. . . ."

"Well, and Berestov?"

"Wait a moment. We sat down to table; the bailiff's wife had the place of honor. I sat next to her . . . the daughters sulked, but I didn't care about them. . . ."

"Good heavens, Nastya, how tiresome you are with your never-ending details!"

"How impatient you are! Well, we rose from the table . . . we had been sitting down for three hours, and the dinner was excellent: pastry, blancmange, blue, red and striped. . . . Well, we left the table and went into the garden to have a game of tag, and it was then that the young master made his appearance."

"Well, and is it true that he is so very handsome?"

"Exceedingly handsome: tall, well built, and with red cheeks . . ."

"Really? And I was under the impression that he was pale. Well, and how did he seem to you? Sad, thoughtful?"

"Nothing of the kind! I have never in my life seen such a madcap. He joined in our game."

"Joined in your game of tag? Impossible!"

"Not at all impossible. And what else do you think he did? He'd catch you and kiss you!"

"With your permission, Nastya, you are fibbing."

"With your permission, I am not fibbing. I had the greatest trouble in the world to get away from him. He spent the whole day with us."

"But they say that he is in love, and hasn't eyes for anybody."

"I don't know anything about that, but I know that he looked at me a good deal, and so he did at Tanya, the bailiff's daughter, and at Pasha from Kolbino, too. But it cannot be said that he misbehaved—the scamp!"

"That is extraordinary! And what do they say about him in the house?"

"They say that he is an excellent master—so kind, so cheerful. They have only one fault to find with him: he is too fond of running after the girls. But for my part, I don't think that is a very great fault: he will settle down with age."

"How I should like to see him!" said Liza, with a sigh.

"What is so difficult about it? Tugilovo is not far from us —only about three versts. Go and take a walk in that direction, or a ride on horseback, and you will assuredly meet him. He goes out early every morning with his gun."

"No, no, that would not do. He might think that I was running after him. Besides, our fathers are not on good terms, so that I cannot make his acquaintance. . . . Ah! Nastya, do you know what I'll do? I will dress myself up as a peasant girl!"

"Exactly! Put on a coarse blouse and a *sarafan,* and then go boldly to Tugilovo; I will answer for it that Berestov will not pass you by."

"And I know how to speak like the peasants about here. Ah, Nastya! my dear Nastya! what an excellent idea!"

And Liza went to bed, firmly resolved on putting her plan into execution.

The next morning she began to prepare to carry out her plan. She sent to the market and bought some coarse linen, some blue nankeen and some copper buttons, and with the help of Nastya she cut out for herself a blouse and *sarafan.* She then set all the female servants to work to do the necessary sewing, so that by evening everything was ready. Liza tried on the new costume, and as she stood before the mirror, she confessed to herself that she had never looked so charming. Then she rehearsed her part. As she walked she made a low bow, and then nodded her head several times, after the manner of a clay cat, spoke in the peasants' dialect, smiled behind her sleeve, and earned Nastya's complete approval. One thing only proved irksome to her: she tried to walk barefooted across the courtyard, but the turf pricked her tender feet, and she found the sand and gravel unbearable. Nastya immediately came to her assistance. She took the measurement of Liza's foot, ran to the fields to find Trofim the shepherd, and ordered him to make a pair of bast shoes to fit.

The next morning, at crack o' dawn, Liza was already awake. Everybody in the house was still asleep. Nastya, at the gate was waiting for the shepherd. The sound of a horn was heard, and the village flock filed past the manorhouse. Trofim, as he passed Nastya, gave her a small pair of colored bast shoes, and received from her a half-ruble in exchange. Liza quietly dressed herself in the peasant's costume, whispered her instructions to Nastya with reference to Miss Jackson, descended the back staircase and made her way through the kitchen garden into the field beyond.

The eastern sky was all aglow, and the golden rows of clouds seemed to be awaiting the sun, as courtiers await their monarch. The clear sky, the freshness of the morning, the dew, the light breeze, and the singing of the birds filled the heart of Liza with childish joy. The fear of meeting some acquaintance seemed to give her wings, for she flew rather than walked. But as she approached the grove which formed the boundary of her father's estate, she slackened her pace. Here she resolved to wait for Alexey. Her heart beat violently, she knew not why; but is not the fear which accompanies our youthful escapades their greatest charm? Liza advanced into the depth of the grove. The muffled, undulat-

ing murmur of the branches welcomed the young girl. Her
gaiety vanished. Little by little she abandoned herself to
sweet reveries. She thought—but who can say exactly what
a young lady of seventeen thinks of, alone in a grove, at six
o'clock of a spring morning? And so she walked musingly
along the pathway, which was shaded on both sides by tall
trees, when suddenly a magnificent hunting dog barked at
her. Liza became frightened and cried out. But at the same
moment a voice called out: *"Tout beau, Sbogar, ici!"* . . .
and a young hunter emerged from behind a clump of bushes.

"Don't be afraid, my dear," said he to Liza: "my dog
does not bite."

Liza had already recovered from her fright, and she immediately took advantage of her opportunity.

"But, sir," said she, assuming a half-frightened, half-
bashful expression, "I am so afraid; he looks so fierce—he
might fly at me again."

Alexey—for the reader has already recognized him—
gazed fixedly at the young peasant girl.

"I will accompany you if you are afraid," he said to her.
"Will you allow me to walk along with you?"

"Who is to hinder you?" replied Liza. "A free man may
do as he likes, and the road is everybody's."

"Where do you come from?"

"From Priluchino; I am the daughter of Vassily the blacksmith, and I am going to gather mushrooms." (Liza carried
a basket on her arm.) "And you, sir? From Tugilovo, I
have no doubt."

"Exactly so," replied Alexey. "I am the young master's
valet."

Alexey wanted to put himself on an equal footing with
her, but Liza looked at him and laughed.

"That is a fib," said she. "I am not such a fool as you may

think. I see very well that you are the young master himself."

"Why do you think so?"

"I think so for a great many reasons."

"But—"

"As if it were not possible to tell the master from the servant! You are not dressed like a servant, you do not speak like one, and you do not call your dog the way we do."

Alexey liked Liza more and more. As he was not accustomed to standing upon ceremony with pretty peasant girls, he wanted to embrace her; but Liza drew back from him, and suddenly assumed such a cold and severe look, that Alexey, although much amused, did not venture to renew the attempt.

"If you wish that we should remain good friends," said she with dignity, "be good enough not to forget yourself."

"Who taught you to be so clever?" asked Alexey, bursting into a laugh. "Can it be my friend Nastenka, the maid of your young mistress? See how enlightenment becomes diffused!"

Liza felt that she had stepped out of her role, and she immediately recovered herself.

"Do you think," said she, "that I have never been to the manor-house? Don't alarm yourself; I have seen and heard a great many things. . . . But," continued she, "if I talk to you, I shall not gather my mushrooms. Go your way, sir, and I will go mine. Pray excuse me."

And she was about to move off, but Alexey seized hold of her hand.

"What is your name, my dear?"

"Akulina," replied Liza, endeavoring to disengage her fingers from his grasp. "But let me go, sir; it is time for me to return home."

"Well, my friend Akulina, I will certainly pay a visit to your father, Vassily the blacksmith."

"What do you say?" exclaimed Liza quickly. "For Heaven's sake, don't think of doing such a thing! If it were known at home that I had been talking to a gentleman alone in the grove, I should fare very badly—my father, Vassily the blacksmith, would beat me to death."

"But I really must see you again."

"Well, then, I will come here again some time to gather mushrooms."

"When?"

"Well, tomorrow, if you wish it."

"My dear Akulina, I would kiss you, but I dare not. . . . Tomorrow, then, at the same time, isn't that so?"

"Yes, yes!"

"And you will not deceive me?"

"I will not deceive you."

"Swear it."

"Well, then, I swear by Holy Friday that I will come."

The young people separated. Liza emerged from the wood, crossed the field, stole into the garden and hastened to the place where Nastya awaited her. There she changed her costume, replying absently to the questions of her impatient confidante, and then she repaired to the parlor. The cloth was laid, the breakfast was ready, and Miss Jackson, already powdered and laced up, so that she looked like a wine glass, was cutting thin slices of bread and butter.

Her father praised her for her early walk.

"There is nothing so healthy," said he, "as getting up at daybreak."

Then he cited several instances of human longevity, which he had taken from the English journals, and observed that all persons who had lived to be upwards of a hundred, abstained from brandy and rose at daybreak, winter and summer.

Liza did not listen to him. In her thoughts she was going

over all the circumstances of the morning's meeting, Akulina's whole conversation with the young hunter, and her conscience began to torment her. In vain did she try to persuade
herself that their talk had not gone beyond the bounds of
propriety, and that the prank would be followed by no serious consequences—her conscience spoke louder than her
reason. The promise given for the following day troubled
her more than anything else, and she almost felt resolved not
to keep her solemn oath. But then, might not Alexey, after
waiting for her in vain, make his way to the village and
search out the daughter of Vassily the blacksmith, the veritable Akulina—a fat, pock-marked peasant girl—and so discover the prank she had played upon him? This thought horrified Liza, and she resolved to repair to the little wood the
next morning again as Akulina.

For his part, Alexey was in an ecstasy of delight. All day
long he thought of his new acquaintance; and in his dreams
at night the form of the dark-skinned beauty appeared before
him. The morning had scarcely begun to dawn, when he was
already dressed. Without giving himself time to load his gun,
he set out for the fields with his faithful Sbogar, and hastened
to the place of the promised rendezvous. A half-hour of intolerable waiting passed by; at last he caught a glimpse of a blue
sarafan between the bushes, and he rushed forward to meet
his charming Akulina. She smiled at his ecstasy of gratitude,
but Alexey immediately observed upon her face traces of sad-
ness and uneasiness. He wished to know the cause. Liza confessed to him that her act seemed to her very frivolous, that
she repented of it, that this time she did not wish to break
her promised word, but that this meeting would be the last,
and she therefore entreated him to break off an acquaintance-
ship which could not lead to any good.

All this, of course, was expressed in the language of a

peasant; but such thoughts and sentiments, so unusual in a simple girl of the lower class, struck Alexey with astonishment. He employed all his eloquence to divert Akulina from her purpose; he assured her that his intentions were honorable, promised her that he would never give her cause to repent, that he would obey her in everything, and earnestly entreated her not to deprive him of the joy of seeing her alone, if only once a day, or even only twice a week. He spoke the language of true passion, and at that moment he was really in love. Liza listened to him in silence.

"Give me your word," said she at last, "that you will never come to the village in search of me, and that you will never seek a meeting with me except those that I shall appoint myself."

Alexey swore by Holy Friday, but she stopped him with a smile.

"I do not want you to swear," said she; "your mere word is sufficient."

After that they began to converse together in a friendly manner, strolling about the wood, until Liza said to him: "Time is up."

They separated, and when Alexey was left alone, he could not understand how, in two meetings, a simple peasant girl had succeeded in acquiring such real power over him. His relations with Akulina had for him all the charm of novelty, and although the injunctions of the strange peasant girl appeared to him to be very severe, the thought of breaking his word never once entered his mind. The fact was that Alexey, in spite of his fateful ring, his mysterious correspondence, and his gloomy disenchantment, was a good and impulsive young fellow, with a pure heart capable of innocent pleasure.

Were I to listen to my own wishes only, I would here enter into a minute description of the interviews of the young people, of their growing inclination toward each other, their confidences, occupations and conversations; but I know that the greater part of my readers would not share my interest. Such details are usually considered tedious and uninteresting, and therefore I will omit them, merely observing, that before two months had elapsed, Alexey was already hopelessly in love, and Liza equally so, though less demonstrative in revealing the fact. Both were happy in the present and troubled themselves little about the future.

The thought of indissoluble ties frequently passed through their minds, but never had they spoken to each other about the matter. The reason was plain: Alexey, however much attached he might be to his lovely Akulina, could not forget the distance that separated him from the poor peasant girl; while Liza, knowing the hatred that existed between their parents, did not dare to hope for a mutual reconciliation. Moreover, her *amour propre* was stimulated in secret by the obscure and romantic hope of seeing at last the proprietor of Tugilovo at the feet of the daughter of the Priluchino blacksmith. All at once an important event occurred which threatened to alter their mutual relations.

One bright cold morning—such a morning as is very common during our Russian autumn—Ivan Petrovich Berestov went out for a ride on horseback, taking with him three pairs of hunting dogs, a groom and several peasant boys with clappers. At the same time, Grigory Ivanovich Muromsky, tempted by the beautiful weather, ordered his bob-tailed mare to be saddled, and started out to visit his Anglicized domains. On approaching the wood, he perceived his neighbor, sitting proudly on his horse, in his cloak lined with foxskin, waiting for a hare which the boys, with loud cries and the rattling of their clappers, had started out of a thicket. If Grigory Ivanovich had foreseen this meeting, he would certainly have proceeded in another direction, but he came upon Berestov so unexpectedly, that he suddenly found himself no farther than the distance of a pistol shot away from him. There was no help for it: Muromsky, like a civilized European, rode forward toward his adversary and politely saluted him. Berestov returned the salute with the zeal characteristic of a chained bear, who salutes the public in obedience to the order of his master.

At that moment the hare darted out of the wood and started off across the field. Berestov and the groom raised a loud shout, let the dogs loose, and then galloped off in pursuit. Muromsky's horse, not being accustomed to hunting, took fright and bolted. Muromsky, who prided himself on being a good horseman, gave it full rein, and inwardly rejoiced at the incident which delivered him from a disagreeable companion. But the horse, reaching a ravine which it had not previously noticed, suddenly sprang to one side, and Muromsky was thrown from the saddle. Striking the frozen ground with considerable force, he lay there cursing his bobtailed mare, which, as if recovering itself, had suddenly come to a standstill as soon as it felt that it was without a rider.

Ivan Petrovich hastened toward him and inquired if he had injured himself. In the meantime the groom had secured the guilty horse, which he now led forward by the bridle. He helped Muromsky into the saddle, and Berestov invited him to his house. Muromsky could not refuse the invitation, for he felt indebted to him; and so Berestov returned home, covered with glory for having hunted down a hare and for bringing with him his adversary wounded and almost a prisoner of war.

The two neighbors took breakfast together and conversed with each other in a very friendly manner. Muromsky requested Berestov to lend him a *droshky,* for he was obliged to confess that, owing to his bruises, he was not in a condition to return home on horseback. Berestov conducted him to the steps, and Muromsky did not take leave of him until he had obtained a promise from him that he would come the next day in company with Alexey Ivanovich, and dine in a friendly way at Priluchino. In this way was a deeply rooted enmity of long standing apparently brought to an end by the skittishness of a bob-tailed mare.

Liza ran forward to meet Grigory Ivanovich.

"What does this mean, Papa?" said she, with astonishment. "Why are you limping? Where is your horse? Whose *droshky* is this?"

"You will never guess, my dear," replied Grigory Ivanovich; and then he related to her everything that had happened.

Liza could not believe her ears. Without giving her time to collect herself, Grigory Ivanovich then went on to inform her that the two Berestovs—father and son—would dine with them on the following day.

"What do you say?" she exclaimed, turning pale. "The Berestovs, father and son, will dine with us tomorrow! No, Papa, you can do as you please, but I shall not show myself."

"What! Have you taken leave of your senses?" replied her father. "Since when have you been so bashful? Or do you cherish a hereditary hatred toward him like a heroine of romance? Enough, do not be a fool."

"No, Papa, not for anything in the world, not for any treasure would I appear before the Berestovs."

Grigory Ivanovich shrugged his shoulders, and did not dispute with her any further, for he knew that by contradiction he would obtain nothing from her, and went to rest after his eventful ride.

Lizaveta Grigoryevna repaired to her room and summoned

Nastya. They both conversed together for a long time about the impending visit. What would Alexey think if, in the well-bred young lady, he recognized his Akulina? What opinion would he have of her conduct, of her manners, of her good sense? On the other hand, Liza wished very much to see what impression would be produced upon him by a meeting so unexpected. . . . Suddenly an idea flashed through her mind. She communicated it to Nastya; both felt delighted with it, and they resolved to carry it into effect.

The next day at breakfast, Grigory Ivanovich asked his daughter if she still intended to hide from the Berestovs.

"Papa," replied Liza, "I will receive them if you wish it, but on one condition, and that is, that however I may appear before them, or whatever I may do, you will not be angry with me, or show the least sign of astonishment or displeasure."

"Some new prank!" said Grigory Ivanovich, laughing. "Very well, very well, I agree; do what you like, my dark-eyed romp.

With these words he kissed her on the forehead, and Liza ran off to put her plan into execution.

At two o'clock precisely, a carriage of domestic make, drawn by six horses, entered the courtyard and rounded the lawn. The elder Berestov mounted the steps with the assistance of two lackeys in the Muromsky livery. His son came after him on horseback, and together they entered the dining room, where the table was already laid. Muromsky received his neighbors in the most gracious manner, proposed that they inspect his garden and menagerie before dinner, and conducted them along paths carefully kept and graveled. The elder Berestov inwardly deplored the time and labor wasted in such useless fancies, but he held his tongue out of politeness. His son shared neither the disapprobation of the economical landowner, nor the enthusiasm of the vain-glorious Anglomaniac, but waited with impatience for the appearance of his host's daughter, of whom he had heard a great deal; and although his heart, as we know, was already engaged, youthful beauty always had a claim upon his imagination.

Returning to the parlor, they all three sat down; and while the old men recalled their young days, and related anecdotes of their respective careers in the service, Alexey reflected as to what role he should play in the presence of Liza. He decided that an air of cold indifference would be the most becoming under the circumstances, and he prepared to act accordingly. The door opened; he turned his head with such indifference, with such haughty carelessness, that the heart of the most inveterate coquette would inevitably have quaked. Unfortunately, instead of Liza, it was old Miss Jackson, who, painted and tightly laced, entered the room with downcast eyes and with a curtsey, so that Alexey's remarkable military move was wasted. He had not succeeded in recovering from his confusion, when the door opened again, and this time it was Liza herself who entered.

All rose; her father was just beginning to introduce his guests, when suddenly he stopped short and bit his lips. . . . Liza, his dark-complexioned Liza, was painted white up to the ears, and was more heavily made up than even Miss Jackson herself; false curls, much lighter than her own hair, covered her head like the peruke of Louis the Fourteenth; her sleeves à l'imbécile stood out like the hooped skirts of Madame de Pompadour; her figure was pinched in like the letter X, and all her mother's jewels, which had not yet found their way to the pawnbroker's, shone upon her fingers, her neck and in her ears.

Alexey could not possibly recognize his Akulina in the grotesque and dazzling young lady. His father kissed her hand,

and he followed his example, though much against his will; when he touched her little white fingers, it seemed to him that they trembled. In the meantime he succeeded in catching a glimpse of her little foot, intentionally advanced and set off to advantage by the most coquettish shoe imaginable. This reconciled him somewhat to the rest of her toilette. As for the paint and powder, it must be confessed that, in the simplicity of his heart, he had not noticed them at the first glance, and afterwards had no suspicion of them. Grigory Ivanovich remembered his promise, and endeavored not to show any astonishment; but his daughter's prank seemed to him so amusing, that he could scarcely contain himself. But the person who felt no inclination to laugh was the prim English governess. She had a shrewd suspicion that the paint and powder had been extracted from her chest of drawers, and a deep flush of anger was distinctly visible beneath the artificial whiteness of her face. She darted angry glances at the young madcap, who, reserving her explanations for another time, pretended that she did not notice them.

They sat down to table. Alexey continued to play his role of assumed indifference and absent-mindedness. Liza put on an air of affectation, spoke in a sing-song through her teeth, and only in French. Her father kept constantly looking at her, not understanding her object, but finding it all exceedingly amusing. The English governess fumed with rage and said not a word. Ivan Petrovich alone seemed at home: he ate like two, drank heavily, laughed at his own jokes, and grew more talkative and hilarious every moment.

At last they all rose from the table; the guests took their departure, and Grigory Ivanovich gave free vent to his laughter and to his questions.

"What put the idea into your head of fooling them like that?" he said to Liza. "But do you know what? The paint suits you admirably. I do not wish to fathom the mysteries of a lady's toilette, but if I were in your place, I would very soon begin to paint; not too much, of course, but just a little."

Liza was enchanted with the success of her stratagem. She embraced her father, promised him that she would consider his advice, and then hastened to conciliate the indignant Miss Jackson, who with great reluctance consented to open the door and listen to her explanations. Liza was ashamed to appear before strangers with her dark complexion; she had not dared to ask . . . she felt sure that dear, good Miss Jackson would pardon her, etc., etc. Miss Jackson, feeling convinced that Liza had not wished to make her a laughing-stock by imitating her, calmed down, kissed her, and as a token of reconciliation, made her a present of a small pot of English ceruse, which Liza accepted with every appearance of sincere gratitude.

The reader will readily imagine that Liza lost no time in repairing to the rendezvous in the little wood the next morning.

"You were at our master's yesterday," she said at once to Alexey. "What do you think of our young mistress?"

Alexey replied that he had not noticed her.

"That's a pity!" replied Liza.

"Why so?" asked Alexey.

"Because I wanted to ask you if it is true what they say——"

"What do they say?"

"Is it true, as they say, that I am very much like her?"

"What nonsense! She is a perfect freak compared with you."

"Oh, sir, it is very wrong of you to speak like that. Our young mistress is so fair and so stylish! How could I be compared with her!"

Alexey vowed to her that she was more beautiful than all the fair young ladies in creation, and in order to pacify her completely, he began to describe her mistress in such comical terms that Liza laughed heartily.

"But," said she with a sigh, "even though our young mistress may be ridiculous, I am but a poor ignorant thing in comparison with her."

"Oh!" said Alexey. "Is that anything to break your heart about? If you wish it, I will soon teach you to read and write."

"Yes, indeed," said Liza, "why shouldn't I try?"

"Very well, my dear; we will commence at once."

They sat down. Alexey drew from his pocket a pencil and notebook, and Akulina learned the alphabet with astonishing rapidity. Alexey could not sufficiently admire her intelligence. The following morning she wished to try to write. At first the pencil refused to obey her, but after a few minutes she was able to trace the letters with tolerable accuracy.

"It is really wonderful!" said Alexey. "Our method certainly produces quicker results than the Lancaster system."

And indeed, at the third lesson Akulina began to spell through *Natalya the Boyar's Daughter,* interrupting her reading by observations which really filled Alexey with astonishment, and she filled a whole sheet of paper with aphorisms drawn from the same story.

A week went by, and a correspondence was established between them. Their letter box was the hollow of an old oak tree, and Nastya acted as their messenger. Thither Alexey carried his letters written in a bold round hand, and there he found on plain blue paper the scrawls of his beloved. Akulina perceptibly began to acquire an elegant style of expression, and her mind developed noticeably.

Meanwhile, the recently formed acquaintance between

Ivan Petrovich Berestov and Grigory Ivanovich Muromsky soon became transformed into a sincere friendship, under the following circumstances. Muromsky frequently reflected that, on the death of Ivan Petrovich, all his possessions would pass into the hands of Alexey Ivanovich, in which case the latter would be one of the wealthiest landed proprietors in the province, and there would be nothing to hinder him from marrying Liza. The elder Berestov, on his side, although recognizing in his neighbor a certain extravagance (or, as he termed it, English folly), was perfectly ready to admit that he possessed many excellent qualities, as for example, his rare resourcefulness. Grigory Ivanovich was closely related to Count Pronsky, a man of distinction and of great influence. The Count could be of great service to Alexey, and Muromsky (so thought Ivan Petrovich) would doubtless rejoice to see his daughter marry so advantageously. By dint of constantly dwelling upon this idea, the two old men came at last to communicate their thoughts to one another. They embraced each other, both promised to do their best to arrange the matter, and they immediately set to work, each on his own side. Muromsky foresaw that he would have some difficulty in persuading his Betsy to become more intimately acquainted with Alexey, whom she had not seen since the memorable dinner. It seemed to him that they had not liked each other much; at least Alexey had not paid any further visits to Priluchino, and Liza had retired to her room every time that Ivan Petrovich had honored them with a visit.

"But," thought Grigory Ivanovich, "if Alexey came to see us every day, Betsy could not help falling in love with him. That is in the nature of things. Time will settle everything."

Ivan Petrovich was less uneasy about the success of his designs. That same evening he summoned his son to his study, lit his pipe, and, after a short pause, said: "Well,"

Alyosha, you have not said anything for a long time about military service. Or has the Hussar uniform lost its charm for you?"

"No, Father," replied Alexey respectfully; "but I see that you do not like the idea of my entering the Hussars, and it is my duty to obey you."

"Good," replied Ivan Petrovich; "I see that you are an obedient son; that is a consolation to me. . . . On my side, I do not wish to compel you; I do not want to force you to enter . . . the civil service . . . at once, but, in the meanwhile, I intend you to get married."

"To whom, Father?" asked Alexey, in astonishment.

"To Lizaveta Grigoryevna Muromsky," replied Ivan Petrovich. "She is a fine bride, is she not?"

"Father, I have not thought of marriage yet."

"You have not thought of it, and therefore I have thought of it for you."

"As you please, but I do not care for Liza Muromsky in the least."

"You will get to like her afterwards. Love comes with time."

"I do not feel capable of making her happy."

"Do not fret about making her happy. What? Is this how you respect your father's wish? Very well!"

"As you choose. I do not wish to marry, and I will not marry."

"You will marry, or I will curse you; and as for my estate, as true as there is a God in heaven, I will sell it and squander the money, and not leave you a farthing. I will give you three days to think about the matter; and in the meantime, keep out of my sight."

Alexey knew that when his father once took an idea into his head, even a nail would not drive it out, as Taras Skotinin[2] says in the comedy. But Alexey took after his father, and was just as headstrong as he was. He went to his room and began to reflect upon the limits of paternal authority. Then his thoughts reverted to Lizaveta Grigoryevna, to his father's solemn vow to make him a beggar, and last of all to Akulina. For the first time he saw clearly that he was passionately in love with her; the romantic idea of marrying a peasant girl and of living by the labor of his hands came into his head, and the more he thought of such a decisive step, the more reasonable did it seem to him. For some time the interviews in the wood had ceased on account of the rainy weather. He wrote Akulina a letter in the neatest handwriting, and in the wildest style, informing her of the misfortune that threatened them, and offering her his hand. He took the letter at once to the post office in the wood, and then went to bed, well satisfied with himself.

The next day Alexey, still firm in his resolution, rode over early in the morning to visit Muromsky, in order to explain matters frankly to him. He hoped to excite his generosity and win him over to his side.

"Is Grigory Ivanovich at home?" he asked, stopping his horse in front of the steps of the Priluchino mansion.

"No, sir," replied the servant; "Grigory Ivanovich rode out early this morning, and has not yet returned."

"How annoying!" thought Alexey. . . . "Is Lizaveta Grigoryevna at home, then?" he asked.

"Yes, sir."

Alexey sprang from his horse, gave the reins to the lackey, and entered without being announced.

"Everything is going to be decided now," thought he,

directing his steps toward the parlor. "I will explain everything to Lizaveta herself."

He entered . . . and then stood still as if petrified! Liza . . . no . . . Akulina, dear, dark-skinned Akulina, no longer in a *sarafan*, but in a white morning dress, was sitting in front of the window, reading his letter; she was so preoccupied that she had not heard him enter.

Alexey could not restrain an exclamation of joy. Liza started, raised her head, uttered a cry, and wished to fly from the room. But he held her back.

"Akulina! Akulina!"

Liza endeavored to free herself from his grasp.

"Mais laissez-moi donc, monsieur! . . . Mais êtes-vous fou?" she repeated, turning away.

"Akulina! my dear Akulina!" he repeated, kissing her hands.

Miss Jackson, a witness of this scene, knew not what to think of it. At that moment the door opened, and Grigory Ivanovich entered the room.

"Aha!" said Muromsky. "It seems that you have already arranged matters between you."

The reader will spare me the unnecessary obligation of describing the dénouement.

The End of the Tales
of I. P. Belkin

The Queen of Spades

The Queen of Spades signifies secret ill-will.
NEW FORTUNE-TELLER

I

When bleak was the weather,
The friends came together
To play.
The stakes, they were doubled;
The sly ones, untroubled,
Were gay.
They all had their innings,
And chalked up their winnings,
And so
They kept busy together
Throughout the bleak weather,
Oho!

THERE WAS a card party at the rooms of Narumov of the Horse Guards. The long winter night passed away imperceptibly, and it was five o'clock in the morning before the company sat down to supper. Those who had won, ate with a good appetite; the others sat staring absently at their empty plates. When the champagne appeared, however, the conversation became more animated, and all took a part in it.

"And how did you fare, Surin?" asked the host.

"Oh, I lost, as usual. I must confess that I am unlucky: I never raise the original stakes, I always keep cool, I never allow anything to put me out, and yet I always lose!"

"And you have never been tempted? You have never staked on several cards in succession? . . . Your firmness astonishes me."

"But what do you think of Hermann?" said one of the guests, pointing to a young engineer. "He has never had a card in his hand in his life, he has never in his life doubled the stake, and yet he sits here till five o'clock in the morning watching our play."

"Play interests me very much," said Hermann: "but I am not in the position to sacrifice the necessary in the hope of winning the superfluous."

"Hermann is a German: he is prudent—that is all!" observed Tomsky. "But if there is one person that I cannot understand, it is my grandmother, the Countess Anna Fedotovna."

"How? What?" cried the guests.

"I cannot understand," continued Tomsky, "how it is that my grandmother does not punt."

"What is there remarkable about an old lady of eighty not gambling?" said Narumov.

"Then you know nothing about her?"

"No, really; haven't the faintest idea."

"Oh! then listen. You must know that, about sixty years ago, my grandmother went to Paris, where she created quite a sensation. People used to run after her to catch a glimpse of 'la Vénus moscovite.' Richelieu courted her, and my grandmother maintains that he almost blew out his brains in consequence of her cruelty. At that time ladies used to play faro. On one occasion at the Court, she lost a very considerable sum to the Duke of Orleans. On returning home, my grandmother removed the patches from her face, took off her hoops, informed my grandfather of her loss at the gaming table, and ordered him to pay the money. My deceased grandfather, as far as I remember, was a sort of butler to my grandmother. He dreaded her like fire; but, on hearing of such a heavy loss, he almost went out of his mind; he calculated the various sums she had lost, and pointed out to her that in six months she had spent half a million, that neither their Moscow nor Saratov estates were near Paris, and finally refused point-blank to pay the debt. My grandmother slapped his face and slept by herself as a sign of her displeasure. The next day she sent for her husband, hoping that this domestic punishment had produced an effect upon him, but she found him inflexible. For the first time in her life, she condescended to offer reasons and explanations. She thought she could convince him by pointing out to him that there are debts and debts, and that there is a great difference between a Prince and a coachmaker. But it was all in vain, grandfather was in revolt. He said 'no,' and that was all. My grandmother did not know what to do. She was on friendly terms with a very remarkable man. You have heard of Count St. Germain, about whom so many marvelous stories are told. You know that he represented himself as the Wandering Jew, as the discoverer of the elixir of life, of the philosopher's stone, and so forth. Some laughed at him as a charlatan; but Casanova, in his memoirs, says that he was a spy. But be that as it may, St. Germain, in spite of the mystery surrounding him, was a man of decent appearance and had an amiable manner in company. Even to this day my grandmother is in love with him, and becomes quite angry if anyone speaks disrespectfully of him. My grandmother knew that St. Germain had large sums of money at his disposal. She resolved to have recourse to him, and she wrote a letter to him asking him to come to her without delay. The queer old man immediately waited upon her and found her overwhelmed with grief. She described to him in the blackest colors the barbarity of her husband, and ended by declaring that she placed all her hopes in his friendship and graciousness.

"St. Germain reflected.

" 'I could advance you the sum you want,' said he; 'but I know that you would not rest easy until you had paid me back, and I should not like to bring fresh troubles upon you. But there is another way of getting out of your difficulty: you can win back your money.'

" 'But, my dear Count,' replied my grandmother, 'I tell you that we haven't any money left.'

" 'Money is not necessary,' replied St. Germain. 'Be pleased to listen to me.'

"Then he revealed to her a secret, for which each of us would give a good deal . . ."

The young gamblers listened with increased attention. Tomsky lit his pipe, pulled at it, and continued:

"That same evening my grandmother went to Versailles *au jeu de la Reine.* The Duke of Orleans kept the bank; my grandmother excused herself in an offhanded manner for not having yet paid her debt, by inventing some little story, and then began to play against him. She chose three cards and played them one after the other: all three won at the start and my grandmother recovered all that she had lost."

"Mere chance!" said one of the guests.

"A fairy tale!" observed Hermann.

"Perhaps they were marked cards!" said a third.

"I do not think so," replied Tomsky gravely.

"What!" said Narumov. "You have a grandmother who knows how to hit upon three lucky cards in succession, and you have never yet succeeded in getting the secret of it out of her?"

"That's the deuce of it!" replied Tomsky. "She had four sons, one of whom was my father; all four are desperate gamblers, and yet not to one of them did she ever reveal her secret, although it would not have been a bad thing either for them or for me. But this is what I heard from my uncle, Count Ivan Ilyich, and he assured me, on his honor, that it was true. The late Chaplitzky—the same who died in poverty after having squandered millions—once lost, in his youth, about three hundred thousand rubles—to Zorich, if I remember rightly. He was in despair. My grandmother, who was always very hard on extravagant young men, took pity, however, upon Chaplitzky. She mentioned to him three cards, telling him to play them one after the other, at the same time exacting from him a solemn promise that he, would never play cards again as long as he lived. Chaplitzky then went to his victorious opponent, and they began a fresh game. On the first card he staked fifty thousand rubles and won at once, he doubled the stake and won again, doubled it again, and won, not only all he had lost, but something over and above that. . . .

"But it is time to go to bed: it is a quarter to six already."

And indeed it was already beginning to dawn; the young men emptied their glasses and then took leave of one another.

II

*—Il paraît que monsieur est
décidément pour les suivantes.
—Que voulez-vous, madame? Elles
sont plus fraîches.*

SOCIETY TALK

THE OLD Countess X. was seated in her dressing room in front of her looking glass. Three maids stood around her. One held a small pot of rouge, another a box of hairpins, and the third a tall cap with bright red ribbons. The Countess had no longer the slightest pretensions to beauty—hers had faded long ago—but she still preserved all the habits of her youth, dressed in strict accordance with the fashion of the seventies, and made as long and as careful a toilette as she would have done sixty years previously. Near the window, at an embroidery frame, sat a young lady, her ward.

"Good morning, *Grand'maman*," said a young officer, entering the room. "*Bonjour, Mademoiselle Lise. Grand'maman,* I have a favor to ask of you."

"What is it, Paul?"

"I want you to let me introduce one of my friends to you, and to allow me to bring him to the ball on Friday."

"Bring him direct to the ball and introduce him to me there. Were you at N.'s yesterday?"

"Yes; everything went off very pleasantly, and dancing kept up until five o'clock. How beautiful Mme. Yeletzkaya was!"

"But, my dear, what is there beautiful about her? You should have seen her grandmother, Princess Darya Petrovna! By the way, she must have aged very much, Princess Darya Petrovna."

"How do you mean, aged?" cried Tomsky thoughtlessly. "She died seven years ago."

The young lady raised her head and made a sign to the young man. He then remembered that the old Countess was never to be informed of the death of any of her contemporaries, and he bit his lip. But the Countess heard the news with the greatest indifference.

"Died!" said she. "And I did not know it. We were appointed maids of honor at the same time, and when we were being presented, the Empress . . ."

And the Countess for the hundredth time related the anecdote to her grandson.

"Come, Paul," said she, when she had finished her story, "help me to get up. Lizanka, where is my snuffbox?"

And the Countess with her three maids went behind a screen to finish her toilette. Tomsky was left alone with the young lady.

"Who is the gentleman you wish to introduce to the Countess?" asked Lizaveta Ivanovna in a whisper.

"Narumov. Do you know him?"

"No. Is he in the army or is he a civilian?"

"In the army."

"Is he in the Engineers?"

"No, in the Cavalry. What made you think that he was in the Engineers?"

The young lady smiled, but made no reply.

"Paul," cried the Countess, from behind the screen, "send me some new novel, only, pray, not the kind they write nowadays."

"What do you mean, *Grand'maman?*"

"That is, a novel, in which the hero strangles neither his father nor his mother, and in which there are no drowned bodies. I have a great horror of them."

"There are no such novels nowadays. Would you like a Russian one?"

"Are there any Russian novels? Send me one, my dear, please send me one!"

"Good-bye, *Grand'maman:* I am in a hurry. . . . Good-bye, Lizaveta Ivanovna. What, then, made you think that Narumov was in the Engineers?"

And Tomsky withdrew from the dressing room.

Lizaveta Ivanovna was left alone: she laid aside her work and began to look out of the window. A few moments afterwards, from behind a corner house on the other side of the street, a young officer appeared. A deep blush covered her cheeks; she took up her work again and bent her head over the frame. At the same moment the Countess returned, completely dressed.

"Order the carriage, Lizaveta," said she; "we will go out for a drive."

Lizaveta arose from the frame and began to put away her work.

"What is the matter with you, my dear, are you deaf?" cried the Countess. "Order the carriage to be got ready at once."

"I will do so this moment," replied the young lady, and ran into the anteroom.

A servant entered and gave the Countess some books from Prince Pavel Alexandrovich.

"Tell him that I am much obliged to him," said the Countess. "Lizaveta! Lizaveta! Where are you running to?"

"I am going to dress."

"There is plenty of time, my dear. Sit down here. Open the first volume and read aloud to me."

Her companion took the book and read a few lines.

"Louder," said the Countess. "What is the matter with you, my dear? Have you lost your voice? Wait—give me that footstool—a little nearer—that will do!"

Lizaveta read two more pages. The Countess yawned.

"Put the book down," said she. "What a lot of nonsense! Send it back to Prince Pavel with my thanks. . . . But where is the carriage?"

"The carriage is ready," said Lizaveta, looking out into the street.

"How is it that you are not dressed?" said the Countess. "I must always wait for you. It is intolerable, my dear!"

Liza hastened to her room. She had not been there two minutes, before the Countess began to ring with all her might. The three maids came running in at one door and the valet at another.

"How is it that you don't come when I ring for you?" said the Countess. "Tell Lizaveta Ivanovna that I am waiting for her."

Lizaveta returned with her hat and cloak on.

"At last you are here!" said the Countess. "But why such an elaborate toilette? Whom do you intend to captivate? What sort of weather is it? It seems rather windy."

"No, Your Ladyship, it is very calm," replied the valet.

"You always speak thoughtlessly. Open the window. So it is: windy and bitterly cold. Unharness the horses. Lizaveta, we won't go out—there was no need for you to deck yourself out like that."

"And that's my life!" thought Lizaveta Ivanovna.

And, in truth, Lizaveta Ivanovna was a very unfortunate creature. "It is bitter to eat the bread of another," says

Dante, "and hard to climb his stair." But who can know
what the bitterness of dependence is so well as the poor
companion of an old lady of quality? The Countess X. had
by no means a bad heart, but she was capricious, like a
woman who had been spoiled by the world, as well as avari-
cious and sunk in cold egoism, like all old people who are
no longer capable of affection, and whose thoughts are with
the past and not the present. She participated in all the
vanities of the great world, went to balls, where she sat in a
corner, painted and dressed in old-fashioned style, like an
ugly but indispensable ornament of the ballroom; the guests
on entering approached her and bowed profoundly, as if in
accordance with a set ceremony, but after that nobody took
any further notice of her. She received the whole town at her
house, and observed the strictest etiquette, although she
could no longer recognize people. Her numerous domestics,
growing fat and old in her antechamber and servants' hall,
did just as they liked, and vied with each other in robbing
the moribund old woman. Lizaveta Ivanovna was the martyr
of the household. She poured tea, and was reprimanded for
using too much sugar; she read novels aloud to the Countess,
and the faults of the author were visited upon her head; she
accompanied the Countess in her walks, and was held answerable for the weather or the state of the pavement. A
salary was attached to the post, but she very rarely received
it, although she was expected to dress like everybody else,
that is to say, like very few indeed. In society she played the
most pitiable role. Everybody knew her, and nobody paid
her any attention. At balls she danced only when a partner
was wanted, and ladies would only take hold of her arm
when it was necessary to lead her out of the room to attend
to their dresses. She had a great deal of *amour propre,* and
felt her position keenly, and she looked about her with impatience for a deliverer to come to her rescue; but the young

men, calculating in their giddiness, did not condescend to pay her any attention, although Lizaveta Ivanovna was a hundred times prettier than the bare-faced and cold-hearted marriageable girls around whom they hovered. Many a time did she quietly slink away from the dull and elegant drawing room, to go and cry in her own poor little room, in which stood a screen, a chest of drawers, a looking glass and a painted bedstead, and where a tallow candle burned feebly in a copper candlestick.

One morning—this was about two days after the card party described at the beginning of this story, and a week previous to the scene at which we have just assisted—Lizaveta Ivanovna was seated near the window at her embroidery frame, when, happening to look out into the street, she caught sight of a young officer of the Engineers, standing motionless with his eyes fixed upon her window. She lowered her head and went on again with her work. About five minutes afterward she looked out again—the young officer was still standing in the same place. Not being in the habit of coquetting with passing officers, she did not continue to gaze out into the street, but went on sewing for a couple of hours, without raising her head. Dinner was announced. She rose up and began to put her embroidery away, but glancing casually out the window, she perceived the officer again. This seemed to her very strange. After dinner she went to the window with a certain feeling of uneasiness, but the officer was no longer there—and she thought no more about him.

A couple of days afterwards, just as she was stepping into the carriage with the Countess, she saw him again. He was standing close to the entrance, with his face half concealed by his beaver collar, his black eyes flashing beneath his hat. Lizaveta felt alarmed, though she knew not why, and she trembled as she seated herself in the carriage.

On returning home, she hastened to the window—the officer was standing in his accustomed place, with his eyes fixed upon her. She drew back, a prey to curiosity and agitated by a feeling which was quite new to her.

From that time on not a day passed without the young officer making his appearance under the window at the customary hour. A spontaneous relationship was established between them. Sitting in her place at work, she would feel his approach; and raising her head, she would look at him longer and longer each day. The young man seemed to be very grateful to her for it: she saw with the sharp eye of youth, how a sudden flush covered his pale cheeks each time that their glances met. By the end of the week she smiled at him. . . .

When Tomsky asked permission of his grandmother the Countess to present one of his friends to her, the young girl's heart beat violently. But hearing that Narumov was not an engineer, but in the Horse Guards, she regretted that by her indiscreet question, she had betrayed her secret to the volatile Tomsky.

Hermann was the son of a Russified German, from whom he had inherited a small fortune. Being firmly convinced of the necessity of insuring his independence, Hermann did not touch even the interest on his capital, but lived on his pay, without allowing himself the slightest luxury. Moreover, he was reserved and ambitious, and his companions rarely had an opportunity of making merry at the expense of his excessive parsimony. He had strong passions and an ardent imagination, but his firmness of disposition preserved him from the ordinary errors of youth. Thus, though a gambler at heart, he never touched a card, for he considerd his position did not allow him—as he said—"to risk the necessary in the hope of winning the superfluous," yet he would sit for nights together at the card table and follow with feverish excitement the various turns of the game.

The story of the three cards had produced a powerful impression upon his imagination, and all night long he could think of nothing else. "If only," he thought to himself the following evening, as he wandered through St. Petersburg, "if only the old Countess would reveal her secret to me! If she would only tell me the names of the three winning cards! Why should I not try my fortune? I must get introduced to her and win her favor—perhaps become her lover. . . . But all that will take time, and she is eighty-seven years old: she might be dead in a week, in a couple of days even! . . . And the story itself: is it credible? . . . No! Prudence, moderation and work: those are my three winning cards; that is what will increase my capital threefold, sevenfold, and procure for me ease and independence."

Musing in this manner, he walked on until he found himself in one of the principal streets of St. Petersburg, in front of a house of old-fashioned architecture. The street was blocked with carriages; one after the other they rolled up in front of the illuminated entrance. Every minute there emerged from the coaches the shapely foot of a young beauty, a spurred boot, a striped stocking above a diplomatic shoe. Fur coats and cloaks whisked past the majestic porter.

Hermann stopped. "Whose house is this?" he asked the watchman at the corner.

"The Countess X.'s," replied the watchman.

Hermann trembled. The strange story of the three cards again presented itself to his imagination. He began walking up and down before the house, thinking of its owner and her marvelous gift. Returning late to his modest lodging, he could not go to sleep for a long time, and when at last he did doze off, he could dream of nothing but cards, green tables, piles of banknotes and heaps of gold coins. He played card after card, firmly turning down the corners, and won uninterruptedly, raking in the gold and filling his pockets with the notes. Waking up late the next morning, he sighed over the loss of his imaginary wealth, then went out again to wander about the streets, and found himself once more in front of the Countess's house. Some unknown power seemed to draw him thither. He stopped and began to stare at the windows. In one of these he saw the head of a black-haired woman, which was bent probably over some book or handwork. The head was raised. Hermann saw a fresh-cheeked face and a pair of black eyes. That moment decided his fate.

III

Vous m'écrivez, mon ange, des lettres de
quatre pages plus vite que je ne puis les lire.
A CORRESPONDENCE

LIZAVETA IVANOVNA had scarcely taken off her hat and cloak, when the Countess sent for her and again ordered the carriage. The vehicle drew up before the door, and they prepared to take their seats. Just at the moment when two footmen were assisting the old lady into the carriage, Lizaveta saw her engineer close beside the wheel; he grasped her hand; alarm caused her to lose her presence of mind, and the young man disappeared—but not before leaving a letter in her hand. She concealed it in her glove, and during the whole of the drive she neither saw nor heard anything. It was the custom of the Countess, when out for an airing in her carriage to be constantly asking such questions as: "Who was that person that met us just now? What is the name of this bridge? What is written on that signboard?" On this occasion, however, Lizaveta returned such vague and absurd answers, that the Countess became angry with her.

"What is the matter with you, my dear?" she exclaimed. "Have you taken leave of your senses, or what is it? Do you not hear me or understand what I say? . . . Heaven be thanked, I am still in my right mind and speak plainly enough!"

Lizaveta Ivanovna did not hear her. On returning home she ran to her room, and drew the letter out of her glove: it was not sealed. Lizaveta read it. The letter contained a declaration of love; it was tender, respectful, and copied word for word from a German novel. But Lizaveta did not not know anything of the German language, and she was quite delighted with the letter.

For all that, it troubled her exceedingly. For the first time in her life she was entering into secret and intimate relations with a young man. His boldness horrified her. She reproached herself for her imprudent behavior, and knew not what to do. Should she cease to sit at the window and, by assuming an appearance of indifference toward him, put a check upon the young officer's desire to pursue her further? Should she send his letter back to him, or should she answer him in a cold and resolute manner? There was nobody to whom she could turn in her perplexity, for she had neither female friend nor adviser. . . . At length she resolved to reply to him.

She sat down at her little writing table, took pen and paper, and began to think. Several times she began her letter, and then tore it up: the way she had expressed herself seemed to her either too indulgent or too severe. At last she succeeded in writing a few lines with which she felt satisfied.

"I am convinced," she wrote, "that your intentions are honorable, and that you do not wish to offend me by any imprudent action, but our acquaintance should not have begun in such a manner. I return you your letter, and I hope that I shall never have any cause to complain of undeserved disrespect."

The next day, as soon as Hermann made his appearance, Lizaveta rose from her embroidery, went into the drawing room, opened the wicket and threw the letter into the street, trusting to the young officer's alertness.

Hermann hastened forward, picked it up and then repaired to a confectioner's shop. Breaking the seal of the envelope, he found inside it his own letter and Lizaveta's reply. He had expected this, and he returned home, very much taken up with his intrigue.

Three days afterward, a bright-eyed young girl from a milliner's establishment brought Lizaveta a letter. Lizaveta opened it with great uneasiness, fearing that it was a demand for money, when suddenly she recognized Hermann's handwriting.

"You have made a mistake, my dear," said she; "this letter is not for me."

"Oh, yes, it is for you," replied the pert girl, without concealing a sly smile. "Have the goodness to read it."

Lizaveta glanced at the letter. Hermann requested an interview.

"It cannot be," said Lizaveta Ivanovna, alarmed both at the haste with which he had made his request, and the manner in which it had been transmitted. "This letter is certainly not for me."

And she tore it into fragments.

"If the letter was not for you, why have you torn it up?"

said the girl. "I should have given it back to the person who sent it."

"Be good enough, my dear," said Lizaveta, disconcerted by this remark, "not to bring me any more letters in future, and tell the person who sent you that he ought to be ashamed. . . ."

But Hermann was not the man to be thus put off. Every day Lizaveta received from him a letter, sent now in this way, now in that. They were no longer translated from the German. Hermann wrote them under the inspiration of passion, and spoke in his own language, and they bore full testimony to the inflexibility of his desire and the disordered condition of his uncontrollable imagination. Lizaveta no longer thought of sending them back to him: she became intoxicated with them and began to reply to them, and little by little her answers became longer and more affectionate. At last she threw out of the window to him the following letter:

"This evening there is going to be a ball at the X. Embassy. The Countess will be there. We shall remain until two o'clock. This is your opportunity of seeing me alone. As soon as the Countess is gone, the servants will very probably go out, and there will be nobody left but the porter, but he, too, usually retires to his lodge. Come at half past eleven. Walk straight upstairs. If you meet anybody in the anteroom, ask if the Countess is at home. If you are told she is not, there will be nothing left for you to do but to go away and return another time. But it is most probable that you will meet nobody. The maidservants all sit together in one room. On leaving the anteroom, turn to the left, and walk straight on until you reach the Countess' bedroom. In the bedroom, behind a screen, you will find two small doors: the one on the right leads to a study, which the Countess never enters; the one on the left leads to a corridor, at the end of which is a narrow winding staircase; this leads to my room."

Hermann quivered like a tiger, as he waited for the appointed time. At ten o'clock in the evening he was already in front of the Countess' house. The weather was terrible; the wind was howling; the sleety snow fell in large flakes; the lamps emitted a feeble light, the streets were deserted; from time to time a sledge, drawn by a sorry-looking hack, passed by, the driver on the lookout for a belated fare. Hermann stood there wearing nothing but his jacket, yet he felt neither the wind nor the snow.

At last the Countess' carriage drew up. Hermann saw two footmen carry out in their arms the bent form of the old lady, wrapped in sables, and immediately behind her, clad in a light mantle, and with a wreath of fresh flowers on her head, followed Lizaveta. The door was closed. The carriage rolled away heavily through the yielding snow. The porter shut the street door; the windows became dark.

Hermann began walking up and down near the deserted house; at length he stopped under a lamp, and glanced at his watch: it was twenty minutes past eleven. He remained standing under the lamp, his eyes fixed upon the watch, impatiently waiting for the remaining minutes to pass. At half past eleven precisely, Hermann ascended the steps of the house, and made his way into the brightly illuminated vestibule. The porter was not there. Hermann ran up the stairs, opened the door of the anteroom and saw a footman sitting asleep in an antique soiled armchair, under a lamp. With a light firm step Hermann walked past him. The reception room and the drawing room were in semi-darkness. They were lit feebly by a lamp in the anteroom.

Hermann entered the bedroom. Before an ikon case, filled with ancient ikons, a golden sanctuary lamp was burning. Armchairs, upholstered in faded brocade, and sofas, the gilding of which was worn off and which were piled with down cushions, stood in melancholy symmetry around the room, the walls of which were hung with China silk. On the wall hung two portraits painted in Paris by Madame Lebrun. One of them represented a plump, pink-cheeked man of about forty in a light green uniform and with a star on his breast; the other—a beautiful young woman, with an aquiline nose, curls at her temples, and a rose in her powdered hair. In all the corners stood porcelain shepherds and shepherdesses, clocks from the workshop of the celebrated Leroy, boxes, roulettes, fans, and the various gewgaws for ladies that were invented at the end of the last century, together with Mont-golfier's balloon and Mesmer's magnetism. Hermann stepped behind the screen. Behind it stood a little iron bed; on the right was the door which led to the study; on the left—the other which led to the corridor. He opened the latter, and saw the little winding staircase which led to the room of the poor ward. . . . But he retraced his steps and entered the dark study.

The time passed slowly. All was still. The clock in the drawing room struck twelve; in all the rooms, one clock after another marked the hour, and everything was quiet again. Hermann stood leaning against the cold stove. He was calm; his heart beat regularly, like that of a man resolved upon a dangerous but inevitable undertaking. The clock struck one, then two; and he heard the distant rumbling of carriage wheels. In spite of himself, excitement seized him. The carriage drew near and stopped. He heard the sound of the carriage step being let down. All was bustle within the house. The servants were running hither and thither, voices were heard, and the house was lit up. Three antiquated chambermaids entered the bedroom, and they were shortly afterwards followed by the Countess who, more dead than alive, sank into an arm-chair. Hermann peeped through a chink. Lizaveta Ivanovna passed close by him, and he heard her hurried steps as she hurried up her staircase. For a moment his heart was assailed by something like remorse, but the emotion was only transitory. He stood petrified.

The Countess began to undress before her looking glass. Her cap, decorated with roses, was unpinned, and then her powdered wig was removed from off her white and closely cropped head. Hairpins fell in showers around her. Her yellow satin dress, embroidered with silver, fell down at her swollen feet.

Hermann witnessed the repulsive mysteries of her toilette; at last the Countess was in her nightcap and nightgown, and in this costume, more suitable to her age, she appeared less hideous and terrifying.

Like all old people in general, the Countess suffered from sleeplessness. Having undressed, she seated herself at the window in an armchair and dismissed her maids. The candles were taken away, and once more the room was lit only by the sanctuary lamp. The Countess sat there looking quite yellow, moving her flaccid lips and swaying from side to side. Her dull eyes expressed complete vacancy of mind, and, looking at her, one would have thought that the rocking of her body was not voluntary, but was produced by the action of some concealed galvanic mechanism.

Suddenly the deathlike face changed incredibly. The lips ceased to move, the eyes became animated: before the Countess stood a stranger.

"Do not be alarmed, for Heaven's sake, do not be alarmed!" said he in a low but distinct voice. "I have no intention of doing you any harm, I have only come to ask a favor of you."

The old woman looked at him in silence, as if she had not heard what he had said. Hermann thought that she was deaf, and, bending down toward her ear, he repeated what he had said. The old woman remained silent as before.

"You can insure the happiness of my life," continued Hermann, "and it will cost you nothing. I know that you can name three cards in succession—"

Hermann stopped. The Countess appeared now to understand what was asked of her; she seemed to be seeking words with which to reply.

"It was a joke," she replied at last. "I swear it was only a joke."

"This is no joking matter," replied Hermann angrily. "Remember Chaplitzky, whom you helped to win back what he had lost."

The Countess became visibly uneasy. Her features expressed strong emotion, but she soon lapsed into her former insensibility.

"Can you not name me these three winning cards?" continued Hermann.

The Countess remained silent; Hermann continued: "For whom are you preserving your secret? For your grandsons? They are rich enough without it; they do not know the worth of money. Your cards would be of no use to a spendthrift. He who cannot preserve his paternal inheritance, will die in want, even though he had a demon at his service. I am not a man of that sort; I know the value of money. Your three cards will not be wasted on me. Come!"

He paused and tremblingly awaited her reply. The Countess remained silent; Hermann fell upon his knees.

"If your heart has ever known the feeling of love," said he, "if you remember its rapture, if you have ever smiled at the cry of your new-born child, if your breast has ever throbbed with any human feeling, I entreat you by the feelings of a wife, a lover, a mother, by all that is most sacred in life, not to reject my plea. Reveal to me your secret. Of what use is it to you? . . . Maybe it is connected with some terrible sin, the loss of eternal bliss, some bargain with the devil. . . . Consider—you are old; you have not long to live—I am ready to take your sins upon my soul. Only reveal to me your secret. Remember that the happiness of a man is in your hands, that not only I, but my children, grandchildren, and great-grandchildren, will bless your memory and reverence it as something sacred. . . ."

The old woman answered not a word.

Hermann rose to his feet.

"You old witch!" he exclaimed, clenching his teeth. "Then I will make you answer!"

With these words he drew a pistol from his pocket.

At the sight of the pistol, the Countess for the second time exhibited strong emotion. She shook her head and raised her hands as if to protect herself from the shot . . . then she fell backward and remained motionless.

"Come, an end to this childish nonsense!" said Hermann, taking hold of her hand. "I ask you for the last time: will you tell me the names of your three cards, or will you not?"

The Countess made no reply. Hermann perceived that she was dead!

IV

7 mai, 18 — —
Homme sans moeurs et sans religion!
A CORRESPONDENCE

LIZAVETA IVANOVNA was sitting in her room, still in her ball dress, lost in deep thought. On returning home, she had hastily dismissed the sleepy maid, who reluctantly came forward to assist her, saying that she would undress herself, and with a trembling heart had gone up to her own room, hoping to find Hermann there, but yet desiring not to find him. At the first glance she convinced herself that he was not there, and she thanked her fate for the obstacle which had prevented their meeting. She sat down without undressing, and began to recall to mind all the circumstances which in so short a time had carried her so far. It was not three weeks since the time when she had first seen the young man from the window—and she already was in correspondence with him, and he had succeeded in inducing her to grant him a nocturnal tryst! She knew his name only through his having written it at the bottom of some of his letters; she had never spoken to him, had never heard his voice, and had never heard anything of him until that evening. But, strange to say, that very evening at the ball, Tomsky, being piqued with the young Princess Pauline N., who, contrary to her usual custom, did not flirt with him, wished to revenge himself by assuming an air of indifference: he therefore engaged Lizaveta Ivanovna and danced an endless mazurka with her. All the time he kept teasing her about her partiality for officers in the Engineers; he assured her that he knew far more than she could have supposed, and some of his jests were so happily aimed, that Lizaveta thought several times that her secret was known to him.

"From whom have you learned all this?" she asked, smiling.

"From a friend of a person very well known to you," replied Tomsky, "from a very remarkable man."

"And who is this remarkable man?"

"His name is Hermann."

Lizaveta made no reply; but her hands and feet turned to ice.

"This Hermann," continued Tomsky, "is a truly romantic character. He has the profile of a Napoleon, and the soul of a Mephistopheles. I believe that he has at least three crimes upon his conscience. . . . How pale you are!"

"I have a headache. . . . But what did this Hermann— or whatever his name is—tell you?"

"Hermann is very much dissatisfied with his friend: he says that in his place he would act very differently. . . . I even think that Hermann himself has designs upon you; at least, he listens not indifferently to his friend's enamored exclamations."

"But where has he seen me?"

"In church, perhaps; or promenading—God alone knows where. It may have been in your room, while you were asleep, for he is capable of it."

Three ladies approaching him with the question: *"Oubli ou regret?"* interrupted the conversation, which had become so tantalizingly interesting to Lizaveta.

The lady chosen by Tomsky was the Princess Pauline herself. She succeeded in effecting a reconciliation with him by making an extra turn in the dance and managing to delay resuming her seat. On returning to his place, Tomsky thought no more either of Hermann or Lizaveta. She longed to renew the interrupted conversation, but the mazurka came to an end, and shortly afterward the old Countess took her departure.

Tomsky's words were nothing more than the small talk of the mazurka, but they sank deep into the soul of the young dreamer. The portrait, sketched by Tomsky, agreed with the picture she had formed in her own mind, and that image, rendered commonplace by current novels, terrified and fascinated her imagination. She was now sitting with her bare arms crossed and her head, still adorned with flowers, was bowed over her half-uncovered breast. Suddenly the door opened and Hermann entered. She shuddered.

"Where have you been?" she asked in a frightened whisper.

"In the old Countess' bedroom," replied Hermann. "I have just left her. The Countess is dead."

"My God! What are you saying?"

"And I am afraid," added Hermann, "that I am the cause of her death."

Lizaveta looked at him, and Tomsky's words found an echo in her soul: "This man has at least three crimes upon his conscience!" Hermann sat down by the window near her, and related all that had happened.

Lizaveta listened to him in terror. So all those passionate letters, those ardent demands, this bold obstinate pursuit—all this was not love! Money—that was what his soul yearned for! She could not satisfy his desire and make him happy! The poor girl had been nothing but the blind accomplice of a robber, of the murderer of her aged benefactress! . . . She wept bitter tears of belated, agonized repentance. Hermann gazed at her in silence: his heart, too, was tormented, but neither the tears of the poor girl, nor the wonderful charm of her beauty, enhanced by her grief, could produce any impression upon his hardened soul. He felt no pricking of conscience at the thought of the dead old woman. One thing only horrified him: the irreparable loss of the secret which he had expected would bring him wealth.

"You are a monster!" said Lizaveta at last.

"I did not wish her death," replied Hermann: "my pistol is not loaded."

Both grew silent.

The day began to dawn. Lizaveta extinguished her candle: a pale light illumined her room. She wiped her tear-stained eyes and raised them toward Hermann: he was sitting on the window sill, with his arms folded and frowning fiercely. In this attitude he bore a striking resemblance to the portrait of Napoleon. This resemblance struck even Lizaveta Ivanovna.

"How shall I get you out of the house?" said she at last. "I thought of conducting you down the secret staircase, but in that case it would be necessary to go through the Countess' bedroom, and I am afraid."

"Tell me how to find this secret staircase—I will go alone."

Lizaveta arose, took from her drawer a key, handed it to Hermann and gave him the necessary instructions. Hermann pressed her cold, unresponsive hand, kissed her bowed head, and left the room.

He descended the winding staircase, and once more entered the Countess' bedroom. The dead old woman sat as if petrified; her face expressed profound tranquillity. Hermann stopped before her, and gazed long and earnestly at her, as if he wished to convince himself of the terrible reality; at last he entered the study, felt behind the tapestry for the door, and then began to descend the dark staircase, agitated by strange emotions. "At this very hour," thought he, "some sixty years ago, a young gallant, who has long been moldering in his grave, may have stolen down this very staircase, perhaps coming from the very same bedroom, wearing an embroidered caftan, with his hair dressed *à l'oiseau royal* and pressing to his heart his three-cornered hat, and the heart of his aged mistress has only today ceased to beat. . . ."

At the bottom of the staircase Hermann found a door, which he opened with the same key, and found himself in a corridor which led him into the street.

V

That night the deceased Baroness von W. appeared to me. She was clad all in white and said to me: "How are you, Mr. Councilor?"

SWEDENBORG

THREE DAYS after the fatal night, at nine o'clock in the morning, Hermann repaired to the Convent of ——, where the burial service for the deceased Countess was to be held. Although feeling no remorse, he could not altogether stifle the voice of conscience, which kept repeating to him: "You are the murderer of the old woman!" While he had little true faith, he was very superstitious; and believing that the dead Countess might exercise an evil influence on his life, he resolved to be present at her funeral in order to ask her pardon.

The church was full. It was with difficulty that Hermann made his way through the crowd. The coffin stood on a sumptuous catafalque under a velvet baldachin. The deceased lay within it, her hands crossed upon her breast, and wearing a lace cap and a white satin gown. Around the catafalque stood the members of her household: the servants in black caftans, with armorial ribbons upon their shoulders, and candles in their hands; the relatives—children, grandchildren, and great-grandchildren—in deep mourning.

Nobody wept; tears would have been *une affectation*. The Countess was so old that her death could have surprised nobody, and her relatives had long looked upon her as not among the living. A famous preacher delivered the funeral oration. In simple and touching words he described the peaceful passing away of the saintly woman whose long life had been a serene, moving preparation for a Christian end. "The angel of death found her," said the preacher, "engaged in pious meditation and waiting for the midnight bridegroom."

The service concluded in an atmosphere of melancholy decorum. The relatives went forward first to bid farewell to the deceased. Then followed the numerous acquaintances, who had come to render the last homage to her who for so many years had participated in their frivolous amusements. After these followed the members of the Countess' household. The last of these was the old housekeeper who was of the same age as the deceased. Two young women led her forward, supporting her by the arms. She had not strength enough to bow down to the ground—she was the only one to shed a few tears and kiss the cold hand of her mistress.

Hermann now resolved to approach the coffin. He bowed down to the ground and for several minutes lay on the cold floor, which was strewn with fir boughs; at last he arose, as pale as the deceased Countess herself, ascended the steps of the catafalque and bent over the corpse. . . . At that moment it seemed to him that the dead woman darted a mocking look at him and winked with one eye. Hermann started back, took a false step and fell to the ground. He was lifted up. At the same moment Lizaveta Ivanovna was carried into the vestibule of the church in a faint. This episode disturbed for some minutes the solemnity of the gloomy ceremony. Among the congregation arose a muffled murmur, and the lean chamberlain, a near relative of the deceased, whispered in the ear of an Englishman who was standing near him, that the young officer was a natural son of the Countess, to which the Englishman coldly replied: "Oh!"

During the whole of that day, Hermann was exceedingly perturbed. Dining in an out-of-the-way restaurant, he drank a great deal of wine, contrary to his usual custom, in the hope of allaying his inward agitation. But the wine only served to excite his imagination still more. On returning home, he threw himself upon his bed without undressing, and fell into a deep sleep.

When he woke up it was already night, and the moon was shining into the room. He looked at his watch: it was a quarter to three. Sleep had left him; he sat down upon his bed and thought of the funeral of the old Countess.

At that moment somebody in the street looked in at his window, and immediately passed on again. Hermann paid no attention to this incident. A few moments afterward he heard the door of the anteroom open. Hermann thought that it was his orderly, drunk as usual, returning from some nocturnal expedition, but presently he heard footsteps that were unknown to him: somebody was shuffling softly across the floor in slippers. The door opened, and a woman, dressed in white, entered the room. Hermann mistook her for his old nurse, and wondered what could bring her there at that hour of the night. But the white woman glided rapidly across the room and stood before him—and Hermann recognized the Countess!

"I have come to you against my will," she said in a firm voice: "but I have been ordered to grant your request. Three, seven, ace will win for you if played in succession, but only on these conditions: that you do not play more than one card in twenty-four hours, and that you never play again during the rest of your life. I forgive you my death, on condition that you marry my ward, Lizaveta Ivanovna."

With these words she turned round very quietly, walked with a shuffling gait toward the door and disappeared. Hermann heard the street door bang, and he saw someone look in at him through the window again.

For a long time Hermann could not recover himself. Then he went into the next room. His orderly was asleep upon the floor, and he had much difficulty in waking him. The orderly was drunk as usual, and nothing could be got out of him. The street door was locked. Hermann returned to his room, lit his candle, and set down an account of his vision.

VI

"Attendez!"
"How dare you say attendez *to me?"*
"Your Excellency, I said: 'Attendez, sir.' "

TWO FIXED IDEAS can no more exist together in the moral world than two bodies can occupy one and the same place in the physical world. "Three, seven, ace" soon drove out of Hermann's mind the thought of the dead Countess. "Three, seven, ace" were perpetually running through his head and continually on his lips. If he saw a young girl, he would say: "How slender she is! Quite like the three of hearts." If anybody asked: "What is the time?" he would reply: "Five minutes to seven." Every stout man that he saw reminded him of the ace. "Three, seven, ace" haunted him in his sleep, and assumed all possible shapes. The three bloomed before him in the form of a magnificent flower, the seven was represented by a Gothic portal, and the ace became transformed into a gigantic spider. One thought alone occupied his whole mind—to make use of the secret which he had pur-

chased so dearly. He thought of applying for a furlough so
as to travel abroad. He wanted to go to Paris and force fortune to yield a treasure to him in the public gambling houses
there. Chance spared him all this trouble.

There was in Moscow a society of wealthy gamblers, pre-
sided over by the celebrated Chekalinsky, who had passed
all his life at the card table and had amassed millions, accepting bills of exchange for his winnings and paying his losses
in ready money. His long experience secured for him the confidence of his companions, and his open house, his famous
cook, and his agreeable and cheerful manner gained for him
the respect of the public. He came to St. Petersburg. The
young men of the capital flocked to his rooms, forgetting
balls for cards, and preferring the temptations of faro to the
seductions of flirting. Narumov conducted Hermann to
Chekalinsky's residence.

They passed through a suite of magnificent rooms, filled
with courteous attendants. Several generals and privy counselors were playing whist; young men were lolling carelessly
upon the velvet-covered sofas, eating ices and smoking pipes.
In the drawing room, at the head of a long table, around
which crowded about a score of players, sat the master of the
house keeping the bank. He was a man of about sixty years
of age, of a very dignified appearance; his head was covered
with silvery-white hair; his full, florid countenance expressed
good nature, and his eyes twinkled with a perpetual smile.
Narumov introduced Hermann to him. Chekalinsky shook
him by the hand in a friendly manner, requested him not to
stand on ceremony, and then went on dealing.

The game lasted a long time. On the table lay more than
thirty cards. Chekalinsky paused after each throw, in order
to give the players time to arrange their cards and note down
their losses, listened politely to their requests, and more po-

litely still, straightened out the corners of cards that some absent-minded player's hand had turned down. At last the game was finished. Chekalinsky shuffled the cards and prepared to deal again.

"Allow me to play a card," said Hermann, stretching out his hand from behind a stout gentleman who was punting.

Chekalinsky smiled and bowed silently, as a sign of acquiescence. Narumov laughingly congratulated Hermann on ending his long abstention from cards, and wished him a lucky beginning.

"Here goes!" said Hermann, writing the figure with chalk on the back of his card.

"How much, sir?" asked the banker, screwing up his eyes. "Excuse me, I cannot see quite clearly."

"Forty-seven thousand," replied Hermann.

At these words every head in the room turned suddenly round, and all eyes were fixed upon Hermann.

"He has taken leave of his senses!" thought Narumov.

"Allow me to observe," said Chekalinsky, with his eternal smile, "that that is a very high stake; nobody here has ever staked more than two hundred and seventy-five rubles at a time."

"Well," retorted Hermann, "do you accept my card or not?"

Chekalinsky bowed with the same look of humble acquiescence.

"I only wish to inform you," said he, "that enjoying the full confidence of my partners, I can only play for ready money. For my own part, I am, of course, quite convinced that your word is sufficient, but for the sake of order, and because of the accounts, I must ask you to put the money on your card."

Hermann drew from his pocket a banknote and handed it

to Chekalinsky, who, after examining it in a cursory manner, placed it on Hermann's card.

He began to deal. On the right a nine turned up, and on the left a three.

"I win!" said Hermann, showing his card.

A murmur of astonishment arose among the players. Chekalinsky frowned, but the smile quickly returned to his face.

"Do you wish me to settle with you?" he said to Hermann.

"If you please," replied the latter.

Chekalinsky drew from his pocket a number of banknotes and paid up at once. Hermann took his money and left the table. Narumov could not recover from his astonishment. Hermann drank a glass of lemonade and went home.

The next evening he again appeared at Chekalinsky's. The host was dealing. Hermann walked up to the table; the punters immediately made room for him. Chekalinsky greeted him with a gracious bow.

Hermann waited for the next game, took a card and placed upon it his forty-seven thousand rubles, together with his winnings of the previous evening.

Chekalinsky began to deal. A knave turned up on the right, a seven on the left.

Hermann showed his seven.

There was a general exclamation. Chekalinsky was obviously disturbed, but he counted out the ninety-four thousand rubles and handed them over to Hermann, who pocketed them in the coolest manner possible and immediately left the house.

The next evening Hermann appeared again at the table. Everyone was expecting him. The generals and privy counselors left their whist in order to watch such extraordinary play. The young officers jumped up from their sofas, and even the servants crowded into the room. All pressed round

Hermann. The other players left off punting, impatient to see how it would end. Hermann stood at the table and prepared to play alone against the pale but still smiling Chekalinsky. Each opened a new pack of cards. Chekalinsky shuffled. Hermann took a card and covered it with a pile of banknotes. It was like a duel. Deep silence reigned.

Chekalinsky began to deal; his hands trembled. On the right a queen turned up, and on the left an ace.

"Ace wins!" cried Hermann, showing his card.

"Your queen has lost," said Chekalinsky sweetly.

Hermann started; instead of an ace, there lay before him the queen of spades! He could not believe his eyes, nor could he understand how he had made such a mistake.

At that moment it seemed to him that the queen of spades screwed up her eyes and sneered. He was struck by the remarkable resemblance. . . .

"The old woman!" he exclaimed, in terror.

Chekalinsky gathered up his winnings. For some time Hermann remained perfectly motionless. When at last he left the table, the room buzzed with loud talk.

"Splendidly punted!" said the players. Chekalinsky shuffled the cards afresh, and the game went on as usual.

CONCLUSION

Hermann went out of his mind. He is now confined in room Number 17 of the Obukhov Hospital. He never answers any questions, but he constantly mutters with unusual rapidity: "Three, seven, ace! Three, seven, queen!"

Lizaveta Ivanovna has married a very amiable young man, a son of the former steward of the old Countess. He is a civil servant, and has a considerable fortune. Lizaveta is bringing up a poor relative.

Tomsky has been promoted to the rank of captain, and is marrying Princess Pauline.

Kirdjali

KIRDJALI was by birth a Bulgarian. Kirdjali, in the Turkish language, signifies a knight, a daredevil. His real name I do not know.

Kirdjali with his brigandage brought terror upon the whole of Moldavia. In order to give some idea of him, I will relate one of his exploits. One night he and the Arnaut Michaelaki fell together upon a Bulgarian village. They set it on fire at both ends, and began to go from hut to hut. Kirdjali cut throats, and Michaelaki carried off the booty. Both shouted: "Kirdjali! Kirdjali!" The whole village took to flight.

When Alexander Ypsilanti[1] proclaimed the revolt and began to collect his army, Kirdjali brought him several of his old companions. The real object of the Hetaeria was but ill understood by them, but war presented an opportunity for getting rich at the expense of the Turks, and perhaps of the Moldavians, and that was plain to them.

Alexander Ypsilanti was personally brave, but he did not possess the qualities necessary for the role which he had assumed with such ardor and such want of caution. He did not know how to manage the people whom he was obliged to lead. They had neither respect for him nor confidence in

[1] The chief of the Hetaerists, whose object was the liberation of Greece from the Turkish yoke (TRANSLATOR'S NOTE).

him. After the unhappy battle, in which the flower of Greek youth perished, Iordaki Olimbioti persuaded him to retire, and he himself took his place. Ypsilanti escaped to the borders of Austria, and thence sent his curses to the men whom he called traitors, cowards, and scoundrels. These cowards and scoundrels for the most part perished within the walls of the monastery of Seko, or on the banks of the Pruth, desperately defending themselves against an enemy outnumbering them ten to one.

Kirdjali found himself in the detachment of George Kantakuzin, of whom might be repeated exactly what has been said of Ypsilanti. On the eve of the battle of Skulyani, Kantakuzin asked permission of the Russian authorities to enter our territory. The detachment remained without a leader, but Kirdjali, Saphianos, Kantagoni, and others stood in no need whatever of a leader.

The battle of Skulyani does not seem to have been described by anybody in all its affecting reality. Imagine seven hundred men—Arnauts, Albanians, Greeks, Bulgarians, and every kind of riff-raff—with no idea of military art, retreating in sight of fifteen thousand Turkish cavalry. This detachment hugged the bank of the Pruth, and placed in front of themselves two small cannon, which they had found at Jassy, in the courtyard of the governor, and from which salutes used to be fired during name-day feasts. The Turks would have been glad to use grapeshot, but they dared not without the permission of the Russian authorities: the shots would infallibly have flown over to our shore. The commander of our quarantine station (now deceased), although he had served forty years in the army, had never in his life heard the whistle of a bullet, but Heaven ordained that he should hear it then. Several of them whizzed past his ears. The old man became terribly angry, and abused the major of the Okhotsky infantry regiment, which was attached to the station. The major, not knowing what to do, ran to the river, beyond which Turkish cavalrymen were displaying their prowess, and threatened them with his finger. Seeing this, they turned round and galloped off, with the whole Turkish detachment after them. The major, who had threatened them with his finger, was called Khorchevsky. I do not know what became of him.

The next day, however, the Turks attacked the Hetaerists. Not daring to use grapeshot or cannonballs, they resolved, contrary to their usual custom, to employ cold steel. The battle was fierce. Men slashed each other with yataghans. The Turks used lances, which they had not employed till then; these lances were Russian: Nekrassovists[2] fought in their ranks. The Hetaerists, by permission of our Emperor, were allowed to cross the Pruth and take refuge in our quarantine station. They began to cross over. Kantagoni and Saphianos remained upon the Turkish bank. Kirdjali, wounded the evening before, was already within our territory. Saphianos was killed. Kantagoni, a very stout man, was wounded in the stomach by a lance. With one hand he raised his sword, with the other he seized the hostile lance, thrust it further into himself, and in that manner was able to reach his murderer with his sword, when both fell together.

All was over. The Turks remained victorious. Moldavia was swept clear of insurrectionary bands. About six hundred Arnauts were scattered over Bessarabia; if they did not know how to support themselves, they were yet grateful to Russia for her protection. They led an idle life, but not a dissipated one. They could always be seen in the coffee houses of half-Turkish Bessarabia, with long pipes in their mouths, sipping coffee grounds out of small cups. Their figured jackets and

[2] Russian dissidents settled in Turkey (EDITOR'S NOTE).

pointed red slippers were already beginning to wear out, but their tufted skullcaps were still worn on the side of the head, and yataghans and pistols still protruded from their broad sashes. Nobody complained of them. It was impossible to imagine that these poor, peaceably disposed men were the notorious klephts of Moldavia, the companions of the ferocious Kirdjali, and that he himself was among them.

The Pasha in command at Jassy became informed of this, and, in virtue of treaty stipulation, requested the Russian authorities to extradite the brigand.

The police instituted a search. They discovered that Kirdjali was really in Kishinev. They captured him in the house of a fugitive monk in the evening, when he was having supper, sitting in the dark with seven companions.

Kirdjali was placed under arrest. He did not try to conceal the truth; he acknowledged that he was Kirdjali.

"But," he added, "since I crossed the Pruth, I have not taken so much as a pin, or imposed upon even the lowest gypsy. To the Turks, to the Moldavians and to the Wallachians I am undoubtedly a brigand, but to the Russians I am a guest. When Saphianos, having fired off all his grape-shot came here, collecting from the wounded, for the last shots, buttons, nails, watch chains and the knobs of yataghans, I gave him twenty *beshliks*,[3] and was left without money. God knows that I, Kirdjali, have been living on charity. Why then do the Russians now deliver me into the hands of my enemies?"

After that, Kirdjali was silent, and tranquilly awaited the decision that was to determine his fate. He did not wait long. The authorities, not being bound to look upon brigands from their romantic side, and being convinced of the justice of the demand, ordered Kirdjali to be sent to Jassy.

[3] A small silver Turkish coin (EDITOR'S NOTE).

A man of heart and intellect, at that time a young and unknown official, who is now occupying an important post, vividly described to me his departure.

At the gate of the prison stood a *caruta*. . . . Perhaps you do not know what a *caruta* is. It is a low wicker vehicle, to which, not very long since, there were generally harnessed six or eight sorry jades. A Moldavian, with a mustache and a sheepskin cap, sitting astride one of them, incessantly shouted and cracked his whip, and his wretched animals ran on at a fairly sharp trot. If one of them began to slacken its pace, he unharnessed it with terrible oaths and left it upon the road, little caring what might be its fate. On the return journey he was sure to find it in the same place, quietly grazing upon the green steppe. It not infrequently happened that a traveler, starting from one station with eight horses, arrived at the next with a pair only. It used to be so about fifteen years ago. Nowadays in Russianized Bessarabia they have adopted Russian harness and the Russian *telega*.

Such a *caruta* stood at the gate of the prison in the year 1821, toward the end of the month of September. Jewesses who wore drooping sleeves and loose slippers, Arnauts in their ragged and picturesque attire, well-proportioned Moldavian women with black-eyed children in their arms, surrounded the *caruta*. The men preserved silence; the women were eagerly expecting something.

The gate opened, and several police officers stepped out into the street; behind them came two soldiers leading the fettered Kirdjali.

He seemed about thirty years of age. The features of his swarthy face were regular and harsh. He was tall, broad-shouldered, and seemed endowed with unusual physical strength. A variegated turban covered the side of his head, and a broad sash encircled his slender waist. A dolman of thick, dark blue cloth, a shirt, its broad folds falling below the knee, and handsome slippers composed the remainder of his costume. His look was proud and calm. . . .

One of the officials, a red-faced old man in a faded uniform, on which dangled three buttons, pinched with a pair of pewter spectacles the purple knob that served him for a nose, unfolded a paper, and began to read nasally in the Moldavian tongue. From time to time he glanced haughtily at the fettered Kirdjali, to whom apparently the paper referred. Kirdjali listened to him attentively. The official finished his reading, folded up the paper and shouted sternly at the people, ordering them to make way and the *caruta* to be driven up. Then Kirdjali turned to him and said a few words to him in Moldavian; his voice trembled, his countenance changed, he burst into tears and fell at the feet of the police official, clanking his fetters. The police official, terrified, started back; the soldiers were about to raise Kirdjali, but he rose up himself, gathered up his chains, stepped into the *caruta* and cried: "Drive on!" A gendarme took a seat beside him, the Moldavian cracked his whip, and the *caruta* rolled away.

"What did Kirdjali say to you?" asked the young official of the police officer.

"He asked me," replied the police officer, smiling, "to look after his wife and child, who live not far from Kilia, in a Bulgarian village: he is afraid that they may suffer through him. Foolish fellow!"

The young official's story affected me deeply. I was sorry for poor Kirdjali. For a long time I knew nothing of his fate. Some years later I met the young official. We began to talk about the past.

"What about your friend Kirdjali?" I asked. "Do you know what became of him?"

"To be sure I do," he replied, and related to me the following.

Kirdjali, having been brought to Jassy, was taken before the Pasha, who condemned him to be impaled. The execution was deferred till some holiday. In the meantime he was confined in jail.

The prisoner was guarded by seven Turks (simple people, and at heart as much brigands as Kirdjali himself); they respected him and, like all Orientals, listened with avidity to his strange stories.

Between the guards and the prisoner an intimate acquaintance sprang up. One day Kirdjali said to them: "Brothers, my hour is near! Nobody can escape his fate. I shall soon part from you. I should like to leave you something in remembrance of me."

The Turks pricked up their ears.

"Brothers," continued Kirdjali, "three years ago, when I was engaged in plundering along with the late Michaelaki, we buried on the steppes not far from Jassy, a kettle filled with coins. Evidently, neither I nor he will make use of the hoard. Be it so; take it for yourselves and divide it in a friendly manner."

The Turks almost took leave of their senses. The question was, how were they to find the precious spot? They thought and thought and resolved that Kirdjali himself should conduct them to the place.

Night came on. The Turks removed the irons from the feet of the prisoner, tied his hands with a rope, and, leaving the town, set out with him for the steppe.

Kirdjali led them, walking steadily in one direction from mound to mound. They walked on for a long time. At last Kirdjali stopped near a broad stone, measured twelve paces toward the south, stamped and said: "Here."

The Turks began to make their arrangements. Four of them took out their yataghans and commenced digging. Three remained on guard. Kirdjali sat down on the stone and watched them at their work.

"Well, how much longer are you going to be?" he asked. "Haven't you come to it?"

"Not yet," replied the Turks, and they worked away with such ardor that the perspiration rolled from them in great drops.

Kirdjali began to show signs of impatience.

"What people!" he exclaimed. "They do not even know how to dig decently. I should have finished the whole business in a couple of minutes. Children, untie my hands and give me a yataghan."

The Turks reflected and began to take counsel together. "What harm would there be?" reasoned they. "Let us untie his hands and give him a yataghan. He is only one, we are seven."

And the Turks untied his hands and gave him a yataghan.

At last Kirdjali was free and armed. What must he have felt at that moment! . . . He began digging quickly, the guards helping him. . . . Suddenly he plunged his yataghan into one of them, and, leaving the blade in his breast, he snatched from his belt a couple of pistols.

The remaining six, seeing Kirdjali armed with two pistols, ran off.

Kirdjali is now operating near Jassy. Not long ago he wrote to the governor, demanding from him five thousand leus, and threatening, should the money not be forthcoming, to set fire to Jassy and to get at the governor himself. The five thousand were delivered to him!

Such is Kirdjali!

The Negro of Peter the Great

[UNFINISHED]

I

AMONG the young men sent abroad by Peter the Great for the acquisition of knowledge indispensable to a country in a state of transition, was his godson, the Negro, Ibrahim. After being educated in the Military School at Paris, which he left with the rank of Captain of Artillery, he distinguished himself in the Spanish war and, severely wounded, returned to Paris. The Emperor, in the midst of his vast labors, never ceased to inquire after his favorite, and he always received flattering accounts of his progress and conduct. Peter was exceedingly pleased with him, and repeatedly requested him to return to Russia, but Ibrahim was in no hurry. He excused himself under various pretexts: now it was his wound, now it was a wish to complete his education, now a want of money; and Peter indulgently complied with his wishes, begged him to take care of his health, thanked him for his zeal for study, and although extremely thrifty where his own expenses were concerned, he did not stint his favorite in money, adding to the ducats fatherly advice and cautionary admonition.

According to the testimony of all the historical memoirs, nothing could be compared with the frivolity, folly, and luxury of the French of that period. The last years of the reign of Louis the Fourteenth, remarkable for the strict piety, gravity, and decorum of the Court, had left no traces behind. The Duke of Orleans, uniting many brilliant qualities with vices of every kind, unfortunately did not possess the slightest shadow of hypocrisy. The orgies of the Palais Royal were no secret in Paris; the example was infectious. At that time Law[1] appeared upon the scene; greed for money was united to the thirst for pleasure and dissipation; estates were squandered, morals perished, Frenchmen laughed and calculated, and the kingdom was falling apart to the playful refrains of satirical vaudevilles.

In the meantime society presented a most entertaining picture. Culture and the need of amusement brought all ranks together. Wealth, amiability, renown, talent, even eccentricity—everything that fed curiosity or promised pleasure, was received with the same indulgence. Literature, learning and philosophy forsook their quiet studies and appeared in the circles of the great world to render homage to fashion and to govern it. Women reigned, but no longer demanded adoration. Superficial politeness replaced the profound respect formerly shown to them. The pranks of the Duke de Richelieu, the Alcibiades of modern Athens, belong to history, and give an idea of the morals of that period.

---

[1] John Law, the famous projector of financial schemes (TRANSLATOR'S NOTE).

Tems fortuné, marqué par la licence,
Où la folie, agitant son grelot,
D'un pied léger parcourt toute la France,
Où nul mortel ne daigne être dévot,
Où l'on fait tout excepté pénitence.

The appearance of Ibrahim, his looks, culture and native intelligence excited general attention in Paris. All the ladies were anxious to see "le nègre du czar" at their houses, and vied with each other in trying to capture him. The Regent invited him more than once to his merry evening parties; he assisted at the suppers animated by the youth of Arouet, the old age of Chaulieu, and the conversations of Montesquieu and Fontenelle. He did not miss a single ball, fete, or first night, and he gave himself up to the general whirl with all the ardor of his years and nature. But the thought of exchanging these distractions, these brilliant amusements for the harsh simplicity of the Petersburg Court was not the only thing that dismayed Ibrahim; other and stronger ties bound him to Paris. The young African was in love.

The Countess D——, although no longer in the first bloom of youth, was still renowned for her beauty. On leaving the convent at seventeen, she had been married to a man with whom she had not had time to fall in love, and who later on did not take the trouble to gain her affection. Rumor ascribed several lovers to her, but such was the indulgence of the world, that she enjoyed a good reputation, for nobody was able to reproach her with any ridiculous or scandalous adventure. Her house was one of the most fashionable, and the best Parisian society made it their rendezvous. Ibrahim was introduced to her by young Merville, who was generally looked upon as her latest lover—and who did all in his power to attain credit for the report.

The Countess received Ibrahim courteously, but without any particular attention: this flattered him. Generally the young Negro was regarded in the light of a curiosity; people used to surround him and overwhelm him with compliments and questions—and this curiosity, although concealed by a show of graciousness, offended his vanity. Women's delightful attention, almost the sole aim of our exertions, not only afforded him no pleasure, but even filled him with bitterness and indignation. He felt that he was for them a kind of rare beast, a peculiar alien creature, accidentally brought into a world, with which he had nothing in common. He even envied people who remained unnoticed, and considered them fortunate in their insignificance.

The thought, that nature had not created him to enjoy requited love, saved him from self-assurance and vain pretensions, and added a rare charm to his behavior toward women. His conversation was simple and dignified; he pleased Countess D——, who had grown tired of the eternal jokes and subtle insinuations of French wits. Ibrahim frequently visited her. Little by little she became accustomed to the young Negro's appearance, and even began to find something agreeable in that curly head, that stood out so black in the midst of the powdered perukes in her reception room (Ibrahim had been wounded in the head, and wore a bandage instead of a peruke). He was twenty-seven years of age, and was tall and slender, and more than one beauty glanced at him with a feeling more flattering than simple curiosity. But the prejudiced Ibrahim either did not observe anything of this or merely looked upon it as coquetry. But when his glances met those of the Countess, his distrust vanished. Her eyes expressed such winning kindness, her manner toward him was so simple, so unconstrained, that it was impossible to suspect her of the least shadow of coquetry or raillery.

The thought of love had not entered his head, but to see the Countess each day had become a necessity to him. He sought her out everywhere, and every meeting with her seemed an unexpected favor from Heaven. The Countess guessed his feelings before he himself did. There is no denying that a love, which is without hope and which demands nothing, touches the female heart more surely than all the devices of seduction. In the presence of Ibrahim, the Countess followed all his movements, listened to every word that he said; without him she became thoughtful, and fell into her usual abstraction. Merville was the first to observe this mutual inclination, and he congratulated Ibrahim. Nothing inflames love so much as the encouraging observations of a bystander: love is blind, and, having no trust in itself, readily grasps hold of every support.

Merville's words roused Ibrahim. He had never till then imagined the possibility of possessing the woman that he loved; hope suddenly illumined his soul; he fell madly in love. In vain did the Countess, alarmed by the ardor of his passion, seek to oppose to it the admonitions of friendship and the counsels of prudence; she herself was beginning to weaken. . . . Incautious rewards swiftly followed one another. And at last, carried away by the force of the passion she had herself inspired, surrendering to its influence, she gave herself to the ravished Ibrahim. . . .

Nothing is hidden from the eyes of the observing world. The Countess' new liaison was soon known to everybody. Some ladies were amazed at her choice; to many it seemed quite natural. Some laughed; others regarded her conduct as unpardonably indiscreet. In the first intoxication of passion, Ibrahim and the Countess noticed nothing, but soon the equivocal jokes of the men and the pointed remarks of the women began to reach their ears. Ibrahim's cold and dignified manner had hitherto protected him from such attacks; he bore them with impatience, and knew not how to ward them off. The Countess, accustomed to the respect of the world, could not calmly bear to see herself an object of gossip and ridicule. With tears in her eyes she complained to Ibrahim, now bitterly reproaching him, now imploring him not to defend her, lest by some useless scandal she should be completely ruined.

A new circumstance further complicated her position: the consequence of imprudent love began to be apparent. Consolation, advice, proposals—all were exhausted and all rejected. The Countess saw that her ruin was inevitable, and in despair awaited it.

As soon as the condition of the Countess became known, tongues wagged again with fresh vigor; sentimental women gave vent to exclamations of horror; men wagered as to whether the Countess would give birth to a white or a black baby. Numerous epigrams were aimed at her husband, who alone in all Paris knew nothing and suspected nothing.

The fatal moment approached. The condition of the Countess was terrible. Ibrahim visited her every day. He saw her mental and physical strength gradually giving way. Her tears and her terror were renewed every moment. Finally she felt the first pains. Measures were hastily taken. Means were found for getting the Count out of the way. The doctor arrived. Two days before this a poor woman had been persuaded to surrender to strangers her new-born infant; a trusted person had been sent for it. Ibrahim was in the room adjoining the bedchamber where the unhappy Countess lay; not daring to breathe, he heard her muffled groans, the maid's whisper, and the doctor's orders. Her sufferings lasted a long time. Her every groan lacerated his heart. Every interval of silence overwhelmed him with terror. . . . Suddenly he heard the weak cry of a baby—and, unable to repress his elation, he rushed into the Countess' room. . . . A black baby lay upon the bed at her feet. Ibrahim approached it. His heart beat violently. He blessed his son with a trembling hand. The Countess smiled faintly and stretched out to him her feeble hand, but the doctor, fearing that the excitement might be too great for the patient, dragged Ibrahim away from her bed. The new-born child was placed in a covered basket, and carried out of the house by a secret staircase. Then the other child was brought in, and its cradle placed in the bedroom. Ibrahim took his departure, feeling somewhat more at ease. The Count was expected. He returned late, heard of the happy delivery of his wife, and was much gratified. In this way the public, which had been expecting a great scandal, was deceived in its hope, and was compelled to console itself with malicious gossip alone. Everything resumed its usual course.

But Ibrahim felt that there would have to be a change in his lot, and that sooner or later his relations with the Countess would come to the knowledge of her husband. In that case, whatever might happen, the ruin of the Countess was inevitable. Ibrahim loved passionately and was passionately loved in return, but the Countess was willful and frivolous; it was not the first time that she had loved. Disgust and even hatred might replace in her heart the most tender feelings. Ibrahim already foresaw the moment when she would cool toward him. Hitherto he had not known jealousy, but with dread he now felt a presentiment of it; he thought that the pain of separation would be less distressing, and he resolved to break off the unhappy connection, leave Paris, and return to Russia, whither Peter and a vague sense of duty had been calling him for a long time.

II

DAYS, months passed, and the enamored Ibrahim could not resolve to leave the woman that he had seduced. The Countess grew more and more attached to him. Their son was being brought up in a distant province. The slanders of the world were beginning to subside, and the lovers began to enjoy greater tranquillity, silently remembering the past storm and endeavoring not to think of the future.

One day Ibrahim attended a levee at the Duke of Orleans' residence. The Duke, passing by him, stopped, and handing him a letter, told him to read it at his leisure. It was a letter from Peter the First. The Emperor, guessing the true cause of his absence, wrote to the Duke that he had no intention of compelling Ibrahim, that he left it to his own free will to return to Russia or not, but that in any case he would never abandon his former foster child. This letter touched Ibrahim to the bottom of his heart. From that moment his lot was settled. The next day he informed the Regent of his intention to set out immediately for Russia.

"Consider what you are doing," said the Duke to him. "Russia is not your native country. I do not think that you will ever again see your torrid birthplace, but your long residence in France has made you equally a stranger to the climate and the ways of life of half-savage Russia. You were not born a subject of Peter. Listen to my advice: take advantage of his magnanimous permission, remain in France, for which you have already shed your blood, and rest assured that here your services and talents will not remain unrewarded."

Ibrahim thanked the Duke sincerely, but remained firm in his resolution.

"I am sorry," said the Regent, "but perhaps you are right."

He promised to let him retire from the French service and wrote a full account of the matter to the Czar.

Ibrahim was soon ready for the journey. He spent the evening before his departure at the house of the Countess D——, as usual. She knew nothing. Ibrahim had not the heart to inform her of his intention. The Countess was calm and cheerful. She several times called him to her and joked about his being so pensive. After supper the guests departed. The Countess, her husband, and Ibrahim were left alone in the parlor. The unhappy man would have given everything in the world to have been left alone with her; but Count D—— seemed to have seated himself so comfortably beside the fire, that there was no hope of getting him out of the room. All three remained silent.

"*Bonne nuit!*" said the Countess at last.

Ibrahim's heart contracted and he suddenly felt all the horrors of parting. He stood motionless.

"*Bonne nuit, messieurs!*" repeated the Countess.

Still he remained motionless. . . . At last his eyes darkened, his head swam round, and he could scarcely walk out of the room. On reaching home, he wrote, almost unconsciously, the following letter:

I am going away, dear Leonora; I am leaving you forever. I am writing to you, because I have not the strength to tell it to you otherwise.

My happiness could not last: I have enjoyed it in spite of fate and nature. You were bound to stop loving me; the enchantment was bound to vanish. This thought has always pursued me, even in those moments when I have seemed to forget everything, when at you feet I have been intoxicated by your passionate self-denial, by your unbounded tenderness. . . . The frivolous world unmercifully persecutes in fact that which it permits in theory; its cold mockery sooner or later would have vanquished you, would have humbled your ardent soul, and at last you would have become ashamed of your passion. . . . What would then have become of me? No, it is better to die, better to leave you before that terrible moment.

Your peace is dearer to me than anything: you could not enjoy it while the eyes of the world were fixed upon us. Recall all that you have suffered, all the insults to your amour propre, all the tortures of fear; remember the terrible birth of our son. Think: ought I to expose you any longer to such agitations and dangers? Why should I endeavor to unite the fate of such a tender, beautiful creature to the miserable fate of a Negro, of a pitiable creature, scarce worthy of the name of man?

Farewell, Leonora; farewell, my dear and only friend. I am leaving you, I am leaving the first and last joy of my life. I have neither fatherland nor kindred; I am going to gloomy Russia, where my utter solitude will be a consolation to me. Serious work, to which from now on I shall devote myself, will at least divert me from, if not stifle, painful recollections of the days of rapture and bliss. . . . Farewell, Leonora! I tear myself away from this letter, as if from your embrace. Farewell, be happy, and think sometimes of the poor Negro, of your faithful Ibrahim.

That same night he set out for Russia.

The journey did not seem to him as terrible as he had expected. His imagination triumphed over the reality. The farther he got from Paris, the more vivid and nearer rose up before him the objects he was leaving forever.

Before he was aware of it he found himself at the Russian frontier. Autumn had already set in, but the coachmen, in spite of the bad state of the roads, drove him with the speed of the wind, and on the seventeenth day of his journey he arrived at Krasnoe Selo, through which at that time the high road passed.

It was still a distance of twenty-eight versts to Petersburg. While the horses were being hitched up, Ibrahim entered the post-house. In a corner, a tall man, in a green *caftan* and with a clay pipe in his mouth, his elbows upon the table, was reading the Hamburg newspapers. Hearing somebody enter, he raised his head.

"Ah, Ibrahim!" he exclaimed, rising from the bench. "How do you do, godson?"

Ibrahim recognized Peter, and in his delight was about to rush toward him, but he respectfully paused. The Emperor approached, embraced him, and kissed him upon the head.

"I was informed of your coming," said Peter, "and set off to meet you. I have been waiting for you here since yesterday."

Ibrahim could not find words to express his gratitude.

"Let your carriage follow on behind us," continued the Emperor, "and you take your place by my side and ride along with me."

The Czar's carriage was driven up; he took his seat with Ibrahim, and they set off at a gallop. In about an hour and a half they reached Petersburg. Ibrahim gazed with curiosity at the new-born city which was springing up out of the marsh at the beck of the autocrat. Bare dams, canals without embankments, wooden bridges everywhere testified to the recent triumph of the human will over the hostile elements. The houses seemed to have been built in a hurry. In the whole town there was nothing magnificent but the Neva, not yet ornamented with its granite frame, but already covered with warships and merchant vessels. The imperial carriage stopped at the palace, the so-called Czarina's Garden. On the steps Peter was met by a woman of about thirty-five years of age, handsome, and dressed in the lastest Parisian fashion. Peter kissed her on the lips and, taking Ibrahim by the hand, said: "Do you recognize my godson, Katinka? I beg you to treat him as kindly as you used to."

Catherine fixed on him her dark piercing eyes, and stretched out her hand to him in a friendly manner. Two young beauties, tall, slender, and fresh as roses, stood behind her and respectfully approached Peter. "Liza," said he to one of them, "do you remember the little Negro who stole my apples for you at Oranienbaum? Here he is; let me introduce him to you."

The Grand Duchess laughed and blushed. They went into the dining room. In expectation of the Czar, the table had been laid. Peter sat down to dinner with all his family, and invited Ibrahim to sit down with them. During dinner the Emperor conversed with him on various subjects, questioned him about the Spanish war, the internal affairs of France, and the Regent, whom he liked, although he condemned much in him. Ibrahim possessed an exact and observant mind. Peter was very pleased with his replies. He recalled to mind some features of Ibrahim's childhood, and related them with such good-humor and gaiety, that nobody could have suspected this kind and hospitable host to be the hero of Poltava, the dread and mighty reformer of Russia.

After dinner the Emperor, according to the Russian custom, retired to rest. Ibrahim remained with the Empress and the Grand Duchesses. He tried to satisfy their curiosity, described the Parisian way of life, the holidays that were kept there, and the changeable fashions. In the meantime, some of the persons belonging to the Emperor's suite had assembled in the palace. Ibrahim recognized the magnificent Prince Menshikov, who, seeing the Negro conversing with Catherine, cast an arrogant glance at him; Prince Jacob Dolgoruky, Peter's stern counselor; the learned Bruce, who had acquired among the people the name of the "Russian Faust"; the young Raguzinsky, his former companion, and others who had come to make their reports to the Emperor and to receive his orders.

In about two hours' time the Emperor appeared.

"Let us see," said he to Ibrahim, "if you have forgotten your old duties. Take a slate and follow me."

Peter shut himself up in his workroom and busied himself with state affairs. He worked in turns with Bruce, with Prince Dolgoruky, and with the chief of police, General Devier, and dictated to Ibrahim several ukases and decisions. Ibrahim could not sufficiently admire the quickness and firmness of his understanding, the strength and flexibility of his powers of attention, and the variety of his occupations. When the work was finished, Peter drew out a notebook in order to see if all that he had proposed to do that day had been accomplished. Then, issuing from the workroom, he said to Ibrahim: "It is late; no doubt you are tired—sleep here tonight, as you used to do in the old days; tomorrow I will wake you."

Ibrahim, on being left alone, could hardly collect his thoughts. He was in Petersburg; he saw again the great man, near whom, not yet knowing his worth, he had passed his childhood. Almost with regret he confessed to himself that the Countess D——, for the first time since their separation, had not been his sole thought during the whole of the day. He saw that the new mode of life which awaited him—the activity and constant occupation—would revive his soul, wearied by passion, idleness and secret grief. The thought of being a great man's co-worker and, together with him, influencing the fate of a great nation, aroused within him for the first time the noble feeling of ambition. In this disposition of mind he lay down upon the camp bed prepared for him, and then the usual dreams carried him back to far-off Paris, to the arms of his dear Countess.

III

THE NEXT MORNING, Peter, according to his promise, woke Ibrahim and congratulated him on his elevation to the rank of captain-lieutenant of the Artillery company of the Preobrazhensky Regiment, in which he himself was Captain. The courtiers surrounded Ibrahim, each in his way trying to be attentive to the new favorite. The haughty Prince Menshikov pressed his hand in a friendly manner; Sheremetyev inquired after his Parisian acquaintances, and Golovin invited him to dinner. Others followed the example of the latter, so that Ibrahim received enough invitations to last him at least a whole month.

Ibrahim now began to lead a monotonous but busy life, consequently he did not feel at all dull. From day to day he became more attached to the Emperor, and was better able to comprehend his lofty soul. To follow the thoughts of a great man is a most absorbing study. Ibrahim saw Peter in the Senate arguing weighty questions of legislation with Buturlin and Dolgoruky; with the Admiralty committee establishing the naval power of Russia; he saw him with Feofan, Gavril Buzhinsky, and Kopievich, in his free hours examining translations of foreign authors, or visiting the factory of a merchant, the workshop of a mechanic, or the study of a savant. Russia presented to Ibrahim the appearance of a huge workshop, where machines alone move, where each workman, subject to established rules, is occupied with his own particular business. He, too, felt obliged to work at his own bench, and he endeavored to regret as little as possible the gaieties of his Parisian life. But it was more difficult for him to drive from his mind another and dear memory: he often thought of the Countess D——, and pictured to himself her just indignation, her tears, and her despondency. . . . But sometimes a terrible thought oppressed his heart: the distractions of the great world, a new tie, another favorite—he shuddered; jealousy began to set his African blood boiling, and hot tears were ready to roll down his black face.

One morning he was sitting in his study, surrounded by business papers, when suddenly he heard a loud greeting in French. Ibrahim turned around quickly, and young Korsakov, whom he had left in Paris in the whirl of the great world, embraced him with joyful exclamations.

"I have only just arrived," said Korsakov, "and I have come straight to you. All our Parisian acquaintances send their greetings to you, and regret your absence. The Countess D—— ordered me to summon you to return without fail, and here is her letter to you."

Ibrahim seized it with a trembling hand and looked at the familiar handwriting of the address, not daring to believe his eyes.

"How glad I am," continued Korsakov, "that you have not yet died of ennui in this barbarous Petersburg! What do people do here? How do they occupy themselves? Who is your tailor? Have you opera, at least?"

Ibrahim absently replied that probably the Emperor was just then at work in the dockyard.

Korsakov laughed. "I see," said he, "that you can't attend to me just now; some other time we will talk to our heart's content; I will go now and pay my respects to the Emperor."

With these words he turned on his heel and hastened out of the room.

Ibrahim, left alone, hastily opened the letter. The Countess tenderly complained to him, reproaching him with dissimulation and distrust.

"You say," wrote she, "that my peace is dearer to you than everything in the world. Ibrahim, if this were the truth, would you have brought me to the condition to which I was reduced by the unexpected news of your departure? You were afraid that I might have detained you. Be assured that, in spite of my love, I should have known how to sacrifice it for your happiness and for what you consider your duty."

The Countess ended the letter with passionate assurances of love, and implored him to write to her, if only now and then, even though there should be no hope of their ever seeing each other again.

Ibrahim read this letter through twenty times, kissing the priceless lines with rapture. He was burning with impatience to hear something about the Countess, and he was just preparing to set out for the Admiralty, hoping to find Korsakov still there, when the door opened, and Korsakov himself appeared once more. He had already paid his respects to the Emperor, and as was usual with him, he seemed very well satisfied with himself.

"*Entre nous,*" he said to Ibrahim, "the Emperor is a very strange person. Just fancy, I found him in a sort of linen singlet, on the mast of a new ship, whither I was compelled to climb with my dispatches. I stood on the rope ladder, and had not sufficient room to make a suitable bow, and so I became completely confused, a thing that had never happened to me in my life before. However, when the Emperor had read my letter, he looked at me from head to foot, and no doubt was agreeably struck by the taste and smartness of my attire; at any rate he smiled and invited me to tonight's assembly. But I am a perfect stranger in Petersburg; in the six years that I have been away I have quite forgotten the local customs; pray be my mentor; call for me and introduce me."

Ibrahim agreed to do so, and hastened to turn the conversation to a subject that was more interesting to him. "Well, and how is the Countess D——?"

"The Countess? Of course, at first she was very much grieved on account of your departure; then, of course, little by little, she found solace and took a new lover: do you know whom? The lanky Marquis R——. Why are you staring at me so with your Negro eyes? Or does it seem strange to you? Don't you know that lasting grief is not in human nature, particularly in feminine nature? Chew on this, while I go and rest after my journey, and don't forget to come and call for me."

What feelings filled the soul of Ibrahim? Jealousy? Rage? Despair? No, but a deep, oppressing despondency. He repeated to himself: "I foresaw it, it had to happen." Then he opened the Countess's letter, read it again, hung his head and wept bitterly. He wept for a long time. The tears relieved his heart. Looking at the clock, he perceived that it was time to set out. Ibrahim would have been very glad to stay away, but the assembly was a matter of duty, and the Emperor strictly demanded the presence of his retainers. He dressed himself and started out to call for Korsakov.

Korsakov was sitting in his dressing gown, reading a French book. "So early?" he said to Ibrahim, on seeing him.

"Mercy," the latter replied; "it is already half past five, we shall be late; make haste and dress and let us go."

Korsakov, in a flurry, rang the bell with all his might; the servants came running in, and he began hastily to dress himself. His French valet gave him shoes with red heels, blue velvet breeches, and a pink *caftan* embroidered with spangles. His peruke was hurriedly powdered in the antechamber and brought in to him. Korsakov stuck his cropped head into it, asked for his sword and gloves, turned round about ten times before the glass, and then informed Ibrahim that he was ready. The footmen handed them their bearskin greatcoats, and they set out for the Winter Palace.

Korsakov overwhelmed Ibrahim with questions: Who was the greatest beauty in Petersburg? Who was supposed to be the best dancer? Which dance was just then the rage? Ibrahim very reluctantly gratified his curiosity. Meanwhile they reached the palace. A great number of long sledges, old-fashioned carriages, and gilded coaches already stood on the lawn. Near the steps were crowded liveried and mustachioed coachmen; messengers resplendent in tinsel and plumes, and bearing maces; Hussars, pages, and clumsy footmen loaded with the coats and muffs of their masters—a retinue indispensable according to the notions of the gentry of that time. At the sight of Ibrahim, a general murmur arose: "The Negro, the Negro, the Czar's Negro!" He hurriedly conducted Korsakov through this motley crowd. The Court lackey opened the doors wide, and they entered the hall. Korsakov was dumfounded. . . . In a large room, illuminated by tallow candles, which burnt dimly amidst clouds of tobacco smoke, magnates with blue ribbons across the shoulders, ambassadors, foreign merchants, officers of the Guards in green uniforms, ship-masters in jackets and striped trousers, moved backwards and forwards in crowds to the uninterrupted sound of the music of wind instruments. The ladies sat against the walls, the young ones being decked out in all the splendor of the prevailing fashion. Gold and silver glittered upon their gowns; out of sumptuous farthingales their slender forms rose like flower stalks; diamonds sparkled in their ears, in their long curls, and around their necks. They turned gaily about to the right and to the left, waiting for their cavaliers and for the dancing to begin. The elderly ladies craftily endeavored to combine the new fashions with the proscribed style of the past; their caps resembled the sable headdress of the Czarina Natalya Kirilovna,[2] and their gowns and capes recalled the *sarafan* and *dushegreika*.[3] They seemed to attend these newfangled gatherings with more astonishment than pleasure, and cast looks of resentment at the wives and daughters of the Dutch skippers, who, in dimity skirts and red bodices, knitted their stockings and laughed and chatted among themselves as if they were at home.

Korsakov was completely bewildered. Observing new arrivals, a servant approached them with beer and glasses on a tray.

"*Que diable est ce que tout cela?*" he asked Ibrahim in a whisper.

Ibrahim could not repress a smile. The Empress and the Grand Duchesses, dazzling in their beauty and their attire, walked through the rows of guests, conversing affably with them. The Emperor was in another room. Korsakov, wishing to show himself to him, with difficulty succeeded in pushing his way thither through the constantly moving crowd. In this room were chiefly foreigners, solemnly smoking their clay pipes and draining earthenware mugs. On the tables were bottles of beer and wine, leather pouches with tobacco, glasses of punch, and some chessboards.

At one of these Peter was playing draughts with a broad-

[2] The mother of Peter the Great (TRANSLATOR'S NOTE).
[3] A fur-lined or wadded sleeveless jacket (EDITOR'S NOTE).

shouldered skipper. They zealously saluted one another with whiffs of tobacco smoke, and the Emperor was so puzzled by an unexpected move that had been made by his opponent, that he did not notice Korsakov, in spite of the latter's efforts to call attention to himself. Just then a stout gentleman, with a large bouquet upon his breast, fussily entered the room, announced in a loud voice that the dancing had commenced, and immediately retired. A large number of the guests followed him, Korsakov among them.

An unexpected sight filled him with astonishment. Along the whole length of the ballroom, to the sound of the most wretched music, the ladies and gentlemen stood in two rows facing each other; the gentlemen bowed low, the ladies curtsied still lower, first forward, then to the right, then to the left, then again forward, again to the right, and so on. Korsakov, gazing at this peculiar pastime, opened his eyes wide and bit his lips. The curtseying and bowing continued for about half an hour; at last they ceased, and the stout gentleman with the bouquet announced that the ceremonial dances were ended, and ordered the musicians to play a minuet. Korsakov rejoiced, and prepared to shine. Among the young ladies was one in particular whom he was greatly charmed with. She was about sixteen years of age, was richly dressed, but with taste, and sat near an elderly gentleman of stern and dignified appearance. Korsakov approached her and asked her to do him the honor of dancing with him. The young beauty looked at him in confusion, and did not seem to know what to say to him. The gentleman sitting near her frowned still more. Korsakov awaited her decision, but the gentleman with the bouquet came up to him, led him to the middle of the room, and said in a pompous manner: "Sir, you have done wrong. In the first place, you approached this young person without making the three necessary bows to her, and in the second place, you took upon yourself to choose her, whereas, in the minuet that right belongs to the lady, and not to the gentleman. On that account you must be severely punished, that is to say, you must drain the goblet of the Great Eagle."

Korsakov grew more and more astonished. In a moment the guests surrounded him, loudly demanding the immediate payment of the penalty. Peter, hearing the laughter and the shouting, came out of the adjoining room, as he was very fond of being present in person at such punishments. The crowd divided before him, and he entered the circle, where stood the culprit and before him the marshal of the assembly holding in his hands a huge goblet filled with malmsey. He was trying in vain to persuade the offender to comply willingly with the law.

"Aha!" said Peter, seeing Korsakov. "You are caught, brother. Come now, monsieur, drink and don't make faces."

There was no help for it: the poor fop, without pausing to take breath, drained the goblet and returned it to the marshal.

"Look here, Korsakov," said Peter to him. "Those breeches of yours are of velvet, such as I myself do not wear, and I am far richer than you. That is extravagance; take care that I do not fall out with you."

Hearing this reprimand, Korsakov wished to make his way out of the circle, but he staggered and almost fell, to the indescribable delight of the Emperor and the whole merry company. This episode not only did not spoil the harmony and interest of the principal performance, but even enlivened it. The gentlemen began to scrape and bow, and the ladies to curtsey and clap their heels together with great zeal, and out of time with the music. Korsakov could not take part in the general gaiety. The lady whom he had chosen approached Ibrahim, at the command of her father, Gavrila Afanasyevich Rzhevsky, and, dropping her blue eyes, timidly gave him her hand. Ibrahim danced the minuet with her and led her back to her former place, then sought out Korsakov, led him out of the ballroom, placed him in the carriage and drove him home. On the way Korsakov began to mutter indistinctly: "Accursed assembly! . . . Accursed goblet of the Great Eagle!" . . . but he soon fell into a sound sleep, and knew not how he reached home, nor how he was undressed and put into bed: and he awoke the next day with a headache, and with a dim recollection of the scraping, the curtseying, the tobacco smoke, the gentleman with the bouquet, and the goblet of the Great Eagle.

IV

I MUST NOW introduce the gracious reader to Gavrila Afanasyevich Rzhevsky. He was descended from an ancient noble family, possessed vast estates, was hospitable, loved falconry, and had a large number of domestics—in a word, he was a genuine Russian gentleman. To use his own expression, he could not endure the German spirit, and he endeavored to preserve in his home the ancient customs that were so dear to him. His daughter was seventeen years old. She had lost her mother while she was yet a child. She had been brought up in the old style, that is to say, she was surrounded by governesses, nurses, playmates, and maidservants, was able to embroider in gold, and could neither read nor write. Her father, notwithstanding his dislike of everything foreign, could not oppose her wish to learn German dances from a captive Swedish officer, living in their house. This deserving dancing-master was about fifty years of age; his right foot had been shot through at Narva, and consequently it was not capable of performing minuets and courantes, but the left executed with wonderful ease and agility the most difficult steps. His pupil did honor to his efforts. Natalya Gavrilovna was celebrated for being the best dancer at the assemblies, and this was partly the cause of Korsakov's transgression. He came the next day to apologize to Gavrila Afanasyevich; but the grace and elegance of the young fop did not find favor in the eyes of the proud boyar, who wittily nicknamed him the French monkey.

It was a holiday. Gavrila Afanasyevich expected some relatives and friends. In the ancient hall a long table was being laid. The guests were arriving with their wives and daughters, who had at last been set free from domestic imprisonment by the decree of the Emperor and by his own example. Natalya Gavrilovna carried round to each guest a silver tray laden with golden cups, and each man, as he drained his, regretted that the kiss, which it was customary to receive on such occasions in the olden times, had gone out of fashion.

They sat down to table. In the place of honor, next to the host, sat his father-in-law, Prince Boris Alexeyevich Lykov, a boyar of seventy years of age; the other guests ranged themselves according to the rank of their family, thus recalling the happy times when rules of precedence were generally respected. The men sat on one side, the women on the other. At the end of the table, the housekeeper in her old fashioned jacket and headdress, the dwarf, a thirty-year-old midget, prim and wrinkled, and the captive Swede, in his faded blue uniform, occupied their accustomed places. The table, which was loaded with a large number of dishes, was surrounded by an anxious crowd of domestics, among whom the butler was prominent, thanks to his severe look, big paunch, and stately immobility. The first few minutes of the dinner were devoted entirely to the products of our old-fashioned cuisine; the noise of plates and the rattling of spoons alone disturbed the general silence. At last the host, seeing that the time had arrived for amusing the guests with agreeable conversation, turned around and asked: "But where is Yekimovna? Call her here."

Several servants were about to rush off in different directions, but at that moment an old woman, powdered and rouged, decked out in flowers and tinsel, in a low-necked silk gown, entered, singing and dancing. All were pleased to see her.

"Good-day, Yekimovna," said Prince Lykov. "How are you?"

"Quite well and happy, gossip: still singing and dancing and looking out for suitors."

"Where have you been, fool?" asked the host.

"Decking myself out, gossip, for our dear guests, for this holy day, by the order of the Czar, at the command of the boyar, in the German style, to make you all smile."

At these words there was a loud burst of laughter, and the fool took her place behind the host's chair.

"The fool talks nonsense, but sometimes speaks the truth," said Tatyana Afanasyevna, the eldest sister of the host, for whom he entertained great respect. "Truly, the present fashions are something for all to laugh at. Since you, gentlemen, have shaved off your beards and put on short *caftans,* it is, of course, useless to talk about women's rags, but it is really a pity about the *sarafan,* the girls' ribbon, and the *povoinik!*[4] It is pitiable and at the same time laughable, to see the belles of today: their hair fluffed up like tow, greased and covered with French flour; their stomachs laced so tightly that they almost break in two; their petticoats are stretched on hoops,

---

4 The national headdress of the Russian women (TRANSLATOR'S NOTE).

so that they have to enter a carriage sideways, and to go through a door they have to stoop; they can neither stand, nor sit, nor breathe—real martyrs, the darlings!"

"Oh, my dear Tatyana Afanasyevna!" said Kirila Petrovich T——, a former governor of Ryazan, where he had acquired three thousand serfs and a young wife, both by somewhat shady means, "as far as I am concerned, my wife may dress as she pleases, she may get herself up like a blowzy peasant woman or like the Chinese Emperor, provided that she does not order new dresses every month and throw away the outmoded ones that are nearly new. In former times the grandmother's *sarafan* formed part of the granddaughter's dowry, but nowadays all that is changed: the dress, that the mistress wears today, you will see the servant wearing tomorrow. What is to be done? It is the ruin of the Russian nobility; it's a calamity!"

At these words he sighed and looked at his Marya Ilyinishna, who did not seem at all to like either his praises of the past or his disparagement of the latest customs. The other young ladies shared her displeasure, but they remained silent, for modesty was then considered an indispensable attribute of a young woman.

"And who is to blame?" said Gavrila Afanasyevich, filling a tankard with foaming kvass. "Isn't it our own fault? The young women play the fool, and we encourage them."

"But what can we do, when our wishes are not consulted?" retorted Khila Petrovich. "One would be glad to shut his wife up in the women's rooms, but with beating of drums she is summoned to appear at the assemblies. The husband goes after the whip, but the wife after frippery. Oh, those assemblies! The Lord has visited us with this punishment for our sins."

Marya Ilyinishna sat as if on needles and pins; her tongue

itched to speak. At last she could restrain herself no longer, and turning to her husband, she asked him, with an acid smile, what he found wrong in the assemblies.

"This is what I find wrong in them," replied the husband heatedly. "Since they began, husbands have been unable to manage their wives; wives have forgotten the words of the Apostle: 'Let the wife see that she reverence her husband'; they no longer busy themselves about their households, but about finery, they do not think of how to please their husbands, but how to attract the attention of giddy officers. And is it becoming, madam, for a Russian lady to associate with tobacco-smoking Germans and their charwomen? And was ever such a thing heard of, as dancing and talking with young men till far into the night? It would be all very well if it were with relatives, but with outsiders, with strangers, with people that they are totally unacquainted with!"

"I've a word for your ear, but the wolf is prowling near," said Gavrila Afanasyevich, frowning. "I confess that I too dislike these assemblies: before you know where you are, you knock into a drunken man, or are made drunk yourself to become the laughingstock of others. Then you must keep your eyes open for fear that some good-for-nothing fellow might be up to mischief with your daughter; the young men nowadays are so utterly spoilt. Look, for example, at the son of the late Yevgraf Sergeyevich Korsakov, who at the last assembly made such a commotion over Natasha that it brought the blood to my cheeks. The next day I see somebody driving straight into my courtyard; I thought to myself, who in the name of Heaven is it, can it be Prince Alexander Danilovich? But no: it was Ivan Yevgrafovich! He could not stop at the gate and make his way on foot to the steps, not he! He flew in, bowing and chattering, the Lord preserve us! The fool Yekimovna mimics him very amusingly: by the way, fool, give us an imitation of the foreign monkey."

The fool Yekimovna seized hold of a dish-cover, placed it under her arm like a hat, and began twisting, scraping, and bowing in every direction, repeating: "monsieur . . . mamselle . . . assemblée . . . pardon." General and prolonged laughter again testified to the delight of the guests.

"The very spit of Korsakov," said old Prince Lykov, wiping away the tears of laughter when quiet was again restored. "But why conceal the fact? He is not the first, nor will he be the last, who has returned from abroad to holy Russia a buffoon. What do our children learn there? To bow and scrape with their feet, to chatter God knows what gibberish. to treat their elders with disrespect, and to dangle after other men's wives. Of all the young people who have been educated abroad (the Lord forgive me!) the Czar's Negro most resembles a man."

"Of course," observed Gavrila Afanasyevich: "he is a sober, decent man, not like that good-for-nothing. . . . But who is it that has just driven through the gate into the courtyard? Surely it cannot be that foreign monkey again? Why do you stand gaping there, beasts?" he continued, turning to the servants. "Run and tell him he won't be admitted, and in future . . ."

"Old man, are you dreaming?" interrupted Yekimovna the fool. "Or are you blind? It is the Emperor's sledge—the Czar has come."

Gavrila Afanasyevich rose hastily from the table, everybody rushed to the windows, and sure enough they saw the Emperor ascending the steps, leaning on his orderly's shoulder. There was great commotion. The host rushed to meet Peter; the servants ran hither and thither as if they had gone crazy; the guests became alarmed; some even thought how they might hasten home as quickly as possible. Suddenly the thundering voice of Peter resounded in the anteroom; all became silent, and the Czar entered, accompanied by his host, who was beside himself with joy.

"Good day, gentlemen!" said Peter, with a cheerful countenance.

All made a profound bow. The sharp eyes of the Czar sought out in the crowd the young daughter of the house; he called her to him. Natalya Gavrilovna advanced boldly enough, but she blushed not only to the ears but even to the shoulders.

"You grow prettier from hour to hour," the Emperor said to her, and as was his habit he kissed her on the head; then turning to the guests, he added: "I have disturbed you? You were dining? Pray sit down again, and give me some aniseed brandy, Gavrila Afanasyevich."

The host rushed to the stately butler, snatched from his hand a tray, filled a golden goblet himself, and gave it with a bow to the Emperor. Peter drank the brandy, ate a biscuit, and for the second time requested the guests to continue their dinner. All resumed their former places, except the dwarf and the housekeeper, who did not dare to remain at a table honored by the presence of the Czar. Peter sat down by the side of the host and asked for cabbage soup. The Emperor's orderly handed him a wooden spoon mounted with ivory, and a knife and fork with green bone handles, for Peter never used any other table implements but his own. The dinner, which a moment before had been so noisy and merry, was now continued in silence and constraint. The host, in his delight and awe, ate nothing; the guests also stood upon ceremony and listened with respectful attention, as the Emperor spoke in German with the captive Swede about the campaign of 1701. The fool Yekimovna, several times questioned by the Emperor, replied with a sort of timid indifference, which, by the way, did not at all prove her natural stupidity. At last the dinner came to an end. The Emperor rose, and after him all the guests.

"Gavrila Afanasyevich," he said to the host, "I must speak to you in private," and, taking him by the arm, he led him into the parlor and locked the door. The guests remained in the dining room, talking in whispers about the unexpected visit, and, afraid of being indiscreet, they soon drove off one after another, without thanking the host for his hospitality. His father-in-law, daughter, and sister conducted them very quietly to the door, and remained alone in the dining room, waiting for the Emperor to emerge.

V

HALF AN HOUR later the door opened and Peter issued forth. With a dignified inclination of the head he responded to the threefold bow of Prince Lykov, Tatyana Afanasyevna and Natasha, and walked straight out into the anteroom. The host handed him his red coat, conducted him to the sledge, and on the steps thanked him once more for the honor he had shown him.

Peter drove off.

Returning to the dining room, Gavrila Afanasyevich seemed very much troubled; he angrily ordered the servants to clear the table as quickly as possible, sent Natasha to her own room, and, informing his sister and father-in-law that he must talk with them, he led them into the bedroom, where he usually rested after dinner. The old Prince lay down upon the oak bed; Tatyana Afanasyevna sank into the old brocaded armchair, and placed her feet upon the footstool; Gavrila Afanasyevich locked all the doors, sat down upon the bed at the feet of Prince Lykov, and in a low voice began: "It was not for nothing that the Emperor paid me a visit today; guess what he wanted to talk to me about."

"How can we know, brother?" said Tatyana Afanasyevna.

"Has the Czar appointed you governor of some province?" said his father-in-law. "It is high time that he did so. Or has he offered you an ambassador's post? Men of noble birth— not only plain clerks—are sent to foreign monarchs."

"No," replied his son-in-law, frowning. "I am a man of the old school, and our services nowadays are not in demand, although, perhaps, an orthodox Russian nobleman is worth more than these modern upstarts, pancake vendors[5] and heathens. But this is a different matter altogether."

"Then what was it, brother," said Tatyana Afanasyevna, "that he was talking with you about for such a long time? Can it be that you are in trouble? The Lord save and defend us!"

"Not exactly trouble, but I confess that it is a matter for reflection."

"Then what is it, brother? What is it all about?"

"It is about Natasha: the Czar came to speak of a match for her."

"God be praised!" said Tatyana Afanasyevna, crossing herself. "The girl is of marriageable age, and as the match-maker is, so must the bridegroom be. God give them love and counsel, the honor is great. For whom does the Czar ask her hand?"

"H'm!" exclaimed Gavrila Afanasyevich. "For whom? That's just it—for whom!"

[5] The allusion is to Menshikov, who is said to have sold pancakes or pies on the Moscow streets in his youth (EDITOR'S NOTE).

"Who is it, then?" repeated Prince Lykov, already beginning to doze off.

"Guess," said Gavrila Afanasyevich.

"My dear brother," replied the old lady, "how can we guess? There are a great number of eligibles at Court, each of whom would be glad to take your Natasha for his wife. Is it Dolgoruky?"

"No, it is not Dolgoruky."

"It's just as well: he is much too conceited. Is it Shein? Troyekurov?"

"No, neither the one nor the other."

"I do not care for them either; they are flighty, and too much imbued with the German spirit. Well, is it Miloslavsky?"

"No, not he."

"It's just as well, he is rich and stupid. Who then? Yeletzky? Lvov? No? It cannot be Raguzinsky? I cannot think of anybody else. For whom, then, does the Czar intend Natasha?"

"For the Negro Ibrahim."

The old lady exclaimed, and struck her hands together. Prince Lykov raised his head from the pillow, and with astonishment repeated: "For the Negro Ibrahim?"

"My dear brother!" said the old lady in a tearful voice. "Do not ruin your own child, do not deliver poor little Natasha into the clutches of that black devil."

"But how," replied Gavrila Afanasyevich, "can I refuse the Emperor, who promises in return to bestow his favor upon us and all our house?"

"What!" exclaimed the old Prince, who was now wide awake. "Natasha, my granddaughter, to be married to a bought Negro!"

"He is not of common birth," said Gavrila Afanasyevich,

"he is the son of a Negro Sultan. The Mussulmen took him prisoner and sold him in Constantinople, and our ambassador bought him and presented him to the Czar. The Negro's eldest brother came to Russia with a considerable ransom and—"

"My dear Gavrila Afanasyevich!" interrupted the old lady, "we have heard the fairy tale about Prince Bova and Yeruslan Lazarevich. Tell us rather what answers you made to the Emperor's proposal."

"I said that we were under his authority, and that it was our duty to obey him in all things."

At that moment a noise was heard behind the door. Gavrila Afanasyevich went to open it, but felt some obstruction. He pushed it hard, the door opened, and they saw Natasha lying in a swoon upon the bloodstained floor.

Her heart had sunk within her, when the Emperor shut himself up with her father; some presentiment had whispered to her that the matter concerned her, and when Gavrila Afanasyevich ordered her to withdraw, saying that he wished to speak to her aunt and grandfather, she could not resist the promptings of feminine curiosity, stole quietly along through the inner rooms to the bedroom door, and did not miss a single word of the whole terrible conversation; when she heard her father's last words, the poor girl lost consciousness, and falling, struck her head against an ironbound chest, in which her dowry was kept.

The servants hastened to the spot; Natasha was lifted up, carried to her own room, and placed in bed. After a while she regained consciousness, opened her eyes, but recognized neither father nor aunt. A violent fever set in; she spoke in her delirium about the Czar's Negro, about marriage, and suddenly cried in a plaintive and piercing voice: "Valeryan, dear Valeryan, my life, save me! There they are, there they are. . . ."

Tatyana Afanasyevna glanced uneasily at her brother, who turned pale, bit his lips, and silently left the room. He returned to the old Prince, who, unable to mount the stairs, had remained below.

"How is Natasha?" he asked.

"Very bad," replied the grieved father, "worse than I thought; she is delirious, and raves about Valeryan."

"Who is this Valeryan?" asked the anxious old man. "Can it be that orphan, the son of a *streletz*,"[6] whom you brought up in your house?"

"The same, to my misfortune!" replied Gavrila Afanasyevich. "His father, at the time of the rebellion, saved my life, and the devil put it into my head to take the accursed wolf-cub into my house. When, two years ago, he was enrolled in the regiment at his own request, Natasha, on taking leave of him, shed bitter tears, and he stood as if petrified. This seemed suspicious to me, and I spoke about it to my sister. But since that time Natasha has never mentioned his name, and nothing whatever has been heard of him. I thought that she had forgotten him, but apparently this is not the case. It's settled: she shall marry the Negro."

Prince Lykov did not contradict him: it would have been useless. He returned home; Tatyana Afanasyevna remained by the side of Natasha's bed; Gavrila Afanasyevich, having sent for the doctor, locked himself in his room, and the house grew silent and gloomy.

The unexpected proposal astonished Ibrahim quite as much as Gavrila Afanasyevich. This is how it happened. Peter, being engaged in business with Ibrahim, said to him: "I perceive, my friend, that you are downhearted; speak frankly, what is it you want?"

Ibrahim assured the Emperor that he was very well satisfied with his lot, and wished for nothing better.

---

[6] A soldier in the standing army of old Muscovy (EDITOR'S NOTE).

"Good," said the Emperor. "If you are dull without any cause, I know how to cheer you up."

At the conclusion of the work, Peter asked Ibrahim: "Do you like the young lady with whom you danced the minuet at the last assembly?"

"She is very charming, Your Majesty, and seems to be a good and modest girl."

"Then I shall take it upon myself to make you better acquainted with her. Would you like to marry her?"

"I, Your Majesty?"

"Listen, Ibrahim: you are a man alone in the world, without birth and kindred, a stranger to everybody, except myself. Were I to die today, what would become of you tomorrow, my poor Negro? You must get settled while there is yet time, find support in new ties, become connected by marriage with the Russian nobility."

"Your Majesty, I am happy under your protection, and in the possession of your favor. God grant that I may not survive my Czar and benefactor—I wish for nothing more; but even if I had any idea of getting married, would the young lady and her relations consent? My appearance—"

"Your appearance? What nonsense! You are a capital fellow! A young girl must obey the will of her parents, and we will see what old Gavrila Rzhevsky will say, when I myself am your matchmaker."

With these words the Emperor ordered his sledge, and left Ibrahim sunk in deep reflection.

"Get married?" thought the African. "Why not? Am I to be condemned to pass my life in solitude, and not know the greatest pleasure and the most sacred duties of man, just because I was born in the torrid zone? I cannot hope to be loved: a childish objection! Is it possible to believe in love? Does it then exist in the frivolous heart of woman? As I have renounced forever these sweet delusions, I choose other, more substantial attractions. The Emperor is right: I must think of my future. Marriage with the young Rzhevsky girl will connect me with the proud Russian nobility, and I shall cease to be a sojourner in my new fatherland. From my wife I shall not require love: I shall be satisfied with her fidelity; and her friendship I will acquire by constant tenderness, confidence, and indulgence."

Ibrahim, according to his usual custom, wished to occupy himself with work, but his imagination was too active. He left the papers and went for a stroll along the banks of the Neva. Suddenly he heard the voice of Peter; he looked around and saw the Emperor, who, having dismissed his sledge, advanced toward him with a beaming countenance.

"It is all settled, brother!" said Peter, taking him by the arm. "I have arranged your marriage. Tomorrow, go and visit your future father-in-law, but see that you humor his boyar pride: leave the sledge at the gate, go through the courtyard on foot, talk to him about his services and distinctions, and he will be perfectly charmed with you. . . . And now," continued he, shaking his cudgel, "lead me to that rogue Danilych, with whom I must confer about his recent pranks."

Ibrahim thanked Peter heartily for his fatherly solicitude on his account, accompanied him as far as the magnificent palace of Prince Menshikov, and then returned home.

VI

A LAMP shed a soft light on the glass case in which glittered the gold and silver mountings of the old family ikons. The flickering light faintly illuminated the curtained bed and the little table set out with labeled medicine bottles. Near the stove sat a servant-maid at her spinning wheel, and the subdued noise of the spindle was the only sound that broke the silence of the room.

"Who is there?" asked a feeble voice.

The servant-maid rose immediately, approached the bed, and gently raised the curtain.

"Will it soon be daylight?" asked Natasha.

"It is already midday," replied the maid.

"Oh, Lord! And why is it so dark?"

"The curtains are drawn, miss."

"Help me to dress quickly."

"You must not do so, miss; the doctor has forbidden it."

"Am I ill then? How long have I been this way?"

"About a fortnight."

"Is it possible? And it seems to me as if it were only yesterday that I went to bed. . . ."

Natasha became silent; she tried to collect her scattered thoughts. Something had happened to her, but what it was she could not exactly remember. The maid stood before her, awaiting her orders. At that moment a dull noise was heard below.

"What is that?" asked the invalid.

"The gentlemen have finished dinner," replied the maid. "They are rising from the table. Tatyana Afanasyevna will be here presently."

Natasha seemed pleased at this; she waved her feeble hand. The maid drew the curtain and seated herself again at the spinning wheel.

A few minutes afterwards, a head in a broad white cap with dark ribbons appeared in the doorway and asked in a low voice: "How is Natasha?"

"How do you do, Auntie?" said the invalid in a faint voice, and Tatyana Afanasyevna hastened toward her.

"The young lady has come to," said the maid, carefully drawing a chair to the side of the bed. The old lady, with tears in her eyes, kissed the pale, languid face of her niece, and sat down beside her. Just behind her came a German doctor in a black *caftan* and the wig worn by the learned. He felt Natasha's pulse, and announced in Latin, and then in Russian, that the danger was over. He asked for paper and ink, wrote out a new prescription, and departed. The old lady rose, kissed Natasha once more, and immediately hurried down with the good news to Gavrila Afanasyevich.

The Czar's Negro, in uniform, wearing his sword and carrying his hat in his hand, sat in the drawing room with Gavrila Afanasyevich. Korsakov, stretched out upon a soft couch, was listening to their conversation, and teasing a venerable greyhound. Becoming tired of this occupation, he approached the mirror, the usual refuge of the idle, and in it he saw Tatyana Afanasyevna, who through the doorway was vainly signaling to her brother.

"Someone is calling you, Gavrila Afanasyevich," said Korsakov, turning around to him and interrupting Ibrahim's speech.

Gavrila Afanasyevich immediately went to his sister and closed the door behind him.

"I am astonished at your patience," said Korsakov to Ibrahim. "For a full hour you have been listening to a lot of nonsense about the antiquity of the Lykov and Rzhevsky lineage, and have even added your own moral observations! In your place *j'aurais planté là* the old liar and his whole tribe, including Natasha Gavrilovna, who puts on airs, and is only pretending to be ill—*une petite santé*. Tell me candidly: are you really in love with this little *mijaurée?*"

"No," replied Ibrahim, "I am not going to marry for love, I am going to make a marriage of convenience, and then only if she has no decided aversion to me."

"Listen, Ibrahim," said Korsakov, "follow my advice this time; in truth, I am more sensible than I seem. Get this foolish idea out of your head—don't marry. It seems to me that your bride has no particular liking for you. Don't all sorts of things happen in this world? For instance: I am certainly not a bad-looking fellow myself, and yet it has happened to me to deceive husbands, who, Lord knows, were in no way worse-looking than me. And you yourself . . . do you remember our Parisian friend, Count D——? There is no dependence to be placed upon a woman's fidelity; happy is he who can regard it with indifference. But you! . . . With your passionate, pensive, and suspicious nature, with your flat nose, thick lips, and coarse wool, to rush into all the dangers of matrimony . . . !"

"I thank you for your friendly advice," interrupted Ibrahim coldly. "But you know the proverb: It is not your duty to rock other people's children."

"Take care, Ibrahim," replied Korsakov, laughing, "that you are not called upon some day to prove the truth of that proverb in the literal sense of the word."

Meanwhile the conversation in the next room became very heated.

"You will kill her," the old lady was saying. "She cannot bear the sight of him."

"But judge for yourself," replied her obstinate brother. "For a fortnight he has been coming here as her bridegroom, and during that time he has not once seen his bride. He may think at last that her illness is a mere invention, and that we are only seeking to gain time in order to rid ourselves of him in some way. And what will the Czar say? He has already sent three times to ask after the health of Natasha. Do as you like, but I have no intention of quarreling with him."

"Good Lord!" said Tatyana Afanasyevna. "What will become of the poor child! At least let me go and prepare her for such a visit."

Gavrila Afanasyevich consented, and then returned to the parlor.

"Thank God!" said he to Ibrahim. "The danger is over. Natasha is much better. Were it not that I do not like to leave my dear guest Ivan Yeografovich here alone, I would take you upstairs to have a glimpse of your bride."

Korsakov congratulated Gavrila Afanasyevich, asked him not to be uneasy on his account, assured him that he was compelled to go at once, and rushed out into the hall, without allowing his host to accompany him.

Meanwhile Tatyana Afanasyevna hastened to prepare the invalid for the appearance of the terrible guest. Entering the room, she sat down breathless by the side of the bed, and took Natasha by the hand; but before she was able to utter a word, the door opened.

Natasha asked: "Who has come in?"

The old lady turned faint. Gavrila Afanasyevich drew back the curtain, looked coldly at the sick girl, and asked how she was. The invalid wanted to smile at him, but could not. Her father's stern look struck her, and uneasiness took possession of her. At that moment it seemed to her that someone was standing at the head of her bed. She raised her head with an effort and suddenly recognized the Czar's Negro. Then she remembered everything, and all the horror of the future presented itself to her. But she was too exhausted to be perceptibly shocked. Natasha laid her head down again upon the pillow and closed her eyes . . . her heart beat painfully. Tatyana Afanasyevna made a sign to her brother that the invalid wanted to go to sleep, and all quitted the room very quietly, except the maid, who resumed her seat at the spinning wheel.

The unhappy girl opened her eyes, and no longer seeing anybody by her bedside, called the maid and sent her for the dwarf. But at that moment a round, old figure rolled up to her bed, like a ball. Lastochka (for so the dwarf was called) with all the speed of her short legs had followed Gavrila Afanasyevich and Ibrahim up the stairs, and concealed herself behind the door, in accordance with the promptings of that curiosity which is inborn in the fair sex. Natasha, seeing her, sent the maid away, and the dwarf sat down upon a stool by the bedside.

Never had so small a body contained within itself so much energy. She meddled. in everything, knew everything, and busied herself about everything. By cunning and insinuating ways she had succeeded in gaining the love of her masters, and the hatred of all the household, which she controlled in the most autocratic manner. Gavrila Afanasyevich listened to her tale-bearing, complaints, and petty requests. Tatyana Afanasyevna constantly asked her opinion, and followed her advice, and Natasha had the most unbounded affection for her, and confided to her all the thoughts, all the emotions of her sixteen-year-old heart.

"Do you know, Lastochka," said she, "my father is going to marry me to the Negro."

The dwarf sighed deeply, and her wrinkled face became still more wrinkled.

"Is there no hope?" continued Natasha. "Will my father not take pity upon me?"

The dwarf shook her cap.

"Will not my grandfather or my aunt intercede for me?"

"No, miss; during your illness the Negro succeeded in bewitching everybody. The master dotes upon him, the Prince raves about him alone, and Tatyana Afanasyevna says it is a pity that he is a Negro, as a better bridegroom we could not wish for."

"My God! my God!" moaned poor Natasha.

"Do not grieve, my pretty one," said the dwarf, kissing her feeble hand. "If you are to marry the Negro, you will have your own way in everything. Nowadays it is not as it was in the olden times: husbands no longer keep their wives under lock and key; they say the Negro is rich; you will have a splendid house—you will lead a merry life."

"Poor Valeryan!" said Natasha, but so softly, that the dwarf could only guess what she said, rather than hear the words.

"That is just it, miss," said she, mysteriously lowering her voice; "if you thought less of the *streletz* orphan, you would not rave about him in your delirium and your father would not be angry."

"What!" said the alarmed Natasha. "I have raved about Valeryan? And my father heard it? And my father is angry?"

"That is just the trouble," replied the dwarf. "Now, if you were to ask him not to marry you to the Negro, he would think that Valeryan was the cause. There is nothing to be done; submit to the will of your parents, for what is to be, will be."

Natasha did not reply. The thought that the secret of her heart was known to her father, produced a powerful effect upon her imagination. One hope alone remained to her: to die before the consummation of the odious marriage. This thought consoled her. Weak and sad at heart she resigned herself to her fate.

VII

IN THE HOUSE OF Gavrila Afanasyevich, to the right of
the vestibule, was a narrow room with one window. In it
stood a simple bed covered with a woolen counterpane; in
front of the bed was a small deal table, on which a tallow
candle was burning, and some sheets of music lay open. On
the wall hung an old blue uniform and its contemporary, a
three-cornered hat; above it, fastened by three nails, was a
cheap print representing Charles XII on horseback. The
notes of a flute resounded through this humble abode. The
captive dancing-master, its lonely occupant, in a nightcap
and nankeen dressing gown, was relieving the tedium of a
winter evening, by playing some old Swedish marches which
reminded him of the gay days of his youth. After devoting
two whole hours to this exercise, the Swede took his flute
to pieces, placed it in a box, and began to undress. . . .

Just then the latch of his door was lifted and a tall, handsome young man, in uniform, entered the room. The Swede
rose, surprised.

"You do not recognize me, Gustav Adamych," said the
young visitor in a moved voice. "You do not remember the
boy to whom you used to give military instruction, and with
whom you nearly started a fire in this very room, shooting
off a toy cannon."

Gustav Adamych looked closely. . . .

"Eh, eh," he cried at last, embracing him. "Greetings!
How long have you been here? Sit down, you scapegrace,
let us talk."